Even the air seemed soft around her...

"If I kissed you, you would have to call me North."

"You will do no such thing," she hissed, even though she prayed he would do just that. She should not encourage him. She should not lean her head back against his collar bone, but she did. What in the world had come over her?

It was the darkness. It had to be. If there was even a hint of light, she would not dare act as she was. But perhaps that was a trick men used.

She tried to straighten but was immobilized by chills as first his hair brushed against her ear, then his breath skimmed over her neck. Warm lips against her shoulder turned her knees to liquid and they failed her.

He caught her, lifted her, held her up while he continued. She sighed as she had never done before. He laughed quietly against her skin, then straightened.

"Forgive me, Livvy. That was quite unfair of me."

"Hmm?" She could think of not a word to say, or a muscle that might help her say it. With chills down the front of her and Northwick's warm form behind her, she felt quite content to remain that way until she woke in the morning. For the mist covering her brain had to be a dream. Only in her dream would Northwick choose her over his precious Plumiere.

"Livvy?"

"Shhh."

"Livvy," he growled in her ear.

Chills began their waterfall all over again.

"When Ashmoore kisses you, compare it with this. Remember me standing here, holding you this way. Remember how you are trembling."

"You made me cold. Clearly not my fault."

"Yes, it is all *my* fault. I did this to you. I will be the only one to make you cold and make you hot. Only me. I cannot stand by and smile, Livvy darling. You are meant for no one but me. Remember that, when Ashmoore takes your hand—"

She shook off the mist, pulled her shoulder out from beneath that waterfall of chills, and turned to confront the darkness.

*

To Marlin—

my Thor

and the inspiration

for every step I take.

*

Just me and you.

Blood for Ink © 2012 Lesli Muir Lytle
All rights reserved

ISBN: 978-1492176329

Cover Design by Kelli Ann Morgan
www.inspirecreativeservices.com

Interior book design by
Bob Houston eBook Formatting

BLOOD

FOR

INK

The Scarlet Plumiere Series

Book One

By L. L. Muir

Published By

Ivy & Stone

www.llmuir.weebly.com

CHAPTER ONE

The Capital Journal, January 31ˢᵗ, Saturday edition, Fiction section

A rumor currently circulates among the gentry in The Grand City that the white-blond Viscount F had a visitor one recent morning, or rather, visitors, as the woman who claimed to be his wife brought with her a pair of identical offspring closely resembling the viscount himself. Piercing blue eyes and straight white hair adorned both cherubs whose mother was blessed with the dark hair of her Spanish ancestors.

Not believing the woman, or his own eyes it seems, Viscount F shooed the little family from his noble steps and into the halls of a certain hotel where they have taken up residence until a higher authority might be able to hear their tale.

It was also rumored the mistress of Viscount F has moved out of his grasp as she deemed it unwise to associate with a man who possesses untrustworthy...eyes.

It remains to be seen whether or not the current fiancée of this poor-sighted creature is also saved from his company.—The Scarlet Plumiere

"Well, Stanley, you cannot very well sue the paper for libel when they did print this in the fiction section." Ramsey Birmingham, Earl of Northwick, kept a straight face but only just. His friend, Stanley Winters, Viscount Forsgreen, was not the first to be chastised by the red-penned writer. That he was being so dramatic about it, so early on a Saturday morning, was an invitation for torment.

"But North! I tell you there was no woman. No wife. No children with my blue eyes and white hair."

"White hair, even. Not blond." Presley Talbot, Marquess of Harcourt and the worst tease among them, prodded poor Stanley from behind, then walked around the man and offered him a much needed drink.

Stan raised the glass, then paused. "It is early."

"Drink!" Harcourt slapped him on the back, nearly spilling the shot of courage.

Stanley needed no more prompting and emptied the glass, then stared into its empty depths. "Yes, white hair. There are no such creatures, I assure you. I have only been to Spain two years ago and... Oh, dear."

"Well, the vixen got that right at least." Earnest Meriwether, the unfortunately named Earl of Ashmoore, chimed in from the far stacks of North's immodest library. His given name was spot-on, as if his mother might have read the sobriety in his eyes the moment he was born, but the family name was far afield. Ash was never merry; he was deadly serious, and deadly otherwise. After everything that transpired in France, North was no longer quite as dedicated to England as he was to his sober friend; if the Earl of Ashmoore decided to turn coats, North would turn his as well rather than face his dark friend in any skirmish. No man did so and lived.

"But Ash, I am telling you, there is no such woman." Stanley looked at a chair, but North frowned and shook his head, as if to say the morning's business was so serious the viscount should keep on his toes.

Stanley's shoulders fell. Poor man, so easily manipulated. The Scarlet Plumiere really should not have picked on such a harmless chap. North was of half a mind to hunt her down and tell her so.

"Well, The Scarlet Plumiere has yet to accuse an innocent man, even if she is a bit inaccurate on the specificity of the crime." Ash joined the rest, eyes fixed on an open volume of

Shakespeare—the red leather set. He lowered his dark form into the seat Stanley had been eyeing.

"He is right, of course. Let us hear it, Stanley. What have you done?" Harcourt threw North a conspiratory wink, then hooked a leg over the corner of a table and leaned forward for the details, his interest and enthusiasm more than making up for Ash's lack of both.

Of course, Stanley broke.

"I have done nothing! Nothing the rest of our lot has not done from time to time."

North could not bring himself to prod the viscount further. The poor chap had asked his three closest friends to meet that morning to find a solution to his newest problem— fresh as the morning paper. They really should get 'round to the business of helping him.

Harcourt was in no such hurry. He folded his arms and lifted a brow.

"Stanley, you are trying our patience. Spit out your confession, or I do not see us making much of an attempt to save your sorry hide."

Stan flushed from his pinned cravat to the roots of his snowy hair—a shade of red that might well have been the only color that did not become the overly-blessed viscount. He braced himself, as if for the executioner.

"I set Ursula aside."

"You what?" Three baritones in unison sounded almost rehearsed.

North shook his head. "I am sorry, old boy. You did what?"

"He set her aside." Harcourt slapped his knee.

North turned to Ash. "He set her aside."

"Yes, blast you. I set her aside!"

Ashmoore closed the book, laid Shakespeare on the overstuffed arm, and shook a lock of black hair from his forehead. "Pardon my slow wit, but just how does one put an *Ursula* aside?"

Ash was right. Stanley Winters had enjoyed the pick of females since the four of them were in knee breeches together.

Now he had *the* pick of all mistresses and had chosen very well. *Ursula* was indisputably the most sought after mistress in all of London, and it was quite possible Stan, old pal, was the first man to actually end an affair with the woman. *Ursula* did the shopping for a new lover. *Ursula* let that lover know when he was no longer welcome. But the mighty Viscount Forsgreen had *set her aside*.

"I suppose he picked her up by the shoulders, turned, and set her down again." Harcourt demonstrated with an invisible model, then dusted his hands. "Out of his way, presumably. Is that accurate, Stanley?"

The viscount's blush looked to be seeping into his actual hair.

"I let her go," he said quietly.

"Ah. Like fishing, then? You took the hook from her mouth, so to speak, and put her back in the water." North could not help but laugh at Harcourt's miming skills.

"Can she swim, do you suppose?" Ash's usual sobriety fled. He dissolved into laughter at his own jest, as did they all—except poor Stanley of course.

The viscount stood straighter, if possible. "You know perfectly well what I mean. I ended our affair. I told her she was free to do as she pleased."

North nodded and composed himself. "And you paid her a nice settlement, of course."

"Actually, she would not take it. She was not at all happy that I offered it."

A giggling Harcourt bent over and dove onto the couch like a man run through the gut with a saber.

Ash rubbed a hand over his face then stiffened. "That has to be it! Ursula found The Scarlet Plumiere and had you punished. Severely punished, it appears; if night follows day, and things play out the way The Plumiere has predicted, you, my dear *Viscount F*, are about to be released from your engagement."

"But that's why I let her go, you see? It would be poor form to keep one's mistress while one is preparing for marriage, and honeymoon, and fatherhood, and…"

"And death." Having solved the mystery, Ash's nose was back in the book.

"Yes, that too. If Irene Goodfellow breaks it off, Mother will have me fed to the fish, and even though she is doddering, she will find a way to bear another son to replace me."

"It is unsettling the way that woman tosses that threat about," North admitted. "Love her as I do, it fairly gives me nightmares thinking about it."

"Well, thinking about it put me off seeing Ursula," Stan mumbled.

"Quite so. Quite so." North nodded, thinking. The mystery was solved, but what were they to do about it?

"It would be best to have her put down, Stanley. For your own good," Harcourt mumbled against a cushion. With all his antics, his gold-brown hair was coming loose from its tether.

"Who? The Scarlet Plumiere? I cannot have a woman murdered, even if she has essentially ruined my life with her blasted article, using my very blood for her ink, as it were. Why, I cannot believe you would suggest such a thing."

"Oh, not her, man. Your mother." Harcourt rolled onto his back and spoke to the ceiling. "Have your mother put down and enjoy the reprieve. Marry in another ten years."

"Put down my mo...you are mad!"

"No. Actually, it is not a bad idea a 'tall." Ash closed his book again and tossed it onto the side table.

"All right. You are both mad. I will not be having my mother put down, for God's sake."

"Oh, Stanley. Do keep up." Ash folded his hands and unexpectedly grinned. He must have had a grand idea; he did not smile easily. "I mean The Plumiere, of course, not your dear mother."

"You mean it? You can stand here in front of God and good whisky and say such things? Good lord, man. Perhaps I do not know you at all. Perhaps you could actually do the deed yourself!" Stanley straightened his waistcoat as if preparing to leave in a huff.

"Oh, I would rather not do the deed myself, of course." Ashmoore frowned and scrubbed a finger back and forth across his mouth.

North could take it no more. He tossed up his hands. "I surrender as well, Ash. What are you thinking? You cannot be talking about having The Scarlet Plumiere murdered."

"Not murdered. Put down. Removed from power—or The Capital Journal at least." Ash leaned in and lowered his voice. "The only way to control a woman these days, gentlemen, is to marry her off."

Harcourt rolled back onto his face and mumbled, "I'd rather plan a murder than a wedding."

Callister stepped into the library with a small white box tied with crimson ribbon. North nodded his butler over and reached for the package, but the old man shook his head.

"I beg your pardon, my lord, but this just arrived for Viscount Forsgreen."

Something yawned and stretched inside North's breast, something that had been sleeping for two years. Usually, when it woke, he drugged it with brandy until it slept again. He was not sure, but it might have been his soul. And with some sort of premonition which he had never been known to possess, he suspected that *thing* within him would somehow be affected by Stanley's box.

He watched, as did they all, while Stanley slowly pulled a crimson tail, as if he expected a cat to jump out.

The ribbon fell away. Nothing happened. Stanley sat the box upon the table, lifted the lid, and set it to one side. He frowned, looked at North, then reached into its depths. He pulled out a pair of spectacles...and a bubble burst in North's chest.

He laughed.

Stanley did not seem to understand.

"Who knew about this meeting, *Viscount F*?" Ash had to raise his voice to be heard.

North laughed harder. Watching Stanley's face as realization dawned, struck him as particularly amusing.

"Untrustworthy eyes." Harcourt's grin widened further than the confines of his face. "I say, she is a clever minx."

North agreed. The Scarlet Plumiere was clever. And had he a heart, she might have just won it over with her wit alone.

CHAPTER TWO

Monday evening all the most eligible bachelors currently in London, Torreys and Whigs alike, gathered for the lottery on the second floor of White's Gentlemen's Club. Corralling such a group was the unattainable dream of every matchmaking momma of the *ton,* but this was no time to have a woman about.

Of course the younger bachelors were excluded from entering their names; it would have been unbelievably cruel to expect the more innocent among them to participate. North and his friends had deduced that if the winner, or loser rather, were over the age of thirty, there was a better chance the chap deserved his fate in some way. Those young men who had not received invitation were in attendance of course. It would be too good a show to miss.

"I wish we would have been able to do this more privately," Stanley murmured next to North. "There's not a chance of keeping this a secret with so many witnesses."

"Sorry, Stanley." Ash stood to the other side of *Viscount F.* "You came to us for help and this was the best we could think of on short notice and tall whiskeys. I am rather regretting it myself."

North was nauseous, but for a reason all his own. The suggestion of a lottery had come from his own tongue and now his friends were in jeopardy of paying the price. His mind raced for a way to stop the madness, as it had been racing all day, since he had awakened with a pain in his head and a piece of parchment in his hand. It was nothing less than a copy of the missive he'd sent to many of the gentlemen present—a call to arms.

And the fools had come.

He could tell them it was simply a grand joke, but judging by the sober faces before him, they were in no mood to believe it. And considering the turnout, many must view The Scarlet Plumiere as serious a threat as he had, at least while deep in his cups.

Harcourt joined him and the others. Forsgreen and Ashmoore to his right, Harcourt to his left—The Four Kings, as they liked to call themselves—facing a mob of nervous and determined goats, waiting to see who among them would be sacrificed.

Harcourt snorted. "Perhaps our chances will be better on this side of the table, eh?"

Like North and every man who had received the missive, Harcourt had paused at the head of the stairs and written his name on a lot to be added to the barrel, and North feared for his odds of losing a friend today. If one of them were chosen, he would never forgive himself. If his own name were pulled from the pile, he would surely be forced to live out his years in the country, or hiding from Society altogether in a secluded cottage in Scotland. Either way, his friends would be lost to him, and that was entirely unacceptable. Not a thing in this world could drag the four apart—certainly no woman had yet managed it, nor had his weakness in France—but with one flippant suggestion of a lottery, he had placed their brotherhood in jeopardy.

Sweat broke out on his forehead and he dabbed it away, but he was hardly the only one doing so.

The Count Germaine stepped forward. White hair, steel eyes. Mustache nearly large enough to conceal a weapon. No doubt the man had hundreds of little secrets he would like to keep safe from The Plumiere, not to mention polite society.

"I would like to clarify a few things before the lot is drawn," he said. "The chosen man must only marry the chit if she is a relatively young gentlewoman in good standing, correct?"

"Correct." North's voice showed none of his nerves. The thought of Count Germaine getting his hands on his clever little writer made him angry.

"And if she is not?" The count smiled a greasy smile.

North's stomach turned. He had never imagined his writer to be anything but.

"I suppose," sober Ash offered, "we simply threaten her with exposure in order to still her pen."

Stanley nodded vigorously. "Yes, yes. The goal is to stop her from writing. That's all. I will not have the woman harmed, no matter what she might have done to my current plans."

"Well said, *Viscount F.*" North gave Stanley a hearty slap on the back. "I pledge one thousand pounds to the man whose lot is drawn, to offset the cost of wooing the lady."

"Doubt she is a lady," someone murmured.

Heads turned, but whoever had given the insult was wise enough to slither away.

What if the offender were chosen?

North's cravat tightened of its own accord. He resisted dabbing his forehead again.

"If my lot is not chosen, I will throw in a yearling from my racing stock in York." The Earl of Strothsbury grinned.

Harcourt laughed. "Very generous, Strothsbury, but you realize such a gift will not miraculously remove your name from the barrel."

"I have a small property in Scotland I will donate!"

North shook away that earlier image of that Scottish cottage and laughed along with most of the crowd. The Marquis of Landover had been trying to lose that very property in card games for over a year, but had found none foolish enough to risk the winning of it. Now the Marquis had managed to make the most dreaded of lotteries even more distasteful; even if the woman proved a lovely surprise, every man among them feared what Landover's dubious property held in store.

"Too generous of you, Landover," North said as sincerely as he could manage.

"Not at all." The Marquis beamed and rocked up onto his toes.

North could not help but rock him right back on his heels. "Of course, you may well have just donated the property to yourself."

Landover was suddenly the only one *not* smiling. The man's luck was terrible where that property was concerned. It was an Australian boomerang of which he could never rid himself. Perhaps he had sealed his fate in the offering. Perhaps his lot was, at that moment, waiting to jump into North's hand.

North looked hard at the barrel and the room fell silent.

The woman's fate lay before him, through no fault of her own. What in the bloody hell had he done to her?

Stanley slapped the back of his shoulder and held. Whether his friend was offering support, or needing some, he did not know. Likely a bit of both.

He reached forward, laid his fingers on the rim, and took a deep breath. His hand moved into the opening, but Harcourt reached out to stop it.

North looked to his friend.

Harcourt nodded at the back of the room where two out-of-breath gentlemen were signing their names to lots. "Wait but a moment and our odds will improve."

Only when his own heart resumed beating did North discern it had stopped in the first place. He then realized his dread had not been for pulling his lot from the barrel nor for winning Landtree's property—he'd dreaded drawing out anyone's name *but his own!*

He needed to sit down. He needed a brandy. He needed time to think.

But there was no time for consideration. The two tardy gentlemen found a spot in which to stand, and Gibson, the doorman, was making his way toward the barrel with their lots in hand. North had the ridiculous urge to fold his arms over the opening and tell Gibson their lots were not welcome, as if The Scarlet Plumiere was inside that barrel and he wanted her all to himself, as if his band of brothers was secondary.

Did he want her all to himself? Were a few clever lines in a newspaper all it took to pique his interest? To risk his friends?

And do not forget the spectacles, prodded some devil on his shoulder.

In a flash of light from the chandelier above the table, North realized he had gone utterly mad. As poetically just as it might be for Landover's name to be drawn, or as relieving as it might be for some mild acquaintance to be chosen, there was not a man in the room or in the building for that matter, whom he could trust to treat his Scarlet Plumiere fairly.

His friends could fend for themselves when necessary. Surely this woman could not.

Miraculously, a small grain of bravery lying dormant in his chest somehow got splashed with a drop of rain, or whiskey as the case may be, and started to sprout. A delicate tendril of hope stretched tentatively for the light. If nothing else, he owed the mysterious woman for that.

He would not leave her fate to chance.

He nodded at Gibson and allowed the man to drop two white tiles in with the rest. Then he reached for the opening again.

"Stir the lots!" More than one man suggested it.

And so he stirred them...

CHAPTER THREE

The Capital Journal, February 3ʳᵈ, Morning edition, Fiction section

A wild tale is spreading like the black plague through ladies' drawing rooms at this very hour. Supposedly, the men of The Grand City (or at least those allegedly eligible for marriage), held a meeting in the honor of a particularly talented writer and drew lots. The 'alotted' is to be the lucky so-and-so who must not only ferret out the identity of said writer, but must marry her in order to control her...uh, plume...thereby removing the threat to his fellows' reputations. These gentlemen fail to comprehend that said writer's reporting might very well be the last resort for some women to find justice in this world.

Bravo, Mr. Lott! Did you think of this scheme by yourself or with your fellow Kings? I cannot imagine a sweeter justice than for the man who imagined such a lottery to be its first selected victim. I say "first" because after you wave your white kerchief in surrender, undoubtedly there will be a few boisterous fools who think they can succeed where you are about to fail.

However, I will be sporting and wish you bon chance! —The Scarlet Plumiere

North's first reaction, besides smiling into his breakfast coffee, was relief that his family name had miraculously escaped the papers, even though its readers would by now know full well the identity of Mr. Lott. Another favor he owed the mysterious woman.

His second reaction was to berate himself, yet again, for the stupidity of his actions. What if he ultimately failed to unmask her? What if the entire city bore witness to his utter humiliation at being thwarted by a female?

He could never allow that to happen. He was already the unworthy remnant of his line, and if it was the last thing he accomplished, he would ensure that name did not die in disgrace. It was the very least he owed his parents after they had lost their lives trying to reach him, to save him from his kidnappers in France. And all the while, he had wallowed in the darkness, cursing them for failing him.

What he really owed them was a better son.

He shook off his dark thoughts and read The Plumiere's letter once more. By the end, he was smiling again.

"Callister!"

"I am here, my lord."

"Dye my kerchiefs red."

"Red? Sir?" His man's face froze.

"Yes, red. And die a few cravats as well." He folded the page carefully and handed it to the butler. "Place this on my desk."

"Red, sir? You want some red cravats, sir?" Callister failed to reach for the paper, so North dropped it on the table while the butler got hold of himself.

"Yes, just a few. No need to ruin the lot." He bent to his meal.

"Of course not, sir." Callister took the paper, then headed for the door, but hesitated.

"What is it man?"

"I was just wondering, sir, if you would prefer them to be dyed, or if you would like me to arrange to have them made from new red cloth?"

"As long as some are available by this evening." He dismissed the old man with a wave.

"Very good, my lord."

"Oh, and one more thing."

"Sir?" Poor Callister looked as if his eyes might jump from his skull.

"I would like someone to take a letter to The Capital Journal for the evening edition, in say...an hour."

"Very good, my lord."

It really was too bad of him not to wait until after the old butler had quit the room before he let out his rush of excitement, whooping like a boy who had just been told he was getting a pony for his birthday. It did rather feel like a birthday, however. He had been given a gift, in a way. The wit of The Scarlet Plumiere was just as sharp as he'd hoped. He had not been misled by one or two clever lines.

Someone knocked quietly on the dining room door, no doubt of two minds about entering if they had heard his carrying on.

"Come!"

Chester, a young footman, poked his head around the door, his eyes wide.

"Mister Callister sent me, my lord. I will be just here in the hallway, when you have your missive ready."

"Thank you, Chester."

He finished his breakfast and hurried to his study, rubbing his hands together and gathering his thoughts as he went.

My dear SP...

***

His friends arrived at a quarter of seven. The evening edition of The Capital Journal would be arriving soon after the hour. They set up their watch in the library as was their habit. Harcourt sat on the arm of the couch spinning a miniature globe, stopping it with his finger, then picking it up to examine the chosen spot more closely, only to set it down and repeat the procedure. Ash sat in the overstuffed chair and inspected the toes of his boots, scuffed them up a bit, then examined them again. Stanley looked out the French windows at the snowy garden beyond, his back to his fellows, his shoulders slumped as if paying some sort of penance by again denying himself a seat.

North sat on the edge of a particularly uncomfortable chair with very little in the way of a cushion—something his late mother had shipped home from the African continent. She was gone now. He was perfectly safe getting rid of the thing, but it did bring a bit of interest to the room, or so he had been told by a woman with a decorating bent.

His elbows rested on his knees, his thumbs provided a shelf for his chin, and his entwined fingers helped hide his excitement. If he managed to keep his brows together, his friends might never know just how miserable he *was not*. The image of a mysterious property in Scotland did a better job of wiping his smile from his face completely, however. And for that, he was grateful.

The minutes ticked by. Chester should have picked up a copy of the paper by now. How long would it take him to reach the townhouse? Might traffic cause a delay?

He could not help but harbor some hope that The Scarlet Plumiere had been warned of his letter and might have added a rebuttal. Of course he tried to brace himself for disappointment. The woman did not live at the newspaper office, after all. Did she?

"Does the owner of The Capital Journal have a daughter do you think?" He asked it of the room at large.

"I have no knowledge of the man," said Harcourt, spinning the globe again without looking up. "Perhaps his wife?"

Well, *that* was not encouraging. Due to some here-to-fore unknown insanity, he had grown wildly fond of his little writer only now to worry she might be already married and not *little* in the least. A stout woman with a quick wit? Of course it was possible. In fact many stout women he had known through his life had been memorable. Stanley's mother, for instance, the Duchess of Rochester, overfilled her plate and thus overfilled a chair as well. The only thing quicker than her wit was her understanding of the young male mind; the simple need to catch frogs for days on end; a distraction from the sorrow when all those frogs died in their new cage when left too long in the sun; and lately, the distraction from being a motherless son.

If The Plumiere were stout but unmarried, he supposed the woman might make an excellent choice of mother for his children. That was, if the getting of children were not too difficult...should the visage of his friend's mother intrude.

"Oh, dear God." He mumbled into his fingers.

"You are certainly not going to let your imagination run rough-shod, are you North?" Ash tucked his boots beneath him and sat straighter. "Let's not worry too much until we find out if she is marriageable."

"You are right, of course." North had had enough of the African chair, and he found himself on his feet, pacing behind Stanley.

"But on the brighter side, if she is already married, he is off the proverbial hook. Her looks would not matter." Harcourt pointed out the obvious.

"So really," Stanley turned away from the window, "her looks do not matter one way or the other."

He stopped his pacing. Of course her looks mattered, but he was not about to debate the point with his friends. No doubt it was why they had come, to distract him. But he did not want to be distracted, blast it!

The opening of the front door echoed down the marble hallway. North marched over to Ash and tilted his head. The earl nodded, stood, and moved to the couch. North was grateful his friend understood. Coherent thoughts were suddenly impossible, let alone a coherent sentence. He had just settled his equally grateful behind into the softer chair when Callister entered with four copies of the paper. Four. If he remembered, he would give the old man a nice raise for his quick thinking.

"The Capital Journal, my lords." Callister handed them around then walked to the sideboard and began pouring drinks. The sweet smell of brandy mingled with that of leather and fresh ink. The only thing missing was the aroma of his father's pipe. If he leaned close to the leather, he would likely smell that as well.

He found the personal section and set the remainder of the paper aside.

> *The Capital Journal, February 3, Evening edition,*
> *Personal section*
> *My dear SP,*
> *You cannot imagine my pleasure at reading your latest installment of fiction. It gave me hope you will run and hide and not allow yourself to be caught too soon, now that you know the name of your hunter. If you were to swoon at my feet, I would be sorely disappointed. So run, my dear. Give me a merry chase, even though the ending may not be so 'marry.'*
> *–Mr. Lott*

That was all. Nothing from her. He sought out the fiction section. Nothing there either. He could not stifle a sigh of disappointment.

The room was surprisingly quiet. Surely his friends were not slow readers. He looked up.

Ash's glower rivaled his battlefield demeanor. Above the earl's shoulder, the chronically jovial Harcourt glowered as well. Stanley's mouth hung open, his arms still holding up the paper.

"Would you care to explain this?" Ash nodded at his paper. "I assume yours reads the same as mine."

"What?" He did not understand what he might have written that offended his friends so. He even stuck his nose back in his paper and read his own words again.

"So you wrote this?" Harcourt shook his head, still frowning.

"Of course I wrote it. What's wrong with it?"

Stanley moved forward and leaned against the couch. "There's nothing wrong with it, but...but..."

Harcourt helped him. "But it hardly sounds as if you are unhappy about the situation."

"Unhappy?" *What the devil did he mean?*

"Yes. Unhappy." Ash folded his arms and leaned back as if expecting the kind of confession Stanley had made just days before.

"Do you want me to be unhappier about it? I assure you I can find a thing or two about which to complain."

Callister cleared his throat and passed brandies to all, then slipped from the room, as if he weren't even tempted to hang about and listen. And North decided the raise in wages was not necessary after all. The man had likely ordered more than just four copies of the paper and was scurrying off to read his own.

He raised his staff's wages too often as it was.

Once the door was closed, Ash tisked. "You owe our *Viscount F* an apology."

"Really? Why?" North gripped the sides of his chair. He honestly could not understand why his friends were displeased with his note to his...prey.

"He has been downright despondent," Harcourt nodded in Stan's direction.

North looked up at his too-blond friend. "Have you, Stanley? Because you think all this is your fault?"

"Actually, yes." The viscount's bottom lip stuck out a bit further than usual.

"Well, that is completely silly." *Wasn't it?*

"Yes, it is silly if you are happy about your new situation," said Ash.

"Of course I am not happy about it."

Harcourt stood. "Oh, I think you are. In fact, I have not seen you so enthused about anything since...France." The other men nodded rather vigorously.

Nosey, overly-observant friends! Why on Earth was an improvement of his mood a bad thing?

"I have just been...bored, that is all. You must admit she is anything but tedious."

Ash suddenly jumped to his feet. "Where is it?"

Harcourt swung wide to the left. Stanley came around the end of the couch, though he was frowning at Ash. Stan did not know what was going on either, but regardless, joined Ashmoore's side of a battle.

"Where is what?" *Devil take them all.*

"The lot." Ash grinned. At least it resembled a grin, and it was not the most pleasant of grins either. He really must refine his smiling techniques if he was going to make it a regular habit.

"What lot?" North concentrated on not sweating. The library fire was...ah, not lit.

Damn.

It was a lucky thing his current seat was so cushioned and forgiving, since North was determined to back his way out of it. He had been interrogated before and lived. This should be no different.

His friends stepped closer.

"*The* lot, North. The one you took from the barrel. What did you do with it?" Ash was frightening when he enunciated carefully.

"I burned it. In effigy."

"Liar. They were made of bone." His dark friend's eyes sparkled.

"How could you keep this from us? How could you not tell us?" Harcourt halted, his hands on his hips.

"I do not know what you mean." Even the chair did not believe him and as he scrambled backward, it dumped him out on his arse.

"Hold him down! Callister and I will find it!" Harcourt rounded the African chair and ran for the door.

Ash jumped over the toppled furniture and straddled North's chest, trapping his arms in the doing. Ash was gasping for breath and North realized the man was laughing. North was pretty amused himself, watching his fastidious friend wallow about on the floor, hair swinging in his eyes, as if they were back at Eaton, fighting in the dormitory. And he was hardly worried—they'd never find the cursed thing.

He tried his damnedest to unseat his gasping friend, but to no avail. He, too, had little breath with which to fight; any moment he would be passing out. In fact, passing out was not a bad idea.

Something dripped on his face and he stopped squirming. Had he given Ash a bloody nose?

There. Wet. Again.

He shook the liquid from his face. Standing over him with his fingers in what must be his glass of fine brandy, Stanley grinned down at him.

"Chinese water torture should loosen his tongue, do you suppose, Ash?"

"That could take all night to work." Ash grabbed his chin and held him steady.

"Yes. Yes it could." Stanley had definitely finished with his pouting, damn him. "Confess, North."

"I confess nothing."

Thirty minutes of torture and one soaked Aubosson carpet later, Harcourt rejoined them, a shaking Callister in tow.

"We found it."

Impossible! He'd chucked it onto the top of his impressive ten-feet-tall wardrobe!

"I beg your pardon, my lord, but *you* found it. I distinctly remember trying to prevent you from going through His Lordship's things."

Harcourt rolled his eyes. At least North thought he did. It was hard to tell upside down with stinging whisky blurring his vision.

"You can let me up now," he growled. It was a fact he could do little more than growl with all the yelling he'd done. He had laughed a bit, of course, but how could he not? At least during the majority of his torture he'd been quite convincingly furious.

He twisted beneath Ash and caught the man off guard. Before he could launch any kind of assault, however, Ash was out of reach.

Ever-prepared Callister handed him a wet towel. After North got a fraction of the liquor off his face, Ash moved closer to Harcourt, and thus closer to North—careless man. An instant later, he received an incredibly satisfying snap of the towel. At least North found it satisfying.

Stanley snatched the towel from behind and tossed it over North's head and into Callister's waiting hands.

"You are all against me," North said, glaring at each man in turn. At least his butler had the decency to look sorry for it.

"Well, go on. Whose name was on it?" Ash stood out of towel-reach, even though North's weapon had been removed.

"You will not believe it." Harcourt grinned at North as if inviting him to beg. North would never beg.

"Come now. We have waited long enough." Stanley reached for Harcourt's hand, but the latter pulled it out of reach just in time.

"I think you might wish to sit down." Still, he grinned at North. Not wanting to tip his hand, apparently.

"Ridiculous. Whose name, man? Who is this fellow who owes the Earl of Northwick his freedom?" Ash grinned.

"I warned you to sit down."

"You will tell him anyway, so tell him." North righted the comfortable chair and sat in it.

"Dear God." Stanley walked to the African chair and sat, dropping his head into his hands.

"Read the name." Ash's quiet order was not one any would refuse, even the teasing Marquis of Harcourt.

The latter lifted the tile and read, carefully, simply, "Ashmoore."

CHAPTER FOUR

The Scarlet Plumiere paced.

She paced before the sitting room fire until she grew hot. She paced in her father's dark gardens until the chill from her toes began moving up her calves, until her nose was so cold she feared it might break off like an icicle if she touched it. She then decided to pace in her own room and hoped the upstairs staff would not consult the downstairs staff and note just how much pacing she had accomplished. She so hated people to worry over her.

After donning her nightdress and wrap, she sat before her mirror and allowed Stella to brush out her hair. She had no need to sort through her thoughts. She was fully aware of the choices before her and the choice she would make in the end. But there was something glorious in standing at a crossroads, with possibilities waving to you from down the lane. Once she turned down her chosen road, there would be no one, and nothing, waving to her again.

Though allowing Lord Northwick to find her and marry her seemed a romantic dream, he was, in reality, her enemy. His honor demanded he find a way to prevent her writing; marriage was merely a means to that end.

But nothing could keep her from continuing her work. No temptation would be great enough to leave the ladies of London without a champion. After coming frighteningly close to marrying a monster, she could not live with herself if another young lady endured such a fate if it had been within her power to stop it. It would be as unforgiveable a sin as anything Lord Gordon might have done, or had planned to do, to her.

She would carry on as always. Men more desperate than Northwick had tried to find her before, and failed, as would the earl. If she could refrain from toying with the man, he would become bored and surrender soon enough.

Toying with him *in her mind* was another thing altogether. It would hurt nothing, harm no one, if she indulged in a daydream or two before she turned her back on temptation. She imagined him thoroughly enchanted by her clever wit, then deliriously happy when he discovered it was she, the woman he had always loved from afar.

She had certainly admired him from afar, in spite of only seeing him twice before; once, when she was eleven; the second time at her last ball where she realized he was a man grown, broad of shoulder, handsome as Satan himself must be. But he had not danced, and he had not appeared happy to be there. Later she'd learned he had only recently returned to England. His friends had forced him to attend. That he had looked at no other women soothed her feelings a bit, after failing to catch his eye all night.

And then Lord Gordon came along and changed everything. She had hardly laid eyes on any gentlemen since. Men in her father's employ hardly signified.

In her dreams, late that night, her mind forgot the plan, and she found herself running down that forbidden road and into Northwick's outstretched arms. His kisses began soft, then turned wild, consuming. Then they tapered off to a tiny flick of his tongue on her cheek.

She woke to find her late mother's dog on her pillow, licking her face. She was perfectly furious she might have had even a tender thought for the little rat, even in her sleep. And The Rat knew it too. He shot off the bed and out the door before she let go of the heavy pink bed-pillow. Instead, it landed in what was surely meant to be her breakfast. There was not a reasonable doubt in her mind The Rat had planned the whole episode.

"I am so sorry, Stella," she called as the maid disappeared into the hallway with juice splashed on her face and apron, stoically carrying the tray away with the offending pillow on top, as if she always served breakfast in that manner. "I will break my fast in the dining room, shall I then?"

As she scrubbed at her face, she vowed again that someday she would kill that dog—as soon as she believed her father would survive without it. The man seemed to view the animal as proof his late wife was still about. Often, he would hear the tinkling of The Rat's collar entering the room and begin talking to the woman. And dutiful daughter that she was, The Scarlet Plumiere would slink away, refusing to discover how long the conversation might have gone on before he remembered.

It had been three years...

Knowing there would be no letter in the paper from the earl, she was in no hurry to go downstairs. Stella returned with a cup of tea and a wink. All was forgiven, but the girl punished her head a bit, trying her hand—three times—at a new hairstyle. The end result was both beautiful and sad. Such a pity no one but her father would see it.

At breakfast, she pushed her food around her plate as she was wont to do on occasion. The footman would never come to collect the mess until she walked away from it. They were that familiar with her oddities.

Finally, four capers remained on her plate. Four little green bumps, like miniature hats for her smallest finger.

She separated them. North, South, East, and West. North was straight ahead, the path she was determined to walk. South was the past so she swallowed it whole. No need to go there. Mother was gone. The only threat from that front was her constant worry she might forget the woman's face, and voice, and a hundred other things. But that threat was lessened by the knowledge that she would never be leaving her father's household, and thus never leaving the sights and smells that kept the woman's memory alive.

The aftertaste of the bitter caper was an apt reminder that her reputation was well and goodly dented. There was nothing for it but to go forward. Spilled milk and all that. Lots and lots of spilled milk. Of course it had been washed away, thanks to her quick thinking and dear friend whose husband owned The Capital Journal, but a stain remained.

She could live with a stain. She could not have lived with Lord Gordon.

And there he was. The caper to the East. Her ex-fiancé was currently hiding abroad, probably waiting for memories and gossip sheets to fade. He may well come home with a wife on his arm, to try and push those memories along, but surely that would not happen while The Scarlet Plumier was still at her post.

Thank heavens the man is afraid of something.

Using her fork, she smashed the eastern caper until it was completely unrecognizable.

That left the caper to the West. The Earl of Northwick. But should not he be the caper to the North?

She turned her plate until West became North. But that left her uncomfortably close to Lord Gordon, so she quickly turned it back. For just a tingly moment, it had looked so easy to go in Northwick's direction. Just as she had in the dream...

If she allowed herself to be wooed by the caper to the West, the blob to the East would realize she was truly The Scarlet Plumiere and hurry home to murder her. There was no doubt about that. And there were all those girls about to enjoy their debuts. All those fathers happy to marry them off to whomever they deemed worthy. All those future groomsmen who would be, for the majority, as worthy as they seemed. But those few who proved unworthy? Who would call them to justice for their offenses? Who would rescue those innocent brides from the secrets those men kept from Society? If not for The Scarlet Plumiere, then who?

She gobbled up the caper to the West, took a knife and scraped the Lord Gordon blob off her plate completely and wiped it on her napkin. The caper to the North was the only one remaining, so she left the table, confident in her decision to change nothing about her life.

Definitely, absolutely confident.

***

North woke late with a hundred emotions churning in his belly, but there was only one he could truly put a finger on— regret. He regretted writing that note to The Plumiere, only because it exposed him to his friends. He never intended for them to learn the truth. And they still did not know the whole of it.

They believed North had sacrificed himself for the sake of a friend. It was probably the first time since France that he had appeared worthy of their circle. But he was worthy in appearance alone. He had always belonged with his fellow Kings due to their lifelong friendship, but whether or not he was deserving of that position was a question he asked himself often. His friends never wondered of course. That's what made them the most spectacular chums in the world.

How could he crush their newfound veneration by telling them he had decided to call out his own name before he picked his friend's lot from the barrel? How could he confess he did not actually know it was Ashmoore's until after he had finally taken a look at the blasted tile, after he was safely ensconced in his own bedchambers?

As it was, they treated him like the most noble of martyrs, apologizing for the whiskey torture, eating their words. It would have been even more satisfying had he deserved it.

Ash had been moved, and Ash was rarely moved. If only he had not been moved quite so immediately, North might have been able to blurt out the truth before it was too late. Now, his confession would only embarrass them all. It might affect their friendship and that was a risk he would not take.

And there really was no reason for them to ever find out. After all, he was the only one who knew his intentions before the lot was drawn. He was the only one who knew how long it had taken before he had read Ash's name. If he could control his own tongue, he had nothing to worry about. Life would go on. Their admiration would fade back to the weak color it had been. The world would be righted. And perhaps there would be a clever female addition in his life.

His friends had finally quit the place and gone home, deep in their cups. He would have been quite drunk himself if so much of his whiskey had not gone in through his eyes. But he had been careful. A loose tongue was a dangerous thing. *And a loose lot.* Why the blast had not he destroyed it?

The bright sunlight sneaking through a gap in the curtains told him he had slept late—which meant The Capital Journal's morning edition should be waiting with his breakfast. He was downstairs in record time. The paper lay on the table, but just in case the staff was watching for their own amusement, he filled his plate first and pretended that the paper was not all he felt like devouring.

The eggs were a bit cold. They bounced around in his mouth until he washed them away with hot coffee. The sausages resisted chewing as well. Was he being punished for something?

He remembered calling Callister a traitor or something to that effect. That was probably it. His breakfast was usually ready and warm whatever hour he happened to rise in the morning, unless he had harmed the feelings of one of his staff. He was always made to pay. They were a terribly loyal bunch, and if he wanted a decent lunch, he had best apologize to his butler and do so before witnesses.

He eyed the paper and decided his butler's feelings were a bit more important. There was probably no word from The Plumiere inside anyway. Who knew how slow she might be to respond. Or perhaps she would not respond at all. Perhaps his lottery and his missive had frightened her away.

He stood and headed for the kitchens, to search for Callister while he ruminated.

If the lottery had frightened her, she would not have responded to it the morning after the event. Unless she had suffered a change of heart after his first public assault. If so, she might have gone into hiding and his quest might take a very long time indeed. In addition, he would very much miss a lively repartee.

He found his staff huddled over a table, listening as Chester read to them. The boy had only recently confessed he could not read and so the staff had vowed to teach him. But this was no lesson book from which he read.

"Dear Lott," Chester read, pronouncing carefully, if haltingly, leaving his audience to strain forward as they simultaneously listened and urged him on. Not a soul noticed their employer's presence.

"I...suppose...you meant...that last as a pun. Marry, as...opposed...to merry. Does this mean you plan to...elude...the...agreement...of the...gentlemen's...lottery...and not marry your...quarry? If you find her, that is. She will not run, hide, nor...faint...at your feet...and still you will...never catch her. I also...hear...you did not get a...chance...to show...off your new...ward...robe last even...ing. Pity. The Scar...let Plum...oh, Plumiere."

The staff erupted in a dissonant chorus of outrage and laughter.

"How the devil did she know about his red drawers?"

"Mary! It weren't his drawers they made red, it were his cravats and shirts."

"Sarah, do not be ridiculous," Callister snapped. "Of course His Lordship did not order red shirts."

"No more ridiculous than—Cor! Forgive me, Yer Lordship!"

By the time Sarah's outburst stopped echoing around the room, his staff had lined up, sealed their lips, and turned red, in that order. If they had not re-arranged themselves, he might have been able to separate the outraged persons from those highly entertained so he might give the former a nice bonus for their sympathy. But the thought of disappointing half of them never sat well. He always ended up paying everyone.

But that gave him an idea.

"Well, Chester?"

The lad stammered and shook. If he did not stop his teasing, he would put the boy off reading altogether.

"Do you have an opinion, Chester, as to how I should respond to The Scarlet Plumiere this time?"

Chester's shaking finally reached his head.

North looked to the rest. "Well?"

Callister came forward and stood like a shield between himself and the nervous staff. "Well what, sir?"

"Well, what do you suggest I write in my reply?"

A woman stepped forward. Cookie. She was likely the person to blame for his cold breakfast.

He encouraged her with a nod.

"I would tell her you were in conference all night with your band o' spies, that you are closin' in, like." Cookie opened her mouth again, then shut it tight.

"Go on. I insist."

Mary, the maid to her right stepped on her toe, but brave Cookie shook her off.

"I would give 'er the thumb to the nose, sir."

"I beg your pardon?"

"I would put on all my red finery and gad about town in them all day, no matter how many folks laugh at me."

"You would?"

Cookie blushed. "Oh, no sir. I would never!"

North laughed. "That's all right, Cookie. I think it is a fine idea. I like that a bit better than the spy idea." That band of spies was a little too close to home. In fact, he was hoping to have a few reports before his friends arrived that evening. The tables had turned from the night before. He was now mindful of keeping his friends distracted instead of the other way 'round. If he failed to do so, Ash might get the daft notion to relieve him of his writer—or rather, his duty.

His staff fidgeted and stole glances at one another. Clearly, they were uncomfortable having him in their quarters.

"You know, I do expect perfect loyalty in my staff."

"Yes, my lord, we are aware," Callister said.

"I expect there are some who would come with bribery to learn anything they can from you."

From the way a few people looked away, he suspected it had already happened.

"I know you are loyal bunch. I am sure every seamstress in town was happy to spread the news of my new...wardrobe." He walked the line, inspecting his troops, so to speak. "If...no, *when*...anyone tries to bribe you, I want you to do two things."

"What is that, my lord?"

"I want you to remember that they may well have been sent by The Scarlet Plumiere."

A dozen white mob caps nodded slowly. They would unite in his defense if they believed there was an enemy to thwart. They would all be outraged the next time The Scarlet Plumiere exposed too much information to all and sundry.

"And what else would you have us do, my lord?" Callister also seemed pleased with the sudden unity in his own ranks.

"I want you to report to me how much you were offered and I shall double it."

"Cor!" Sarah's eyes bulged.

"And trying to bribe each other does not count."

Sarah frowned. "Oh, no, sir." Then her brows rose in understanding. "*Oh!* No, sir!"

North turned to his butler. "Callister?"

"My lord?"

"I apologize for calling you a traitor last evening. I'm sure if my mother were here, she would have clouted my ears on your behalf."

"Thank you, my lord."

"And Cookie?"

"Yes, my lord?"

"An early luncheon, if you please."

The round woman laughed. "Of course, my lord."

"Now, if you will excuse me, I have a letter to write."

CHAPTER FIVE

As it turned out, that letter took the better part of the day to compose.

By noon he had been called upon by three Bow Street runners offering their services for various, but exorbitant sums. None were happy to be turned away. In fact, the last man was not the type to take no for an answer. He seated himself before North's desk without invitation and went on listing his successful missions for both the crown and the common man.

"I beg your pardon, what was your name?" North asked politely—too politely, but the man remained oblivious.

"Mister Wilbur T. Franklin at your service, your lordship. Now, as I was saying—"

"Franklin, are you by chance familiar with the Earl of Ashmoore?"

The man's mouth snapped shut and his eyes widened. He nodded. He waited.

North smiled pleasantly and took a sip of his tepid tea. Took another. Cleared his throat. Set down his cup.

"I only ask—Franklin is it? I only ask because Lord Ashmoore is expected at any moment. And you happen to be sitting in the chair he favors."

The man's rump shot up off the seat as if fired from a canon. Then he wheeled, arse first, toward the door, mumbling the word 'appointment'.

North went on as if he hadn't noticed. "He prefers to keep his back to the wall. I am sure you understand."

Wilbur T. Franklin swung the study door wide, peeked his red face toward the front of the house, then scurried down the hall in the opposite direction. Callister ran—yes, actually ran—past the opening in close pursuit, no doubt to ensure the Bow Street Runner was assisted in his exit. North was half tempted to follow just to watch, but he abstained, vowing to lure the details out of his butler at the first chance.

It was rather poor form to use Ash's name as a threat, but the earl would hardly mind. He rather enjoyed his dark reputation as the most lethal man of the aristocracy. It ensured he was left in peace. North was also given a wide berth, as it were, but whether it was due to his association with Ashmoore or his own mysterious reputation, he could not say. That this Franklin fellow seemed oblivious of both bothered him slightly, but he would rather suffer oblivious buffoons than to have all of London learn the details of those missing years in France.

While he awaited Ash's arrival, he was content to allow his mind to wander into more pleasant arenas, such as the possible form and figure of a certain writer. However, his imagination functioned so well that by the time his friend made an appearance, he was nearly out of his mind with determination to find the woman before night could fall.

Ash stopped in the doorway, but North felt compelled to finish walking the length of the windows before turning to his friend.

"That bad?" Ash waited.

North nodded to the chair Franklin had recently vacated and forced himself behind his desk once more.

"It is a sickness now. I spend every moment perusing the lists we compiled, conjuring up this image, you see. One particular form seems to push the rest aside and I am afraid I will be inconsolable if she does not at least resemble that image."

"Voluptuous?" None but Ash could ask such a thing and remain objective.

"Quite."

"Beautiful?"

"Of course." North began to feel like a silly boy.

"Dark or light?"

"Dark, I think."

"Tall or short?"

"Tall. Definitely tall."

Ash frowned for a moment, and when he looked up, North expected the man might just spit out the true identity of The Scarlet Plumiere then and there.

"That's it then. We must convince ourselves she is a flat-chested, plain woman. Short, and blond. If we can do that, we will not be disappointed. The question is, can we do it?"

That's how it had always been with the four of them. It had always been 'we'.

North closed his eyes and gave it a go.

The small, less-than-fairly endowed woman was not an entirely unpleasant package. After all, she possessed a quick wit. And she must be blessed with a dazzling smile, a smile sculpted from genuine laughter.

"At least you have stopped pouting," Ash interrupted.

"I do not pout."

"No. You do not. At least not lately." Ash looked away, then down at his hands.

North could not remember a moment of awkward silence between them. Even in France, when horror lay at their feet and painted their hands red, they had always been at ease with each other. Surely, with just the two of them in the study, Ash would feel comfortable discussing anything. The fact that he did not filled North with dread.

"Now who's pouting?" North teased, but sat back and braced his hands on the arms of his chair.

Ash continued to look at his hands. "I came early this morning because you and I have things to discuss—things that do not concern Stan and Harcourt." Finally, he looked North in the eye.

The dread in his chest turned to fire. Some things he would never discuss. Some things Ash would never discuss. They had an agreement.

"You are thinking of France. Do not." Ash shook his head vigorously.

North expelled a breath and waited. The fire in his chest took a moment to smother, but he managed it. Then for good measure, he imagined pouring cold water on the ashes, just in case.

"In spite of how much I drank last night," his friend began, "I still remember the conversation."

"As do I." North swallowed and tried not to imagine his writer being tugged from his grasp. Of course he could hardly be in love with a woman he'd never met, but he was rather fond of his new sense of hope—a sense he might not have known had she not stirred up his soul. And hope seemed as worthy a mast as any to which to tie himself.

"My lot was drawn," Ash said.

"No."

"No? You deny that my lot was drawn?"

"Yes. I mean, no." *Breathe.* "Of course your lot was drawn, but it should not have been. There should never have been a lottery in the first place. It was my idea. It is my responsibility to see it through."

Ash stood abruptly and walked to the window, wrapping his fist in his hair, then smoothing his unruly locks back into place. He turned and faced North across the room—across a battlefield of sorts. But North could not allow his friend to win this one. The undefeatable Earl of Ashmoore must be defeated! And just this once, North prayed he might be the man to do it.

"I cannot allow you to make such a sacrifice for me." Ash squared his shoulders, as prepared for battle as *he* was, it seemed.

"I am not doing it for you, if that helps." North decided to take a tip from Wilbur T. Franklin and refuse to take no for an answer. "I am doing it for myself. It is time I settled anyway, and with whom better to settle down than a woman who intrigues me?"

"I will not allow—"

"See here," North got to his feet. "I am going to find this woman. If God is merciful, I am going to find her today. You can either help me, as a true friend would do, or you can fight me. But understand this—you will not take my writer from me!" Dear lord! He had gone and said it aloud! With his words ringing in his ears, he grimaced at how childish he had sounded.

"Someone's going to fight the Earl of Ashmoore? Do tell." Harcourt stood in the doorway that had been closed a moment before. Stanley strained to see around him, then gave up and shoved the Marquis out of his way.

"Pardon me, Harcourt, but I would like a front row seat for this myself." Stan ungraciously flung himself into a chair and waited.

North shut his eyes and willed them all to go away. The room stilled. When he checked to see if his wish had been granted, he found Stan and Harcourt watching Ash, who had turned to face the window. But the man's shoulders were shaking. Then the man began to sob.

At least he would have thought his friend was sobbing if he did not know the Earl of Ashmoore so bloody well.

Stan looked to North. "What is the matter with him?"

Harcourt looked equally concerned.

"Nothing is the matter with the son of a bitch. He is laughing. At me."

Ash apparently took that statement as an invitation to vent any and all emotion he might have been suppressing for the last decade. He whooped. He hollered. He drenched his face with tears.

Callister came to the doorway. "I beg your pardon, my lord. Should I fetch a doctor for His Lordship?"

"You see, Ashmoore? You have upset my staff. I insist you control yourself."

"Ashmoore lost control of himself? Never!" Stanley turned to their dark friend. "What gives, old boy? You must let us in on the joke."

The ever-decorous earl finally folded his legs beneath him and sat upon the floor. Callister appeared at his side, offering a towel with which Ash first dried his face then blew his nose.

"Shall you tell them, or shall I?" Ash asked ominously.

"Oh, by all means." North made a grand gesture and dropped into his chair, prepared to lose all respect of his fellows.

"It seems North has fallen madly—" He look at North. "Vehemently?"

"Indeed." He'd be damned if he'd try to explain *hope* to the jackal now.

Ash gave a nod. "Vehemently then...in love with The Scarlet Plumiere, sight unseen."

Harcourt frowned. "Amusing, yes. But enough to throw you into fits?"

"Oh, I am not amused. I am relieved. North did not throw himself on the sword for me after all. It seems our Earl of Northwick was not completely honest with us last evening, were you old chum?"

"Apparently not," North murmured.

"More secrets, North?" Stanley tisked.

North tried distraction. "It occurs to me, Ashmoore, that your detecting skills might be put to better use today—"

"Shut up, North. Ashmoore was about to tell us something. Go ahead, Ash." Harcourt waved a royal hand of permission.

Ash gave Harcourt a nod, then continued. "He never intended to allow anyone else's name to be drawn, did you old boy?"

"Of course I did. In the beginning."

"And when did you change your mind? When Germaine spoke up?" Ash stood and brushed imaginary dust from his trousers, then sought a seat with his back to a wall.

"No."

"When Strothsbury offered one of his horses?" Stan grinned.

"No."

Harcourt frowned. "Well, you could not possibly have done it to keep from giving that thousand pounds away."

North's face grew uncomfortably hot before he opened his mouth to confess.

"If you must know, it was right after Landover donated his Scottish property."

A few moments later, Callister sent for four dry towels.

***

Over dinner, Stan made his report.

"The owner of The Capital Journal is a hen-pecked man by the name of Malbury. He is a minor baronette. Lady Malbury is said to run the establishment, but only in the afternoons. Her mornings are apparently spent in the parlors of the gentry, collecting gossip for various scandal sheets that are printed between editions of The Journal. She was accused once of being The Plumiere, but she denied it, of course. As far as I have learned, no one suspects her now."

"Whose houses does she frequent? Do you know?" North speared a beet with his knife. The mystery gave him an appetite he had not known in years.

"Everyone's."

"Everyone's?" That was hardly helpful.

"I beg your pardon. She frequents only those households in which ladies reside."

"Well, thank you, Stanley. That narrows it down a little." Harcourt snorted.

"My driver spoke with her driver. She visits different ladies each day. None of them twice in a week."

"Does she have a daughter?" Ash was back to his sober self. Not a trace of a laugh line on his tan face.

"Two sons who fight over who will inherit the business. No daughters."

North was relieved. There was still a good chance she was a member of the *ton*.

"We should assign three men to the building. One to follow anyone suspicious. One to report to us. One to stay on the building." North plotted and ate at the same pace, shoveling food into his mouth as quickly as he could empty it.

"Already done." Stanley, too, was eating like a starved man. "And Malbury's driver was happy to join my employ."

"Have you written your response yet?" Harcourt studied a roll as if he could not detect a way inside it.

"Not yet. I have written it in my mind a hundred times of course."

"Excellent." Harcourt ripped open the roll and buttered it generously. "I have an idea."

CHAPTER SIX

The Capital Journal, February 5ᵗʰ, Morning edition, Personal advertisements

To The SP from Mr. Lott

If the quarry is found not to be marriageable in some way (say, she is already "taken," so to speak) then the appropriate thing to do would be to murder this husband whose failure to control his...chattel...has resulted in these works of fiction. Thus another might take up the reins, or the whip, so to speak.

I do pray this is not the case, as I am more than willing to woo and win you in a traditional manner. But rest assured, I will stand by my word as I gave it to my fellows.

Oh, but The Scarlet Plumiere was furious. There had been nothing in the evening edition, and now she had choked on insults for breakfast!

"Stella!"

Though she had never been introduced to the Earl of Northwick, she had been led to believe he was one of the few men of the *ton* whose honor was without question. Since she had entered society years before, she had listened for his name. But alas, he had been so rarely the subject of conversation, her suspicions should have been roused long before.

Of course, he had never been betrothed before. And he was not betrothed now, admonished a little angel in her ear, but she was in no mood to be listening to angels. She would

send a note to Lady Malbury by the usual means and have the
man investigated on the morrow. But her response to his
insults could not wait.

"*En guarde*, Mr. Lott. If you have got skeletons in your
closet, they will not remain for long!"

A presence behind her made her jump. It was Stella. She
did not look as though she had heard her little monologue, but
merely waited to hear why she'd been summoned.

"I have an errand to attend to. Please make me
presentable." The lad who usually picked up her letters for
The Journal would not come around until it was dark again.
The staff must never know her alternate persona, so she could
not very well send one of them.

"An errand? Outside the house?" Stella's hand froze as
she reached for the brush.

"Of course. I am not a prisoner here."

"Of course not, my lady." Stella looked doubtful, but
picked up the brush and set herself to her task.

The Scarlet Plumiere felt a little doubtful herself. But the
insults ringing in her ears pushed her on. Despite her earlier
decision to let the matter drop, to cease playing cat and mouse
with the Earl of Northwick, she could not retreat now.

Silly man. He thought he was the cat.

***

""My lady, will not you consider waiting for Mr. Hopkins
to return?"

The Scarlet Plumiere stopped with one foot on the
carriage step. "Why would I need to wait for him?"

Stella stammered. "Perhaps he can see to your errand for
you. Perhaps *I* can!" Her eyes were wild. Poor thing had not
seen Livvy leave the house without her father since joining the
staff a year before.

"Stella, I assure you there is nothing to worry over. It is
not as if I'll be strolling in Hyde Park. I have one stop to
make, then I will return straight away."

"You will not let me come along, my lady?"

"No. It is something I must do alone. Of course John will be with me. I will be perfectly safe."

Her dutiful maid gave the large carriage driver a warning look that made the poor man swallow nervously. Perhaps she'd underestimated the girl's mettle.

"Are you sure you should leave your father, my lady?" Stella was so busy wringing her hands, she had forgotten herself.

"If my father needs comforting, find The Rat. He will be perfectly happy until I can return. And the only danger I am in at the moment is that of freezing to death." And with that, she pulled the carriage door shut before the maid could force her way inside. Livvy checked her reticule to be sure she had not forgotten the letter in all the quibbling. It was there, tucked neatly in the pink lining of her mother's pearl studded reticule. It smelled of the woman. Next to the letter lay a perfume laden handkerchief, forgotten for three years. She pulled it out and held it to her nose, rubbing her fingers over the stitches that created a border of tiny blue flowers.

"I wish you were here, mama."

But that was not entirely true. She would love to have had her mother at her side through her ordeal, but she doubted she could have played the role of her own savior had Lady Telford been hovering about. The woman had been so clever. After the first post by The Plumiere, her mother would likely have recognized her daughter's handiwork and been too proud to keep her discovery to herself.

So, motherless and unable to disappoint her mourning father, she had thought of a way to fend for herself. And with no daughters of her own, Lady Malbury had jumped at the chance to help. Too bad The Plumiere could not risk spending more time with the woman who ran The Capital Journal. Someone would surely suspect her. And if suspicion reached the ears of Lord Gordon, she would be dead in a week.

The carriage made its way deeper into the city, though she dared not sit too near the window to see what might have changed since last she was out and about. She and her father spent only half the year in town, but since the scandal, she only saw it on her way to and from their country home. Perhaps that was why it always seemed The Great City in her eyes; it was a great mystery she would never have a chance to solve.

She caught sight of a hack for hire and was blessed with inspiration. Without a parasol, she rapped on the wall with her knuckles.

"Stop the carriage! John! Stop the carriage!"

The big man obliged and was at her door before she reached for the handle.

"What is it my lady?"

"Hand me out."

"Here, my lady?"

"Yes, here. I wish to hire that carriage to take me the rest of the way. Do not be offended, but I cannot risk someone recognizing this carriage when I arrive at my destination. Trust me on this."

"But, my lady—"

"No buts about it, John. Wait for me here."

John did not wait, however. He abandoned the carriage to accompany her to the hack, then paid the man.

"Thank you, John," she said as he helped her into the hack.

"Hopkins will have my head in a basket. Just see if he don't, my lady." And with that, he closed the door.

The hired driver opened the hatch. "Where to, Miss?"

The street on which The Journal was located was particularly congested that day. Whether or not that congestion was usual, she could not say. The last time she had set foot inside the building she had been clutching that first letter in her hand and a prayer in her heart that she might find someone inside those doors willing to help her.

Traffic came to a complete stop and those memorable doors still a half-block away. It was such a cold day she was not even tempted to walk, even if she had had the nerve to do so. She reached for the window, conceding a breath of cold air might bolster her courage a bit. Beyond the glass, a man sat on the steps outside The Journal, holding up a paper, as if

reading, but avidly watching the crowd instead. Not far from
him, a man leaned against a pillar, acting in much the same
manner. Were they watching for her? Was she incredibly vain
to think such a thing?

A woman started up the steps and three men came to
attention, the two she had noticed, and a third young man who
stood near the roadside, presumably to earn a coin by holding
horses. But he was not watching for customers; he was
watching the lady. With his head, the man on the steps
gestured for the young man to follow her. The boy had taken
only a few steps when another man caught up to the woman
and took her elbow—likely her husband. The boy fell back to
his post.

Dear heavens! They were watching for a lone woman. A
woman like her! She could not go inside now, no matter if the
trio might only be a band of pick-pockets and not spies sent by
the Earl of Northwick. And she certainly could not trust
anyone to deliver the letter for her. There was too much at
risk—her work, her very life! Better for her to just go home
and stew in her anger until her usual messenger could come
for her letter. She only trusted him because the lad worked for
Lady Malbury. No doubt he believed Lady Malbury was
carrying on an affair with Papa.

The hack lurched forward and she moved back against
the seat, watching the watchers as she neared the wide set of
steps and suddenly, the hack stopped! She'd forgotten to tell
the driver she had changed her mind!

All three men turned their heads. The young one, near the
road, tried to see into the depths. He seemed to look directly
into her eyes! The hack shook. The driver was there in an
instant, opening her door, holding out a gloved hand. The boy
moved close, tilting his head one way, then another.

"My lady?" The driver peeked inside.

"No! I have changed my mind," she whispered loudly.

"Eh?"

"Take me back. This instant!"

The boy lunged for the door as it snapped shut. She held
onto the handle as if her very life depended upon her ability to

do so. The hack rocked wildly as the driver mounted, nearly pulling the handle out of her grasp. Still the boy tried to open the door.

"Dear Lord, help me!"

"'Ere, now. Get away from there. That's a lady inside."

The driver's whip descended with a whack. The pulling ceased. But suddenly the boy's face was against the window. She quickly turned her head away. The hack lurched forward and the boy disappeared.

Had he seen her? Would he recognize her again? Could he describe her to someone—say, Mr. Lott?

The driver's voice came from a small hole in the roof. "My lady, be warned. That lad still follows. I cannot get away from 'im in this 'ere crowd, y' see."

"I understand," she called out, assuming the driver would hear.

"Do you still wish to return to your carriage?"

Her carriage? And John!

"Yes, to my carriage. Hurry if you please!" Her heart would surely explode, beating as it was.

What might happen once the hack stopped? Surely John would not harm the boy, but how would she be able to keep the lad from giving her away?

The hack sped up and gave her hope. She peeked out the window but could not tell if she was still pursued. She imagined the boy running but unable to keep up. Giving up. Turning back. She took a deep breath, then another. Her heart did not slow its beating. They turned left at a corner. Then left again, and once again. The hack came to a halt, and the door opened instantly, but it was John leaning into her view.

"Grateful I am, my lady, that you did not dawdle. I might have worried myself plum to death, I might."

"John!" She took his hand and his help.

"'Ere now. She is been followed, she has. And there's the blighter now!"

She looked up and saw the driver pointing his thumb behind him. Then she looked around John to see the young man, hands on his knees, catching his breath at the corner. John pushed her behind him, then headed for the boy.

"No! John, I forbid you to harm him. Let me speak to him." John stopped, his mouth open on an argument. She hurried past him and only got nervous when she realized the boy was walking toward her, not intimidated by John in the least.

She slowed. He kept coming. When she took a step back, the boy stopped. He looked around her, not to John, but to the coach. She stepped sideways to block his view. Only then did he seem to notice her and gave a little bow. "Please forgive me, my lady, if I frightened you. It is not my job to frighten you."

She was no judge, but he looked to be about 15 years old.

"It is only your job to find out who I am?"

He grinned. "It is, my lady...?"

She laughed. "Oh, no. I will not make it easier for you."

"It was worth a go?" He grinned.

She laughed again, but sobered. "My very life is in danger, young sir."

He frowned, looked offended. "You are in no danger from my master, I assure you."

"But if your master succeeds in unmasking me, there is another lord who will come to murder me."

The lad looked at her askance, likely trying to decide how truthful she might be.

"I realize it is just a game to your master, but it is a deadly game. He does not realize how many others anxiously wait for him to point me out."

John's heavy footsteps came closer. Without looking, she reached back a hand to stay him.

"I recognize the carriage," the lad confessed.

"You do?" Her stomach sank. Was it already too late?

He took one last look. "Yes, I do."

"Please," she said simply and put a hand to her heart.

The boy stopped smiling. Eventually, he nodded.

She walked forward, took his face in her hands, and kissed him on the cheek. He pulled away, hopped backward and turned, sprinting back down the street. When he rounded the corner, his hand was pressed to his cheek, as if holding the kiss in place.

"My lady!" John stuck his elbow in front of her, giving her little choice but to take it.

She sighed. "He was a handsome boy. I should have kissed him on the lips."

From the sounds he was making, she thought John might have swallowed his tongue. She released his elbow to pound him on the back.

"I was jesting, John. Only jesting."

But of course she had not been jesting at all. It might have been her only kiss and she had gotten it wrong! She may as well have been kissing her own hand.

When the carriage arrived home, Stella was huddled in a thick shawl, standing at the window. She opened the front door before Livvy reached it.

"My lady, Mr. Hopkins said he would like an audience as soon as you returned, if it is convenient."

"Oh? Of course." She handed her mantle to Chester, then followed Stella. John followed her. No doubt the big man was eager to tattle on her for the reckless kissing of a street boy. But he had not been a street boy at all. He had been dressed well enough. Not liveried, but dressed well. Was his master the Earl of Northwick? Would the boy be bullied into telling her identity? Would he tell his master about the kiss?

Oh, dear heavens, what a fool she would appear in the papers tomorrow.

She shook her head. Better not to lose faith in the boy before he had had a chance to prove himself. He had nodded. That was as good as a promise. Either way, she would know in a day or two, as soon as Mr. Lott responded.

She passed her father in the hallway. He nodded but did not stop chattering to the maids at either side, telling them the tale of how he had met his bride. It was his favorite story, always leaving him in a fine mood. She smiled, wondering if the maids had encouraged the recitation or if it had come to him on his own.

Stella preceded her to her father's study where she found Hopkins sitting behind the desk. It was unusual, to be sure, especially when the butler rose a bit slowly when she entered.

"What is the meaning of this, Hopkins?"

John came in and closed the door. Stella moved to the other side of the room, joining the gardener, the cook, and the housekeeper, Mrs. Wheaton. Hopkins rolled his eyes and shook his head, then he moved to one side and indicated the chair he'd occupied.

"Please, my lady. Sit."

Stella took great interest in her own boots. No help there.

"Very well." She took her seat and tried not to look as confused as she felt. "I have had a rather tiring day, Hopkins. I hope this will not take long."

"I am sorry to disappoint you, my lady, but it will take as long as it must needs take." The man lifted his chin and rested his fingertips on the desk. Had he raised his voice? Hopkins? His face was a bit redder than usual. His nostrils flared.

"Why, Hopkins! You are angry with me!" She laughed. "You have not been angry with me since I was, what, twelve?"

"Fourteen, actually." He cleared his throat. "But that is neither here nor there." He cleared his throat again. Stella poured him a glass of water, but he shooed her away. "You left the house."

"Yes. I did. And before John is forced to tell you what transpired, I will confess all. I forced him to stop and hire a hack for me, and then proceeded to mysterious places without him." She lowered her voice for effect. "When I returned, I had been followed by a young man. I demanded that John allow me to speak with him, then I kissed him and he went away."

"You kissed *John*, my lady?" Hopkins turned to find the driver trying—and failing—to blend in with the mahogany-paneled wall.

"Not John. The young man. I only kissed his cheek." She stood. "If there's nothing more..."

"Sit."

Hopkins had not ordered her to sit in a good ten or twelve years, but she had been trained well by that tone of voice that said, *I do not care who your father is. You will behave as a lady.*

She sat.

"So, you felt so compelled to run your errand that you left the house without a chaperone, then abandoned your only protector behind with the carriage and galloped into town."

"We could not gallop," she mumbled.

"I beg your pardon, my lady?"

"I said, we could not gallop. There were too many rigs on the road. That is why the boy was able to follow."

"Ah. I see. So we can place the blame squarely on the shoulders of all those who chose to drive on Shetland Road this morning."

Livvy felt as though she'd just been struck in the stomach.

"How could you possibly know which road I chose?"

"You went to the offices of The Capital Journal did you not?"

"Were you having me followed Hopkins? Truly?"

Hopkins closed his eyes and took a patient breath. "No, my lady. There is no need to have you followed. Correct me if I am wrong, but there is only one place The Scarlet Plumiere might be tempted to go these days."

She suddenly experienced a dozen prickles inside her nose, then behind her eyes. It was no wonder tears filled her vision.

"You *know*?"

"Yes, my lady. Only those of us in this room."

Stella and the others beamed and nodded.

"And you have told no one?"

"Of course not, my lady."

"Thank you, Hopkins. Thank all of you."

"Not at all. Not at all." He took that glass of water from Stella then, and took a long drink. "Now, who is this young man you kissed, and where is your next letter?"

CHAPTER SEVEN

The Capital Journal, February 5ᵗʰ, Evening Edition, Fiction Section,

And so, in The Great City, a certain Mr. Lott publicly slanders a writer, insinuating not only her lack of virtue, but also the lack of proper supervision by a husband who may or may not exist, and then only until Mr. Lott hunts him down and ceases that existence. What then, Mr. Lott? Will you take the place of this deceased man and beat his wife in his stead?

Beware, any young ladies who might have imagined to find happiness at the side of anyone known as such, for Mr. Lott will no doubt beat his wife and children regularly and with the support of his fellows! —The Scarlet Plumiere

Soon after the evening edition arrived at Northwick's residence, Viscount Forsgreen sent word that he had news to impart and for North, Ash and Harcourt to await him at White's Gentlemen's Club. A short while later, North sat in a comfortable chair in a private corner, sipping on a brandy and marveling that he could not, for the life of him, remember his ride across town. Had he walked? Ridden? Flown?

Flying would not surprise him in the least, as hopeful as he was that his search was at an end. In fact, if he had not stuffed himself into a rather over-stuffed chair, he might at that moment have been flitting about the room like a bird looking for access to the sky. The large establishment had hardly enough room to contain his excitement. And there was little or no space available for worry; the fact that Stanley had not hinted whether the news might be good or bad hardly registered.

Ashmoore and Harcourt arrived, followed soon after by a disappointingly sober *Viscount F*. North's hopes took one look at Stanley's face and promptly fled through the front window. When they plummeted to the street below, North winced.

"We have a problem," the viscount announced as he joined his fellows and signaled to a footman. "Four brandies."

North raised his glass. "Already have one, thanks."

"You will need another." Stan nodded to the footman and chose the seat to North's left.

"You have found her?" North could not put off the question another second.

"Is she disfigured?" Harcourt whispered. "Married? Actually a man?"

North glared at the Marquess now seated to his right. He had not considered the last.

"Oh, she is a *she* no doubt about that." Stanley still looked none too pleased about it. To North he warned, "Drink up," and went so far as to put a finger to his glass and lift the bottom.

He swallowed to keep from getting drenched in liquor for the second time that week. Perhaps the act of choking started his heart again. He damned Stanley in any case.

"You will thank me." His helpful friend took the fresh brandies from the footman and passed them around.

"Bottoms up."

North did not touch his glass. His tongue was not the one needing to be loosed.

"Spit it out," he demanded.

"All right then. She went to the newspaper offices this morning."

"Then we have her!" Harcourt jumped out of his seat.

"Not so fast," Stan said. "I had three men on the place. A hack pulled up. She must have been spooked, somehow. When the driver tried to hand her out, she told him to take her back."

"Back where?"

"To her own carriage, as it turned out. My lad tried to get a look at her through the window. He even tried to pull the door open before they drove away, but the clever chit held it shut!"

"So he followed her." Ash picked up his glass and took a distracted sip, but North knew the man was far from indifferent.

As for North, he had to concentrate on breathing. On keeping his heart from giving out. On refraining from screaming at his friend to get to the end of his tale before he, too, went out the front window!

"Yes, he followed her. He was about to give up when the hack stopped. Her carriage was waiting. Her driver started after my lad, but she stopped him, said he was not to harm the boy, then insisted she be allowed to speak with him."

"Your boy...spoke with her?" North's voice broke, but his friends pretended not to notice.

She was real—not a figment of his mind, not an apparition conjured by his lonely soul.

"Yes, he spoke with her."

"What did she say?"

Stan looked him in the eye. "I have no idea."

"Why? The boy was not killed?" North could honestly think of no other reason for the tale-telling to stop short.

"No. He was not harmed." Stan smiled.

"Did he suddenly fall mute?" Harcourt asked.

Stan shook his head, then faced North. "Now listen. The boy's not talking. He will not say a word. He recognized the carriage, but he will not tell me to whom it belonged. I do not know what the woman said to him, but it won him to her side. I am afraid there is no budging him."

"We can get the boy to talk, if you insist upon it." Ash's voice implied so much more than his words.

"You know me well enough not to make such an offer." North scoffed.

"Do I? I know Ramsay Birmingham, Earl of Northwick. I do not know Mr. Lott so well. Mr. Lott in love is another man altogether. This love of yours has made you...unpredictable."

"Blarney. The both of you." Harcourt sighed. "I refuse to believe love can change a man that much. In spite of all that happened in France, we still know each other inside and out. A little infatuation cannot do more damage than that. Especially if an infatuation with someone they have never met. Eh, North?" Harcourt slapped him on the shoulder. "Besides, if anyone has changed since this farce began, it is you, Ash. All that smiling. Laughing like a hyena at the zoo." He nudged Ash's knee with his own. "You sure you are not just as smitten as North?"

Ash's eyes flashed at North for the length of a heartbeat, then flashed back to the drink he coddled between his hands.

What the devil was that?

"Do not be ridiculous, Harcourt," said his dark friend. "*I* would have to see her first."

Their eyes met again. This time, Ash did not glace away. And he was smiling.

North lifted his glass to accept the challenge, grateful his hand did not shake when he did so. It was a race then.

He turned to Stanley. "I would still like to speak to the boy, if you do not mind."

Stan finished off his drink and slapped his empty glass onto the small solid table between them.

"I thought you might. He is outside, waiting in my carriage."

***

Two men stood before the carriage door bearing the ducal crest of Stanley's father. North recognized one of them as the viscount's driver.

"You do not have the boy tied up inside, do you Viscount?" He asked it lightly, but he was worried. For the first time in his life he felt as if he did not know his friends so well after all. In the name of friendship, Ash was willing to torture the boy, or so he'd offered. If kind-hearted Stanley Winters had the poor lad tied up in his carriage, then he would never take another thing for granted. The Marquess of

Harcourt might confess to be an imposter and North would not be surprised.

"Is he still inside?" Stanley asked his driver.

"Aye, sir." The men stepped to the side.

Stan opened the door. A lantern lit the interior. It took a bit of maneuvering, but the four of them managed to fit inside. Stanley and Harcourt sat on one side with the blanket-wrapped boy wedged between them—no telling yet if the lad's hands were tied. North and Ash faced them.

Stan clapped the boy on the shoulder. "I gave you my word you would be in no danger. I am pleased you did not run."

"No need to run, sir." The boy lifted his chin. "What would you like to know, my lords?"

Ash went first. "Did she bribe you?"

"No, my lord."

"So you choose not to reveal her identity?"

"Yes, my lord." The boy smiled as if he cared not whether his answer displeased his audience.

Harcourt elbowed the witness. "A kiss is as good as a bribe, you know."

The boy stiffened. It took North a moment to understand what that meant.

Damn it! What kind of a lady was she to go about kissing boys?

He took a deep breath and considered his emotions. Was there a chance the woman had done the deed in hopes of tormenting him? He pictured her in his mind, sitting at a delicate writing desk, the end of a red quill caught between her teeth and her bottom lip while she wondered how best to vex Mr. Lott.

Of course she had planned it. No doubt in his mind. And with his emotions back in check, he dared speak.

"I assume she kissed you then?"

The boy's chin held steady and high, as did his blush. "She did, my lord. But it was only to thank me."

"For?" Ash's voice was controlled as always.

"For agreeing not to rat her out, my lord." The boy's eyes darted to Ash, then away again.

"But you have already ratted her out, have you not?" Ash's voice was smooth, hypnotic.

The boy laughed and a hand, free of bindings, worked its way out of the blanket to shake a finger at Ashmoore. "Oh, no, my lord. You may be clever, but she is doubly so."

"And she is...?"

"The Scarlet Plumiere, my lord."

"The daughter of...?"

"Her father, I would think, my lord." The boy was unable to stifle his grin for long.

"Clever lad." Ashmoore shrugged and leaned back.

North could stand it no longer.

"Look here. Did she ask you to keep secret the fact that she is beautiful...or not?"

The boy considered, then nodded. "She is beautiful, my lord. I will give you that."

Ash shook his head. "I would not put much trust in that. He has been kissed by her."

"I beg your pardon, my lords, but I thought her most beautiful before she kissed me, or spoke to me, or told her man not to harm me."

Harcourt nodded. "I believe him."

The boy seemed pleased by it.

North tried to hide just how pleased he was. It was a wonder he did not jump out of his seat and knock himself unconscious on the low ceiling. He distracted himself by thinking of something else to lure the lad out.

"Ashmoore here bet the gentlewoman would be a blonde. My guess was a brunette."

The lad looked at the dark earl and swallowed. He lowered his chin a bit, but his words remained bold.

"I have forgotten the lady's hair, my lords."

Harcourt laughed. North forged on, no longer trying to hide his enthusiasm. The boy was too clever by half.

"Unmarried?"

"Last I heard, sir."

"What of her height, then? You can tell us if she is short or tall, surely."

"Who is to say how tall is tall?" The boy winked, damn him.

"Did she have to rise up to kiss you? Or bend down?"

"Neither."

"So she is of a height with you, then?"

"Yes, my lord." The boy's grin widened while North looked him over.

Damn! His teeth clenched, but he managed to speak through them. "I do not suppose you would like to step out of the carriage."

"Aw, no my lord. I have taken a chill, I have. And Lord Winters here did promise me a carriage ride home."

Half an hour later, the Four Kings sat 'round a table playing Whist. They had lost a battle, that was all. They had yet to lose the war.

It was not the *tête-à-tête* in the carriage that disturbed North. It was the boy's parting words, given sincerely.

"Give up the game, Lord Northwick. Please. For her."

So, The Scarlet Plumiere would be in danger if he found her out? Was it just an impression she gave to a smitten young man to persuade him to keep her secret? Or would she truly be in danger? Of course there were many gentlemen who held grudges. But as the wife of the Earl of Northwick, would she not enjoy complete protection?

He resisted the thought, but it came anyway; *would Ash be better able to protect her?*

"Well," came Harcourt's voice, through a haze of cigar smoke swirling around his head. "We at least know my plan worked. We provoked her, and she appeared."

With all the commotion, North had completely forgotten about the plan.

"Well, then," he said. "Let's do it again."

CHAPTER EIGHT

The Scarlet Plumiere sat at her dressing table searching the mirror before her for any sign of her mother. The slant of her nose, perhaps. Something similar there. And a look about her eyes.

Papa always told her there was a bit of her mother in her eyes when she laughed.

Summoning a false smile, she could not see it. Nothing mischievous. Nothing cunning in her eyes this morning. Perhaps if she had enjoyed a more successful night of sleep, she would look a bit more intelligent. But how could she expect to sleep when her fate might be revealed in the next edition of The Journal? As soon as she could get a paper in her hands, she would know if the boy had kept her secret.

The suspense kept her mind from settling 'til nearly dawn. Had she remembered how early the paper would arrive, she would not have been able to sleep even then. But she'd forgotten, then she'd slept like the dead, and now it was too late.

If she did not get up earlier than her father, she had to wait for the man to finish with his morning read before she could have her turn. Sometimes it took him all of the morning, depending on the news of the day. And worse, sometimes the man forgot he had read the thing and started over once again.

But it was not the waiting that most concerned her, or even her fate, it was the reminder that her father's mind was slipping further by the day.

Stella toed the door open, breakfast tray in hand and a grin on her face.

"Hopkins thought you might enjoy your own copy of The Capital Journal today, my lady." The maid quickly placed the tray before her.

And so he had! There, next to her usual fare lay a lovely, crisp copy of the paper. But she restrained herself. First, she took two sips of tea and two bites of a warm roll, fortified herself with a bite of sausage, then chased it all down with a larger mouthful of tea. If the tray were returned to the kitchens untouched, she would be served enormous amounts of food all day. Best not to insult the cook or concern Mr. Hopkins. Since the butler had confessed his knowledge of her clandestine deeds, he had been a bit more bossy than usual. But she knew it for the affection it was.

She could wait no longer and pushed the tray to the side. The nosey staff would just have to face the fact that the morning was a bit too tenuous to include the cleaning of one's breakfast tray.

With shaking hands, she picked up the paper. She leafed through the pages and could not find the personal section!

"It has to be here! They have never let me down before."

She started again, from the beginning. It was right where it always was, directly after the fashion page. She sighed in relief.

Stella leaned over her shoulder.

"I do not see why they do not put it right there on the front page. I am sure it is the first thing everyone will be reading this morning."

"Nonsense. Only gossipy women read my articles, and the men who get exposed."

Stella snorted. "Surely you do not really believe that, my lady. Common and gentlemen alike go after the newsies like the last fish in the basket. When you are after someone, the paper does triple their business to be sure."

The Plumiere had never considered what affect she might have on the newspaper. Still, it was flattering to know she was the source of entertainment for some. She had thought herself quite clever at times, but a quick look around at her situation humbled her soon enough.

If she were so clever, why had she not found a way back into society? Why was she not dancing at balls, invited to dine with clever people, taken to the Opera on the arm of a handsome gentleman? Why was she resigned to her father's home with only his company, and only when her appearance did not upset the man...or his rat?

No. She was not clever. She was lucky.

She almost regretted finding the personal section so soon. One last letter from her might-have-been pursuer—that was all she would have. No matter what the man had written, she would not respond. Until another young woman needed her help, The Scarlet Plumiere would go silent. She had realized, for her own health, it would be far too risky to indulge any longer in her cat-and-mouse play with Northwick. If he found her, she was as good as dead. Truly.

And then, what of her father? If Lord Gordon hunted her down and put her head on a pike, her father would not last for long, whether Gordon got to him or not. The staff would be able to keep the truth from him for a while. But sometimes, when they least expected it, her father would become completely lucid. What then? What if he read in the papers that his daughter had died? Perhaps he would only remember her as the girl who so resembled his wife. But what if he did remember? What if he remembered over and over again?

The blow would be too much. Lord Gordon will have killed two birds with one stone.

The Plumiere shook off her morbid thoughts and reached for that one last thrill. One final dessert on the tray that was her life.

It was there. A note from Mr. Lott. But why had he made this, of all notes, so terribly brief?

No matter. At least there was something.

> *The Capital Journal, February 6ᵗʰ, Morning edition, Personal section*
> *My Dear SP,*
> *You tempt me to be just as you have painted me. Pray, bring a switch and meet me in Hyde Park Sunday afternoon, if you dare. –Mr. Lott*

The boy had kept his word! He had not revealed her to the earl! She was safe!

She took just a moment to enjoy her relief before reading the message once again. And again. Then a slow smile curled her lips that caused her maid to take a step back.

There were a few times in The Plumiere's life when inspiration struck her like a lightning bolt from Heaven itself. Sometimes she had known, instantly, what to write in order to help a young woman. She experienced such inspiration as she read Mr. Lott's short, but rousing note.

Rousing, because she had no choice but to act, and inspiring, because she knew precisely what action she must take. It was plain as the type with which the note had been set.

A dignified but silent withdrawal was not possible now. If she did not RSVP to his invitation, The Plumiere's reputation would suffer, she reasoned. And the one weapon she possessed in her war against the dishonorable gentlemen of the *ton* would become but a dull-edged sword. If she were mocked, she had no power.

And if anyone was going to be mocked in the papers this season, it was going to be Ramsay Birmingham, Earl of Northwick.

"Do you need to answer straight away, my lady? John could see to it your missive is delivered to The Journal in time for the evening post."

She considered for only a moment, then reached for her breakfast once again. She would need her strength for this day.

"I believe it might serve me better to let Mr. Lott stew, at least until morning." Besides, she had other correspondence to write.

CHAPTER NINE

The Capital Journal, February 7ᵗʰ, Saturday edition

> *Let it be known throughout The Grand City that a certain writer will present herself and her switch at Hyde Park on Sunday, noon. Come rain. Come shine. Come the Lord.*

Saturday evening, North could not contain his excitement. When a knock was heard at the front door he scurried down the stairs to answer it himself and flung the door wide. As usual, his friends were prompt. Stanley and Harcourt laughed in surprise and Ash, being Ash, frowned.

"You are not dressed," Stanley said as he entered.

"And neither are you!" North fidgeted like a school boy while their hats and coats were taken by Callister, then he led them up the stairs.

"What are you talking about?" Harcourt trotted up behind him.

North reached his own rooms and urged them inside. "We are going to set a new fashion, gentlemen."

"We are?" Stanley lined up with the other two and Chester came from the dressing room with a pile of red clothing.

"Yes, *we* are."

Harcourt laughed as he was handed a red cravat and kerchief. "You could not have made this fashion statement on your own?"

"Let's just say I wish to make a louder statement than one man can make."

Ash sighed but made no complaint as he began tugging off his own cravat.

After passing the scarlet items around, Chester retrieved a package from the dressing room and set it on the bed.

Stanley pointed with his elbow while his hands were busy working a stickpin through the fabric at his neck.

"What's that?"

"Another set." North grinned and lifted his chin while Callister made a smarter shape of the red stuff beneath.

"For whom?" Harcourt met North's eyes in the mirror.

"Beau Brummel."

Of course he'd been prepared to share Brummel's participation in order to gain his friends' cooperation, but his fellow Kings had capitulated without fuss. Their sudden inability to speak was rather gratifying, however.

Finally, Ash spoke. "I would never complain, of course, but might I ask why we are making this fashion statement?"

"To make her laugh," he explained.

"The Plumiere?"

"Of course."

Harcourt snorted. "I will bet you a crown she will not be the only one laughing."

North sighed. "Does it matter?"

"Not really, no."

Ashmoore studied North a bit too closely. "There must be something you are not telling us. You cannot seem to look me in the eye. A bad habit you have lately acquired."

North tipped back his head and grimaced. "Fine." He looked at his dark friend. "I suppose I was hoping I might somehow recognize her laugh. Are you satisfied?" He then braced himself for ridicule.

His three friends exchanged looks, then Ashmoore turned back to him. "We will accept that."

"You will?"

"Of course," said Harcourt, heading for the door. "It is not unlike the Cinderella story. Only you will search with a certain type of laughter in mind, instead of a shoe in hand."

Stanley followed next. "Your romantic side is showing, Harcourt. Beware not to let a woman hear you speaking of Cinderella and her slipper. You'll be discovering shoes on your doorsteps every morning."

A moment later, they were descending the wide staircase when a footman came to the door—likely the most smartly dressed footman in all of England, actually. North handed the man the parcel.

"Please be sure His Lordship understands how incredibly grateful I am for his participation tonight."

"I will, Your Lordship."

Callister held up Stanley's coat for the viscount to don, obviously trying not to stare at the man's necktie. While it did not clash with the black and white of his evening clothes, it did nothing whatsoever to improve it. But North wanted it that way. The more shocking the better.

A brilliant idea, but it was hardly his own. Rather the credit belonged to both Brummel and Cookie. As unlikely as it seemed, it appeared the two thought along the same lines, that North should done his Scarlet finery and strut about the city. He was already prepared to wear the red stuff that night, but Brummel had called upon him with the same idea, adding an offer to join in the prank. North had merely allowed the famous man believe the idea had been his own.

Resembling bandy roosters more than Kings, the four climbed into Ash's carriage and headed off to the first of many events that evening.

In the back of North's mind rose the ridiculous notion that the lady may not accept him, but he tamped down the thought like a hot coal, a nuisance that would hopefully die out if he left it alone.

"I will believe it when I see it." Stanley harrumphed out the window.

North feared he had been thinking aloud, but when Ash spoke, he relaxed.

"I would not bet against him, Stanley. If Beau Brummel says he will wear something daring, he will wear it."

Harcourt nodded. "Too bad he does not know a good spy or two to help us find the chit."

"So you have had no luck either, hm?" Ash shook his head faintly. "My sources can find nothing."

"You have to admit," Stanley interjected. "She smacks of a female Robin Hood. And she must be quite clever about hiding herself. Otherwise, her supposed gentlemen victims would have found her out. Some, I am sure, are more than capable of murder. "

The parting words of Stanley's young spy threatened to surface, but North tamped them down as well. It was not a night for worries, but a night for making merry.

At Lady Emerson's they walked through the ballroom like a parade of black and red swans, dipping their heads now and again as they wandered past the ladies. Of course North kept his ear cocked for some magical note of laughter but was not terribly discouraged when he did not hear it. It was only their first party.

They repeated the parade through the second floor of Lady Harper's fete, pausing here and there for a word of greeting with the gentlemen. The ladies seemed leery of conversing with them rather than being amused by their costumes, dashing all hopes of sampling their laughter. In the ballroom, however, the laughter was free for the listening. Too free, truth be told. Even the orchestra was forced to stop playing in order to catch their breath. Of course all Four Kings laughed along—they had intended for the evening to be a lark, after all—but inwardly, North was cursing himself for not anticipating such a reaction. How in the world could he discern the heartfelt laughter of one woman amidst the guffaws of so many?

Once the hilarity died down, he took heart again and went in search of a dance partner. He rather hoped The Plumiere might turn out to be Natalia Somersby. Such a nice long neck on that one. So elegant when she moved. But when he begged a dance from her, she took one look at his cravat and spooked like a horse. Her mother was quick to apologize, but it was clear the older woman suspected he and his friends were mad.

At Irene Goodfellow's party, poor Stanley spent an hour in the study with the girl's father, assuring him that Lord Brummel himself was in on the joke, and all would be made right in the papers. The older man spent the rest of the hour lecturing on the cost of practical jokes, how truly impractical they were in light of the blunt he had paid for his daughter's party and he would see no peaceful return for the investment.

It was not until Brummel himself stood at the top of Irene's stairs, proud as a scarlet peacock, that North stopped worrying about the Goodfellow's tarnished opinion of Stanley. Having the man attend one's event was the favor of a lifetime, even had the man shown up dressed as a cat with whiskers painted on his face.

What Brummel did wear was shocking enough. The red of his cravat was repeated, perfectly, in the red of his breeches. His waistcoat was of red and puce stripes, and his puce coattails announced to all and sundry that only the most talented of tailors could have constructed the entire ensemble.

North would be damned if his fashionable friend had not taken his little joke and created a furor that would reach Paris, be copied a hundred times, and touted the greatest stroke of Avant Guard since Adam picked up a fig leaf.

North offered to speak to Goodfellow, to take responsibility for making Stanley dress the way he had, but the latter just laughed and shook his head.

"I am afraid if Lord Goodfellow has to spend one more second staring at a piece of red cloth, he will charge like a bull. No. If the wedding is called off because of this, then it is not a family to which I would like to attach myself for the rest of my days. I will be the perfect gentleman for the rest of the evening. That will have to suffice."

He must have been sincere, too, for Stanley immersed himself in the role of a responsible fiancée for the rest of the night, drinking only punch and the odd glass of sherry.

As the hour grew late, he conceded defeat. Surely he would never hear the honest laughter from any woman in such a public setting where every movement of a fan, every inflection of speech, and every batted lash was watched so closely.

And then he heard it. Off to his left, a woman laughed.

He turned and strode toward the balcony doors. Could it be she? Was The Plumiere, at that moment, watching him from beyond the windows?

A young man stood in the shadows, murmuring in the ear of a young woman as he wrapped his coat about her shoulders. She laughed again. It was the very music he'd been listening for.

She glanced up and gasped, then turned her back to him. There had been no recognition in her eyes, no attention given to his clothes, the color of which was still discernible from the light of the ballroom shining through the windows.

His smile faded when the young gallant stepped forward to block North's view of his lady.

It was not until the long ride home in the odd blue darkness before dawn that he was actually tempted to give up the chase. How the devil was he supposed to recognize her? By the look of guilt in her eyes? A bit of ink on her fingers? His only chance, truly, was that the woman was foolish enough to bring a switch to Hyde Park.

Please, God. Let her be foolish.

CHAPTER TEN

North paced while his horse was saddled. He had dressed rather quickly. The poor stable lad had needed a moment more, but rather than insult the boy by finishing the job for him, he paced—as far away from the stable doors as he could stand. It would not do to make the boy or the horse nervous too.

Harcourt arrived at twenty of twelve. The cloud from his breath mingled with that from his horse. The tips of his ears were pink, the rest of him was safe from the cold morning air by a handsome new greatcoat collared with fur.

"Has your stable lad got an extra bridle do you think?"

North spared a glance at his friend's tack. It all looked sound.

"Of course. Is there a problem?"

"I do not need one, actually, but *you* may. There is no controlling you, I fear. I might ask the lad for a lasso, in case you bolt for the park without your mount."

North did not trust his tongue, so he merely ignored the man.

"Do you believe she will be there?" Harcourt continued, undaunted.

"Of course. She said she would. To all her readers, she promised to be there." And he was one of her readers. "I doubt she is the type to be afraid of the cold."

"I think she will be sitting across the road, huddled in a carriage, watching you make a fool of yourself so Society will have plenty to laugh about in the morning edition."

North froze in his tracks.

Was she purposefully making sport of him? Of course she was. It is what their little dance was about. But surely she would keep her word. And if she did not, well, perhaps she was not the woman for him after all.

That's what he had come to; building up bitter feelings toward The Plumiere just in case he was disappointed yet again. He worried his rusty heart might not be up to her toying with it.

The lad brought 'round his horse and he mounted in a much more controlled fashion than he had been capable of just a moment before. It was better this way, more dignified. If he entered Rotten Row, anxiously bouncing in his saddle, he would be fodder for more than one newspaper.

Sedately, they made their way to Hyde Park. A patch of snow remained here and there, but the winter had been a mild one thus far. Although the air was frigid at the moment, the sun pierced the middle of a clear sky and promised to make mud out of the frozen paths before much longer.

Two blocks from the park entrance, Ash and Stanley waited. Together, in thick brown coats, they looked like four fashionable bears.

"What the devil took you so long? I would have expected you to be early this morning, of all days." Stanley adjusted his seat, then adjusted it again, his jostling demonstrating just how ridiculous North would have appeared had Harcourt not tossed cold water on him.

He turned to the latter. "Thank you, my friend."

"Not at all." Harcourt had also taken note of Stanley's fidgeting and apparently knew why he'd been thanked.

They moved on and finally Stanley settled. A block further and North's stomach tied itself into knots, but he kept his attention straight ahead. Was she watching him even now?

"I suppose we must make a circuit, make damn good and sure you are seen." Ash was not the most gregarious of men. That he had agreed to march in yet another parade said much about his loyalty—or else it said much about his interest in The Plumiere. North would be damned before he would ask which.

They rode by twos and when they headed through the gate, Stanley and Harcourt reined in. North and Ash nearly collided with them, but it had been no one's fault; the park was packed to bursting with carriages. In fact, he would not have been surprised if every carriage in London were attempting to crowd onto the lane.

There were plenty of people afoot as well. Mostly women, he noted, and unafraid of muddying their skirts. They all carried what looked to be willow branches. Every last damned one of them! Even a few carriage drivers were using a thin branch to control their teams!

Harcourt turned and grinned. "Rather like sending Stanley a pair of spectacles."

North had no time to be amused. No time to be disappointed. He had to act quickly. He had to find her! Somehow.

"All right, gentlemen. We split up. Try to remember every woman you see!"

He divided the park and gave his friends their assignments, then headed down the center of Rotten Row.

She was here. She had kept her word. Now, by hell he was going to keep his.

As the sun warmed the winter scene before him, he felt inspired to search, not for The Scarlet Plumiere, but for his own heart. She would be the one holding it.

***

"Damn her to hell!"

"Now, North. Do not be so bitter." Stanley got up from the dining table and headed to the sideboard to fill his plate. Again. He had only done so half a dozen times that afternoon.

The dining room had become the war room out of necessity. For some silly reason, his friends refused to work long hours without food. And of course the table was needed for all their reconnaissance.

Every now and then, Callister would slide a small plate of sustenance past North's elbow and hover about until he ate the last bite. He might have collapsed on top of the lists and been absorbed into the heap otherwise, so he should be grateful. But at the moment, he was not capable of feeling gratitude.

"Cold tea, sir." Callister was at his elbow again. "It might help to revive you."

"Better pour it on his head, then," suggested Harcourt from his left.

"It is no use," said Ash. "Everyone I can think of now has already been added to the list." He pushed aside the peerage register. "I am beginning to believe every woman in London was in that park today. Even Lord Telford's daughter was there, and she has not been seen in public for nearly two years."

"I would wager young lads were minding their manners today. All those women about with switches in their hands." Harcourt laughed.

"She has made it rather difficult to find a lead, has not she?" Ash smiled. "She is a clever, clever woman."

North sat up. No cold drink needed. His friend's frightening smile did the trick.

"Cannot have her, Ash." Harcourt tossed a balled piece of parchment toward the far end of the table. "North will lose all respect if he fails to woo and win her now. No one will believe a recant."

"True." North tried a sober nod, but Ash narrowed his eyes. Better to change the subject of the conversation and do it quickly. "But I cannot very well woo and win her if we cannot find her lads."

"Have you an idea?" Stanley returned to the table and North reached across and relieved him of a cross-bun.

"We know she is somewhere on this list." And damn if it was not all they knew.

"Then how do we eliminate names?" Stanley asked the question for the tenth time.

North pushed back his chair and rose. It was maddening, knowing her name was there, on his table, waiting for him to pick up the right bit of parchment and read her identity. He paced around the table once, twice, then reached out and took up the nearest list. Mimicking Harcourt's game with the globe, he looked away, pointed at the list, then looked to see what name lay nearest his finger.

Whether or not he had been divinely led to the name, it gave him a brilliant idea.

"If the daughter of Lord Telford was there, The Plumiere's other liberated women had to have been there as well. The poor, showing up to support their Robin Hood, as it were." North smiled.

"If we take her rescued damsels from the list, we will eliminate less than a dozen," Stanley pointed out.

"We do not eliminate them. We eliminate everyone *but* them. We will do whatever we must to get these women to confess."

"Including seduction?" Harcourt laughed.

"Why not?" He threw his hands in the air and caution to the wind. Finally, he had a solid plan.

"You had better be very, very careful, North." Stanley appeared genuinely concerned. "Some young lady might one day need saving from you."

CHAPTER ELEVEN

After spoiling The Plumiere once with her own copy of the paper, Hopkins must have realized he could never turn back. The morning edition peeked over the edge of her breakfast tray as Stella strode into her room. Not realizing her mistress was already awake and waiting, the maid placed the tray on an ottoman while she went about opening the curtains.

"Good morning, Stella," Livvy sang.

The maid nearly jumped from her skin. "Cor! Good morning, my lady."

Stella scooped up the tray and hurried to the bed.

"No need to rush this morning. It is my own letter I will be reading today. Tomorrow should be much more exciting."

"Yes, my lady." The maid stood fidgeting next to the bed in any case.

The Plumiere let the breakfast wait for a moment and opened the paper. She found the fiction section, then noticed Stella straining her neck to read what she could.

"Would you like to read something?"

In answer, the maid scooped up the remainder of the paper.

The Plumiere laughed. Then, in case Stella was anxious to hear what she herself had written after the episode at the park, she read it aloud.

> *The Capital Journal, February 9ᵗʰ, Morning edition, Fiction Section*
> *And so it happened in The Great City that a certain Mr. Lott was unable to locate the writer he sought at Hyde Park on a Sunday afternoon. Perhaps*

*the man suffers from the same poor eyesight with
which his dear friend, Viscount F, suffers. Or perhaps
his long evening of the night before affected his ability
to see the woman with the switch who was right before
his eyes.*

    *Speaking of which...Was it terribly devastating
this writer wonders, when Mr. Lott and his fellows
found they were not as fashion-forward as they
presumed? It seems they were upstaged by The Great
City's own Lord B whose valet—or possibly Lord B
himself—lent a much more talented hand to the tying
of His Lordship's scarlet cravat.*

    *In short, Lord B's ensemble was stunning, I am
afraid Mr. Lott and associates merely stunned.*
—The Ever-Scarlet Plumiere"

She giggled. Poor Mr. Lott. He would believe she had
been present at one or more of the soirees attended by the four
ridiculously clad lords the previous night, and all because of a
little detail her driver was able to glean from another driver—
that Lord Northwick had difficulty keeping his cravat straight
all night.

It was a delicious detail to which she had never been
privy had her staff not come forward and unmasked her. The
little gathering from the study consisted of her most loyal
servants, thank heavens, so her secret was completely safe.

Stella gasped.

The Plumiere turned the find the girl white as a sheet,
holding out a page as if it were covered in blood.

"My word, Stella. What is it?"

"He's answered you, my lady, in the personal notices."

"That is not possible. He could not have known what I
was going to write!"

She refused to panic. The maid must be mistaken. It
could not be from Mr. Lott.

She scanned the sheet.

    To A Certain Writer from a Mr. Lott
    My dearest Scarlet Plumiere,

*...I feel it only sporting to warn you, I have you
now.*

A dozen emotions flooded her body and clashed in the
center of her chest. She could not breathe. She had turned to
stone, surely!

The man was bluffing. He had to be. It would be
impossible for the man to have learned her identity from the
farce at the park. Thanks to Lady Malbury's ability to spread
gossip from one end of the country to the other in a matter of
hours, she had secretly invited all the women of the *ton* to find
a willow branch and come to Hyde Park for a bit of
entertainment. Out of so many, how could he have settled on
her?

Unless a certain young man had been tortured into
confession!

An hour later, she was still fuming at Northwick's
attempt to draw her out. It was obviously the only strategy he
had. There were truly no leads to follow. There was no way he
would find her out.

"He is bluffing," she said for the twentieth time since
Stella had begun working on her hair. Nothing of her mother
in the mirror now. She did not even resemble herself. Pale.
Worried. But her hair looked marvelous. Stella had only
needed to start over once this time. The new style looked even
better on her than it had the first time. Her dark hair held the
ringlets naturally. The weaving in the front looked much more
like a crown than it had before.

Her gaze dropped back to her own eyes.

"He is only bluffing," she promised herself.

Stella nodded, a bit too vigorously.

The door burst open. Hopkins stood just outside, catching
his breath. He had not knocked. Had he, too, read the personal
notices? Or was it—

"My father?"

Hopkins shook his head. "Your father is quite well this
morning, my lady. Forgive the intrusion, but you have a
visitor.

"Lady Malbury?" That was a frightening possibility. If the woman came to her home, it would put her secret in danger. In order to get the woman's aid for Sunday afternoon, she had merely left a note for the woman under the pot on Friday night. Reliable as clockwork.

"No, my lady. You have a...*gentleman* caller."

Hopkins looked at the salver in his hand as if debating the necessity of showing her the card placed ominously on its surface. But if the butler was uncertain, who was she to sway him? So she waited.

Hopkins brought it forward as if it were the calling card of The Prince Regent.

The Scarlet Plumiere found her courage and took the card.

Earl of Northwick.

The newspaper screamed from her bedside table. *"I have you now!"*

"Hopkins," she tried to do more than whisper, but failed.

"Yes, my lady?"

"Tell His Lordship that I do not accept callers."

"I have already assured the man you do not."

"And he did not leave?"

"No, my lady. He asked me to tell you he cannot leave until he has been heard."

Her maid fainted, rather dramatically in fact. She wondered why she did not do the same herself. And truly, a good look at Hopkins made her wonder if the man had not fainted, then recovered just outside her door. He was still breathing strangely, poor man.

"Well, then. We shall just let him wait until he tires of the futility."

Hopkins shook his head.

"Hopkins?"

"I am sorry, my lady, but your father is already entertaining Mr.—that is to say—His Lordship is already entertaining Lord Northwick.

The Plumiere jumped to her feet. "My father?" The devil was in her house and alone with her father?

Hopkins stepped in her path and bowed. "Begging your pardon, my lady, but your father is quite himself this morning. He is doing admirably if you do not mind me saying so."

She exhaled in relief. A good day for Papa meant a good day for her. Lord Northwick be damned.

But how on earth had he found her? *He cannot be that clever. He cannot. What can he hope to find here? Signed confessions? Inky fingers?*

"Stella, I need gloves!"

Stella was blissfully unaware of her needs, so she tossed a shawl over the woman and found her own gloves.

"The only hint of who I am was far back in the first article. Is he that clever? Has he guessed it? If that is where he learned my name, then he cannot be sure. He must be guessing that The Plumiere has something to do with me."

"Unless the boy confessed, my lady."

"I refuse to believe it. Unless they tortured him... Surely they would not have tortured him!"

"Please sit, my lady. You cannot allow him to see you so upset. If he does not know already, he might guess if you panic."

She sat and fanned her face. Hopkins poured her a glass of sherry.

She held up a hand. "No, Hopkins. I will need my wits, thank you."

She imagined the man conversing pleasantly with her father, unaware he was able to do so only because the older man was having a particularly good day. What would he expect her to say when they met? Would he accuse her in front of Papa? Would he be disappointed she was not more beautiful? Was he there to announce he had no intention of marrying a woman with so sullied a past? Would he expect tears? A duel?

"Hah!"

She thought frantically. No telling how long her father's excellent day would last. And there might actually *be* a duel if the man hurt her father's feelings in any way.

"So," she thought aloud. "If he thinks to find the brave-hearted Scarlet Plumiere here, at my home, he will be sorely disappointed. I will deny it. I will be anything but brave. I will be anything but clever. He will be sniffing in circles until he tires and goes away!"

Inside, of course, she was huddled in a corner of her mind, rocking nervously, waiting for her doom.

***

"Mr. Lott, I presume."

North should have been prepared for such a greeting, but had supposed the Earl of Telford was above reading gossip sheets.

"I must confess to it, my lord." He bowed deeply.

The old man simultaneously pounded him on the back and pulled him into the drawing room. "I supposed I have made my own confession, have not I? Read the fiction section first, myself." The earl gestured to one chair and stood before another, waiting for North to sit first.

"After you, my lord."

Telford laughed. "Oh, my boy. Please call me Telly. Everyone does."

North doubted there were many in that circle. From what Ash had learned, the man rarely made an appearance since the death of his wife three years before. Even his attendance in the House of Lords had ceased. So why come to London at all?

Since The Incident with Lord Gordon two years ago, his daughter had been as much a recluse. But she had pried herself out of her home long enough to find a switch and join the parade at Hyde Park.

And if she was willing to make an appearance in public, she could bloody well accept a caller!

"Telly it is then. And you must call me North."

Telford beamed. "I shall. Thank you."

A maid fluttered in, looked strangely at her master, then bowed her way back out of the room.

"Josie! Some tea, if you please!" Telford ordered. "Now, North. You must tell me everything. I shant allow you to leave until you share all you know about The Scarlet Plumiere."

"If you insist." It was a fact it suited him perfectly—since he did not plan on leaving until he had had a nice long visit with Lord Telford's daughter.

***

North was shocked at how well he got on with Lord Telford. The man had all sorts of advice for him, as if he were passing down generations of wisdom that he would have shared with a son. But having had a single daughter, he had heaped it all on the head of the first available younger man that came by the house.

The man was obviously still mourning Lady Telford, as the majority of his advice had to do with the proper treatment and respect for one's wife. And there were times during their conversation when the gentleman emanated a very real desperation, as if he were afraid the information would be lost otherwise.

North listened sincerely, reveling slightly in the temporary facade of a father instructing his son. A Father without a son. A son without a father. Was that it? He suspected there was something else, some current churning beneath the man's words. And so he listened and watched for some clue, but clarity never presented itself.

Finally, the conversation turned to The Capital Journal and that morning's edition.

They were laughing nigh to tears when the butler stepped into the room and cleared his throat. He, too, looked strangely at Lord Telford, then announced, "Pardon me, my lords. Your tea."

The nervous maid returned, but her eyes were down, her nose was high, and there was no sign of her earlier confusion.

"Thank you, Josie. I am sure Lord Northwick has a steady hand."

"I supposed we shall see," North said, then reached for the pot.

***

"Well, Hopkins? Do you suppose he knows?" She stood to the side of the stairway, dreading her first encounter with the handsome Mr. Lott.

"I am sorry, my lady. There was no telling, though I doubt they would have been laughing so outlandishly had either of them supposed you were The Scarlet Plumiere."

Mrs. Wheaton cleared her throat. Her eyes were the size of billiard balls. Only when the shadow behind her shifted, was the source of her alarm made clear.

"Lord Ashmoore to see you, my lady." The housekeeper hesitated, gave her a popping sort of curtsy, then scurried away. Hopkins moved behind her, ready to come to her aid should she need him.

The looming shadow moved forward and bowed. When he lifted his eyes, The Scarlet Plumiere knew he had heard every word.

"Have you harmed the boy?" She kept her voice low, hoping her surprise guest would do the same.

"What boy would that be, my lady?" He did not smile. Was he disappointed The Plumiere had not turned out to be someone more exciting?

"The boy who followed my hack. I presumed he was the only one who could have identified me."

"Ah, that boy. I assure you, he keeps your secret still, my lady." Finally, the man smiled. "You quite won him over."

"Then how did you and Lord Northwick find me out?"

"Oh, but he has not. Not yet."

"So I have just given the game away." She let her head drop forward, took a slow breath, then looked up. "I suppose you have no choice but to tell him."

The man only stared at her. It was quite unnerving—the way the bright light of morning did not seem to reach his face, although it shined brilliantly through the windows above the front door and reflected through the hallway. It might have something to do with how his hair hung over his eyes. Perhaps the black of his clothes. He might have seemed quite imposing, intimidating actually, had it not been for those remarkable eyes...and the way he had smiled. She had the impression he did not smile often enough. She had heard him laugh before, but of course that had been nearly a decade ago.

"Have we met before?" He seemed embarrassed to have to ask.

"You tipped your hat to me at the park yesterday."

"Before then?"

"I am sure not, my lord. I spied on you and your friends once, when we were all much younger. Nearly ten years ago, at a party in the country."

"Ten years ago? Oh, dear."

"Not to worry, my lord. You were all rolling down a hill, squealing like girls, laughing yourselves silly. It was quite entertaining. Lord Northwick was..." She stopped and shook her head.

"You meant to say he was handsome, even then?"

"He was quite...full of life."

"Yes, I remember. We all were. Then."

"And now?"

"And now, we are mostly full of brandy and of ourselves." He looked away for a moment.

"I have been terribly rude." She stepped to the side and made a sweeping gesture toward the drawing room. "Be my guest, Lord Ashmoore. Let your celebration begin."

"Nothing for you to celebrate?"

"I am afraid not, my lord. I will not celebrate the demise of The Scarlet Plumiere, nor my own imminent murder."

"You will be in danger, to be sure."

She was relieved to find someone else could see it.

"Yes. And yet you still searched for me."

"Lads playing at being heroes, I am afraid."

"The lads from the hill will not be able to protect me, sir." She clasped her hands and looked at the floor.

"We are no longer the lads from the hill, my lady." He lowered his voice and took her elbow, moving them further away from the drawing room. She searched his face for a reason, but found no emotion there. It was impossible to tell what the man was thinking.

"I stand corrected. At least one of you is the deadliest gentleman of the *ton*."

He grimaced. "I did not know ladies heard that kind of talk."

"We just pretend we do not." She gave him a wink and it won her a genuine smile.

"I understand how you won the boy over." He shook a dark curl from his eyes, the one soft detail among a dozen harder ones. "I would like to offer you my services, my lady. Consider me at your beck and call. You need only send word and I will come as quickly as my horse can bring me."

She nodded. How does one respond to such an offer?

"I apologize, but I am afraid I have remembered an urgent engagement. Please give my apologies to Northwick— or better yet...*do not*." There it was again, that amused smile. He bowed, then spun on his heel. A moment later, Hopkins was closing the door behind him and the hallway lightened.

Now, to see if Lord Northwick was as clever as he seemed to think.

CHAPTER TWELVE

North and Lord Telford had settled into a comfortable silence when a small person coughed. Or it had sounded like a small person.

A beauty stood in the doorway. He jumped to his feet. When Telly sat down his cup and struggled to follow suit, the beauty rushed forward.

"Heavens, Father. Please sit."

The man looked closely at the pretty bird fluttering over him and smiled. "It is a very good day today, Livvy."

She tried to tuck a shawl about the man's knees, but he kept pulling it off, first one side and then the other. Finally, she put her hands on her lovely hips and leaned close.

"Yes, Father, it seems to be a very good day indeed." The smile she gave the man could have brought tears to a softer man's eyes. "Suit yourself," she said sternly, but then winked at the old man, who winked back.

"Lord Northwick, may I introduce my daughter, Olivia Reynolds? Livvy, I give you Mr. Lott."

The bird had dipped into a curtsy, but popped up quickly and stared, open-mouthed, at her father.

"Oh, now. You know I read the papers, Livvy."

North found his voice. "Indeed. Your father is possibly The Scarlet Plumiere's most devoted fan."

Since he finally had her attention, he inclined his head.

She blushed as if he were standing before her bare-chested.

"Miss Reynolds, I am sure you must have guessed why I am here, and why I insist on speaking with you."

She side-stepped, behind her father's chair, then shook her head once, glancing at her father, then back up again. Finally she spoke.

"Of course, Lord Northwick. Would you care to take a turn in the garden?"

"I am at your service." He bowed and excused himself. "Will you not need a wrap at least?

She smiled and shook her head.

"Be careful with my daughter, Lord Northwick, or I am sure we shall read about it in the papers."

"I have no doubt, sir. It has been my greatest pleasure making your acquaintance."

"Mine as well." The man waved from his seat.

The pretty bird led him to the French doors and opened one, then insisted he precede her.

"Enjoy yourself," she sang. "I shant be terribly long." And with that, she shut the door before he could protest.

He paused only long enough to pick up his chin and close his mouth before turning toward the garden. Poor thing. She had been out of society for so long, her manners were rusty. That was all. And a pretty thing, too. It was no wonder Ash had wanted to call upon her. His friend had obviously noticed her beauty when he'd seen her in Hyde Park, but had kept that detail to himself. And so it was no wonder the man wished to be the one to call upon her. But it had been the name *Olivia Reynolds* that struck North with inspiration. He felt strongly that the trail leading to his future wife would begin at her door.

Finding The Plumiere soon was imperative or he would look a fool for the note he had placed in the personal pages. But how could he resist taunting her when she rose so consistently to the bait? If he flustered her enough, she was destined to make a mistake. Absolutely destined.

He glanced back at the house.

Miss Reynolds was another matter. It was a lucky thing he had not chanced upon her before now. Otherwise he might have been intrigued in an entirely different direction. Could his reaction to her be attributed to the fact he'd been more concerned with mourning his family than ensuring the family name be carried on? Had it been so long since he'd noticed the women around him? Was Miss Reynolds only a sample of what had been dancing beneath his nose for the past two or three years?

Surely not. One look into her dark eyes and he would have paid very, very close attention.

And yet they'd just met. Only a sentence or two between them—not unlike his relationship with The Plumiere herself. Good lord, was he going to fall for every female in sight? Perhaps it hadn't been his soul stirring to life, but a more primitive instinct.

Perhaps I've been lonely long enough.

That was it. He had finally lost his senses. He'd only recently decided to allow a woman into his life; he certainly did not need two. What he did need was to learn The Plumiere's identity, then he would likely never see Miss Reynolds again. Unless, of course, she might prove helpful in distracting Ashmoore. The man was far too fascinated by North's *bride to be*—enough so to make North a bit nervous. So perhaps he might have been wise to have allowed the man to come meet with Miss Reynolds after all. His dark friend would have forgotten all about hunting down another man's woman.

He would simply arrange for the pair to meet.

***

Livvy hurried back to her father's side and sat on the floor at his knee. No matter if the Lord God Himself were waiting in the garden, she was not about to miss a moment of her father's good day.

He beamed down at her while Hopkins lowered her heavy white cloak around her shoulders.

"Take it easy on the man, Livvy. Will you? He seems an awfully decent sort."

"You are referring to Lord Northwick, Papa?"

"I am. Poor man—tortured man, even after he returned from France."

"I did not realize you knew him so well."

"I knew his grandfather." He waved his hand and frowned. "There was something I wanted to tell you, Livvy. Something important."

The frown faded, then returned with a vengeance, like a wind dying down, then intensifying in an entirely new direction.

"What?" Her father pulled back from her then, and just that quickly, the good day was gone. The gleam in his eye was gone. The man seated before her was confused, frightened. "Where's my wife?" He peered closely at her. "You are not my wife."

"No, my lord. I will see if I can find her, shall I?" She rose and walked stiffly to the garden door.

"She will have a small dog with her. She has lovely dark hair, like yours. Very like yours."

"I understand." She paused, hoping her father's bad spell might have been only momentary this time, but the man in the chair paid her no mind, captivated as he was by the miniature he had pulled from his pocket. He frequently asked about the woman in the painting. She hadn't the heart to tell him it was only a portrait of his daughter.

Livvy could not indulge in the luxury of grieving for her father's illness at the moment; the devil was likely melting the snow in her rose garden.

I must act frightened and timid. Even if Northwick was sure she was The Plumiere, she had to create doubt. *Life or death. Life or death.*

She made her way slowly down the path.

He stood with his back to the house, his hands clutched behind him. Such a tall man. Such wide shoulders. He had barely fit through the door when she had ushered him outside. His boots had brushed her skirts. He had smelled of...well, he had smelled quite different from her father. And even in the wintery garden, he gave off a warmth she could sense as she neared. Perhaps depicting him as the devil was not so far afield.

She stopped, took a silent step backward, then another. When a carriage could have fit nicely between them, she broke the silence.

"Ahem."

He spun. His eyes assessed her face, her hair. She looked away. Her blush was real enough.

"Please forgive my intrusion this morning, Miss Reynolds. I am sure you can understand why I had no choice but to come."

The best way to remove all doubt was to open her mouth, so she bit her lips and shrugged. The man was so dastardly handsome face to face she worried she might confess all in a moment of weakness and beg him to follow through on his promises. And of a surety, she was weakened, if not by the handsome man before her, then by her heartache for her papa. One of these days he was going to remember that important thing he planned to tell her. *One of these good days.*

"Your father seems well apprised of the situation between Mr. Lott and The Scarlet Plumiere."

She nodded, but frowned. She'd had no idea her father had bothered himself with gossip, though she was pleased he had noticed her—at least that other 'her.' Though she could not see it, she apparently resembled her mother so closely, her presence often brought on his confusion. But as The Scarlet Plumiere, she could not disappoint him.

"Come, now. Will you say nothing? Are you so beholden to this woman that you will not give me her name, even if it might be for her own good?"

He does not know I am The Scarlet Plumiere! The relief drained her of all strength, but only for a heartbeat. Her knees held, but only just. She gave him her back lest he notice the surprise on her face. She took a few steps before she could get her brows to return to their original positions, then she turned to face him. She would rather squeal like a little girl and hurry off to share the news with Stella and Hopkins, but that would have to wait. Besides, it was only a matter of time before Lord Ashmoore would give her away.

"I am sorry, my lord, but I am a bit unpracticed in the art of conversing with strange gentlemen. Pray have pity." And pray give her a moment to stifle her emotions before she forgot the timid role she was playing. If she was unable to do so, she might just tell him what she thought of men who believed they knew what was best for a woman, especially a woman he'd never met. And to be outspoken in his presence? She might as well be waving a red-plumed pen under his nose.

He hurried forward. "Forgive me. I am a man possessed these days. Please. Be seated." He led her to a bench. "I blame your friend completely of course."

She sat carefully, beautifully—she would have rather kicked his shin bone.

The Scarlet Plumiere was responsible for his rudeness? The man was a dolt. If she did not end their meeting immediately she was likely to bite completely through her tongue! Or perhaps she would earn the blame she'd been assigned and drive him completely mad.

He had turned his back once again, so she stuck out her tongue before she responded.

"My friend? I do not understand, my lord."

He spun on his heel again. "The Scarlet Plumiere of course. I am possessed with finding her."

She frowned, trying to appear as though thinking caused her pain.

"Forgive me, but did you not say you believe her own good might be served by your finding her? Or did you mean to say *your own* good would be served?"

"Touché, Miss Reynolds. You have me there."

The pear trees were woven into an arbor creating a tunnel of branches through which one could see the far end of the garden. Northwick stood at its entrance, as if tempted to walk the length of it if only he weren't so tall. Most men would not have that problem.

He reached a tanned hand to the stark branches and snapped off a small twig, then watched it twist between his fingers, seeing, but not seeing. His voice turned reverent.

"Of course I wish to find her for myself, for my own good. I must confess, only to you of course, that I am fairly enthralled by her and I have yet to see her face."

Dolt or no, she could not help but forgive him. The man was enthralled with her? How terribly romantic. It would come to nothing of course, but he had given a lovely reason to have laid that blame at her feet.

"I only *hope* that our meeting might prove to be for her good." He tossed the stick away then moved to the bench and sat down beside her, then looked plaintively into her eyes. "I think she believes herself to be in danger, but I have some rather capable friends who would help until the danger had passed. I would like to boast that I can provide adequate protection for her myself, but surely four are better than one."

"I am sure every woman in London would love the chance to ask you this, my lord, so I must not waste the opportunity to do so..."

"Ask whatever you will."

"Do you mean to fulfill the terms of the gentlemen's lottery?" Surely it was a reasonable question. Of course her life would certainly be easier if he said no, but she found herself praying the opposite.

He scooped up her gloved hands, turned her shoulders toward him. "I do."

His eyes fell to her lips and remained for heartbeat after heartbeat. She barely breathed. As he exhaled, he seemed to move closer. Then a deep line formed between his brows. His gaze flew to her eyes, then he dropped her hands and jumped to his feet as if her simple white gloves had burst into flame.

She was quite sure it was only her face that had done so. But hopefully any redness could be attributed to the chill in the February air.

"I humbly beg your pardon, my lady. I was but caught up in the moment, thinking of...*her*."

Well, that was hardly flattering. Perhaps she would not pardon him after all.

"Please, say you will forgive me." He stood a safe distance away while he begged.

"I do not know what you mean, sir. For what do you beg forgiveness?" Oh, but playing the simpleton was becoming easier by the moment. And to hear him admit what he had been about to do would sound lovely, she was sure.

He frowned. Apparently he was not going to say it. But even in her disappointment, it was all she could do not to burst out laughing. Not noticing that he'd nearly kissed her seemed to dent his pride.

Too bad she had not leaned toward him. He'd pulled on her hands; it would have seemed a natural thing to do. But too late did she realize what was happening, and yet another chance for a real kiss slipped her by. And this time, by a grown man—and quite possibly the most dashing man she had ever known. Strong chin. Serious brow, and a triangular plane below his cheeks that urged her to smooth her thumbs across them. But she would never have that chance.

It was certain he would never try to kiss her again, not with how he felt about The Scarlet Plumiere. And he would never find out who that was if his friend held his tongue. So again, no kiss.

CHAPTER THIRTEEN

North began to pace. He glanced up once, to see if she minded, but Miss Reynolds just smiled and waved for him to continue. He inclined his head, then did just that.

He could easily imagine how The Plumiere must have felt when this lovely creature was about to become the mistreated property of Gordon. The man was a scoundrel and all the *ton* knew it. Correction, all the *men* of the ton knew it, and yet no man had come forward to save the lass, leaving the saving to the women.

Well, one woman at least.

Thank goodness Miss Reynolds seemed not to have noticed how close he'd come to kissing her! He blamed it entirely on the fact that she so resembled the original image he had conjured of his future bride. Except for the over-large—

He shook the image from his head.

If she had not possessed dark hair, or been so lovely, he reasoned, he would not have been drawn to her side, drawn to her lips. He had been distracted, but what man would not be?

Yes, what man would not be?

An image flashed in his mind of a large barrel containing both The Plumiere and Miss Reynolds over which he stood, trying to cover the opening with his arms and shoulders so that other gentlemen could not drop in their lots as they passed.

It was only further confirmation that he was, indeed, losing his mind.

Since he had already promised himself to one woman, he had best create a bit of distance between himself and Telford's daughter. And the best way to do that would be to attach her to the arm of someone else—and not one of his friends. Heaven forbid he should be tortured within his own circles! No. Better to get her back into the ballrooms and allow other gentlemen compete for her. If The Scarlet Plumiere had finished the job she started, and returned the woman to Society, North would not have found himself in such a predicament...leaning over barrels...

He stopped pacing and cleared his throat. "Did not I see you at the Sharpton's fete the other night?"

"I am afraid not, my lord. I have not been to a fete of any kind since my broken engagement, what with the scandal and all. I hardly need to remind you of the scandal. Honestly, one day I bless the woman who saved me from Lord Gordon, and the next I curse her for it. How I wish I could undo the whole of it, take back the last two years of my life and live it over. Some days I even wonder if it would have been better to have married Lord Gordon. At least I would still be able to shop in public." She smiled sadly.

Poor woman did not even go shopping? What was the world coming to?

He found himself next to her again, so he placed his hands on his knees and held tight.

"Never believe you would be better off with than man, Miss Reynolds. The Scarlet Plumiere did you a great service that day, believe me. Some of us men wish we would have been clever enough to bring his misdeeds to light and rescued you ourselves." His voice had dropped dangerously low. What the devil was wrong with him?

In the silence, however, he heard her breathing pick up a pace. Was she affected by his proximity? He did not dare turn his head to see.

Face forward. Face forward.

"I will try to remember that, sir. On sunny shopping days when I am feeling less than charitable." There was something terribly honest in her statement and an honesty in her tone that demanded his attention. He could not help but turn and look closely. She was such a sweet thing he doubted her capable of strong resentment, but perhaps he was wrong.

"Well, perhaps I can mitigate the injustice done to you. Allow me to take you shopping tomorrow."

It was she who jumped to her feet. He, of course, had to follow. He was a gentleman, after all. But now, blast it, they stood facing each other, only a step apart. And how easily he could cover that step.

"Oh no, sir. I could not possibly." She brought a white glove to her mouth which only served to show the intensity of her blush. It was a clever maneuver, actually; it at least placed a barrier between his lips and hers. She'd known full well how close he had come to kissing her!

But then she bit her lips as if she had just let slip her darkest secret.

Interesting.

"May I ask why not? Surely The Scarlet Plumiere has written nothing incriminating about my past. I do not claim to have read her fiction before my friend became a victim, but surely I would have heard had I been slandered. And I assure you, I have given no reason for my name to be in the paper— well, until recently."

Her glove fell away and her eyes narrowed. Perhaps she did not care to have her writer-friend referred to as a slanderer.

"But that's just it. You are Mr. Lott. If I am seen on your arm when every soul in London knows you plan to woo and win the hand of The Scarlet Plumiere... Well, you can see who everyone would assume me to be, can you not? Every gentleman in town would shun me, if they do not already because of my unpleasant situation. And those who do not shun me might wish to murder me for the sins of my rescuer, thinking they are mine."

Her nostrils flared. It was a small thing, but he had noticed. He looked in her eyes, to discover just how upset she truly was, but just as the door to her thoughts began to open, she stepped back and dropped her eyes. He would have given a hundred pounds for a trellis to have sprung up behind her so she could not run away.

Come back, he urged silently. *Face me. Tell me everything! Do your worst!*

Dear heavens, baiting Olivia Reynolds was as invigorating as baiting The Plumiere!

She suddenly pulled her cloak tighter around herself with shaking hands and he felt ashamed for even thinking such a thing. He gestured back to the bench, then stepped well out of her way. As long as she did not complain about the cold, he was determined to talk with her as long as possible. He could surely keep his distance.

"First of all, Miss Reynolds, had the gentlemen of the *ton* known you were here, hiding behind your door, they would have beaten the thing down by now. I assure you, Society awaits, and I can ease your return to it if you will allow me. And secondly, I would be sure to bring another gentleman upon whose arm you might safely lean."

She considered the sky for a moment, then looked straight into his soul.

"I am sorry, my lord. I cannot accept, but you are gallant to have offered. After all, you would hardly be helping me to serve your own purposes."

He waved away the compliment and her piercing gaze. Unable to look her in the eye, he wandered down the path to the right and took great interest in the denuded branches of an actual trellis. Miniature roses, no doubt. He wondered what color they would be in summer rather than examine the guilt lying heavy in his stomach. None of his motives could be considered selfless.

"I would like to tell you the identity of The Scarlet Plumiere, my lord. I would give you that gift, to help you in your suit for her hand..." Her voice sang through the garden.

He hurried back to her side. The prize! She was about to hand him the prize... But his first thought was whether or not it might be improper to thank her with a kiss. What the devil had come over him?

"That is, if I only knew." She shrugged her shoulders. "But alas, I have no idea whom she may be. One day I was engaged and worrying myself ill over the rumors I had heard concerning my future husband, and the next I was free, Society demanding that I be released from any promise and assuring me of my clear reputation. It is entirely my fault I have not dared trust that reputation."

He gave her his back to avoid showing utter frustration. But was he more disappointed she could not give him the woman's name or that he had lost a reason to kiss her? The pretty little bird could not have teased him more painfully if she had tried!

That barrel popped into his mind again.

A small dog began barking. The barking grew nearer and around the edge of a leafless shrubbery, propelled by its inappropriately short legs, flew a pretty little dog with a red bow around its neck. Without slowing in the slightest, it flung itself at Olivia Reynolds. North smiled, expecting to see an unabashed display of affection, but soon realized the little beast was attacking the woman! No biting, however, just barking and rolling its eyes as if it were furious and trying desperately to convey it.

North stood at the ready to rip the animal away if necessary.

"Get off me, Rat!" The sweet voice of Olivia Reynolds had changed so completely, he expected another woman to be seated on the bench when she lowered her arms.

The dog flew sideways, landed on the bare branches of a hedge, and bounced back at the woman without so much as a yelp. Having little momentum, however, it failed to make the jump to her lap.

Then Telly's daughter began to laugh. *Hysterically.*

The little dog did not seem to be in on the joke and attacked her slipper, pulling it nearly off her foot. And still she laughed.

It was the kind of laughter he had listened for Saturday night. Well, without the hysterical edge of course. And then it struck him, like a club to his belly—

Here sits Cinderella.

The beast growled and thrashed his head from side to side, determined to damage something at least. The sharp little teeth began to slide through the satin.

"Fine," she said, composing herself. "Fine, I will take it off."

The beast stopped thrashing about but held the slipper hostage while it watched the woman's hands coming at him.

She untied the bow and pulled it free. The dog barked and snapped at her hand; she pulled back just in time. Still growling, the little monster walked away, sideways, keeping its eyes fixed on the woman who seemed intent on chasing the thing away with her laughter alone. Finally, she shook the crimson bow at the wee beast and it turned tail and ran.

"Serves you right, Rat," Miss Reynolds mumbled. When she turned back to North, she paled before she could blink.

He could see her reverting back to the timid woman as if she had reached for a mask and was sliding it into place. Gone was the harrier of poor little dogs. Back was the pretty little bird. But he would hardly pounce on her. He would continue the game, pretending innocence. An unconsidered move with the clever Plumiere would be unwise.

"I must apologize," she chirped. "My late mother's dog hates me unconditionally. Sometimes I must revert to childish pranks to keep The Rat—that's to say, the *dog*, from taking over the household entirely."

"She dislikes bows?"

She grinned, tried to suppress it, but failed. "He."

They laughed together for a moment, then he realized he was laughing alone. She was looking at him in an odd manner. He felt the need to apologize.

"I beg your pardon. I seldom laugh like that without my friends about. I quite forgot I was in the presence of a lady."

"You flatter me, sir." She did not look flattered at all as she reached down to shake her skirts over her damaged slipper.

"Oh, dear. I see what you mean. Perhaps I should take a lesson from the dog and attempt to stay in your good graces."

"Or perhaps you will wake up from a nap with a scar—a crimson bow around your neck." She turned a strained smile to the frozen flower bed to her right, as if admiring the ghosts of flowers past.

Surely she he had intended to say 'scarlet', but he pretended not to notice.

"How did you manage it? I have never known a dog that would sleep through such a thing."

Her smile turned genuine once again. "The Rat is fond of sherry. Oh, he would never take it from my hand, of course, but if someone happened to spill a little in his water bowl..."

"I see. That explains why his own barking appeared to cause him pain. Remind me never to imbibe in your presence."

That smile fell away. He took a hasty step forward, as if he might catch it before it was too late. How foolish.

"What have I said?"

She looked at her hands and shook her head.

"Please, tell me what I have said to erase your beautiful smile."

When she looked up, she was the bird again. Two versions. Perhaps one was Olivia and the other was Livvy. Yes, she had worn that honest smile for her father, when he'd called her Livvy. Olivia was the bird.

"I must admit it has been lovely to have met you, my lord. But I am afraid our association must end here. I cannot risk the consequences. I am sure you understand."

North understood but had no intention of ending their association as she put it. Of course he would keep her close. It was, after all, his duty to protect his wife.

His wife! His Cinderella. His little writer.

He'd done nothing in his life to deserve her. But he would.

Her butler hurried down the walk holding an envelope and gasping for breath. Surely there was someone younger on the staff who might perform the old man's leg work.

"Hopkins? What is it?" She jumped to her feet.

The man shook his head. "I beg your pardon, my lady, but a messenger just delivered this. He directed me to deliver it personally and said a life hangs in the balance."

She took the letter and opened it.

The butler continued to gasp. "Forgive me, my lady, if I have alarmed you for no reason..."

North grasped her elbow, certain she might collapse otherwise. Her face was drained of all color as she handed the note back to her butler and watched him wide-eyed while he read it. The butler then walked to a bench and sat down!

What the devil?

"Forgive me, your lordship," said Hopkins. "I'm a bit out of breath at the moment." He tried to rise.

"Sit, man!" North released the woman and rushed to the old man's side. He took the note before anyone thought to stop him.

"No!" Miss Reynolds held up a hand, but was obviously still reeling from a blow and was forced to sit.

"Forgive me, Miss Reynolds." He opened the paper and read.

How fares your father?

That was all.

His Cinderella had one arm wrapped around herself and was trying to cover her face with her other hand.

North pulled back his lips and gave a shrill whistle in the direction of the house and waved an arm. Surely someone was watching from the windows. A heartbeat later a large fellow loped toward him from the direction of the carriage house.

"John!" Miss Reynolds smiled weakly.

"John, is it? Could you assist Hopkins into the house? He is not feeling well. And have some tea delivered to..." He looked at her and raised a brow. Surely she understood he was not going to leave without an explanation.

"The study will do," she said, but none too happily.

John nodded and did as he was asked. North waited for the men to reach the doors before turning back to the lady and she nearly got away from him. Had he not caught her hand, she likely would have run into her house and locked him outside.

"I insist you take my arm, my lady. You were unsteady yourself but a moment ago." He tucked her hand into his

elbow and walked her to the house, careful to slip inside first
so she could not repeat her earlier trick.

They walked down the hallway as if strolling along the
Serpentine. She was obviously in no hurry to explain the note.
He was happy to spend the day in her company if need be.

A maid was waiting in the study when they entered, so
North closed the door. After tea was poured, he began.

"Do you know who sent the note?"

She started to shake her head but then frowned and
nodded.

"Lord Gordon?"

Her eyes widened in surprise, then she nodded again.

"Tell me. And I beg you not to prevaricate. I will not
leave without the truth."

Livvy was finding it difficult to concentrate, so she took a
sip of her tea. Then another. Then she wondered if she might
drink the cup dry before Lord Northwick pressed her for
details. The man was far too patient. She would never outlast
him.

What would it hurt to tell him?

Besides her pride? Nothing. In point of fact, it might be a
relief to share her burden with a man whom God had gifted
with shoulders broad enough to carry more than his share.

But to whom else could she turn? The Scarlet Plumiere
could hurt Gordon no more than she already had. And as
Olivia Reynolds, she had only her servants and her wits to
save her. She should have been spending more time learning
swordplay.

"Miss Reynolds?" Lord Northwick leaned forward and
squeezed her hand upon the desk. "Please allow me to help
you." He released her and sat back. "I promise whatever you
share will go no further than the Four Kings."

Perhaps she would live to regret it, but for the life of her,
Livvy could think of no argument against confiding in him,
other than the fact he was, after all, her enemy.

"I shall try to be brief," she said.

"Take all the time you need."

"Very well. Two years ago, when Lord Gordon asked for my hand, I felt flattered enough. I found him handsome. Compelling, even. But at our engagement party I found him... I heard him telling another man of some horrible plans he had for me..."

"I can only imagine. Go on."

"He discovered me then, listening." She would hardly share how worthless he made her feel that night. "Later, he pulled me aside and threatened my father's life if I did not go through with the marriage."

"And you did not go to your father for help?"

"I did not. Father was...not himself. He loved my mother very much, you see. His mourning went beyond the norm. I could not add to his burden. After The Scarlet Plumiere came to my rescue, I simply told my father Lord Gordon and I did not suit. I had no idea he might be reading the gossip sheets. Perhaps that was more than he could bear..."

"I do not understand."

She shook her head. Her father's condition was no longer relevant. "Lord Gordon came to me again, before he left the city with his tail between his legs. He blamed me for sharing his secret with The Plumiere. He vowed when he returned that he would kill me, slowly, but only after I watched him kill my father."

"He is a monster!"

"He told me when my father goes missing, I will know he is back in London. This is why I stay at home, my lord. I have little care for my reputation, but my father is everything to me."

"And will you tell your father now?"

She shook her head frantically. "No! His condition is...delicate now. I can tell him nothing."

"Your servants are obviously loyal, but you and your father lack real protection. I will see to it. It will mean a few others, beyond my circle of friends, will have to be told about Gordon. They need not know the whole of it."

"I know not what to say, my lord. I cannot express the relief I feel."

"It is only right. It was my lottery that likely drew the man's attention back to London. But in honesty, I cannot regret it if it brought me to your door."

***

The Scarlet Plumiere! Damn him if he had not found her the very day his message reached her. *I have you now.* Later, when her pride had healed and Gordon was dead, he would inform her he'd discovered her secret that very day. They would laugh about it with their children, perhaps their grandchildren.

It had been a close thing. Her warring personalities had not tipped him off. The ribbon and the way she had avoided the word 'scarlet' would have done it, surely, if he hadn't already recognized her laugh—just as he'd imagined.

He was so pleased, he allowed himself to relax for the first time since the hunt had begun. The carriage squabs had recently been replaced, he remembered, as he leaned back against them and let out a loud breath. Why did he not take his carriage more often? It was so private, watching all of London pass by his windows while those looking his way wondered who might be inside. He loved the anonymity of it, avoiding being the subject of random conversations.

Except when people spoke of Mr. Lott and The Plumiere.

His little stunt at the gentlemen's lottery guaranteed that Stanley did not suffer the spotlight for long. He had accomplished that at least. In fact, Stanley's name had fallen from the gossips sheets rather quickly. The lottery had been held so soon after The Plumiere's attack the tongue-waggers had never heard about the gift of spectacles from the cheeky writer. The whole of London was having a hearty laugh over the joke in the park, but she had gotten no credit whatsoever for the little box tied smartly with a red ribbon. Correction, *scarlet* ribbon. Quite like the one Olivia Reynolds had used to torment that dog.

In his mind, he saw her waving the thing, scaring the little creature into running away once and for all. He heard, once more, the way her shameless laughter filled the garden

like the first breeze of spring. It was a wonder her pear arbor
had not burst into bloom.

That laughter, the search for which had him stalking
about the dance floors of the *ton* with a bent ear.

Would you care to take a turn about the garden, my lord?
She had meant to send him out there alone. That innocent
persona was only an act. And she had nearly given herself
away when he spoke of slander. Her nostrils had not flared
due to her attraction to him. She'd been livid! And he'd loved
every tense moment. Baiting her *was* just like baiting The
Plumiere, and now he understood why.

The truth struck him again. Olivia Reynolds was The
Scarlet Plumiere! He had bloody well found her! He wanted to
jump about and bellow the news to the world. He wanted to go
back and kiss her. He wanted to rush to each of his friends'
houses and give them the news, but they were all out doing
reconnaissance. They were still looking. He would not see
them again until he collected them all for that evening's party.

He had half expected to find Ashmoore joining him in
Telford's drawing room and thanked God that he had not.
Who knows how the meeting would have progressed. He
might never have guessed. And worse, Ash might have. The
man had been overly interested in Telford's daughter. Had he
deduced The Plumiere was most likely the first one spared by
the writer? That the woman, out of desperation, might have
discovered her own way out of a doomed engagement?

Of course Ashmoore would have wondered. The man
was as clever as he was dangerous. And North pitting himself
against his dark friend in a race to find The Plumiere could be
added to the long list of the most foolish things he had done in
his life. But he'd won!

So there he sat, boiling in a sea of excitement, and able to
tell no one. If he did, Ashmoore would take a keener interest
in his future bride. Of course Stan and Harcourt could keep a
secret, but not from one of their own. And he would never ask
them to do so. Nothing was worth the risk to the brotherhood.

Callister? The poor man would burst his buttons trying to keep his secret, but no good would be served. No need to torment the man.

The only news he would be sharing was the note from Gordon and what it meant. He'd already sent a message to Ashmoore's men so that Lord Telford's home would be watched around the clock, until they had a solid plan.

But for The Plumiere's identity, he was destined to bite his tongue and keep his own council. Perforce, he would need to do a bit of dissembling himself. He only hoped he was better at it then Miss Olivia Reynolds.

CHAPTER FOURTEEN

The Capital Journal, February 9th, Evening edition, Personal section.

To Mr. Lott from The Scarlet Plumiere
Dear Mr. Lott,
I am afraid your boast of yesterday had me quite excited. All day I sat out on my balcony, overlooking the drive. But alas, you did not come. Perhaps you should retire to your newly acquired Scottish property and leave The Great City in my capable hands.

Directly below read another note.

To The Scarlet Plumiere from Mr. Lott
Dear SP,
Regarding my claim of this morning, dear writer, I beg your patience as I will be spending a bit of time tidying up some unfinished SP business. It seems a fine young lady had been rescued by a mysterious writer, but then left by the roadside with no transportation back to Society. After I ensure the lady is well on her way, I will have time to collect you.

Stanley jumped into North's carriage before it had come to a complete stop, for which he was grateful. He was in no mood to dawdle.

"Which lady did you call upon this morning, Stan?"

His friend shook his head. "Ursula. But it was of no use."

"She refused to see you?"

"Not at all. She was more than happy see me, if only so I would see how well she is getting on without me. She has taken on Lewiston." Stan rubbed his hands together, then stuck them under his arms. North had not thought to have the brazier filled since his own excitement had kept him over-warm all day.

"Oh? I heard it was Landtree." He had not wanted to mention it before.

"I believe she has taken on the pair of them."

"Really?"

"Really." Stanley grinned. "But it is flattering, I think, that it took two men to replace me."

They both laughed.

North sobered first. "She would not say, though?"

"No. She said if I were a woman, I would know exactly how to contact The Scarlet Plumiere. What the devil does that mean?"

"I have no idea."

Ash would be waiting at Harcourt's residence which was next on the route to Lord and Lady Stevenson's anniversary party. The couple had wed twenty years ago and their wedding was still touted as the Season-opening soiree to which all openers would be compared. There would be enough champagne to drown a coach-and-eight. And every woman present would have weddings on their minds and tongues.

The carriage stopped again.

"Harcourt."

"North. Stan. Any luck?" The Marquess asked it before he landed on the seat.

"Nothing," said North. "The women we called upon claim not to know who she is."

"Same here. I called on Cynthia Stark—now Lady Grey. Same story."

Stan perked up. "Was not it Marquardt who—"

"Yes." North and Harcourt interrupted in unison. Before she had become Lady Grey, Miss Stark had been engaged to Viscount Marquardt—a man The Scarlet Plumiere exposed as a villain who had disposed of two of his maids after he had gotten them with child. To prove the writer wrong, the man had but to produce both maids hale and healthy. The man could not be bothered with such nonsense, as he was preparing an extended tour of the Mediterranean.

"She was right about that one." Harcourt pulled his feet in to let Ashmoore climb aboard and get settled.

"Who was right about what?" Ash demanded once his arse was no longer the center of attention. Once the door closed, the carriage began to warm quickly with little room for cold air.

"The Plumiere was right about Marquardt," said the Marquess.

"She did not know the half of it, I would say. She was lucky the man did not come after her." Ash turned and looked at North.

His gut clenched. He knew what his friend was about to say before he opened his mouth.

"North, I want you to consider that we might be putting this woman in much more danger than we realized."

He agreed with a nod and concentrated on keeping a tight rein on his secret. "What have you learned?"

"Nothing. I spoke to three of her worshippers today. All have the same story. Nearly verbatim."

Harcourt grinned. "Well, gentlemen. I believe we should consider the possibility that the women of London have a secret network all their own. How else could she have arranged for so many ladies to show up on Sunday afternoon with willows in hand?"

"Ursula said something odd to Stan this morning," he said, preferring not to discuss branches for fear of it leading the conversation to include small boxes and scarlet ribbons. It truly was killing him to keep a secret from his friends, but what really worried him was that they would smell the lie on him and worry at him until he confessed. After all, he had not been able to keep the damnable lot to himself, had he?

"She *spoke* with you?" Harcourt's shock was plain.

"Yes. I think she misses me." The viscount's grin returned.

Harcourt rolled his eyes. "She does not have time to miss you, Stanley."

"I know, Lewiston and Landtree." Stan rolled his eyes in return.

"I heard it was Pierce Lange." The marquess said it a bit too innocently.

"Perhaps she is taking on all the 'L's at once then," Ash suggested with a straight face.

Stan shook his head and turned to the window. "See if I ever speak to you lot again."

Ash and Harcourt turned to North. As usual, they expected him to bring Stan back around.

"Come, Stanley. They are only teasing," he chided, but the white head would not budge. "Ursula told Stan that if he were a woman, he would know exactly how to contact The Plumiere."

"What does that mean?" Harcourt demanded.

"That is what I said." Stan's words fogged his window.

Ash looked out his own. "Interesting. We need only to think like a woman, and we will have her. But what then? If we learn her name, what then?"

"I had a nice chat with Lord Telford's daughter this morning." He could at least admit that.

Harcourt looked interested at least. "I hear she was a handful in her day," he said. "What is she now, nineteen? Twenty?"

North's instinct was to rise to the woman's defense, but he had to tread carefully. He had to act as if he could not possibly suspect her of being The Plumiere.

"You must be thinking of someone else. This woman, Olivia, was quite lovely and refined. Her manners were a little rusty, but that was to be expected. She has not been out in Society for two years, and I would believe they have few visitors. The entire staff seemed a bit rusty, actually. But I discovered why."

"Oh?" Ash lifted a brow.

"Lord Gordon threatened the girl before he left town. He accused her of sharing his secret with The Plumiere and promised to come back and murder her—after he forced her to witness her father's murder."

"And she volunteered this information?" Harcourt shook his head. "After only meeting you this morning?"

"I gave her no choice but to explain—"

"I beg your pardon?" Ash sat up straight, his frown enough to cower any other man. "What did you do to Miss Reynolds?"

"I did nothing untoward, I assure you. We discussed The Plumiere for the most part. There was only a moment or two when... Well, it was as if...as if we had been in a moonlit garden after a heated dance instead of two strangers talking in the cold morning air."

"You kissed her!" Harcourt hissed.

"I did not, but it was a close thing."

Ash took a deep breath and settled back, but his jaw flexed. Was the man taken with Telford's daughter after only seeing her in the park? If so, he had best wash that image from his mind completely. The Scarlet Plumiere was his, and thus Olivia Reynolds was his, he did not care whose name was on the damned lot!

"Is there more you should be telling us?" Stanley nudged him.

North tried to swallow, but choked. Good lord! He would be telling them the whole tale if he was not careful.

"Yes, there is." He coughed again, still recovering. "While we were in the garden, the butler brought her a note. From Gordon. It read, *How fares your father?*"

"Bastard!" Stanley and Harcourt shouted in unison.

"I sent for Peter and the others, Ash. I did not think you would mind."

Ash shook his head. His curls fell forward to cover his scowl. "I have a question."

North waited.

"Are you now willing to end your pursuit of The Plumiere now that Miss Reynolds has caught your eye?"

"Absolutely not. The Scarlet Plumiere is mine. I will find her. I will wed her, and damn any man who tries to stop me."

"Then Miss Reynolds is available," Ash pronounced.

"Perhaps." It took all his discipline to keep from jumping on Ash to beat him as hard and as long as possible before the man turned the tables, but all it would accomplish would be to make the pair of them unfit to attend the party. He would just have to find another way to discourage his friend. "I had nearly convinced her to allow me to re-introduce her to society, but she will have nothing to do with me. She fears any woman seen on my arm will immediately be suspected as The Scarlet Plumiere. She is sure Lord Gordon would believe it and hurry all the faster to get his hands around her neck."

"I thought as much." Ash said. "On Sunday I sent men off to find him, and Marquardt, and a few others who felt it necessary to leave England altogether. I have men watching at Calais and Dover as well."

"You have been busy. Thank you." Later, he planned to punish himself for not thinking to do the same. Thank goodness for Ash.

"Would you like a confession?" His dark friend smiled from the shadows.

"From you? Absolutely not."

"It occurred to me that if one of these blokes have a poor aim and murders you, I will need to come to the rescue of our little writer."

"Our writer? You mean *my* writer." North tried not to sound too emotional about it, but feared he had failed miserably.

"I am not so sure. Perhaps you have been seduced by Telford's daughter."

The image of Olivia's lips popped into his mind. Seduction had been far from his plan, in spite of their earlier jest about any means necessary. But how far from hers? Had this Livvy been more cunning than he gave her credit for? Had she been trying to win his sympathies from the start? Then why turn down his offer? Was it just to tease him further, get him well and goodly hooked, like a fish?

He remembered Harcourt's mime of Ursula with a hook in her mouth, and of Stanley removing the hook and letting her go. Of its own accord his tongue began searching the bottom of his own mouth.

CHAPTER FIFTEEN

As it turned out, Olivia Reynolds appeared to be a prophetess.

The only thing dampening spirits at the Stevenson's anniversary party was the Earl of Northwick. Not one woman was available to dance with him that night. He was a bit of dirty lamp oil dropped into a pristine bowl of water. No one could leave his side fast enough.

"Do you suppose a communication was sent out through the female spy network that no one was to speak to us tonight?"

He looked up to find Harcourt bending over his shoulder. As he looked about the room with tables arranged for card playing, he noted Ashmoore and Stanley were entrenched in games of their own. It was a balm, actually, to know his friends were being snubbed as well.

"I think you are right, Marquess," North said. "Perhaps if you take a moment and try to think like a woman, you will find a way to lure someone onto the dance floor."

North's elderly partner gave him a strange look across the card table.

"A private joke. Forgive me."

The man continued to glare at him for the rest of the set, and when he could bear the man no longer, North went in search of some fresh air.

It was bitterly cold and dark on the second story balcony, so even if someone chose to glare at him, there was little chance he would see it. There was also less of a chance of interrupting couples who were intent on stealing a chilly kiss on the veranda below.

He leaned over, to see if such couples had braved the temperature, but found only a trio of women hovering with their shoulders close to keep warm. Were they mad? Why did they not find a quiet alcove inside in which to share their little secrets?

"You must place your letter beneath her potted azaleas. She will make sure it gets to The Scarlet Plumiere."

"Do you think she will really have time to help me, what with that odious man searching for her? Perhaps she is in hiding and will not find my letter. What if someone else finds it?"

"How silly. Who would be poking around under potted plants in the middle of winter? I would think summer would be much more dangerous."

"True! But how in the world will I recognize an azalea plant if it is not in bloom?"

Silence.

"I have not the slightest. I suppose you will have to ask a gardener."

"I can stand it no longer. I do not care who you have to marry. It is not worth catching our death."

A second later, the orchestra grew loud as the ballroom doors were opened, then the music cut off once more.

Potted azaleas? How many women in London had a potted azalea plant, he wondered?

Likely all.

He did not wish to get ahead of himself, but Mr. Lott thought he might have just discovered the mode of communication for the London Women's Secret Network. And if anything could keep his friends busy while he decided how to handle The Scarlet Plumiere, it would be keeping watch on the azalea pots of *The Great City*.

He rushed back inside to find those friends and share what he had just learned. As he reached the bottom of the stairs, Ash and Stanley were just emerging from the card room. A small cloud of smoke escaped with them before the door was completely closed.

"Is Harcourt inside?"

"He is not." Stan looked around. "There. On the dance floor."

North looked across the entry to the room beyond where their jovial friend had indeed found at least one woman willing to forget with whom the marquess had arrived. The music ended, the man grinned at them, then took his time walking the woman back to her companions. For a moment, North's excitement was overshadowed by curiosity.

"How did you manage that?" he asked when the marquess joined them.

"I give you full credit, Northwick. You told me to try and think like a woman, and it worked."

He would demand more details later. At the moment, he was more interested in sharing his own news.

"I have just overheard the most interesting conversation. Shall we adjourn to Ashmoore's residence, or did you wish to enjoy a few more dances?"

"Oh, no. I have been dancing a' plenty. Lead on."

If he could keep his friends busy trying to track down The Plumiere, he could spend some time getting to know Miss Olivia Reynolds before Ashmoore was aware he was losing the game. If he could win her heart, his friend would not stand a chance.

***

Lord Telford passed his most difficult night yet, waking up and wandering through the house for who knew how long before his valet found him, terrified and barely clothed in the study, about to escape into the garden. In winter! The possibilities frightened her so, Livvy sat outside her papa's door for the rest of the night. They had bundled him up nicely and convinced him he would feel more himself on the morrow. He had eventually gone to sleep, snoring late into the morning.

Livvy felt terribly guilty climbing into her own bed when she should see how her father was faring with his breakfast but was confident she was on the brink of collapsing. She was merely choosing a soft surface upon which to do so.

It was afternoon when she woke, thanks to the staff who had closed her curtains against the warmth and light of the afternoon sun. It was her father's voice that woke her, in fact, coming from the garden. She listened closely for a moment, to hear it again, but heard another man's voice instead.

Lord Northwick!

She flew to the curtains and flung them apart, then did the same with her terrace windows. There was no time for thought. If her father suffered another episode like the one the night before...

She burst out onto the balcony and ignored the cold.

"Stop!"

And they did. All four of them.

Her father was dressed finely, as she had not seen him in a year. His hair had been trimmed. His greatcoat made him look a bit more robust than he had been of late, and there were roses in his cheeks. Hopkins had outdone himself. And what a day to have done so—a day when more gentlemen had come calling. The old man appeared to be reveling in their attention and she sighed in relief.

To her father's right stood Northwick, imposing as ever, wearing nothing more substantial than his morning coat, as if the chilly February air gave him a respite from the heat he emanated no matter the weather.

The man standing at her father's left shoulder was Ashmoore. No other man could have cast such a shadow in bright sunlight. His clothes, though fine even from her vantage point, were as dark as before—grey as ashes, black as coal. He was smiling, though barely. Then he looked away.

The gardener stood to one side, looking down, shaking his head.

Northwick grinned up at her and a chill went up her spine—and another up her sleeping gown.

"We have stopped, daughter. Did you need something?" Her father called out, all smiles. He was having a very good day, it seemed. And she was missing it!

"I will be right down," she called.

"No hurry, my dear. Do find some clothes first!"

Northwick continued to grin up at her. What could she have possibly given away? Other than the fact she had danced about with nothing on...in a nightdress he might have been able to see beneath.

Oh, dear heavens!

She screamed for Stella, then began brushing out her hair. There was no time for fashion; a chignon would have to do.

Stella ran into the room, took one look at Livvy's face and headed for the wardrobe. She pulled out the green morning dress.

"Not warm enough."

The blue?

"Too pretty. I do not want the man to think I am pretty."

Stella snorted.

The peach? The peach was a fine choice. Warm. Unflattering. Perfect.

She was downstairs and headed toward her father before they had had a chance to move on. They were still standing around the potted azalea—the pot under which all her correspondence with Lady Malbury waited for her nightly message carrier. Thank heavens there was nothing beneath—unless Lady Malbury had sent a message to her!

She affixed her calmest smile and raised her brows.

"Good heavens, Father. Why are you entertaining in the cold garden this morning?" She kissed his beloved cheek.

"Lord Ashmoore, may I present my daughter, uh..."

Livvy's heart stopped. *Please remember me, Papa.*

"Miss Olivia Reynolds. Livvy? The Earl of Ashmoore."

The dark man moved forward and lifted her hand. She could not help but meet his gaze. She knew she was blushing over what the man might have seen before he had looked away, but she refused to be ashamed. She had been doing whatever necessary to protect her father, even if he did not currently need protecting.

Her chin went up a notch.

So did his. In fact, his lids lowered a bit as he studied her. Then he smiled. What that smiled meant, she had not the foggiest. Had he told her secret after all?

Northwick cleared his throat.

"And you remember Lord Northwick of course. He is the grandson of Alexander Birmingham, an old acquaintance. Is he still among the living, son?

"I am sorry, my lord, but he is not. I am all that's left of my family, I am afraid." A dark shadow seemed to move over the Earl of Northwick then, or perhaps it was just his large dark friend moving closer to him, then whispering something in the man's ear.

Northwick shook his head and looked up. The shadow was gone. His smile returned.

"We have just been debating, Miss Reynolds, on what an azalea plant looks like in winter. Since I had planned to call on your father today, I thought to bring Ashmoore with me so we could put the question to your gardener and put the discussion to rest, as it were. Do you mind?"

"Of course I do not mind." *The devil with the plant.* "May I ask what your business with my father involves?"

"Nothing serious, my dear, I assure you. She is awfully protective of me in my old age you know." Her father moved forward and pulled her hand through his elbow, then patted her. It was the most wonderful feeling. "Mr. Lott just came by to tell me the latest news on The Scarlet Plumiere. He remembered my infatuation with the woman."

Infatuation? Did her father recognize something of her mother in the way she wrote her posts?

She smiled as innocently as she could. "I am afraid I have not read the paper this morning. Perhaps he can enlighten me as well."

Ashmoore inserted himself back into the conversation, demanding her attention, his shoulders pushing Northwick slightly behind him.

"The Scarlet Plumiere is strangely silent this morning, my lady."

She put her hand to her throat. "Oh, I do hope nothing has happened to her."

Northwick came around his friend and stood beside her.

"Fear not, Miss Reynolds. I promise you we are just as concerned about The Plumiere's safety as you are."

For some reason she was unable to tear her gaze away from Ashmoore. He seemed to be trying to communicate with his eyes alone. A strange man, to be sure.

Then suddenly, he looked away. "We have bothered these good people long enough, I think. We have satisfied our curiosity about the plant, have we not?" He moved swiftly to the pot where Juris, the gardener stood guard. "Do these azalea things thrive with wet roots, do you know? Or do they prefer the water to drain through?" He swiftly pushed the edge of the pot forward, toward Juris. The bottom came up, off its plate and Livvy could not stifle her gasp.

But there was nothing there. Nothing on the plate, at least. But beneath the plate, the smallest edge of an envelope peeked out.

She looked up at Ashmoore. He had been watching her, not the pot. Just how did this man know so many of her secrets? Perhaps he had known her identity before he overheard her conversation with Hopkins.

He glanced down, seemed to not notice the little paper from his angle, then allowed the pot to settle back into place.

Juris was unearthly pale.

"Well, man?" Ashmoore asked it kindly, but Juris jumped.

"Sorry, my lord?"

"Does the plant prefer to drain?"

"Drain? Oh. Oh, yes, my lord. Lots of water, but they do not like to soak in it."

"Thank you. North?"

"Right. Well, we will take our leave now. No need to go back through your lovely home. We will just walk 'round to the front." He stepped up to her father and shook his hand. "It has been a pleasure seeing you again, Lord Telford. I so enjoyed our conversation the last time I was here."

He turned to Livvy.

"Miss Reynolds, I beg you to reconsider my invitation to take you shopping. Not a lady in London would dare be seen

with me now, especially The Scarlet Plumiere, so it stands to
reason that anyone caught on my arm could not possibly be
her."

"Shopping? I think it is a splendid idea," said her father.
"Would you mind if I came along?"

For once, Livvy wished her father had not understood the
conversation!

"Of course. We will make a day of it. On Thursday?"
Northwick was taking complete advantage, the rat.

Livvy fought as strongly as she dared without making her
father suspicious. Ultimately, they agreed to make a morning
of it at least. She knew her father was best in the morning. If
God was in his Heaven, her father would last until they were
safely home again.

As Ashmoore led Papa away, Lord Northwick offered his
elbow, then held her to a slower pace.

"Miss Reynolds?"

"Yes?"

"Do you see me as an awkward man?"

"Awkward? I would not think so, my lord."

"Well, do try to remember it when you read the next
installment from your writer-friend. I fear she will not be kind
to me."

"Indeed? Have you committed such an unpardonable sin
since last you were here, my lord?"

He grimaced.

"I suppose," he confessed, "there are those who might
look upon clumsiness as a sin."

"Oh, dear." She tried not to laugh. "What happened?"

"Truly, I have no idea what tripped me, but trip I did. On
the dance floor." He closed his eyes tightly, then opened one.
"At the Stevenson's Anniversary Party."

She laughed then. He opened the other eye and grinned
back.

"So you won't think too badly of me? You'll still be my
friend once I'm outed?"

She sobered. "Oh, I shall need to consider, my lord. That
is a bit much to ask. After all, the Stevenson's Party? All the

important people in my circle would have been in attendance. I must match my reaction to that of my friends." She burst out laughing again. He grinned down at her.

"I shall just have to hope your friends are a tender-hearted lot."

She bit her lip and shook her head, as if to say there was no hope for him. And they laughed again.

"You know, some call The Plumiere a Robin Hood in a ball gown. Perhaps she is capable of pity."

"I suppose that was apt in my circumstance, my lord."

"I believe she is very brave. I think she will be able to handle herself well, no matter what happens next."

"I hope so. But if you, sir, believe I might be able to contact her in some way, that I might sway her hand. I assure you, I cannot. "

CHAPTER SIXTEEN

*The Capital Journal, February 10th, Morning
edition, Personal section
To Mr. Lott from The Scarlet Plumiere
Oh, how the mighty have fallen.*

And oh, how his heart soared.

There was no doubt now. After picking apart his arguments for believing her to be The Plumiere, his reasoning had sounded a bit shaky, but no longer. Only Olivia—Livvy—had been told he had stumbled. If she had told The Plumiere, the latter would have corrected her, if she were active in Society, as The Plumiere claimed to be. If he had fallen, all of the city would have known—all but one poor woman who was holed up in her father's home.

Callister stood by waiting to dress him. He needed to show a different reaction to The Plumiere's message, or he would feel the need to explain. After all, his staff was involved in his hunt as well as his friends. He pretended to search through the paper again, then return to the notice.

"That is all? Nothing in the fiction section? What is that supposed to mean?" Oh, but his acting needed work.

"I have no idea, my lord." Callister managed to get him dressed while he ranted and raved about his lack of satisfaction with The Plumiere. His acting improved by the minute. The excitement over catching his little writer red-handed was easily transformed into outrage.

"I waited two days to hear from her and this is all she gives me?"

"Just like a woman, my lord."

"What?" He turned to Callister and tried to discover whether or not the man was mocking him. The old man looked deadly serious. Not mocking then. Excellent.

He considered his butler for a moment. The man was getting on in years. North really should allow the man to remain below stairs and stop expecting him to also serve as his valet. Would the man welcome a change, or would he be offended by it?

Chester stood in the hallway, waiting for Callister.

"It is all right, Chester. Come in. What is it?"

"The Earl of Ashmoore is waiting in your study, my lord."

"Stand straighter," snapped Callister.

North put his shoulders back and grew an inch before he realized his butler had been speaking to the young man. "You too, Chester."

The boy giggled, then bowed, then giggled down the hallway.

"Please do not encourage him, my lord."

"And why not? You are grooming the lad to be your replacement someday, are you not?"

Callister paused. "Yes, sir. If that is all right with your lordship."

"Then we may as well train him to be as much like you as possible."

"My lord?"

"Cheeky."

Callister stiffened, bowed, then backed into the hall. After the door was closed, North was certain he heard the man giggle.

***

Ash sat behind the desk, scribbling away.

"You did not even notice me enter. What have you got there? A brilliant response to The Scarlet Plumiere's elaborate message this morning?"

"No. Just thinking on paper is all." Ash sprinkled a bit of sand on the ink, dumped it off, then folded the paper and stuffed it into his pocket.

"You afraid you will forget those thoughts?"

"Precisely." Ash's grin was unsettling in any case, but his current smile made North consider hurrying out the door. "I have an idea and a proposition."

"Which one am I going to like?"

"The idea."

"Then tell me that one first. Will I need a drink before I hear the proposition?" He walked to the decanter and started to pour.

"Probably."

"That means *definitely*. Give me a moment."

Stan walked in unannounced as usual, noticed North pouring whisky. "It is early."

"Drink!" Ash bellowed.

"Anyone else suffering *deja vu* this morning?" Harcourt leaned on the doorframe.

North raised a glass in question.

Harcourt shook his head in answer. "It seems to me that all morning drinking can be attributed to The Scarlet Plumiere these days."

"Here, here." North downed the contents of his glass, gasped, then sucked in a breath. "Ash is about to tell me his idea, then depress me with a proposition. Go on, old boy."

"Thanks, old boy. My idea is simple. We think of the five or six places we might catch The Plumiere and assign men to watch their azalea pots."

"Azaleas again?" Harcourt found a seat and slumped into it. Apparently flowers did not impress their merry friend.

"Since Miss Reynolds happened to have a letter beneath her pot yesterday morning, I believe it is our best lead."

"You did not tell me you saw a letter! I saw nothing." North added a dram more to his glass. If this was the likeable news, he needed to be prepared for the other.

"It was under the plate. I did not think to lift the plate. And what's more, the gardener was in on it. He was guarding over that dead plant like an eagle over its fledglings."

"I did notice that. But Miss Reynolds did not seem terribly concerned."

"She gasped when I lifted it. I would say it was not there for the gardener."

"True. True." Damn but his friend was too observant by half.

"So we watch the pots. Whose pots?" Harcourt tried to get into the spirit, but failed.

"I think we should see if there are any pots around the newspaper building. Then check Lady Malbury's house for them. Ursula said we should think like a woman. And if I were a woman—"

Stanley snorted.

Harcourt scowled at him. "Do not underestimate the idea, Stanley. I had ladies willing to dance with me the other night. Did you?"

"I say, if I were a woman," Ash continued, "and I needed to contact The Scarlet Plumiere, I would think of the newspaper first."

"And there's only one woman there." Stanley, at least, was excited.

"Precisely."

If North were still aggressively searching for The Plumiere, he would have been gung-ho for the plan.

"Next time you see Ursula, my friend, give her a kiss from me," he said.

"Gladly."

"If she is not too busy, of course," Harcourt muttered. One would think he had been up all night watching azalea pots already.

"Shut up, Presley dear." Stanley threw a pillow. Harcourt plucked it from the air and used it to cushion his head, then closed his eyes. The man must have been up all night to fail to rise to Stanley's bait; he loathed being called Presley.

Stanley was the only one among them to be called by his Christian name. Since he would eventually inherit his father's title as Duke of Rochester, his Forsgreen title was temporary. Thus, to avoid a change later, they'd agreed to call him Stanley in private. They'd done so long ago, as boys in fact, just after they'd all found themselves standing on the winning side of a schoolyard fight. It was also that day they began calling themselves the Four Kings.

"So we should have a report back by morning." Ash steered the conversation back to mysteries and azalea plants.

"Excellent." North rubbed his hands together, though he felt quite ill. That meant he would not have much time to *win fair maiden*. "Now, what is your proposition?"

"The whiskey working yet?"

"I believe so."

"Then sit down. You are going to hear me out before you tell me to go to Hell. Agreed?"

"As long as I get to tell you to go to Hell in the end."

"Of course." Ash made no move to vacate North's chair, so he settled in the empty seat before the desk. Harcourt and Stanley laughed, but did not enter the conversation.

North nodded to Ash. "By all means, proceed."

"You claim to be in love, or smitten, or vehemently *something* with The Scarlet Plumiere."

North nodded.

"And you also admire Lord Telford's daughter, Olivia. Do not speak, just nod."

He frowned but nodded.

"You agree that The Plumiere faces sure danger from the men whom she has exposed?"

One nod. That was all he was getting.

"We must find her in any case, so we will know which woman needs protection. Also, your honor as a gentleman is at stake if you fail to marry her and stop her from ruining the lives of perfectly good gentlemen like our Stanley here."

Stanley's head inclined to Ash.

North nodded. It was time for the bad news.

"However..." Ash braced his hands on the desk as if he expected an attack, smart man. "In our search for The Plumiere, we have stumbled across a woman who is in real danger from Lord Gordon. If you find and marry our mysterious writer, do you suppose Lord Telford's daughter would be safe moving about in Society with that man in town?"

North shook his head. "Not at all."

"So, you must choose which woman you wish to protect. You can let The Plumiere go along her merry way and allow your reputation to suffer a little. But then, if it is your preference, you will be free to pursue Lord Telford's daughter. Or you can search out your writer and protect her with your life."

"What is the proposition, as if I need to ask?"

"You must choose between them. I, out of friendship and my duty to you, shall do what is necessary to protect the other woman."

It was time to tell his friend to go to Hell. He wanted to pull Ash from his chair and heft him over the desk so when he struck the man in the face, the blow would have all his weight behind it. But he also knew the man was correct. Now was his chance to confess the identity of The Plumiere. But what then? What if the woman fell in love with Ashmoore? If she were intelligent, which she was, she would know that Ashmoore was the safest choice. He could protect her like no other.

But North knew in his soul the woman could make him happy. And he was quite sure he could make her just as happy, even if it took him years to prove it. Could he risk all that in order to save his friends a bit of pot-watching? Certainly not. And if he explained it just that way—say, in a month from now—they would completely understand.

But what to say at the moment that would not lead to his destruction?

He had no choice but to pretend they were two different women. Both women needed protection. The wise thing to do would be to hand Livvy's care over to Ashmoore, but he was not going to enjoy doing it.

He held up his glass. "Take care of Olivia," he said simply. "And Stanley? Get me another whisky."

Stan laughed. "What happens if Miss Olivia ends up being The Scarlet Plumiere?"

He let the comment wash over him instead of lifting him from his chair.

"I will just have to kill Ashmoore, and the rest of us shall live happily ever after," he said.

Ashmoore's mouth curved into what was surely meant as a smile. "Or vice versa, of course."

"Of course."

They all laughed again—all but Ashmoore. North pretended that things were just getting back to usual when he knew full well he was about to enter the gates of a new kind of Hell.

CHAPTER SEVENTEEN

Livvy stood well behind her father's chair while he complained to Hopkins about his breakfast. No doubt the sight of her would upset him further, so she dared not try to escape the room. Northwick and Ashmoore would arrive any moment to collect them for their promised shopping excursion, but her father seemed to be slipping quickly toward a very bad day. She would have to beg off, of course, but she needed to get out of the room in order to do so. She prayed her father forgot the appointment altogether.

Hopkins dropped a plate on the floor, bless him. Her father turned toward the sound and she scurried past. She was nearly through the door when loud voices floated down the hall from the entry. Men's voices.

"Who is that now?"

She hoped her father was not referring to her.

Over her shoulder, she called, "I will just go see, shall I?" She closed the door behind her and ran, calming herself before stepping into the drawing room. Both men ignored the warm fire as if they were unaware their noses and ears were red from the cold morning.

"Good morning, gentlemen." She moved into the room but avoided getting too near. This was not a day to have Ashmoore looking too deeply into her eyes, or Northwick going on about his fascination with the damned Scarlet Plumiere. For all she knew, Ashmoore had already spread the news; she need only wait for the eminent confrontation. But there was another confrontation she had to worry about first— the one between a demented father and the men who held her future in their hands.

She skirted over to the fire and rubbed her hands together as if she were chilled. "I am sorry you have come all this way for naught. My father isn't feeling quite himself this morning, and I could not bear to leave him—"

"Nonsense!" Her father walked into the room, quite a new man from only a moment before. "Good morning, gentlemen."

They exchanged bows. Livvy could not seem to get her mouth to close.

"Good to see you again, Birmingham." Her father sat in his favorite chair.

"And you, sir. You were going to call me North." Ah, but the man was lovely in the morning, red ears and all. He wore a cravat the color of buttermilk that set off his tanned face. His coat was a warm brown above buff breeches. His Hessians shined nearly as brightly as his smile.

"Was I? Isn't that what you call that grandson of yours? The one who was held for ransom in France. Did you ever get him back?"

Northwick's shine dropped away. His face twisted. His mouth opened, but nothing came out.

Ashmoore shot him a worried glance and stepped up to block her father's view of his friend.

"As a matter of fact, Lord Telford, we did get him back. Safe and sound."

"Glad to hear it. Worried about his mind. Heard he was tortured." Her father said, frowning at nothing in particular.

Ashmoore turned to face his friend. Northwick shook his head and Ashmoore stepped aside, though not far. Finally, the darker man looked to Livvy. She could only shake her head in apology. The earl nodded at her, then continued to watch Northwick.

The latter found a cheery smile. "Are you up to our outing this morning, my lord?"

Her father stopped frowning and looked up as if noticing his company for the first time. "Northwick! Good of you to come. My Livvy would have been sorely disappointed I think.

She has not been shopping for quite a while. That reminds me. Any news from The Scarlet Plumiere, my boy?"

"All is quiet on the newspaper front, my lord."

"Yes, well. Perhaps the child has been busy." Her father looked around at her then. "There's something important I wanted to tell you, Livvy. Do not let me forget." Then her father winked.

She looked at Ashmoore. The man nodded and smiled, though Northwick could not see it. Was he trying to tell her that her father knew she was The Scarlet Plumiere? The pair had spoken privately the other day while leaving the garden.

He nodded again.

Extraordinary! Could that possibly be the thing her father was always trying to tell her, but never got around to doing so? She so longed to relieve his mind.

"Father, you have already told me." She swallowed her tears before they could splash out of her eyes. "Remember?"

"Have I? That's fine then." He swatted North's leg to gain his attention. "Do not forget your promises, young man."

"Of course, my lord. Does this mean you will not be accompanying us this morning?"

"I think not. I am told I am not feeling up to it, though it may turn out to be a good day after all."

"But Papa, I could not possibly!"

"Of course you can, my dear. Stella will go along. See to it Hopkins."

"Yes, my lord." Hopkins hurried from the room.

"Lord Ashmoore?"

"Sir?"

"You will watch over them both, I trust. I hear you are a handy sort of fellow to have about."

"He is that, my lord." North smiled. "That is the very reason why I bear his company."

"I trust you both to see that she spends an embarrassing amount of my money. Two years' worth for a start."

"We will see to it, my lord." Northwick looked at her then with the strangest expression upon his face. If she had to guess, she would think it was regret. But what could he be regretting? That her father was not in his right mind? Did that make her unworthy in some way?

Her thoughts began swirling in her stomach and she took a deep breath to try and calm the storm stirred up by her imagination alone. She would wait and see how the rest of the morning played out before she would declare the man an ass. She had come to admire Mr. Lott. In truth, she had collected an array of emotions where the Earl of Northwick was concerned. It would be a pity to end up disliking the man in the end.

Livvy bid her father goodbye and joined the men in the cold foyer. Ashmoore helped her don her white cloak, then pulled on his gloves as he walked out the door. Northwick dropped his gloves in his hat and stepped into the doorway, then held out a hand to her. She took it and waited for him to step outside, but he pulled her into the doorway instead. For a moment, her skirts kept them wedged together, at least from the knees down.

"Livvy, I—"

Ashmoore cleared his throat. He stood beside the carriage, waiting, watching.

"We have men guarding your house, even at this moment, so please do not fear for your father," he said. She got the feeling that was not at all what he had wished to say— and what was he trying to say by rubbing his thumb against her hand as he held it?

He took a breath, frowned, then took another. Poor man, he was going to try again.

"Livvy, if things were different, I would be kissing you this minute. I just wanted you to know that."

"And now she knows." Ashmoore gestured toward the now open carriage. "And the brazier is cooling."

Good heavens!

His strange declaration repeated in her mind while she and Stella shivered under a large fur blanket on one side of the carriage, their toes warming above the brazier hidden in the floor. The men faced them, unaffected. Thankfully, Northwick sat across from Stella so Livvy need not be uncommonly aware of where his knees rested in relation to her own, regardless of the blanket that would have come between them. The man was pure heat, but rather than the warmth that might stop her shivering, it likely would increase it. Ashmoore had no such effect upon her, and so she closed her eyes and imagined the floor beneath her feet to be a bit warmer than it was and willed her teeth not to chatter. When her chills finally ebbed away, she opened her eyes in time to see Northwick's gaze move quickly away from her. She wished desperately to know what he was thinking, and yet was fearful at the same time.

"I must apologize for my father," she began.

"Think nothing of it," interrupted Northwick. "He is not the first gentleman afflicted so. And he will not be the last."

"I trust..." Oh, blast it, but she could think of no better way to ask. "I trust that my father's condition will remain between the pair of you."

Northwick frowned. "You mean, will I refrain from mentioning it in, say, a *newspaper?*"

"That is exactly what I mean." She raised her chin, then realized she had a role to play that day and lowered it.

Ashmoore coughed into his black glove. Had she been looking elsewhere, she might have missed his brief smile. The earl still had not shared her identity with his friend. Why?

"I will mention his condition to no one. You have my word. I am surprised you would think otherwise, Miss Reynolds." Northwick shifted in his seat. "I trust you will not discuss with your lady friends anything your father might have mentioned concerning me."

"I do not know what you mean." She looked at her lap to keep from staring too intently at the man, from trying to pry his secrets from him.

"*Any* of your lady friends, my lady, not just those with a penchant for the pen."

"I am afraid I was worried about other matters this morning, my lord, and did not pay particular attention to his discussion with you. And there are no such lady friends with whom to gossip, even if I were so inclined. In truth, it surprises me you would think it of me."

Although it was true that Stella was her only confidant, she should not have admitted it. Now he would think her deserving of his pity!

Her maid sneaked a hand over to briefly squeeze her own beneath the blanket. Livvy lifted her face to the window to chase away the maudlin thoughts that threatened to bring tears to her eyes. She dared not look at the Earl of Ashmoore to see if she had amused the man yet again.

"I beg your pardon. That was hardly the foot upon which I wished to begin this morning." Northwick signaled the driver with a knock on the wall. The carriage slowed and stopped.

"Are you tossing me out, my lord?" She smiled, trying to lighten the mood.

"Never, Miss Reynolds." He looked at Stella. "I would like to let you in on a little secret, my lady. Would you care to have your maid step outside for a moment?"

Her heart jumped. Was he going to call her out, at the side of the road?

"Stella is most loyal, my lord. I would prefer she stay inside, where it is warm."

"Very well." He glanced at his friend, who only raised a brow. "I have decided you are in far too much danger from Lord Gordon, or his lackeys, and need protection."

"Is that so?" It was the most cautious thing to say at the moment.

"Yes." He cleared his throat while Lord Ashmoore watched him, smiling.

Northwick turned to the latter. "Do you suppose you could do this any better?"

Ashmoore nodded. "Absolutely, but for all the world I would not deprive you of the chance to make an arse of yourself." He turned and bowed to Stella and her. "Forgive my language, ladies."

Stella giggled. Livvy squeezed her hand and she stopped.

"I beg your pardon, Lord Northwick, but what exactly are you trying to *do*?"

"I have decided—"

"Skip to the next bit. You have said that already." She tilted her head and raised her brow, the epitome of patience in her manner at least.

A laugh burst from Ashmoore.

She pointed at him. "You are not helping."

The earl bowed his head and bit his bottom lip. He was rather handsome when he did so—a bright flash of white teeth in the midst of all that darkness.

Northwick growled. "Since you are in danger—"

"Through no fault of my own."

"Well, that is debatable—" He stopped when he noticed her mouth open. He held up one hand as if swearing on the bible. "I admit to placing you in danger."

"Better."

"But nevertheless, you need protection."

"And you think you are the best man for the job?" She tried not to sound doubtful, but failed. And damn it if the man did not appear deflated.

Ashmoore's smile was gone.

"Lord Ashmoore's the best man for the job, actually." Northwick smiled briefly, then gestured toward his friend before folding his hands back in his lap. "There is not a man alive with whom you would be safer."

He was handing her off?

"I will be safe at home. If I stop the charade of rejoining Society, I will be perfectly safe going back to—"

"I am afraid that is not true. I am certain, if it has not yet occurred to Gordon, it will soon, that if I can find The Plumiere, he can do the same."

"But you have not found her!" She swallowed, but not easily. "Have you?"

Ashmoore would not meet her eye.

"Not yet. But I will. I must."

She rolled her eyes. "Oh, I remember. You are *enthralled*. You are *possessed*."

Ashmoore's eyes widened.

Northwick turned red.

Was that to have been a secret between them? How had he said it? *I will admit this, only to you of course...* Dear heavens!

She held up a hand. "I apologize. I had forgotten you said such things in confidence. Please forgive me."

"No need. It is perfectly true. But she must be protected also. Therefore I must go on looking. And while I am searching, Ashmoore can see to your safety as I cannot."

"Because you will be hunting for your lady love."

"Because he is the best man for the job." He sounded as if he believed it, but the admission caused him pain.

"But if I am not out in public, he has no need to protect me."

"He will protect you at home as well." Northwick delivered his edict with no emotion whatsoever.

"In my home? Absolutely not!" The last thing she needed was an audience making her father nervous. The man deserved his peace. "What reason could I possibly give my father?"

"The truth. Your father will appreciate the truth. And he will appreciate the fact that his daughter is well looked after." Northwick knocked on the carriage wall and they started moving again. "I think we should shop somewhere cheerful this morning. Madame Bouchard's?"

The light tone in his voice was a bit forced. She had embarrassed him in front of his friend. He could be no happier to proceed on their morning excursion than she was.

"I have no need of the latest fashions, Lord Northwick." She hoped he would adopt the excuse and turn the carriage 'round, but she knew, the moment he was out of her sight once again, she would be wishing him back.

"Ah, my lady, but you do." Ashmoore sat forward. "Would you be so kind as to accompany me to a small dinner party Saturday evening? At the home of our friend, The Viscount Forsgreen?"

A laugh bubbled up from some forgotten sunny corner and she relaxed instantly. "You mean the famous *Viscount F?*"

"The very same. He is determined to show his fiancée that he is capable of domestic tranquility. But we all fear he cannot do so without help."

"You are quite the band of brothers, are you not?"

"We are."

"Are we?" Northwick interjected. "I have yet to hear of this intimate dinner party."

Ashmoore straightened. "But of course not, North. Even *Viscount F* does not know about it yet." He turned back to Livvy and dug her hand out from beneath the blanket to enclose it between both of his own. "But if I am to help introduce this young lady back into society, I had best get started."

She tried to pull her hand away, but the earl held tight. Finally, she glanced at Northwick to see how he was reacting to his friend turning so...friendly with her. But the man was back to looking out the window. His strong jaw flexed beneath his clean-shaven skin. Was he thinking about her father's comments? Ashmoore's teasing? Or the fact that his friend was holding her hand?

She flattered herself to even imagine it; he was thinking about that writer woman. He was in love, enthralled! And for all her trying, she could not seem to take consolation in the fact that his writer woman was she!

As for Ashmoore, the man seemed satisfied enough to let her hand slip free after a moment or two, then he sat back with a wink. For a man who seemed naturally inclined to wear a scowl, he had certainly found their ride entertaining. Either he reveled in his friend's discomfort—which could not be true of such dear friends—or he was not right in the head.

She looked into his eyes, searching for some sign of lunacy, even though she had no idea what those signs might resemble. He stared back, unflinching.

Northwick growled. Ashmoore laughed in response.

Heaven help her. She was penned inside a carriage with a pair of mad men.

CHAPTER EIGHTEEN

North had enjoyed a fine night's sleep, which was a miracle considering he had planned to hand his Plumiere into Ashmoore's hands that morning. At the last moment he had weakened and caught her in the doorway, waiting for some miracle to present itself. But obviously he had used his miracle allotment for the week.

Livvy needed protection and he wanted her as safe as possible. A second-hand body guard who might succumb to a dark oblivion in the midst of a fight, was no protection at all. So it was a lucky turn of fate that there was no other woman out there in need of protecting. Ashmoore was performing double duty and he was not even aware of it.

Again, it would be much simpler to confess his knowledge to them both so he might end the pretense, but deep in his soul he felt it imperative that he win her heart first. That feat would now be doubly difficult to accomplish after placing her in the care of someone else, so he had to resign himself; he needed to wait to woo her after the threats were negated.

Surely he had the fortitude to hold off.

After what she'd revealed about Gordon, there was no doubt in his mind her former fiancé would be slinking back into town at any moment, anticipating the unmasking of The Scarlet Plumiere. Marquardt was less of a worry. The man had been accused of murder and fled. Eliminating The Scarlet Plumiere would do nothing to recover his reputation and might even worsen it.

Gordon was the enemy on the horizon. But from which horizon would he come? All roads led to London. He could arrive from any direction. And what of the menace the woman faced in the city? What a fool he had been not to recognize the threat she faced from those gentlemen who had shown up for the lottery, men whose secrets were still well hidden, but who felt the need to protect them.

Best for her to be protected at all times, and by someone capable of doing so. He was hardly a candidate. Of course he held his own on the Peninsula, but he hadn't been able to save himself in the end, had he? He'd survived his ordeal only because his friends were too stubborn to give up the search. And when Ashmoore had found him, even in his defeated state, he had been able to rise to the occasion and take his revenge before collapsing. The journey home was a fuzzy memory of waking to excruciating pain when his back had been tended. But gratefully, losing consciousness was a talent he had honed.

What if that talent should come to the fore while defending Livvy? What if a blow from Gordon, or another, brought on those memories that turned his mind black, made his blood still in his veins while he waited for the memory to pass? What might Gordon do to Livvy in the meantime?

No. He would never be able to trust himself to be her only protection. And if North should suddenly take up residence in her home along with Ashmoore? Who among the readers of The Journal would fail to assume she was The Scarlet Plumiere?

And therein lay another threat. Ashmoore would send his carriage home each evening, but if it was discovered the man was residing in Telford's home, after taking her about on his arm a few times, there would be a new scandal—a scandal that might end in the two needing to marry!

Good lord! What had he done? It was no better a plan than the lottery had been!

The carriage ride was a new kind of torture. Staring at the window, trying to discern the reflections of his shopping companions and what might be going on between them, did nothing but strain his eyes. After the pair stared at each other for a ridiculous amount of time, he was unable to stifle a growl, but a moment later, Livvy's head had turned toward her window and remained there until they arrived. If she had not, he might have been forced to stop the carriage and get out.

Ash was begging for a good fight, it seemed. And if he did not stop poking at North, deliberately trying to make him jealous, the man would likely go home with a black eye or a towel to his nose.

Damn the man for knowing him so well.

And Miss Reynolds was far from innocent in the matter. What the devil had she been thinking, giving Ash one of those looks? Did she have no idea what affect she might have on a man? And just how had she affected Ash anyhow? Had their little moment resembled the one in her garden, where he had so lost himself in the wonderful depths of her deep brown eyes that he had forgotten his purpose?

Well, he would just make damned sure the dark earl kept that purpose foremost in his mind.

North was the first to exit the carriage and stood to one side to hand out Stella, but when he turned a hand back to Livvy, Ash already had her firmly in his grasp.

The woman looked at his friend and blushed.

What the bloody hell is that supposed to mean?

North turned and pretended not to care, but thought he heard a mild snort from his friend. Perhaps both a bleeding nose and a black eye would be in order before the morning shopping was concluded. Or better yet, directly after.

"Ash," he called over his shoulder as the man led his would-be wife up the steps.

"Yes?"

"I was wondering if you might like to head 'round to Jackson's after lunch."

"I am not surprised in the least. I am all for it of course."

"Excellent."

On the top step, Livvy paused.

"That is where you gentlemen go to fight, is it not?"

"It is," Ash said with a grin.

"Ridiculous." She mumbled a few other things on her way inside, but one look at Ash told him his friend had not understood a word either.

***

Livvy was relieved to step back onto female territory and leave the fighting dogs to follow—or not.

"Oh, Miss Reynolds!" Madame Bouchard, Roxelle, set aside her usually professional demeanor and hurried forward to give Livvy a hug. "Lord Northwick, when you asked for a bit of privacy ziss morning, you should have told me it was for Our Livvy. I thought you were bringing in zee Scarlet Plumiere with all your concern for her privacy. I told no one, of course. No use having a mob waiting outside when you leave, *n'est ce pas?* If I had let slip one word about you bringing a woman for a fitting ziss morning, people would be assuming Our Livvy was the famous writer! Can you imagine the danger to her?"

"I can indeed. I thank you for making special arrangements this morning. Our Miss Reynolds' safety is our foremost concern at the moment. Is it not, Ashmoore?"

Ashmoore stepped forward. "It is, Madame. We are all most grateful."

"May I introduce Lord Ashmoore, Madame? Ashmoore, Madame Bouchard."

The seamstress practically placed the back of her hand against the taller man's lips before he could catch it. "*Enchanté,*" she whispered.

"*Y moi,* Madame."

"Roxelle, I was only informed moments ago we would be coming to you." Livvy drew her friend's attention away from Ashmoore before the woman could do anything embarrassing—for instance, sitting on the man's lap before he could find a seat.

The seamstress came to the townhouse every year when she and her father returned from the country, to make sure Livvy was at least presentable enough to run into the street if the house caught on fire. Their yearly appointment would have come in a few weeks, after the rest of the ton had the bulk of their new wardrobes in their clutches and out of Roxelle's hands. The woman gave Livvy all the glorious details, of course, so she could almost imagine what the dance floors would look like even if she never attended the parties. Those tidbits, along with the notes she received from Lady Malbury almost daily, left her well supplied with information for her articles. With ease, she could convince her readers that she had attended the events, that The Scarlet Plumiere was an active member of the *ton*.

"Oh, Livvy, my dear. I am so happy to see you away from zat dreadful house."

"Roxelle!"

"You know what I mean, of course. Dreadful only because you never escape."

"Yes, well, we have liberated her now." Northwick gave Ashmoore a pointed look.

Ashmoore shook himself and took a deep breath, and she would be damned if he did not become someone else altogether. His face lightened, his brows rose, and she got a glimpse of those bright white teeth yet again.

"I am very pleased *Our Livvy* has agreed to let me escort her about the city for more than just shopping."

Roxelle's eyes nearly popped from her face, then she put an arm around Livvy's shoulders.

"You must be very careful with Our Livvy, monsieur. She must not be a victim of scandal again."

"I will see to it, Madame. But the only scandal endangering her at the moment is a lack of wardrobe for the new Season, is it not?"

Roxelle clapped her hands and the curtains parted. A model emerged, her attention on the ground.

"It is quite alright, Michelle. He did not bring zee Scarlet Plumiere. You need not avert your eyes."

The girl looked up and curtsied, but did not smile.

"She would have averted her eyes for The Scarlet Plumiere? I do not understand," Northwick said.

"*Oui,* monsieur. No woman in London would willingly give away the identity of zee Scarlet Plumiere. She saves us all by holding the gentlemen of the city to a high standard, *mais non?*"

"But of course." Northwick inclined his head. "That makes us the enemy then, does it not?"

Roxelle grinned and curtsied. "Of course, my lord, but I will be happy to take your money without prejudice."

"I will be spending my own money today, Roxelle, no matter what these gentlemen have to say on the matter.

"But of course." The woman winked at Ashmoore.

Ashmoore turned and winked at Livvy.

What was the man thinking? If he was not careful, Roxelle would believe... Ah. So that was the game. Well, a good game took at least two players and Livvy refused to be dealt out.

"Let's get started then, shall we?" But she was not talking about the clothes.

CHAPTER NINETEEN

Michelle emerged in a new creation of light pink with a dark pink skirt. Even with the black embroidered flowers, it looked far more appropriate for a sixteen year old, so Livvy shook her head. Then she looked to Lord Ashmoore, who shook his as well. They shared a smile.

She did not look to see Lord Northwick's reaction, and after the same happened with the next of Madame Bouchard's creations, the seamstress stopped watching for his reaction as well.

Fashion plates were considered while Michelle changed since the other models had been sent along with the rest of the seamstresses for home appointments. Except for Mrs. Fortescue, the milliner, who brought a collection of hats from Lock and Company next door, their appointment remained quite private.

No one seemed to consider Lord Northwick might like a look at a plate until he stuck his hand out like a beggar.

The dress he took over-long considering was a frumpy frock with ribbons trailing from a billowy waist. By the time he passed it back to Livvy, she merely placed in the pile of undesirables without asking his opinion. He did not ask to see another plate.

From the corner of her eye, she could see the man's hackles rise when Lord Ashmoore reached over to feel a sheer organza Madame Bouchard had draped across her shoulder.

"Does not ziss white look exquisite next to your hair, Livvy?" Madame sighed.

"I agree," said Lord Ashmoore. "Though the garments made from such things should not be ordered with men about, I dare say."

Northwick jumped to his feet. "Perhaps we should step outside."

"*Absolument non!*" Roxelle stomped her French slipper. "It will only do harm for Lord Northwick to be seen hanging about my door. And Cherie and I can discuss her delicate lingerie while she is in a dressing room having her measurements taken."

"You are perfectly correct, Madame." Lord Northwick inclined his head. "I will sit here and try to do no harm."

Roxelle nodded, as if giving him her royal permission to remain.

"When I do find my lady writer," he continued, "we will wish to be married quickly. How long would it take to create something original for a wedding gown?"

Livvy giggled. "I thought you said you have not yet located The Scarlet Plumiere. You are confident she will have you? And so quickly?"

"I am confident, yes. I am quite sure we are compatible. She is a clever girl."

"And you are a clever boy?"

"Most days. Today just does not seem to be one of those days." He tugged at his sleeves.

She laughed again. "And what color do you suppose is her hair? Will puce look lovely with her skin?"

Ashmoore opened his mouth to speak, but Northwick stopped him with a quick shake of his head.

"What have I missed?" She looked to Ashmoore. "I demand to know."

"Well, Lord Northwick is hoping she is blond...and less than fairly—"

"Ash!" Northwick scowled at his friend, then turned to her. "I did not wish her to be blond. Ashmoore and I agreed that to hope for a blond woman would be the safest—"

"Safest? How so? If she had dark hair like mine, she would put you in some sort of danger?" She felt her spine might snap, but relaxing was not something she could accomplish at the moment.

"No, no. That's not what we meant at all." Northwick stood and began to pace. She was glad to have made him at least a little nervous.

She turned to Ashmoore. "We?"

The dark earl held up his hands. "North had created an image of the woman. We thought that if he, *we*, imagined her the opposite of this image, he, er, *we* would be less likely to be disappointed."

"Truly? You had hoped...The Plumiere would be a brunette?"

"A beautiful brunette," Ashmoore added.

"Of course."

What man would not require his wife to be beautiful? For a heartbeat, she wished her face were a bit lopsided, a bit swollen. She wrinkled her nose at Northwick and he immediately blushed.

"I assure you, her appearance has no bearing." Northwick looked off, seeing something that was not there. "I am sure, somehow, I will recognize her."

"How can you say so, since it is likely the two of you have already met?" Such a statement was dangerous, but she could not resist pointing out the error in his logic.

"Perhaps." He had lowered his voice, sounded almost reverent. Good heavens but the man was in love!

Perhaps it was her duty to prepare him for disappointment.

"And perhaps, if she is such a clever woman, you will never find her," she said gently.

"Perhaps." He began a close examination of the blue lace circling the crown of a particularly horrid hat from the brim of which dangled a bird that appeared frozen in death rather than frozen in flight.

"Can your honor not handle such a blow?"

His eyes raised to meet her own. "Can my heart?"

L . L . M u i r

The room went silent. No fabric rustled in the back rooms. No fashion plates tilted and slid from their piles. For once, Ashmoore was in no hurry to torment his friend.

Madame Bouchard came forward and took Livvy's hands from her lap.

"Come, Livvy. Let us see if your measurements have changed much in a year."

Northwick raised his hand to get their attention. "I beg your pardon, ladies, but I think perhaps it would be better for me to go now, so when Miss Reynolds departs she is seen with only Ashmoore." He turned to his friend. "Take care of her."

"I will."

The dark earl suddenly seemed her personal knight, pledging his life to see to her safety. But as Northwick bowed and walked to the door, she realized the knight she very much wanted, the knight she could never have, was the one leaving.

The door closed slowly. She felt like that road of possibilities, the one from her dream, had just closed for her as well. But it was a blessing. At least now she could stop tempting herself.

Was it the after taste of her breakfast or the memory of a certain caper that left her tongue bitter as she preceded Roxelle through the curtains?

The heavy velvet drape creating the fourth wall of the dressing room muffled the sound of the street and whatever little noises Ashmoore might make. Even the air seemed soft around her as she undressed. In the distance, perhaps at the millinery, a door squeaked slowly open.

Roxelle held a pencil between her teeth but managed to say, "Zat is only Michelle, leaving."

Finally, the woman measured six places on each arm and wrote the numbers in a small notebook. "You are a little smaller this year. I hope you are eating enough, Cherie."

Livvy laughed. "I am. And far too many capers."

Roxelle raised her brows in question.

"Pay me no mind. It was a private jest."

"Shall I call for your maid?"

"I can manage with this dress, I think."

"Then I will go upstairs and record your measurements in my secret notebook, then I will burn this page. Some people might commit murder for a peek at another woman's numbers." The woman backed through the curtains and was gone.

The velvet fell into place and she reached for her dress. It would be nice to have some warmer gowns this year, no matter that she would have few places to wear them. The winter was mild, yes, but there was a chill in her bones that might have nothing to do with the weather. And there was a draft in the room, she realized, as she pulled her dress over her head. Before she made her way through the bodice, the light next to the mirror went out. The thick velvet prevented the light from the hallway from penetrating the darkness except for a jagged line above the curtain rail.

She was not too worried. She had no problem buttoning her front in the dark. Then she reached out to push the velvet aside and a hand gripped her own while another covered her mouth! A man stood behind her, pulling her back against him!

"Do not scream, Miss Reynolds. It is only I," a deep voice whispered in her ear, pouring dark chills down her neck, continuing through her, all the way to the floor. "You know my voice by now, surely."

She nodded her head carefully, and he took his hand away.

"How dare you," she hissed, no more anxious to have his presence discovered than he would be. "What if I had screamed?" She tried to turn but he held her shoulders still, held her against him.

"I think you are of sterner stuff, Livvy, even if you pretend not to be."

She dared not respond to that. She had done a poor job at acting the part of the simpering miss who had needed The Scarlet Plumiere to save her. The man should have suspected her by now. He was just so blinded by that image in his head—so blinded he did not realize that image might resemble her!

"I have never given you permission to call me by my Christian name, Lord Northwick."

"North. Please."

"I am sorry, my lord. I could not possibly."

"If I kissed you, you would have to call me North."

"You will do no such thing," she hissed, even though she prayed he would do just that. She should not encourage him. She should not lean her head back against his collar bone, but she did. What in the world had come over her?

It was the darkness. It had to be. If there was even a hint of light, she would not dare act as she was. But perhaps that was a trick men used.

She tried to straighten but was immobilized by chills as first his hair brushed against her ear, then his breath skimmed over her neck. Warm lips against her shoulder turned her knees to liquid and they melted beneath her.

He caught her, lifted her, held her up while he continued. She sighed as she had never done before. He laughed quietly against her skin, then straightened.

"Forgive me, Livvy. That was quite unfair of me."

"Hmm?" She could think of not a word to say, or a muscle that might help her say it. With chills down the front of her and Northwick's warm form behind her, she felt quite content to remain that way until she woke in the morning. For the mist covering her brain had to be a dream. Only in her dream would Northwick choose her over his precious Plumiere.

"Livvy?"

"Shhh."

"Livvy," he growled in her ear.

Chills began their waterfall all over again.

"Livvy, listen to me. Are you listening?"

"Mm. Yes." She began rocking slightly, pleasantly. Side to side. Side to side.

"When Ashmoore kisses you, I wanted you to have something to compare it with. I want you to remember me, standing here, holding you this way. I want you to remember how you are trembling."

"You made me cold. Clearly not my fault."

"No, Livvy. It is all my fault. I did this to you. I will be the only one to make you cold and make you hot. Only me. I cannot stand by and smile, Livvy darling. You are meant for no one but me. Remember that, when Ashmoore takes your hand—"

She shook off the mist, pulled her shoulder out from beneath that waterfall of chills, and turned toward the darkness.

"Just a moment, Lord Northwick. Just what are you demanding from a woman you do not plan to marry? Were you not speaking of your lady love less than an hour ago? Arranging for her wedding gown? Just what do you think I will mean to you after you have walked her down the aisle? So pray, do not tell me in whose arms I am meant to be!"

His arms pulled her forward. His lips searched and found her own, pressed his argument into their flesh, demanded that she return the kiss. But she knew not how. She could only mimic his movements to keep from looking a complete fool.

She wanted him to remember this kiss as well, for it was the only one he would ever have from her.

He growled into her mouth and she knew she had succeeded. He would remember. God knew she would remember. And remember. And wish she had never kissed him back. She would wish she would have screamed—wish she had not driven him to desperate actions with her teasing.

"*Cherie*!" Roxelle's voice carried from down the hall.

"Tell her you will be right there," he whispered against her lips.

She turned her head and obeyed.

"Miss Reynolds!" Ashmoore's voice boomed. "Are you quite all right?"

"I am fine, my lord. I will be with your directly." She called to the ceiling, hoping her voice would carry over the curtain rod. Then she whispered, "Good-bye, Lord Northwick. And happy hunting to you."

He found her hand, pulled her back again. His other hand pulled her face around. Their noses touched. "Have I ever given you a reason not to trust me, Livvy?"

"Not until now."

How she got disentangled from both him and the curtains, she would never know. But a heartbeat later, she was walking into the light and toward the dark form of the Earl of Ashmoore. There were no white teeth, no smiling eyes to greet her, and as she neared, she realized the man held a long knife in his right hand. He must have had it hidden on his person.

Suddenly she realized why Northwick had said Ashmoore was the best man for the job.

They had whispered. Surely the man had not heard Northwick's voice! Was it possible the man was angry enough to hurt his friend?

She stepped up to him, smiling, gently placing her hand upon the glove that clutched the knife.

"You can put that away, my lord. I am in no danger, I assure you. However, I promise to scream myself sick if I see so much as a spider."

He relaxed not a whit. His eyes remained on the corridor behind her. She dared not look back for fear of appearing as guilty as she felt.

Roxelle stood at the counter, wrapping some underthings in paper, nattering on about something. Livvy dared not spare any attention for her words.

"Lord Ashmoore. I beg you, be at ease." She glanced at Roxelle. The man's eyes followed and he nodded. Then his head shot up at the same moment his body tensed, his arm raised. He saw something behind her, then he relaxed and looked at her face.

Not able to bear what he might read there, she closed her eyes and dropped her chin.

"Come," he said. "Let me find you a fine meal before I meet Northwick at Jackson's."

She shook her head, but did not look up.

"I am sorry, my lord, but I must decline. I have seen quite enough excitement for one morning, and must return and see to my father."

Once in the carriage, with parcels sliding about on the seat to either side of them, she had plenty of excuses not to meet his gaze. Her hands darted here and there, pushing at the packages, catching them before they slid off the seat. Stella finally piled some of them on the floor and contained them between her skirts and the door.

Livvy eventually thought of something to converse about other than Lord Northwick.

"Lord Ashmoore, since your friend is no longer with us, I would like to ask your opinion on a matter."

The man took a deep breath, then nodded.

"You have now witnessed my father's condition," she began. "I assure you, he is usually much worse."

"I am sorry."

She shook her head. "What I need to understand is the reason my father seems so much improved the moment other gentlemen walk into the room, while I seem to have the opposite effect upon him."

There. She had finally said it aloud. Although she teetered on the brink of tears, it was a relief, truly, to unburden herself. After also unburdening herself about Lord Gordon, she was beginning to believe that having friends with whom one could share one's concerns was highly underrated.

Ashmoore leaned forward and took her hands in his. His smile all but begged her tears to fall, but she would not let them.

"My dear Miss Reynolds, your father adores you. The condition of which you speak is sometimes known as "King of the Hill.""

"Like the game I watched you and your friends play all those years ago?"

"The very same. You see it in nature, of course. When one male comes upon another, he puffs out his chest, or something similar, to show himself at his best. When one boy sees another standing triumphantly at the top of a hill, his natural instinct is to run up the hill and fight for that place."

"So my father is a peacock, or a boy?"

"Absolutely both. All men are. So whatever it is that makes him react so—to fight his way to the top of the hill— also sharpens his mind. He would have no control over it, of course. So as much as he might wish to be his best while with you, his wishes have no bearing."

"If this is true, then I am not the reason for his episodes."

"Decidedly not." He released her hands and sat back.

The relief of it nearly dried her tears.

"And he does love me."

Ashmoore nodded, "As does another gentleman, I'm afraid."

She lowered her chin, trying to hide her face beneath the brim of her new capote.

"I shouldn't have said that," he murmured. "Please, Miss Reynolds, you have nothing to be ashamed of. Northwick was in the wrong, not you. And I will be happy to explain that to him this afternoon. Not in so many words, of course." He laughed. "In fact, I will use no words whatsoever."

She looked at him then and neglected a slippery box to place a hand on his glove.

"You would not hurt him?"

"Not permanently, I promise."

She looked for his blade but saw no sign of it. "He was right, was he not? About you being the best man to protect me?"

"Actually, no. He *thinks* I am. It is a long story. Not one I should be telling. Not one I am proud of."

"About his experience in France?"

"No. Mine."

"Were you tortured?"

"Every day, my lady. Every blessed day." With his eyes, he dared her to ask for more, but she was not so foolish.

"I fear I am feeling a bit tortured as well at the moment." She said it lightly, to try and lift his mood from the dark place to which he seemed so smoothly to retreat. If his ensuing

laughter was any indication, she was better with levity than
she had thought. "I am sorry if you find my comparison
amusing. I assure you—"

"Stop. I beg you." He held up a hand. "I assume you feel
tortured by the fact that Northwick is pursuing you while he
also claims to be enchanted with The Scarlet Plumiere."

She nodded, realizing what he had found so humorous.
"It is quite silly, is it not? And yet, I do feel tortured,
nonetheless."

"I can only imagine what it is like, my lady...to be
incredibly jealous...of one's self."

CHAPTER TWENTY

Paris, France

Sarah Mason huddled in the center of her French aunt's large bed, afraid of what she might hear through the wall at her back, afraid to sleep, afraid of staying awake. For the past three nights, since she had arrived on Aunt Maude's doorstep carrying everything she owned, she had been left alone while her aunt went off with anyone who might come knocking on her door, in need of the woman's doctoring skills.

Sarah covered her ears to keep from listening to the sounds of a dangerous city going about its business in the dark. She'd been told to open the door to no one, not even to say Maude was not at home. She was not to make a sound or light a candle. If the landlord discovered Sarah spending the night, the rents would be raised.

And so she rolled herself into a tight, shivering mass of bones and covered her head with a pillow. If she could only sing, she could chase away the images that formed in her mind to explain the noises from the streets—the laughter, the screams, the moaning. She prayed her thanks to God that the gentleman in the room above had a loud and constant snore, but that could only drown out so much. A few times in the night, the snoring would cease and she would hold the pillow tight against her ears.

The night wore on, the hours dragged by, like the light of the moon sliding slowly across the curtains. But there was plenty of time to sleep in the morning, when her aunt would also sleep, when the noises and voices outside were less frightening. But every night she feared her aunt would not return. Sarah was fourteen, old enough to imagine Paris to be the sort of city in which people disappeared with regularity. Hopefully her aunt's skills would give the woman some sort of protection. Perhaps Sarah should learn such skills herself...if she could but understand half of what her aunt mumbled to her in French.

The woman had married her uncle, an Englishman. Had she learned nothing from him?

The man upstairs shifted in his bed. The wood bounced against the wall. She had identified the noise the first night. She waited, lifted the pillow, straining to hear, but the snoring did not start again.

A black shadow moved across the curtains. Something thudded against the door!

She sat up, scooted her back against the cold, damp wall, and clutched the pillow to her chest. She could not pretend to sleep, could not merely hold a pillow over her head and wait for morning—whatever had been placed before the door was still there! The moonlit outline of the door remained interrupted by shadow.

And between Sarah and the street, something breathed.

Panting, strident breaths sneaked their way around the door and into the room, as if a man or animal were standing, invisible, before her.

"*Aidez moi*," it whispered. *Help me.* "*Aidez moi.*" Then it whimpered. "Dear Lord, help me!"

An Englishman!

Sarah flew off the bed and flung the bar from the door before she considered the danger, that it might be the landlord playing some trick to ferret her out. But she could not ignore a plea for help from one of her countrymen, misplaced, like her, in a frightening city.

She dropped the latch and the door was pushed open, throwing her backward. She landed on her bottom and sat staring up at the moon, shivering as the cold air poured past her, filling the room.

The dark form of a man lay halfway into the apartment. A puddle poured out from beneath him. She hoped it was water.

His clothes were soaked as if he had just pulled himself out of the river at the end of the block.

"S'il vous plait," he mumbled. "Maude." His accent was horrible.

"Fear not, sir. I will help you."

His eyes flashed open. "English?"

"Yes." She looked out the door, saw nothing but shadows, but she had no time to worry what or whom they might be. She picked up the man's feet and swung his legs out of the way, then shut the door.

How had he survived being wet outside? She must be turning blue herself.

She picked a small blanket off the bed and put it over his chest. She would save the clean ones for later, after he was out of his wet things. Then she took out Maude's last lump of coal. If she had to beg on the street all day to replace it, she would, but there was no other way she knew of to get the man warm. *He might be near death even now.*

Sarah determined God was indeed watching over this man when she found a warm ember still glowing at the back of the stove. She reached inside, to place the large fresh lump beside it, but the door burst open and she snatched it back.

The dark figure in the doorway was well protected from the cold in a greatcoat, thick scarf, and hat. The brim lifted, revealing her aunt beneath. A man stood to one side holding a lantern aloft.

"What in zee bloody hell are you doing?"

Sarah smiled. Her aunt could speak English just fine!

"Why do you grin, Sarah? You are about to sacrifice my emergency coal? Not unless your cher prince Regent is coming to call!"

A clicking noise drew her aunt's attention to the floor. The Englishman's teeth chattered.

"Who is ziss?"

"My prince Regent."

Her aunt waved for the lantern and bent over the Englishman saturating her rug, then filled the air with a bit of French she could not possibly expect Sarah to understand.

Another man came inside, listened, then nodded and
disappeared again. The one with the lantern gestured toward
Sarah and mumbled a question. She thought her aunt said
something about sending a child into the cold is ridiculous.

The woman turned to her. "There is wood beneath that
seat. Use it to start the fire, and quickly. Stand near the stove
and warm yourself, but turn your back while Marcel tends to
your prince."

The Englishman moaned and lifted a hand toward Sarah.
She bent next to him and lifted his heavy head. His hair was
wet and sticky, but she ignored it.

"You will be warm soon. My aunt will take fine care of
you."

Maude snorted.

"Ash," he whispered.

"Ash?"

He nodded. "Ashmoore. Lord Ashmoore."

"Did Lord Ashmoore do this to you?"

He shook his head, but the movement caused him great
pain. He winced and lost consciousness. Sarah laid his head
gently on the floor and stood. Her hand was covered with
blood. Maude grabbed her wrist and took a close look.

"Fresh. Not good. And he has been in the Siene. Your
prince will not live until morning."

"Please, Auntie. How can I be of help?"

"Stoke the fire. Turn your back. Unless I ask for you, do
not turn around, no matter what you hear."

A few minutes later, she had done as she was told. The
small room warmed quickly.

"You recognized ziss name? Ziss Lord Ashmoore?"

"Yes. An English earl," Sarah said over her shoulder.

Maude spoke in French to the man called Marcel. If she
understood correctly, Maude said to cut off the boy's clothes,
that he would have no need of them if he died of cold. To
Sarah, she asked in English, "Is he very rich do you suppose?"

"Lord Ashmoore? Most likely he is very rich. But..."

"But what?"

"He is called the deadliest man in England. Do you suppose he did this?"

"Is he blond?"

"They call him The Dark Earl."

"Then impossible. The man who did ziss is most likely the Englishman I have been with ziss evening, sewing shut his thigh." Maude laughed. "And he was very generous. Said I could take anything for payment. He will be leaving the city soon and needed little. Did you notice my new coat?"

"Yes, I noticed."

"And he gave me gold as well. Paid me extra, for just such an occurrence."

"Occurrence?"

"That a wounded man might manage to pull himself from the Seine and find his way to my doorstep. He paid me well...to make sure the young man would die of his wounds."

CHAPTER TWENTY-ONE

A deep blue gown—the sleeves and hem of which were edged in black and silver braided floss—arrived Saturday afternoon. She did not remember ordering it, but she'd forgotten many details of what happened before Northwick accosted her in the dressing room. And since it was the only thing Roxelle had been able to finish, that was precisely what she wore that evening. Lord Ashmoore arrived alone to escort her to the home of Viscount Forsgreen.

Lady Irene Goodfellow acted as hostess and stood beside the viscount to greet them.

"Welcome to my home, Miss Reynolds," said the latter, bestowing her with the most handsome smile she could ever remember witnessing. He certainly had not yet perfected that grin when she saw him as a younger man, rolling down a grassy hill.

For a moment, she completely forgot what other men looked like when they smiled, including Northwick and Ashmoore. Surely this man was mobbed at every dance he attended. Perhaps just walking down the street might incite the same effect.

"Thank you so much for allowing me to join you, my lord."

"Stanley, please. You cannot arrive on the arm of one of the Four Kings and call me anything else. I insist."

"Stanley, then. Thank you." She did not intend to sound out of breath. What the devil was wrong with her?

"May I present my fiancée, Lady Irene Goodfellow. Irene, Miss Olivia Reynolds, daughter of the Earl of Telford."

The blond woman's eyes looked a bit narrow, as if she needed to squint in order to see clearly. But when she smiled, her eyes opened. It was a fascinating transformation.

"Miss Reynolds, may I call you Olivia? Since we both seem to be part of the King's circle?"

"Of course. I would be honored."

"And you must call me Irene."

Livvy nodded, though she would do no such thing. She'd been in a daze when she'd agreed to use Forsgreen's given name, but the fog was fading. Besides, there was something about Miss Goodfellow she did not trust. Until she had more reason to call the woman her friend, *my lady* would have to do.

Ashmoore squeezed her hand and hooked it into his elbow as he led her to the drawing room. Northwick was standing at the front window, looking onto the street, but spun on his heel when they entered.

"You are late." His gaze slid from her to Ashmoore.

"Are we? I was not aware you were waiting for me, old friend. I would have come directly and left Miss Reynolds to find some other form of transportation."

Northwick rolled his eyes.

She was grateful for their little repartee. It gave her a chance to catch her breath and slow her heart, and it had nothing whatsoever to do with Viscount Forsgreen's amazing smile. Just being in the same room with Northwick made the memory of Stanley fade with each breath. Smiling or no, his was the face she most wanted to see that night. As exciting as it had been to be escorted by a man as dashing as Ashmoore, the man did nothing whatsoever to her temperature. He might as well be her brother. Although she had to admit it had been rather nice having another man about the house for the past few days, entertaining her father, making the quiet townhouse seem like a country party.

And he was ever so sensitive to the moments when she felt her father's memory might be slipping. He seemed to disappear at the most convenient of times, though the aura of protection lingered. That, in itself made him seem like a family member—there if she needed him, there even if she did not.

"My Lord Northwick." She curtsied.

"You *will* call me North." He took her hand and dragged it up to his lips in spite of her half-hearted resistance.

"I will not, my lord."

He only smiled. That was, until he glanced again at Ashmoore. The latter was grinning.

"I see you learned nothing at Jackson's the other day, Ash. I shall be happy to repeat the lesson."

"Oh, come now. You know I was the only instructor that day. Jostling your memory would give me nothing but pleasure of course."

"You two stop it." A man walked into the room, straight to Livvy, and took her hand, to lead her to the other side of the room, all without pausing. He spun her around to face the others and her skirt twirled beautifully before coming to a stop. "There. I have saved you. The Marquess of Harcourt, at your service Miss Reynolds." He bowed low over her hand, but did not kiss it.

A woman cleared her throat. Standing in the doorway, in a lovely peach ensemble, could have been none other than his sister. She was identical to the Marquess in every way, from her brown curls to the grin on her face.

"Forgive me." Harcourt left her side and went to the other woman's rescue, leading her past the other men, directly back to Livvy. "Miss Olivia Reynolds, may I present my sister, Miss Anna Talbot. Anna, meet Olivia, the poor chick that has been tucked beneath Ashmoore's wing for the evening."

Anna laughed and pushed her brother aside, as if the ground he had been standing on had been her rightful territory. "Good boy, Harcourt. Now run along. We two have silly things to discuss."

"I am all ears," he leaned in.

"Yes," Anna agreed. "And teeth, and a rather large nose. Now run along." She tried to shoo him away.

"Large nose? I hate to point this out, Sister, but I could don one of your dresses and be mistaken for you at any ball."

"Bother! Mistaken for me on a very, very bad day, after I have reached the age of fifty perhaps. While I could don your breeches and run about London every night playing The Scarlet Plumiere, saving damsels in distress from rogues like you."

"I am not a rogue, Anna. I am a King. I so dislike having to remind you."

"Yes, yes." Anna reached up and patted her brother on the head. "You are a King. Now run along, Your Highness."

She faced Livvy again.

"Where were we? Oh, yes. We were about to become fast friends and you were about to tell me what you think of our Lord Ashmoore."

Livvy laughed. She would have paid a pretty penny to see such entertainment on a stage. What a difference there was between Anna and Irene. She loved Anna immediately. She did not see what the woman could possibly have seen in her during her glide across the room, but Livvy felt as if she had been invited to have tea with the queen.

"Lord Ashmoore? Which King is he?" She made a show of looking 'round the room, staring at Northwick, then Ashmoore, then Harcourt.

"I believe he is the one winking at you, my dear."

And so he was. She felt her face flush. "He does that often, I am afraid," she confessed.

"Does he?" Anna looked back and forth between them for a moment. "Oops," she whispered. "It seems as though Lord Northwick is not happy to have learned Ash's new habit. I will wager they will be at Jackson's tomorrow."

"They were there only Thursday." Livvy whispered, "I thought they were friends."

Anna laughed. "The finest friendship is easily ruined by jealousy, my dear. I am afraid Lord Northwick is smitten. The question is, is our King of Spades?"

Livvy glanced at Ashmoore, but the man was following Northwick from the room.

"Looks like they cannot stand to wait until tomorrow."
Anna grabbed her hand and began to pull. "Hurry. I do not
want to miss a thing."

Harcourt stepped in front of his sister.

"We are going to find the powder room, Brother."

"Liar. You are not going to poke that delicate nose of
yours where it does not belong."

"But it belongs in the powder room!"

"You are hoping to see a fight. Well, I hate to disappoint
you, but there will not be one. They are going to talk."

"I do not know who you mean."

"Then you lost your memory somewhere between here
and the windows."

"Brother. I truly am in a hurry."

"No."

Anna stepped back. She put a hand to her throat. Her
bottom lip quivered.

"Hell, no." He turned to Livvy. "Pardon my language,
Olivia."

Anna rolled her eyes. "I am sure we have already missed
the best part. Aren't you worried Ashmoore will need a
beefsteak for his eye by now?"

"Ashmoore? You mean Northwick."

"I will wager a guinea on Ashmoore."

Harcourt opened his mouth, then grimaced and shook his
head.

Anna turned to Livvy and her grin sent out waves of
dimples. "See that? I nearly had him."

Ashmoore returned looking no worse for wear, a happy
smile on his face.

Harcourt leaned toward his sister. "That will teach you to
bet against Ash, Sister."

Northwick walked inside. Nothing amiss with him either.
In fact, he was smiling as well.

"And I told you they were only going to talk." Harcourt
stepped aside with a sweeping gesture, indicating his sister's
new freedom to walk where she liked.

"Damned Kings. They know each other just too well for anything interesting to happen." Anna shook her head in disgust.

Livvy disagreed. She thought the fact that both men returned with smiles on their faces was very interesting indeed.

Northwick moved to the window and looked out at the street.

"Ah, my dinner companion has arrived. Excuse me," he said.

Since Livvy had never been told who was on the guest list, she had no idea who Northwick was about to bring through the door, but she could not have been more surprised if the man had escorted in the famous Lady Ursula.

The woman could not have been his mother; his mother was deceased. But the woman had to be his mother's age at least. She was lovely. Extremely lovely in fact, but she was quite stout.

The other little detail that caught and held Livvy's attention was the way Northwick smiled at his new companion. He beamed, as if he had just blown out the candles on his birthday cake and his wish was standing in front of him when he opened his eyes.

If he had not looked so sincere, she might have believed he was play-acting, trying to make her jealous—for in honesty, she was jealous. Caper-green with jealousy, in fact. But then the woman smiled and the light from the sconces seemed to dim. Her smile could rival that of her host, in fact.

Stanley's mother, then, The Duchess of Rochester!

North brought the woman toward her and Livvy dropped into her deepest curtsy.

"Your Grace, may I introduce to you Miss Olivia Reynolds, daughter of the Earl of Telford?"

"Miss Reynolds, it is a great pleasure."

"The pleasure is mine, Your Grace." Livvy straightened and smiled.

"The Duke and I used to play cards with Telly and your mother when we were much, much younger. I was so sorry to hear of her passing."

"Thank you, Your Grace."

"Winnie. Please. Aunt Winnie, if you would like. I think your mother would have liked that. And I am happy to see you look so like her."

Livvy only nodded. Tears made it impossible to speak.

"No tears, my dear. This is your first foray back into society, is it not? I hope you can forgive me for not seeing to the task myself. I had no idea you had been hiding."

Hiding?

"Someone as beautiful as you owes it to Society to participate. Give those young bucks a reason to behave themselves.

"You are too kind, Your Grace."

"Oh? You think I am not earnest? Not just any pretty face gets through these walls." She gestured around them, glanced at Irene, then turned back. "The inner sanctum, as it were. You must have a lot of your mother on the inside as well." The woman took Livvy by the arm and walked her away from the others. "Did your parents ever tell you how they met?"

"You mean the story of how she and her friends held up his carriage for a lark?"

"And your father shot her before he realized—"

"They were all women? Yes. It is one of his favorite stories to tell, actually." It took an effort to swallow.

"What is it, child?"

"My father...is not well."

A moment later, she was sobbing against the bosom of The Duchess of Rochester. The rest of the dinner guests had slipped from the room.

"I am so sorry, Your Grace." For the second time, she tried to compose herself.

"Aunt Winnie."

"Aunt Winnie, then. I do not know what came over me. I am not usually such a milquetoast."

"Of course you are not. But you have to give these things their due. One must spill the milk before one can clean it up."

"That's what Mother used to say."

"And she was right. Now. Dry your face and let's allow Stanley's cook to stop re-heating our supper. I am starved."

Livvy was surprised to find she was starved as well. She would have never expected to fit anything but nerves in her stomach that night, but she was wrong.

CHAPTER TWENTY-TWO

Stanley stood at the head of the table. Irene sat to his left. Harcourt sat beside her with an empty chair next. Ashmoore stood behind the chair at the far end of the table. Anna on his left, then Northwick, then another chair.

"I would rather look at your face than your ear, Ramsay." Her Grace walked around the table to take the seat between Harcourt and Ashmoore, but Livvy got the distinct impression the duchess was more concerned that Livvy set next to her son.

She had no choice but to take the seat between Stanley and Northwick. The latter did not seem too dangerous at the moment, only giving her a brief smile as he held her chair. She wondered if he remembered their last conversation as well as she. Could he still smell the dust in the curtains? The strong smell of India dye in the new fabrics. Perhaps it was her new gown that kept that memory alive, down to the smallest detail. She was sure she could look at her arm and recall which hairs had stood on end when his breath had caressed her neck.

"You're blushing," he murmured, quietly enough that no one else could have heard him. "I am happy to see you remembered."

The hair on her arms rose once more, as if Northwick had trained them to do so.

She braced herself to stand. If this was her reaction to being so near him for only a moment, she would not last the meal. But who could exchange seats with her? Not the duchess. She had already voiced her preference. Irene would ask for an explanation. Trading seats with Anna would only put her on Northwick's opposite side! Trading with one of the men would ruin the seating arrangement, and she doubted Irene would allow it.

"Running away?" His voice was still low, thank heavens. "I never took you for a coward."

"Lord Stanley," she said, turning her head and shoulder away from Northwick's whispers. "I have to thank you for holding this little party. I cannot tell you what it means to have met your mother. My own mother spoke of her, of course, but I never dreamed we would find ourselves in the same circles, if only for one night."

"My pleasure, Olivia." He frowned down the length of the table. "But what's all this about one night, Ashmoore? You are not going to allow this woman to hide in her attic again, are you?"

"Of course not." Ashmoore winked at her.

"Something in your eye, Ashmoore?" Northwick laughed.

"No. Something in yours, my friend." Ashmoore rubbed the back of his knuckles against his chin, then held them up. "This."

"So, it is like that, is it?" Winnie looked from one man to the other, then smiled at Livvy. "At least they are not blind, or witless. I have done a fine job, if I do say so myself."

"I do not understand," she confessed.

"She takes credit for raising the four of us." North grinned when the duchess frowned in his direction. "Credit she certainly deserves."

"But you are pledged to The Scarlet Whatsit, are you not, Northwick?" Irene was back to squinting.

Ashmoore grinned. Livvy felt her face heat.

"I am, Miss Goodfellow. At the moment."

"But surely you do not mean to go back on your promise." Livvy could not stop her tongue. She would take it back if she could, for whichever way the man answered, she would be disappointed.

"I will keep my promise if it is possible to do so."

Stanley gestured with his knife. "You see, darling, he is having a devil of a time finding her. He cannot marry a woman he cannot take to the church, now can he?"

"I hope you will not think ill of me, Lord Northwick, but I hope you never find her." Irene's statement took the attention off of Livvy, for which she was grateful.

"Oh? You are another of her defenders, are you? Hoping she can go on as she has, saving innocent maidens from the wolves of the *ton*?" Northwick set down his spoon.

"Absolutely not. I will never defend the woman who put Stanley in the laughing stocks."

"Truly?" Northwick seemed genuinely surprised. "I think you are the only woman I have spoken with in the past month that was not a fan of the famous writer."

"Infamous writer, you mean." Irene's sneer was less than attractive. Livvy wondered if anyone else saw it before it was gone.

Ashmoore had. He glanced at Livvy, shook his head, then resumed glaring at Irene. At least she had one champion. For all her scrambling for the right thing to say, to defend herself, Livvy could not manage.

"Well, I admire her. She saved Our Livvy, after all." North patted her hand where it lay upon the table clutching her napkin.

Irene squinted at her.

"Did she? Do you consider yourself saved, Olivia? Do you mean to say you could not have saved yourself just as well by refusing to marry Lord Gordon?"

Livvy opened her mouth, but her voice failed her.

"Of course she could have, but she was saved the embarrassment." Northwick came to her defense yet again.

"So, The Scarlet Woman saves some embarrassment while serving it to others. I think she has no right to play judge and executioner. Once you discover her identity, my lord, I insist that you sue her."

"Why?" Stanley laughed. "She has never been so inaccurate before. I believe Ursula misled her."

Irene's blood boiled up into her face. "Surely you will not speak of that woman at the dinner table."

Stanley rolled his eyes. Livvy found her voice.

"What do you mean, misled? Were the twins not actually yours, my lord?"

Everyone laughed but Irene.

"There were no twins, Olivia. No Spanish damsel waiting in the halls of some hotel. We believe Ursula was seeking revenge after I put her aside."

Irene huffed and attacked her main course. The food hardly required a knife, but she stabbed at it regardless.

Livvy felt each stroke, pounding home the realization she'd been spread lies.

Lies. Lies. Lies.

She clutched the edge of the table to keep from jumping to her feet and running out the door. How dare she sit there and sup with the man when she'd wronged him so grievously?

"I am so sorry, my lord." She looked at *Viscount F* and begged for forgiveness, even though he could not possibly know why. Hopefully, he saw it as only pity.

He grinned back. "Not to worry, my dear. No harm done. As I said, the blame was Ursula's.

"I think I cannot bear to hear that name again, my lord." Irene drained the wine from her goblet and smiled. The action had stained two areas above her lips and when she smiled, they looked like small red tusks.

Stanley said nothing.

Livvy laughed into her napkin.

"I think this meal is too lovely to sour with vinegar." The duchess looked about the table as if she expected someone to come up with a brighter topic.

Irene was frowned at her future mother-in-law.

"I must agree with my Mother. I am the one The Scarlet Plumiere seems to have attacked, and I am no worse for it. In fact, if it weren't for that letter to me, getting Northwick all worked up, we would never have thought to bring Miss Reynolds into our ranks." Stanley gave Livvy one of those wonderful smiles and squeezed her hand in spite of the spoon he held. He ignored Irene, even when she huffed at him. "Were you perhaps in the park last Sunday, Mother? I did not see you."

Once he shined his charming smile in another direction, Livvy's mind began to settle once again. She put her own situation aside and thought about the other women she had helped along the way. Lady Grey would surely have married a murderer, but instead, she was very happily wed. The rest of her stories of success were far less dramatic, but the ungentlemanly men in those stories suffered nothing they had not earned. The only time she had erred was with *Viscount F.* But Ursula had sought her out, insisted on an audience. They had met at Lady Malbury's home, just that one time. But ultimately, the man had not suffered. His fiancée was still seated beside him. His mistress had eased a little of her heartache. And Northwick had come into her life.

She looked around the table. Except for Irene of course, she felt as if she had been welcomed into an entirely new family. A family with brothers and sisters...and Auntie Winnie.

She regretted nothing.

Ashmoore was frowning at her with concern, but he need not have worried. It only took a moment for her to recover from the verbal slap.

For the majority of the meal, the conversation moved into topics with which she was unfamiliar, but she smiled and nodded and gave an opinion if she had one. The buzzing of pleasant conversation was like music to her ears. Eventually, however, Anna brought the conversation back around to The Scarlet Plumiere.

"North, darling, how much longer are you going to allow this to go on? When will you give up the hunt?"

"Honestly, I do not know how much longer I can last. She is an extremely clever girl."

Anna laughed. "And extremely popular. I am amazed how she was able to fill that park last week at such short notice."

Harcourt waved his hands to get attention while he took a drink of wine. "Mm. We have it figured out. We are very close to finding her."

It was Livvy's turn to laugh. "Mr. Lott made that boast a long time ago."

"Only ten days ago. But we are close." Northwick did not sound too happy about being so, but she refused to examine his tone too closely. She might imagine he was hoping to fail.

"Actually," said Harcourt, "we are convinced there is a secret communications network amongst the women of the *ton*."

"That would be us, brother. Are you sure you want to show your hand?" Anna laughed and leaned Ashmoore's direction while the footman collected her plate.

Harcourt waved away her warning. "We call it the London Women's Secret Network."

"Very clever. And now we are supposed to exchange knowing looks between one another so my brother can cry, *Ahah*!"

Obligingly, Livvy, Anne and the duchess exchanged knowing glances and gestured wildly with their eyebrows. One glance at Irene proved she was unimpressed.

"Ahah!" Harcourt shouted, pointing at his sister. "You, my dear, may very well be The Plumiere herself. Heaven knows you are cheeky enough."

"I take that as the highest compliment, Brother."

"As it was meant, Sister."

Irene rolled her eyes. "If there is a secret network, I have certainly never heard of it."

No one remarked. The silence was a bit embarrassing.

"I will tell you all about it after the men leave us," Livvy offered.

Irene merely rolled her eyes again.

"I think we have been dismissed, gentlemen." Stanley stood and gestured to the door. "If you will be so kind as to take your usual positions in the library."

Harcourt popped to his feet.

Ashmoore and Northwick glared at each other.

"Out of here, the pair of you," the duchess ordered. "We have seen enough of your pretty faces across the table. Now we must swoon and recover. Out!"

It took the second *out* to get the two up from their chairs and a third to get them out the door. Once the four women entered the drawing room, Irene gave Livvy one of her narrow looks.

"Do you play, Miss Reynolds?"

"Not the piano, no. I play the violin, though far from perfectly."

"Your mother played the violin. I had forgotten," said the duchess.

"You do not mind if I play, then, do you?" Irene asked it of the room at large, then sat down and began a dramatic set of scales. Her playing was so passionate, in fact, it was impossible for the rest of them to carry on a conversation.

Livvy looked at Anna and shrugged. Anna threw back her head and laughed. Irene played louder still. Thankfully, she started playing actual concertos. The third piece began a little softer and Livvy was beginning to think her ears may just survive when she noticed something moving from the corner of her eye.

It was Stanley, waving a white kerchief from the doorway.

"Olivia!" He bid her to come to him. "I will return her in but a moment," he yelled to his mother. Despite some pointed notes, he never gave the pianist a glance.

Even after the doors were closed, the music followed them down the hall. Stanley took her hand and pulled her into a study and closed that door, but the music carried through. No doubt his mother and Anna were forced to flee the drawing room or hold their hands over their ears as Irene seemed determined to have the final say of the evening.

They were alone.

"Forgive my kidnapping, but I thought this might be the only time I might have a word with you." He offered her a chair, then sat on the corner of the desk, facing her.

She only nodded, having no idea what the future duke might like to discuss other than to chastise her for toying with the hearts of two of his friends. But she had been doing her best not to toy with anyone. Well, anyone but Mr. Lott, of course.

"I thought I should confess."

Oh, dear. If she had somehow caught the interest of yet a third King, she was going to go home and never leave her house again.

"Are you sure you would not prefer to keep it to yourself, whatever it is?"

"I know the identity of The Scarlet Plumiere."

Now that was a surprise.

After she got her eyes back in her head, she frowned.

"You do?" Best to play innocent. She thought she had been caught before, when Northwick first arrived on her doorstep.

"Yes. I do."

She sucked on her lips, her teeth—anything to keep from letting the wrong thing escape her mouth.

"Let me rephrase. As you are The Scarlet Plumiere, I would like you to know that I am willing to help you however I can."

The blow quite literally knocked her against the wing-backed chair.

"You think I—"

"I know."

"Might I ask what makes you think—"

"You mean, how did I discover it was you?"

She refused to nod. It still might be a trick.

"That second woman, Farrington? You were just trying to cover your tracks, were you not? Her rescue came only weeks after your own."

He gave her one of his smiles—a very knowing smile.

Perhaps Lord Ashmoore had let it slip. Perhaps, when they had left the dining room, they had argued about how Stanley's fiancée had insulted The Scarlet Plumiere, who happened to be seated at his other elbow!

"Miss Farrington happened to be a friend of mine, my lord. Her fiancé broke her arm when she refused to allow him liberties the night of their engagement. Her father took umbrage with *her*."

Stanley leaned forward, no doubt because the music had swelled again, and he did not want to risk having to yell, so she moved forward as well. When his mouth was very near her ear, he whispered, "*Ahah!*"

She straightened. She suddenly understood how Eve must have felt when she realized she had been beguiled by the snake. But in her mind's eye, the snake was rather blond with a smile he had stolen from an angel.

Stanley held up his hands as if he expected her to attack.

"Now, now. Your secret is safe. I will tell no one."

"You are mistaken."

"Come now, Livvy. The game is up." He grinned at her again, proving his weapon was something against which she could not fight and win.

"Fine. You are correct. But tell me why you will not be sharing my secret with Lord Northwick.

The smile disappeared. He leaned forward again, but she did not fall for it. She could resist him if he was not grinning.

"He needs to learn it on his own. He cannot know that I discovered it before him."

"His pride is that easily bruised?" She did not believe it.

"Do you know what happened to him in France?"

"Only that he was kidnapped. Possibly tortured."

"All our lives, it has been North who pulled our fat from the fire. North who came to *our* rescue. He has saved Ashmoore's life half a dozen times. But he does not seem to remember that. He only remembers that we had to save him in France. If he fails to find you, and any of us succeeds, he will just see it as another rescue."

It was easily believed, especially after the way he had placed her in Ashmoore's keeping. He really did not believe himself worthy to protect her. Her heart broke for him, but she could not allow it to sway her.

"You will have to be very good at keeping your secret then, *Viscount F.* Because I will not allow him to find me. I cannot allow him to find me. If one young woman ends up terrorized by her husband, it will be my fault if I could have stopped it."

"I understand why you do it. Well, most of it anyway."

"You do?"

"I do." Dear heavens! That smile again!

If Ashmoore was the King of Spades, surely Stanley was the King of Hearts.

"May I ask what gave me away?"

"Honestly? It was that penitent look in your eye when you realized—for the first time, it seems—that you had been wrong about me. Along with my deductive reasoning, of course."

"Women should be warned about you."

"Really? Why?"

"Your smile should never be trusted." And now that it had returned, she wished to escape the room as quickly as possible. She stood and he did not try to stop her.

"That, my dear Plumiere, has always been true."

She was still standing before him. "I suppose I may say it now, then."

"What is that?"

She leaned close, as if to say *ahah,* but instead whispered, "Forgive me."

Stanley shook his head. "Not your sin, my dear."

"But my mistake for taking Ursula's word on the matter."

"Forgiven. And do you forgive my little deception?" He gestured around the room.

"Forgiven."

They stepped out of the study to find North running toward them. "What the devil, Stanley?"

"The devil indeed," she said, then winked at the viscount.

Northwick growled. She was quite growing fond of the sound and tried to commit it to memory.

"I would like a word with Miss Reynolds, if I might." He was a bit out of breath.

"Absolutely not. Our discussion was concluded at Madame Bouchard's the other morning." She stepped around him.

"I would like to discuss something else with you." He walked sideways to hold her attention.

"I am sorry, but Miss Reynolds is in my keeping tonight, and I forbid anyone to have a private word with her." Ashmoore stood with hands on hips in the middle of the foyer, blocking everyone's progress.

Livvy did not like the sound of that. Big brother was overstepping a bit.

"Wait just a moment, Lord Ashmoore." She stopped at the sound of more running feet.

Harcourt hurried up behind Ashmoore and tapped him on the shoulder. "Now see here. I am not going to be told to wait alone in the study like some child waiting for his punishment."

An ungodly whistle shrieked through the corridor.

The music stopped.

The mob turned toward the doors of the drawing room where the duchess stood holding two fingers in her mouth. Anna's hands covered her ears, but she slowly lowered them while eyeing the duchess suspiciously.

"Northwick, it is no wonder why I have a headache. I would like you to see me home. Olivia? I will take a kiss on the cheek from you. Ashmoore, return Olivia to her father. Harcourt, stop whining and see to your sister. Stanley? God bless you but you have got to teach Miss Goodfellow the meaning of the word *pianissimo* before she is allowed to touch an instrument again."

Everyone jumped to do the woman's bidding. At least Livvy was afraid to hear that whistle again. No doubt it had come in handy while trying to raise four boys, three of which had not been her own.

"Goodnight, Auntie Winnie." Livvy kissed the proffered fuzzy cheek and could not resist adding a brief hug. Ashmoore herded her toward the door, but she turned back to look for Stanley. Instead, her eyes locked with Northwick's. Time stilled. Stopped.

She could have stood there forever, just staring, sharing a dozen thoughts and none at all. She would remember forever the look on his face. Regret. Frustration. Passion? They were a dozen paces apart with nothing but silence between them. No one moved. No one breathed.

No one moved? Dear heavens. The entire party had witnessed the exchange.

She turned and fled out the door. Thankfully, someone had already opened it.

CHAPTER TWENTY-THREE

North was up early, pacing his foyer.

He had not slept well. Callister stood with his back to the front door holding a plate of sausage rolls as if waiting to offer them to anyone who happened by the house and knocked upon the door. North knew the man was not going to allow him to leave without eating first. How he was going to appease the man was a concern, since he felt like he was about to lose the breakfast he had eaten the day before.

Little did Callister know, it was not his innocent blocking of the door, nor the threat of shoving breakfast down his employer's throat that kept North from leaving. It was his own indecision.

He was determined to go to Livvy's home that very morning, push Ashmoore and Ashmoore's men aside, and demand the chance to speak with the woman alone. He would tell her he already knew she was The Scarlet Plumiere, that he was going to woo and win her even if, by some wild coincidence she was not the real SP. He would call out any man that threatened her...and have Ashmoore kill the man.

"Ahhhh!"

Of course he could do no such thing. He had no protection to offer her but his friend. How could he declare himself and admit he was not enough for her, and still expect to win her hand? Impossible!

On the other hand, the charade had to stop. He could not just stand by and allow Ash to make a place for himself in her heart. It was too unfair to expect him to keep silent.

He headed for the door again. Callister raised the plate.
He took a roll and stared the man down, unblinking, while he
sank his teeth into it.

Nothing for it. He would have to bare his soul and deal
with consequences as they arose.

There. He felt much better. Callister looked terribly
pleased with himself and stepped out of his way. North pushed
the rest of the roll into his mouth, brushed his fingers together
and reached for the door, ready to take on the Earl of
Ashmoore himself.

Only the Earl was headed up his steps that very minute.

"What the blazes?" It sounded quite different spoken
around the food in his mouth. He swallowed while his friend
pushed past him into the house and closed the door. "Why are
you not at Telford's?"

"I have five men there. She is safe. For now."

At the tone of Ash's statement, the sausage roll tried to
come back up. Callister handed him a glass of something and
he drank it down, not tasting it until it was too late.

Milk. He hated milk.

"What is it?"

"Harcourt and Stan should be here any moment."

"Ash. Please. Do not make me wait. I'll go mad."

"Very well. Gordon has returned."

"To London?"

"I am sure of it."

"Then we will just have to—"

"No. *We* will do nothing. He will already have someone
watching you—and closely. You are probably the only lead he
has."

Realization dawned. He could not be seen anywhere near
Livvy. Gordon would not be returning if he didn't hope to find
the Plumiere and punish her. And if North stopped searching
for her, the other lord would assume he had already found her.
Those watching him would already know he'd spent time with
her. It was more important than ever that he stay away.

"I see you understand well enough."

"I will go mad if I do not see her, Ash." He grabbed his friend's arms.

"I know you will. But you are a danger to her now. Remember that."

Callister opened the door as Harcourt and Stanley reached the top step. A few minutes later they had taken up their places in the library. Callister left to order tea.

"Tea?" Stanley looked at the spot in which the butler had been standing. "Did he say, *tea*?" The man had learned to distrust the African chair and had claimed a spot on the couch. Harcourt took his turn on the uncomfortable seat.

"Yes, Stanley. We need our wits old boy. Gordon might have been in the city for days now, depending on the route chosen." Harcourt spared a glance at the brandy decanter, then looked away.

"What next for us then?" Stan was looking at Ashmoore.

"North?" Ash asked innocently—too innocently.

"Oh, no you don't. I am the one who created this mess. I cannot be trusted to get us out. My mind is a little clouded at the moment. I cannot be impartial."

"You do not have to be impartial. Sometimes a little emotional involvement makes the difference." Ash stood and walked to the window. "After all, if it weren't for our emotional involvement, we would have never hung about that last night in France, getting drunk off our arses."

North shook his head. "I must have slept through that."

Ashmoore glanced at Harcourt and Stanley, rather dramatically in fact, then looked him in the eye.

"There is something you need to know."

Harcourt jumped to his feet and hurried to face Ashmoore, toe to toe.

"This is not the time, surely," he said quietly. But the room was not so big as to swallow the sound. Stanley dropped his head in his hands and groaned.

Ash put a hand on Harcourt's shoulder. "I think the right time was years ago, old boy."

Harcourt shrugged out of Ash's grasp and moved to the other side of the room. "Shaking his faith in us won't help the situation," he said.

"I assume I am the *he* to whom you refer," North said, though he'd just as soon walk out the door and not learn whatever secrets they had seen fit to keep from him for years. In spite of the stone weighing heavily in his stomach, he forged on. "Too late to change your mind now. Let's hear it then."

Ashmoore began pacing. That stone got heavier each time his friend completed a circuit. "Try to remember that you made me vow not to speak of France."

"I never forget that."

"Good. Then you will understand why we did not discuss this with you before now. You wanted to forget it all. We only wanted to grant you that wish."

"Not the only reason, of course." Stanley mumbled.

"Quite right, Stan. I beg your pardon."

Harcourt spun about and pointed an accusatory finger. "Look here. You have told everyone how heroic we were, to go back for you, to rescue you. You thought we were heroes. It is hard to let someone down who thinks of you as a hero."

He looked at Ash. "I can understand that. You all thought I was terribly heroic for taking Ash's place in the lottery. I hated to tell you otherwise."

"Exactly." Harcourt smiled. "So you will understand why we did not want to tell you—"

"We aren't the heroes you believed us to be." Stanley sounded terribly ashamed. He kept his head down, his hair hanging over his face like a white curtain.

"You saved me. I was there, remember? You never gave up. You found me, after all that time."

"That's where you are wrong, my friend." Ashmoore stopped pacing and backed up to the wall. He dropped his chin to his chest. "We had given up."

"Then you just happened to break into an armed fortress and check the dungeon for pirate's gold but found me instead?"

Stanley sat back, but looked at his knees. "We were not far away, actually. We had come terribly close and we did not realize it."

"We were distraught." Harcourt was looking down again.

"We were drunk," Ashmoore barked. "We were never going to find you and we were drowning ourselves in every available drop of liquor in the province."

"And then? This cannot be the end of the story. Ash?"

His dark friend moved to the fire and leaned his body against a pillar. His face lit up red and yellow as he watched the flames. When it came, his voice was little more than a whisper.

"A woman came to me that night, chiding me for coming so close only to give up."

"A woman. The Scottish woman you speak of? The one I never seem to remember seeing you with?"

"Yes. That woman. She told us where to find you, gave us details."

"It could have been a trap."

"We would have gone anyway."

"I know you would have. So what is this dire confession? Did you somehow decide not to find me, even after you'd been given these directions?"

"Very nearly. We were too drunk to remember, but luckily, the masked woman—"

"Masked? You never mentioned a mask before."

"Well, how could I? You would have wanted to know every detail."

North nodded. "True. So this is your sin? Please tell me this has not plagued the lot of you for years."

Harcourt lunged forward. "Stop it, North. Will you stop it? You are painting us as heroes again. But we were only very lucky friends. That is all. Providence shined on you. The woman saved you. We did not."

Only two years ago, he would have thought Providence and God had forgotten him, so he'd felt no contrition for taking his revenge on that nest of French vipers. Neither had

Ashmoore. But every night he could not stop the memory of each man he'd executed, saw each face. Dear God!

"She wasn't..." He turned to Ash, unable to voice the question.

"No. She was not there. I killed just the one woman, defending myself. You?"

He searched the horrid memory, shocked that he would willingly do so. None of the blood on his hands or soaking his feet, had been from a woman.

"Not unless one had shorn her hair and dressed as a man," he said.

"Not this woman. Black hair. Green eyes. Too beautiful to ever pass as a man."

"Then, no."

Ashmoore moved to the couch and dropped onto it.

"You are forgiven for not telling me sooner. But I see you as no less my rescuers. You were there, available for the telling."

"We were too drunk to leave the country," groaned Harcourt.

"Well, I will drink to that."

"North, do not treat this as if it is nothing," Stanley whispered. "We gave up."

"Stanley, Harcourt, Ash. I forgive you for it. Now forgive yourselves, for pity's sake." He frowned at Ashmoore. "Why tell me now?"

"I did not want you to have too much faith in us. You believe we are more capable than you to guard Olivia. You are wrong. And if something happens to her, it would be best if you know ahead of time that we are not infallible."

North finally understood what all this had to do with Livvy. They were correct—he'd thanked God every day for his friends, that they would be able to rescue her from any foe. And although it relieved his conscience a bit to suppose he might be worthy to walk among his rescuers, it also chilled the blood in his veins. Livvy was in more danger now, than she had been an hour ago, at least in his muddled mind.

"So, what do *we* do for Livvy?"

Ash leaned on his knees. "Think like Lord Gordon, I suppose. What would you do?"

"There would be no avoiding his being recognized," Stanley offered.

"Right. So he could not just slip into town with a sack over his head." Ash nodded. "Good. What else?"

"Knowing Gordon, he will throw a party," said Harcourt with a sneer.

"If he does, at least we will know where he is," Ash said.

North filled his lungs and let the breath out slowly. "It would not surprise me should the monster send us all invitations."

"The *ton* will be his alibi." Harcourt's frown fell away and his usual enthusiasm attempted to return.

Stanley still looked concerned. "Brilliant. But is *Gordon* that clever?"

"Absolutely," said Ash.

"So we watch for his first public display," Harcourt suggested.

"And we act as if he has already made it." Ash was back on his feet. "There is one other thing. Gordon will not make good any threat against Olivia if The Plumiere is still in play. He will go after the writer first."

"Even so, day and night, Olivia and her father cannot be left alone." North feared his friend was looking for a break from his watch.

"I have enough men already at Telford's. No need for the three of you to bring more attention to the place by coming and going."

"No, of course not." Harcourt frowned. "We will just have to keep busy, beating the bushes for The Plumiere, making him believe we have not found her yet."

North bit his lip. Should he tell them? Should he not? Perhaps his friends would be better able to play their parts if they were not told who The Plumiere actually was. For the moment, unless the situation changed, he would keep Livvy's secret.

Callister returned with four teacups on a tray and passed them around. North took a sip and choked.

"Whiskey, with a shot of tea, my lord."

"Thank you, Callister." He had to clear his throat to get his full voice back. "I believe we should pay closer attention to Lady Malbury's azaleas," he suggested.

Harcourt moaned for some reason.

"I wonder, though," said Stanley. "Would it be better for The Plumiere if we did not find her? Would she be safer? Should not North wave the white flag? Let her go?"

"North?" Ashmoore handed the decision to him yet again.

"I suppose it is inevitable. I was prepared to last another week at best." He hadn't meant to say the last aloud but was relieved to find his friends nodding their agreement. It was reassuring to know he was not the only one tiring of the game.

Harcourt raised his teacup into the air. "To protecting The Scarlet Plumiere!"

"To protecting The Scarlet Plumiere!" They each repeated.

"Whomever she may be," Harcourt said, then drained his glass.

Stanley did the same. Then Ashmoore.

The last bit sounded about as sincere as a toast to the Sherriff of Nottingham.

"Damn you all. You know who she is!" His roar echoed against the ceiling.

Stanley choked. Harcourt's eyes doubled in size, and Ashmoore collapsed into the chair behind him.

North turned to Stanley. "How long have you known?"

"My dinner party. I admit to tricking her into confirming it. My smile distracted her, I believe. I told no one."

"And you?" He stepped up to Harcourt.

"You are the one to leave me on that blasted azalea watch. The young man only checks under two pots—those of Lady Malbury and Miss Reynolds. I told no one."

"And you, Ash?"

"The first day you went to see her, I arrived soon after you did, but heard her discussing it with the servants. I asked her not to tell you I had been there. I told no one else."

"So she *knows* you know?"

Stanley raised his hand. "She knows I know."

Harcourt grinned. "She does not know *I* know."

"Your turn, old boy," Ashmoore said. "How long have you been keeping the same secret from us? I notice you didn't immediately ask for her name."

"I knew the day I met her. She was a veritable Jekyll and Hyde, trying to act the timid bird incapable of leaving her father's side one minute, then tormenting her late mother's dog the next." He laughed at the memory of the little rat side-stepping away with its lip curled. "And the ribbon with which she tormented the animal matched that scarlet ribbon on Stanley's gift."

"The Rat. I do believe it thinks I can protect it from her. Hides beneath whichever chair I choose. So I sit as close to Livvy as possible, just to disappoint it." Ash laughed.

North suddenly sobered.

"Livvy now is it? And just how close to her do you sit?"

His dark friend raised his arms in defense, then lifted a knee across his seated body when North advanced on him.

"I will have you know she has been driven insane with jealousy! Damn me if she has not."

North stopped. "I am not an unreasonable man. I will let you say what you have to say before I pummel you."

"It is not the intensity of her jealousy that drives her mad," he said in all seriousness. "It is the fact that the woman of whom she is jealous is herself."

North smiled. It might have been the only thing to save Ashmoore a bit of blood-letting that day. Any denials would have fallen on a deaf ear, but jealousy he could understand. He had been turning green for weeks!

For the remainder of the evening, they fought over which of them was best capable of protecting Livvy. It embarrassed him to admit to his friends that he was, indeed, afraid he might black out at an inopportune moment—as he often had while a captive in France—and wake to find her gone, or worse. He pled with Ash to maintain his guardianship. Ash, in the end, could not deny him.

Stanley gave his reason for allowing North to learn the truth for himself. Harcourt and Ashmoore admitted to the same. He tried to imagine what he might have felt had one of his friends come to him with the news. They had been correct, of course. It would have dealt his confidence a mighty blow. He so prided himself on being clever enough, at least, to be worthy of her.

Harcourt frowned. "Oh, we did not say you were *worthy* of her, just that we wanted you to *believe* you were."

The marquess's chair flew backward and the wind was knocked from his lungs.

"What's that, old boy?" North returned his foot to the floor and lifted a hand to his ear. "You apologize? Well, certainly I forgive you."

"All joking aside, gentlemen," said Ash. "I think it is time Mr. Lott sent The Scarlet Plumiere another message." Then he clasped his hands behind his back and grinned at North. "We need to give him someone to watch besides Livvy."

CHAPTER TWENTY-FOUR

The Capital Journal, February 16th, Morning
edition, Fiction section
Once upon a time in The Great City, a certain Mr.
Lott became unreasonably besotted with a certain
witty writer, a woman possessed of both a clever wit
and a scarlet pen. But one night he came to his senses
and understood the danger he had invited to her door.
He had paid no heed to those hounds of Hell who
watched and waited for his clever writer to be
unmasked. But he is paying heed to them now.

My dear writer. Come to me. Allow me to protect
you from those I have brought to your door. Let me
make amends. Show yourself to me. Show pity. I admit
I cannot find you and should in all reason, leave you
be. But there are those hounds, you see. I cannot leave
you to them. And I have gone quite insane trying to
find you myself, but you are far too clever for me.

Touche, Mademoiselle. Unmask yourself to me at
least. Collect my white flag...and all my red ones. –
Mr. Lott

Chester brought it to him while he sipped his coffee.
North could not even glance at the newpaper without feeling
gut-punched. Callister did not force breakfast on him. He was
left in absolute, miserable peace.

Ashmoore did not come to tease with tales of The Rat. He
and the men he kept at his beck and call were part of Telford's
household now. All the world assumed his friend was courting
Livvy. Any hounds from Hell should have taken note that a

very dangerous man now watched over Miss Reynolds. To approach her was folly. Scandal be damned.

Stanley and Harcourt were off making a show of searching for The Plumiere, in hopes they were being watched and could lead any sniffing hounds on a merry chase.

North was left to man the distraction. The house was being watched. The watchers were being watched. Any woman fool enough to cross his threshold was asking for very real trouble. It was the longest week of his life.

By Thursday, when he had worn the spots off his playing cards and the pattern from more than one carpet, a message came from Ash.

> *Livvy is going to kill The Rat and feed it to her father for supper if she is not allowed out of the house and away from all these "men." We will be going to the opera tomorrow night, or Livvy will be going alone—or so I have been informed. Yes, you may greet her. No, you may not sit in the same box. You may not touch her hand, swoon as she walks by, or pull her into a dark alcove. You keep your bloody eyes to yourself or do not allow those eyes within a block of the place. –Ash*
>
> *Post Script. No, she does not know that you know, or that Harcourt knows, so yes, she is still painfully jealous, though she would cut off her tongue before she would admit it.*

Poor Olivia!

Surely there was something he could do.

***

Sarah stood on the London dock. Her heart thundered as men and beasts bumped into her in the swirling mist of morning. She might be pushed into the water at any moment, but she dared not move. This is where Maude instructed her to stay and even though she feared drowning, she still feared her aunt a little more.

The woman had refused to leave the ship until the captain returned the fares she'd paid for passage. She'd doctored the leg of his bosen and demanded free passage in return, but the captain insisted he'd only agreed to the terms thinking she meant *return* passage to France. So all morning, while the ship was unloaded, Maude made a nuisance of herself, hoping the man would simply pay her to go away. Sarah was to stand in the center of the dock and cause trouble as well. She'd been capable of only the first half of her instructions.

If the woman weren't her last living relative, Sarah would happily run off into the fog and never see the frightening woman again. She'd had a brief taste of the streets of London, however, and she would never willingly return to them. If Lord Ashmoore was displeased with the trouble they were about to bring to his doorstep, she might find herself alone once again. But at least she would be on home soil. Finding herself alone in Paris would have meant the death of her, she was sure.

***

Livvy had waited all day for something horrible to come along and force them to change their plans. It was not possible that her prison doors would open for her that night. It was just a cruel joke; everyone went on acting as if she truly needed to prepare for an evening at the opera.

She had not attended anything public for years. If she did indeed escape through the front door on Ash's arm, she hoped she still remembered how to act. The little dinner party at *Viscount F's* house had been a simple gathering of friends. Tonight she would need to walk gracefully across foyers, climb stairs without a misstep, smile and say the correct thing to the correct people, and with many of the *haute ton* looking on.

Perhaps she did not wish to leave the house after all. She had laid claim to a small sitting room in the center of the house that boasted only a small window, then refused admittance to anyone without bosoms. For a precious hour, here and there, she had been able to pretend there weren't a half dozen men listening to her breathe and routinely checking to see if she had moved from one room to another.

She had enjoyed playing the tyrant of course, putting an apron on one man and a feather duster in his grip. She had ordered him to dust something for each time he had checked on her that day. The next day they hid from her. They became so stealthy in their watching, it only served to make her nervous. Just yesterday, she'd developed a tic in her eye and went to bed until she was rid of it.

She would have called them all together and had a good hearty scream if her father were not about. For some reason, the man was at his best when Ashmoore was in the room, but being at his best was also taxing for him. After consideration, she had decided Ashmoore's company had to be rationed, like an addictive drug.

In addition, Livvy had had enough of the dark earl's brotherly advice to choke a horse. He told her how she might better get along with The Rat, and he had had a number of theories for her to try. Of course she tried them on Ashmoore instead. He was so slow to catch on that one afternoon she placed his tea and crumpets on the floor, then sat next to them, perfectly willing to chatter pleasantly while he ate them.

He was not amused.

She was amused. She was bloody amused until The Rat ran through the room and snatched a biscuit. She lost her temper and leveled another at his disappearing tail, only to watch the treat hit her mother's cuckoo clock. It flew right through the little door.

She spent the rest of the afternoon cleaning crumbs out of small corners of the poor little contraption. When she failed to note the time, the bird would startle her and she would gasp. Eventually, she gave the little bird a very unladylike name.

Ashmoore's laughter traveled well no matter how many rooms separated them.

She put a dozen crumbly biscuits in his bedsheets. The next day, they were still there. She had no idea where he had slept.

With no one at hand to torment, she finally allowed Stella to have a go at her hair.

"My hair need not be perfect, Stella. Someone will have nailed the doors and windows shut. Just you watch."

Thank goodness Stella ignored her and made her look fabulous, because, as it so happened, there was no crisis that evening. Her father gifted her with her mother's pearls. They were the perfect complement to her new gown of russet velvet. Stella quickly added the broach to her hair, above one temple. She fought to keep the tears from her eyes.

"Lovely color, my dear. Best you stay away from red, do you think? Scarlet would give you away." He kissed her on the cheek, winked, then whistled as he walked away.

The tears could not be helped.

"I will kill whichever man made you cry tonight," Ashmoore offered as she reached the bottom of the stairs.

"I beg you not to, as I am rather fond of my father."

"Oh, I see. Well, then, cry on. But try to finish before we arrive or Northwick will pummel me as soon as the lights go down."

"Northwick's going to be there?" Immediately, her heart got into the spirit of the evening. "I thought he was not allowed to see me."

"Isn't allowed to speak with you. Not at length, anyway. And I have ordered him to show no interest in you. It will all be an act, of course. The man is going quite mad not seeing you."

"He is?"

"He is." He closed his eyes at the last. Was he attempting to convince her, or was he prevaricating?

"How do you know? You are always here." She pulled her hand away and stopped.

"I get reports." He lifted his elbow again.

"Hmph." She took his arm but she did not believe a word. At least she tried not to believe a word. Her mind did not seem to want to let the matter go. The carriage was well warmed, but she got goose pimples imagining Northwick waiting at

The King's Theatre, remembering the last look he'd given her at Stanley's.

Unfortunately, when the nightmare of Lord Gordon came to an end, so would her fairy tale. She would have to give up her new friends, like a set of lovely furniture she could no longer afford. It would all have to go back. The women of London needed a champion, and unless another champion presented themselves, they had only The Scarlet Plumiere. She must not forget it. It would be so easy to let the city take care of itself, but she could not bear the possible consequences.

From now on, however, she would trust no one; she would make doubly sure of a man's guilt before reporting it, the fiction section notwithstanding.

"I am sorry, but it looks to be a crush." Ashmoore dropped the curtain and gave Livvy a pained smile.

"Even better, my lord. If I misstep, no one will see my feet. And if I trip I will just hold tight to your arm until I regain my footing with no one the wiser."

She took a deep breath before leaving the comfort of the warm carriage. Once outside, however, the cold air never reached her. The throng pressing into the theatre left little room for air. Ashmoore's hand was warm and his tight grip reassuring. Her whole arm was locked beneath his elbow so that if someone were to snatch her out of the crowd, the earl would easily be able to save the limb at least.

There was no use looking down; she could not see her feet, let alone where to step next. After a second glance, she recognized the tall man ahead of Ashmoore, knew the back of his head very well in fact. It was Peter, the largest of her guards, the one she had bullied into wearing an apron and dusting her mother's figurines.

She looked to her right; Ian.

The man bumping along to her left was Everhardt. She guessed without looking that Milton was just behind her.

How dashing they all looked in their tails. Although their faces would not be identified by the gentry, they certainly fit in well enough. And they glided along so smoothly they did not seem to be protecting her, but they were. A little push here, a shove there kept the crowd from affecting her protective cocoon. A dozen pardons and half as many apologies later, they were inside the building.

A waving fan caught her attention long before she heard her name. It was Anna, tip-toing above the crowd, as un-ladylike as could be.

"Olivia!"

Ashmoore turned toward the sound. After a fierce battle against the flow of the crowd, she found herself in a new cocoon made entirely of friends. Peter and the others were suddenly gone, like ghosts, fading into the walls, their faces replaced by the dinner party from Stanley's. She instantly noticed Northwick's absence, however.

But she'd been wrong, she realized, when Northwick stepped around her. It had not been Milton behind her after all. The realization sent chills up her spine and into her intricately arranged hair.

"Miss Reynolds." He bowed, then maneuvered his way over to Aunt Winnie's end of the circle. He bumped into Stanley's shoulder and an envelope poked out from his jacket.

"I hope you are not bringing love letters to the opera," said Ashmoore.

"Oh!" North tucked the envelope inside his vest. "Letter for The Plumiere."

Irene pushed on his shoulder to gain his attention. "How are you going to give her a letter if you do not know who she is?"

"I will find a way," he said with a smile. He and Ashmoore exchanged a look, but North shook his head.

Other than a glance at her shoes when he had greeted her, North did not spare her another look. He was clearly enjoying himself, grinning at Winnie and laughing heartily at her little quips. Only when he paused to listen to someone did she notice his intense surveying of the crowd. His head was never down. When he leaned this way or that, his eyes were always up, always moving, just never in her direction.

She knew, somehow, that he was aware of her—just as she was aware of him. If she closed her eyes and he began moving through the crowd, she believed she would be able to point in his direction, so acute were her senses where he was concerned. So attuned was her heart.

By not assigning a name to her feelings, she'd hoped they might dissipate. As long as she did not call it love, it would not be love. And her life would go on, enriched by the memory of friends, but it would go on, as planned. Straight forward. It was the only caper left on the plate.

"We have to split up into two sets of four, I am afraid," Stanley was saying.

Someone grabbed her arm in a tight squeeze. Stanley looked in her direction, noticed who had claimed her and laughed. "Looks like Anna and Livvy are inseparable. Northwick, you and Mother with Irene and me." He passed tickets to Ashmoore and Harcourt.

"Oh, thank heavens," Anna whispered in her ear. "If I had to sit with Miss Goodfellow, someone would get her eyes scratched out and I am afraid it might have been me."

Livvy swallowed her disappointment. Who knew if she would get a chance to see Northwick again before she returned to her cage? But she consoled herself with the pleasure of finally being in the company of another woman. She was also grateful she would not be forced to listen to Irene Goodfellow abusing The Scarlet Plumiere. If that came to a cat fight, Irene might not come out the winner.

She checked the length of her nails and laughed when she realized what she was doing.

CHAPTER TWENTY-FIVE

The first act of the *opera buffa* was not long, but it seemed so. There was no *libretta* for translating the words, and the patter song was so fast and so poorly articulated, she would not have been able to follow along in any case. It was all just an excuse to complain to herself, of course. When one dearly wanted to turn and look at someone in another box, it did not matter what was happening on stage. Mozart himself could have been leading the musicians and she would not have given a fig.

Face forward, she told herself a hundred times before intermission.

"You are missing a terrible comedy, my dear. Someone on your mind?" Anna looked over her shoulder at her, then beyond her. Then she held a fan innocently before her mouth. "Would you like to know what North is doing at the moment?"

She clutched Anna's hand. "Is it so obvious?"

"Only to me, because I was one of those to witness your last farewell, my dear. Remember?" Anna gave her hand a squeeze. "No one would suppose I am watching him. He is just past your ear."

Olivia's hand rose and checked her hair just where Anna seemed to be looking.

"Lovely pearls, by the way."

"They were my mother's."

"And he just looked our way when you moved your arm. You mustn't do it again. He really needs to avoid watching your every move."

"What is he doing now?"

"He is being lectured by Winnie. Smiling now. Nodding. Now he is frowning and folding his arms." Anna laughed discreetly. "Winnie just winked at me. She was a witness too remember? We are all here to help."

"Help what?"

"Help you and North marry, of course."

"Marry!" She closed her eyes to block out the image of herself and North standing at the altar in St. James', but she failed miserably. "He will have to find someone else to marry. I am not available."

"Oh, but we were afraid of that." Anna began to ply her fan in earnest.

"Of what?"

"That you have fallen for Ashmoore."

"She has done no such thing." Ashmoore bent forward and whispered harshly. "And if I can hear you, others may hear you as well. Anna, turn 'round and give these singers their due, would you? And leave poor Livvy alone."

Anna gave him a fierce frown, then whispered, "We will finish this at intermission."

"Anna!" Ashmoore tugged on the woman's hair and she turned back to the stage. Apparently the dark earl had adopted more than one sister.

She fought the urge to giggle and tried to focus on the entertainment. A tenor was having a difficult time remembering his words and signaled to another man to come replace him.

It only reminded her of Northwick, how he was only too happy to let Ashmoore protect her in his stead. She was sorely tempted to tug on Anna's hair herself and demand to know what the man was doing at that moment, if he might be staring at her. Then suddenly, the music ended. The audience broke into applause, probably showing more gratitude for the reprieve than the actual performance, or an enthusiasm for possible refreshments.

Livvy stood gracefully, not popping out of her seat as she wanted to do. By the time she pulled her skirts to the side and turned, Northwick was gone. So was Winnie. She would not have expected the older woman to move so quickly.

She looked to Ashmoore. He rolled his eyes, then offered his arm.

"It is a good thing North is a much better actor than you are an actress. Hopefully he is being watched more carefully than you are, but I doubt it. Not in that dress. I do not know what I was thinking."

"I am glad you chose the color, my lord. Northwick suggested puce for this dress."

He leaned close, since the hallway was filling.

"Only because he does not wish other men to appreciate you, my dear."

"You jest."

"I never jest." He frowned. "That is not true, actually. I rarely jest."

"Fie, sir. You have a terrific wit. Your frown is your disguise."

"Oh, I hope that is not true. I am trying to live up to my reputation and you are telling me it is all in my frown? The very idea should frighten you."

"Yes. It should. Perhaps Lord Northwick might be a better man for the job after all."

He looked at her sharply. "I wish he had heard you say that."

At the top of the stairs, they stopped. The formally dressed mob had filled the foyer and the flow of the room was clogged at the head of the refreshment table. Twenty men waited anxiously to fetch punch for their companions. Until they had fulfilled their gentlemanly duty, the rest of the crowd would have to sort itself out, or wait. Livvy did not mind. She had quite a view from where she stood.

Northwick and Winnie must have left their box before the music ended to have gotten as far as they had. In fact, they were nearly back to the area where their little group had gathered before the performance. Was he hoping she and Ashmoore would be able to join them? Would they indeed have a chance for a word or two after all?

Judging from the crush on the stairs below her, she would never reach the bottom before they would be expected to return to their seats! Was the other staircase as crowded? Alas, it was. They might as well return to their box, but she could not bear to give up a chance to merely watch the man from across the room without the crowd being the wiser.

A gentleman stood near Northwick with a lovely woman on his arm. The back of her head was a cascading mass of auburn curls. The most prominent of her curves were currently aimed at the earl. There could only be one woman in all of London who looked like that. Livvy was a little surprised to see her at so public a function where most men had their wives on their arms.

"Ursula."

Ashmoore leaned down as she stood on the step below him. "You know her then?"

"She insisted on meeting. Lady M arranged it." Quarters were far too cramped to even be discussing such a thing. But as she glanced around, she realized she had been boxed in by Everhardt, Ian and Ashmoore. The railing lay to her right. Peter glanced up from halfway down the steps, but his eyes skimmed the crowd and never actually rested on her.

"I must say, my lord, that I have not given your friends nearly the respect they deserve."

"My friends?"

"These friends." She pointed a sly finger at Ian's back.

"I am sure they will be delighted to hear it. But what about me? Am I safe to return to my bed?"

"Of course, my lord."

"And what of the crumbs?"

"I cannot imagine to what you refer."

"Innocent until the end, eh, Miss Reynolds?"

"*Moi?*" She batted her eyes and laughed. Then she sobered when she saw Northwick lean down and kiss Ursula on the cheek. In public. He had kissed her in public! And dear Aunt Winnie stood next to him, laughing! With the former mistress of her own son! Had the world gone mad?

"If it helps," Ashmoore murmured in her ear, "he owed her a kiss."

She swallowed, looked away. Tapped her foot five times. Looked back.

"Owed her? She had given him too many and he needed to return one?"

Finally, she had to turn her back. She hung on to Ashmoore's hands to control herself.

"I would like to go home, my lord."

"You cannot mean it. Would you like to go somewhere else?"

She studied him, standing there, all tall and handsome, his lips the first thing she noticed each time she looked up at him.

"Livvy." It was a warning she did not care to hear.

"I want you to kiss me, Ashmoore. Please."

"What good will it do, besides create a new scandal for the papers in the morning?"

"I will feel better for it. I know I will. And he will feel worse. That is reason enough."

Ashmoore looked past her.

"But he is not even watching, Livvy."

"As soon as he is, then."

"Damn it!" Ashmoore frowned at her, then dipped his head. He tried to pull back quickly, but she pulled on his lapel a heartbeat more. Then another. Then she let him go.

Ashmoore turned and began pulling one of her hands. She looked over her shoulder, down into the foyer. Just as she found Northwick glaring in her direction, the crowd blocked her view, filling in the wake left by her passing.

She was wrong. It did not make her feel better at all.

"Where did you go? We tried to find you." Anna took her seat, then leaned forward to take a peek beyond Livvy's stiff shoulder. "Dear lord, Olivia. What have you done to the man?"

She could only shake her head. The tears came as soon as the lights dimmed. She cried all through the second act. Ashmoore finally took her home.

The earl insisted on escorting her to her room. For a moment she worried the man had been influenced somehow by their kiss, but refused to imagine the possibilities. The situation was complicated enough. She had been out of her mind to insist he kiss her!

She reached for her door, but he took her chin and urged her to face him. Begrudgingly, she looked up. He was laughing at her in his quiet, slightly smirking way.

"Oh, Livvy. What am I to do with you?" Rather than kiss her, however, he pulled her against his chest and enveloped her in his large arms, then proceeded to hug her until she squeaked. "I should murder you for torturing North and forcing me to be party to it. He will not forgive it easily. I shall have to allow him to beat me bloody a time or two, but at least now we know for sure, eh?"

"What is it we know for sure?" She could only whisper with what breath she had saved in the bottom of her lungs.

"That he is madly in love with you. Only I am the one who will suffer in the end." He released her, then tapped his finger on her chin. "You would have never been so cruel to even The Rat, you know. So when all this is over, you are going to make it up to him."

"When all this is over, all this will be over. I will not marry him. I will not cease acting as The Plumiere."

"Ah, but you will. You have no choice in the matter."

"I beg your pardon."

"Forget for a moment the rest of us will threaten to expose you if you refuse him."

Her mouth dropped open and she forgot it altogether. They wouldn't!

"It is your own heart that will not allow it, Livvy. Your heart will give you no choice whatsoever." He reached out and wiped away a tear she'd not noticed shedding. "We will just be patient for a while longer, shall we?"

He opened her door, made a thorough check of her room, then bid her goodnight.

Stella helped her out of her dress, then left her alone.

Livvy removed her mother's pearls and curled them into a little pile. She stared at them as she brushed out her hair. Try as she might, she could not remember much of Ashmoore's kiss. She did remember having to pull on his lapel to make sure it made an impression on Northwick. Thanks to her antics, though, all the newspapers would enjoy a swift business in the morning.

A noise came from her window. She froze, listening. She had promised Ashmoore she would do a better job of screaming the next time someone surprised her, so she took a deep breath to do just that.

"Did he kiss you goodnight as well?"

She jumped from her seat and turned to face her handsome intruder.

"Lord Northwick!" She clutched her brush to her chest. "How did you get past the guards?"

"You think they would stop me? We are on the same side, remember?" He walked toward her, slowly. His foot lifted above the edge of her thick floral rug as if he had walked the room a dozen times and knew what should be avoided. That rug had been there for years and even she forgot at times, until she was flying toward the foot of her bed.

"They will tell Ashmoore."

He paused, removed his jacket, then tossed it on the bed.

"I do not particularly fear the man at the moment. I am much more afraid of you."

He lied. He did not look the least bit frightened.

"Then perhaps you should go. I am hardly dressed for—"

"Do not fret. I will stay but a moment."

"You will?" How could she possibly sound more disappointed?

He laughed, though quietly.

"I need to do only one thing, then I will be on my way."

"One thing?" She did not like the sound of that. "Slit my throat, maybe?"

"Never. Though your throat may be involved."

Her mind flew back to that encounter in the darkness at Madame Bouchard's. He had done lovely things to her neck then. And she had been completely at his mercy!

She edged sideways, toward the door. He took two quick steps to head her off, so she started backing toward the dressing room. She could get inside, close the door quickly, hold tight to the handle while she screamed for help.

He spared a glance behind her.

"You will never make it. Time to surrender, Livvy."

"Never." She held her brush out between them like a sword. He paused. For a moment, she thought she had won.

"I love you, Livvy."

Her mind stuttered, then stopped.

"I beg your pardon?"

"I said, I love you."

Was she already asleep? Had she slipped into bed and started dreaming?

He licked his finger and reached to his left to pinch out the candle on her dressing table. Only one candle remained on the far side of the bed. The warm glow danced across that handsome plane of his cheek.

"Do not be afraid, Livvy. I have only come to kiss you, to make certain you dream of my lips, not Ashmoore's."

"I have forgotten his already." She bit her tongue. Would he still feel the need to kiss her?

He stalked her until her back was against the dressing room door. Only too late did she remember her plan to be on the other side of it. Gently, he pushed the brush to one side, then eased it from her grasp and tossed it on the bed.

"I am very, very happy to hear that." He moved forward and reached out, but he did not touch her. His hands rested to each side of her head, against the wood. That heat he carried about in his veins came at her from three sides. The smell of him was intoxicating. It took all her control not to lean to the side and bury her nose in his shirtsleeve. But watching him watching her was quite compelling as well. His pupils dilated before her eyes. For some reason, she felt she should say something.

"If you must know, I ordered him to kiss me."

"Ordered?" He rolled his eyes. "I will wager he did not question that order."

"Then you would lose that wager." Ashmoore's voice rang out in harsh contrast to the quiet tones they had been using.

Northwick did not flinch. "I will deal with you later, my friend." His eyes never left her face, paying particular attention to her lips. She breathed deeply, willing him to close the distance, wishing some wind would push him from behind.

"You will deal with me now, old man. I am her protector at the moment. I will do what I must."

Still North did not turn away from her. If he had, she might have screamed.

"Ash, relax. I only came to kiss her."

"Be that as it may."

Livvy's frustration could no longer be contained. "Please, Ash. Give us just a moment."

"As you wish, Livvy." The man's footsteps moved to the door. "You do not mind if your father stays, though, do you?"

Northwick's forehead lowered to touch her own. For a moment, they looked into each other's eyes, desperately, as they had that night at Stanley's.

"Long enough moment for you my dear?" Her father did not sound amused. He had picked a fine time to remember he had a daughter.

"Yes, father."

"Good, because it seemed an eternity to me."

***

Livvy had barely gotten to sleep when someone crashed through her bedroom door. A candle rose above her. She lifted her hand to shade her eyes, but the candle moved back to the door.

"Miss Reynolds is here! She is fine!" It was Peter's voice.

She pulled her blanket to her chin.

"What's wrong? Where is my father?"

"He is snoring away. No need to disturb him, Miss."

Footsteps charged down the hallway.

"She is fine," Peter said again.

"Thank God." Ashmoore hurried to her side and took her hand. "Ursula has been murdered. I do not want to leave you, but—"

"I feel perfectly safe with your men, my lord. Do what you must."

"It is just the blasted headline. North will worry. I have got to send a man to Stanley's of course. We will all be back here before breakfast can be cooked. Will that do?"

"Breakfast will be ready for you, my lord."

Ashmoore pressed a newspaper into her hands, then fled out the door.

With large, sure hands, Peter lit the candle on her nightstand. "I will be right outside, my lady. Milton is just beneath your window."

"Thank you. I doubt Lord Gordon would stoop to climbing trellises."

"Doubt nothing, my lady. Doubt nothing."

She picked up the morning edition and moved it into the light. The headline was easy enough to read.

"THE SCARLET PLUMIERE IS DEAD!"

CHAPTER TWENTY-SIX

North was still wearing his clothes from the night before. He had been so uncontrollably giddy only a few hours ago. Livvy had not actually admitted loving him, but he had been sure of it. He did not remember coming home, did not remember how he might have made it up the stairs and into his bed, fully clothed, but he had awakened that way. The real surprise was that he had been able to sleep at all!

Chester shook him for the second time. Where was Callister?

"My lord, the constable's in the drawing room, speaking with Mr. Callister. He asks that you join them."

"What time is it?"

"Half past six, my lord."

At least he did not need to stop and dress before going downstairs. Hopefully, the constable had something helpful to report about Lord Gordon. Perhaps the man's ship had sunk in the channel. It was too much to ask, but he was incapable of rational thought at the moment.

He entered the drawing room a moment later, holding out hope.

"Constable?"

Callister looked horrified. Surely he did not look that bad. He had removed his cravat, and needed a shave of course, but he was hardly standing before company in his small clothes.

"Callister? What's wrong?"

"I have just been telling your man here about a murder last night. Can you tell me where you went, my lord, after the theatre?"

The constable stood in the center of the room. Two officers stood to either side of North as if guarding the door behind him.

"Why?"

"Some say you disappeared for a bit."

"Some?"

"Couple of blokes who have been following you. Someone hired them to do so. They say you slipped away, didn't return until after the time of the murder. I am sorry to put it so bluntly, my lord, but they seem to think you are the man we are looking for. I would not be so interested in their opinions, of course, but the lady was found holding a letter from you."

"A *woman* was murdered? Which woman?" He advanced on the constable. "Which woman!"

"The Scarlet Plumiere, my lord."

"What?" He could not hear past the noise in his head, but then realized it was only his own shouting.

He looked at Callister for verification, but the man looked as confused as he. It could not be Livvy! No one else had figured it out. Except for each and every one of his friends, of course.

It cannot be Livvy!

Blackness started building at the edge of his vision, overwhelming the details of the room, but he did not care. If he had failed Livvy, there was nothing left for him to care about.

"The woman's name, man. Give me the woman's name!"

"Certainly, my lord. Just as soon as you tell me where you went after the opera?"

"He was with me." Ashmoore's voice cut through the darkness, as it had once before.

"Ash!"

"Livvy's fine. She is absolutely fine." His friend rushed forward, took his arm, and led him to a chair. "It was Ursula."

"Ursula? But why?"

"He must have believed her to be The Plumiere."

"My God! Just because the woman spoke to me at the opera? That's ridiculous. I spoke to a dozen women."

"And kissed one."

As horrifying as that realization was, that he might have doled out the kiss of death, it terrified him to think he might have given such a kiss to Livvy, if he'd been the one to kiss her in public instead of Ash. Or perhaps it hadn't been the kiss at all, but the letter. He had given it to Ursula, discreetly, to pass along to The Plumiere. Perhaps she had accidentally shown it to someone. Either way, it was his fault the woman was dead.

"God forgive me." Another thought surfaced in his foggy mind. He grabbed Ash's sleeve. "Stanley!"

"I already sent Harcourt to him. We will all meet back at Telford's. We can face this together."

"I thought...for a moment, I thought—"

"I know what you thought. I am sorry I did not get here sooner."

"But how did you know?"

The constable cleared his throat. "Yes, my lord. How did you know?"

Ashmoore finally turned to the smaller man and gave him a look that would make any soldier crawl into a corner, but the constable did not seem to notice as he was scribbling furiously in a small book.

"It is in the papers, boy."

The word 'boy' seemed to catch the other's attention.

"I beg your pardon, my lord. I did not realize how late it was."

"If you have any further questions for my friend, we shall be at Lord Telford's residence."

The constable gave a stiff bow and departed, taking his silent officers with him. They looked a bit disappointed to be leaving empty-handed.

Gordon had made his first move, a bold move; he believed he had taken the queen off the board. And next, he would attempt checkmate.

Callister returned. "The constable is gone, Lord Ashmoore. Is there anything we can do to help from here?"

"Just keep watching, Callister. I want no one to take unnecessary risks, but if you hear or see anything suspicious, get word to us. After the constable is satisfied, I am going to insist we move everyone to Telford's country estate. We will let you know when we make the move."

"Very good, my lord."

Ashmoore pulled North from his chair and lowered his voice.

"After we are sure Stanley's all right, you can tell me all about this letter."

CHAPTER TWENTY-SEVEN

Hopkins finally returned to the library.

"She politely declines, my lord."

"Do you think she will come down if her father insists?" North hoped that did not sound as childish to everyone else as it sounded to him.

"I can promise you she will not, my lord. She is aware her father is still sleeping. Last night was a bit taxing on him."

Damn! What was wrong with the woman? He'd thought, if only for a moment or two, that she'd been murdered. He needed to see her, to hold her, to feel the blood pumping through her veins, listen to the beating of her heart.

His growl of frustration resembled more of a roar, and when the echo died, he was not ashamed. He hoped the sound might have reached her and she might come running. If it had not been for the promises he had made to her father last evening, he'd go bellow at her door.

"Leave her alone, North. Give her some time to grieve. I am sure she feels responsible." Ash raised the Paris newspaper back to his face.

"We cannot just allow her to blame herself! I am the one who slipped the woman the letter, expecting her to pass it to Livvy or Lady Malbury. I do not know how anyone could have seen me do so. Only Stanley and Irene were close enough to see it happen. And Winnie. It is not like anyone could have seen around Winnie. No offense, Stanley."

"Mmm?" Stanley was looking out the window, his shoulders sagging.

"Nothing. Never mind."

"When she is ready to discuss it, we will help her all we can. When she is ready. Same for Stanley, of course."

Four minutes passed. Exactly four minutes. Ashmoore had not so much as turned the page.

"Do you think she is safe? I got through her windows, remember."

"North."

"What?"

"Read something."

"I have been reading things for a week. Whatever it is, I assure you, I have read it."

"North?"

"What?"

"Shut up or go home."

"Fine."

Three minutes later, he stood and stretched. He walked to the window and tried to find what might be of interest to Stanley. He clapped his blond friend on the shoulder, then walked to toward the library door, fully expecting Ash to bark his name again.

"Harcourt?"

"Yes, Ash?"

"Follow him."

Harcourt nodded and jumped to his feet.

North gave up and went in search of a book of drawings. If he had to settle for a child's book, so be it. He would go mad trying to decipher actual words.

***

Livvy would never be able to leave her room again. The puffiness of her face was destined to remain.

She blew her nose once again, then retrieved the paper from the corner, where she had tossed it after mashing it into a giant awful ball. She laid it on the bed and smoothed it flat for the second time. If Stella was a thoughtful person, she would bring Livvy a new copy. They were a bit expensive, but she could sell one of her new gowns to pay for it. Since she would not be going out in public again, after all.

THE SCARLET PLUMIERE IS DEAD!

How many times that morning had she wished it were true?

Poor Ursula! Poor, poor Ursula!

Livvy had to stop imagining it. She had to stop wondering what it would have felt like to have Lord Gordon standing over her with no one to stop him.

Absolute terror. Absolute hopelessness. And that was what others might experience if she did not take up her pen again and let the man know he had not only killed the wrong woman, but each new sin would still be shouted from the rooftops! She would start her own gossip sheet if she had to. She had a fortune at her disposal. She would see the man hounded to the very gates of Hell.

She smoothed out the next page, the one displaying for the world the letter from the Earl of Northwick to The Scarlet Plumiere. *Damn him as well.*

He was setting her aside? As *Viscount F* had recently set Ursula aside? They had not even been introduced yet, and he was making his decision? How dare he!

It would serve the man rightly if she walked down the stairs, puffy face and all, and introduced herself to him. Then the woman for whom he had just declared his love would set *him* aside!

Naturally, as it had all morning, the tide of tears followed that thought all the way to shore and poured down her cheeks. Someone finally loved her, and she loved him in return. And it made absolutely no difference.

Well, except for the justification of at least one good cry each day for the rest of her years.

Someone knocked on the door.

"Who is it?" She sounded like a petulant child and did not care.

"Stanley."

"Stanley? Are you alone?" She sniffed.

"I am. Might I have a word?"

She moved to the door and leaned her ear against it.

"Do you perchance have a sack I might wear over my head while we speak?"

"I do, my lady, but I am afraid I am wearing it."

The viscount sat patiently while she pressed cool water to her eyes.

"I am so sorry, Stanley. You were together for quite some time, were you not?"

"We were. And thank you. I am also grateful I had a place to hide today."

"You are hiding from the papers?"

"No. I am hiding from Irene. I cannot bear to hear her thoughts on the matter. She was never a fan of The Scarlet Plumiere. She hated Ursula. The belief that the two turned out to be one and the same gives her justification for every mean thing she has ever said about the writer, that is to say, you. I am sure she is bending ever ear within her reach today."

"I am so sorry. But you are welcome to my sanctuary any time, such as it is. I know we should have the door open, but I will not risk Northwick getting inside."

"Yes, well. I noticed the chair in front of the French doors." He stood and went to it. "May I?"

"Of course."

He turned the chair and tipped it.

"Much more effective if you wedge it beneath the doorknob, like so."

"Ah. Thank you. I will be especially comforted at night."

"Yes. I heard about that. Admitted he loves you, did he?"

"He did."

"Was it wonderful?"

"I am sure there is nothing better."

"I wish I would have told Ursula."

"I am so sorry."

"And I fear I have missed the one chance I will ever have to say such a thing."

"Irene?"

"I cannot imagine it."

"Well, I must tell you that my father and I say it often, and it is quite wonderful too."

"Yes. I can see that it might be. I suppose I should hope for wonderful, loveable children."

"Do not give up though."

"I will make you a deal. I will not give up, if you do not."

She got to her feet and headed for the door. "If that was the reason behind your visit, my lord, I am tossing you from the sanctuary."

"I promise you, I did not come to plead North's case."

Her hand paused on the knob. "Then you will not mention him again?"

"As you wish. If we need to refer to him at all, we should call him The Rat."

"I will accept that." She tugged on the bell-pull. "I will order us some food before they think to cut off our supply."

"Excellent thinking." He then gave her a strange look that had her checking herself in the mirror. "I must admit, Olivia, that I did not know you and Ursula knew each other so well."

"I only met her once, my lord. But I feel as though I murdered the woman with my own hands. If I had not been such a coward, if I had let my identity be known, she would not have paid for rage I must have instilled in her murderer."

"You cannot assume a man's sins, Olivia. I worry you are being far too hard on yourself."

Livvy rolled her eyes and fell forward, burying her face in the bedpillows.

"Olivia?"

She groaned.

"Olivia? Are you quite all right?"

She turned her face and wordlessly held out to him the crumpled paper.

"What is it?"

"You have not read the letter?"

"I have not. The newspaper got a peek at it, did they?"

"Apparently so."

"Is it terribly romantic? North—I mean to say, The Rat— acted peculiar about it last night. I never asked him what it said."

She waited for him to find it. "You may have to smooth it a bit."

He read aloud, damn him.

> *"My dear Scarlet Plumiere,*
> *Forgive me. I love another. Help me end this and I will leave you in peace." –Lord N*

The tide returned with a vengeance. There was something about hearing it from someone else that made it sound so much more depressing. Being both the woman he threw over and the one he threw her over for made no difference whatsoever. Her heart was broken. Her heart was full. Together it was just a full broken heart.

"So this is why you are beside yourself."

"No, do you not understand? I am a terrible person. I am responsible for a woman's death and all I can think about is my own silly heart!"

"Ah. Now I see. But you must also realize that Ursula might have played a small part. I would not be surprised if she had not led others to believe she was The Plumiere. She was quite obsessed you know."

"I did not know."

"Ashmoore said she insisted on meeting you."

"She did. I had never allowed it before, but—"

"She would have hounded Lady Malbury until you did. She talked about you incessantly. I think it was the fact that the gentlemen of the ton fear you. She enjoyed a little of that same reputation, so no doubt she saw you as a kindred spirit. No offense."

"None taken. I had a similar thought, actually, when we met."

"She would be thrilled by the newspaper's mistake, by the headline. But if she were here, I would imagine she would be harsh with you, for feeling too responsible."

"Perhaps."

He smoothed the paper and looked again at the contents of the letter.

"No wonder the constable is suspicious of North."

"What do you mean?"

"Well, look at it as the constable would. North—er, The Rat—tries to end things. Ursula refuses to let him beg off, demands he marry her as he promised at the lottery. He kills her so he can have you. Forgets to retrieve his letter... I am sure that is how they will see it. And he did slip out of sight last night, to come see you, of course. But his witnesses are his dearest friend, the woman he loves, and your father. What if your father forgets?"

"Stanley, please. You are frightening me on purpose!"

"I am frightened myself. Gordon we can hide from, defend against. We can do neither with the authorities."

She couldn't very well admit he was in her room at the time without ruining her reputation and forcing herself into marriage, which would only give the gentlemen what they wanted in the first place—the end of The Scarlet Plumiere. But how could she withhold her help when Northwick's life might depend upon her doing just that?

She got down on her knees and began praying that she'd never have to make that choice.

CHAPTER TWENTY-EIGHT

In the evening, Telly wandered into the drawing room and the look on his face gave nothing away. Was he having a good day, or was he confused as to whom all these men were decorating his furniture?

North stood and bowed, preparing to make any explanation necessary and pasting a pleasant smile on his face that felt more like a grimace.

"What is wrong with you, North?" The older man waved at the rest to stay seated.

He felt himself redden as he confessed. "Olivia will not come out of her rooms, my lord."

"What? And you have not sent in the beaters?"

North shook his head. "Stanley tried to convince her—"

"Convince her? You did not go to her door and threaten to break it down?"

"No, sir. I gave you my word, last night, that I'd never again see the inside of that particular room."

"Oh? Oh, I see. Well. No worries. She'll be down in a trice."

"You'll summon her, my lord?"

"I'll do better than that." He turned a shoulder. "Hopkins!"

His butler appeared. "Yes, my lord?"

"Go inform my daughter that there is a room full of gentlemen who are at this minute deciding what she will or will not do for the rest of her life."

"Very good, my lord."

"Talented beater, that one—except when he is siding with the quail."

"Yes, my lord."

"And North? You may kiss her once when she arrives. No more. If she allows it, that is."

"Thank you, my lord."

Telly turned to Ash. "Well, it is not as if I could have stopped him." He lowered himself into his usual chair.

"But *she* may," Ash said. "Have you read the papers today, my lord?"

"Yes, I've been told. Terribly tragedy. My condolences, Forsgreen."

Stanley bowed and went back to watching out the window.

"And the letter?"

Telly laughed. "I believe you are correct, Ashmoore. He may not get that kiss. Would you be willing to make a little wager? I'll take my daughter's side, of course. A crown he is disappointed."

"Done. But fair warning, I've been in the pen with the bull all afternoon, my lord. I do not like her chances."

They all turned in their seats to watch for the imminent arrival of Livvy. North had not a care for his friends or their wagers. He was going to scoop her up the second he saw her and give her absolutely no chance to protest until after he had his kiss and his say.

A figure came to the doorway and he took a quick step before he realized it was a footman.

"Lord Northwick? There's a young man named Chester asking for you. He insists his matter is urgent, my lord."

"Show him in here."

"Yes, my lord."

Chester hurried in and bowed. Livvy arrived just behind him. They both were flushed and out of breath.

North looked from her to the boy and back again. "Livvy, come here," he said.

She clutched her throat and stepped around the boy, looking at Chester as if he had arrived with ominous news, which he likely had.

North took her arm and pulled her against him.

"Just a moment, Chester."

He turned to face her and slipped his right hand behind her head. She had only enough time to gasp, and barely that, before he pulled her to meet his kiss, to show her all the emotions he had endured that day in his worry for her. The room stayed absolutely still for him until both his breathing and hers became a bit audible.

Throats cleared. Many throats cleared.

He pulled back slightly and soaked in the sight of her heavy eyelids and parted lips.

"Ashmoore? Help Livvy to a seat." He felt her pulled from his grasp as he turned back to Chester. "I'm sorry, Chester. What is it?"

Chester shook himself and tore his eyes from Miss Reynolds.

"Mr. Callister wanted you to know, my lord, there is a Bow Street Runner hanging about the kitchen. He claimed to have come to see you this evening, but when he heard you were not at home, he just made himself comfortable and started telling stories. Only he stops now and then to ask questions."

"Mister Wilbur T. Franklin, no doubt. What is he trying to discover?"

"That's his very name, my lord. He wondered if you and your friends would be at that murdered woman's funeral. He also wondered if Miss Reynolds will be attending. Says he only wants to offer his services to help protect the lady, since dangerous men might be attending as well. He is there still, sir. Callister doubts the man will leave until someone feeds him some supper."

"Very good, Chester. Give us a minute to decide just what we want this fellow to know."

"I'll just be in the hall, then, sir."

North turned to face the room.

"Tell Chester whatever you like," Livvy announced. "I will be attending the funeral." She slipped from her seat and moved behind her father, as if she expected no argument while she used him for a shield.

"Surely you see how dangerous it would be." North took a step toward her, but she cocked her head in a manner that stopped him in his tracks. She was angry with him? How could she possibly? He had just freed them from all impediments. They could marry just as soon as Gordon has been put in his place.

"Actually, the funeral might be a very safe place." Ashmoore stood next to the fireplace, resting one arm on the mantle, staring into the flames. "If he uses the funeral as his alibi, he can hardly harm her in a public setting. We wondered if he might throw a party. Perhaps this is it."

"So he's hoping this Wilbur fellow will scare her away from the funeral. Perhaps he means to have someone else attack her while he surrounds himself with witnesses." North glanced at Livvy and tried not to imagine the possibilities.

"No doubt Chester was followed, to ensure the message was delivered," said Harcourt.

"Then let us not disappoint the man. Let him know Livvy will not be attending, when in truth it may be the safest place for her."

"Then you'll allow me to attend?" Livvy frowned from Ashmoore to North.

North caught a twinkle in her father's eye, and took a breath.

"Livvy, darling, you know full well you will do whatever the devil you want, forgive my language. Just keep us informed so we can protect you. When this crisis is over, you will have no need to do even that."

"I beg your pardon?"

Damn him if she didn't sound a bit disappointed. He tried to suppress his smile.

"You have done an admirable job taking care of yourself until I came along. No doubt you can do so again."

He turned his back on her, only to find Ashmoore's eyes jumping from his head. He winked at his friend, to let him know he was only teasing Livvy. He had no intention of leaving her side when the danger had passed. Ashmoore shook his head and buried his face against the mantle.

"Hopkins!"

"Yes, my lady?"

"Step inside and close the door, if you will."

Hopkins did as she asked. North held steady, trying to concentrate on the fire.

The silence was palpable.

"So. Just how many of you know I am The Scarlet Plumiere?"

He spun 'round, then wished he had not. The look she gave him was not unlike Ashmoore's battlefield grimace and for a flash he imagined that Ursula was not the only one who might be in need of a church service—and not a wedding.

He stepped back until his shoulder butted up against the mantle opposite Ashmoore. His friend's eyes were closed. The man did not turn, but he raised his hand.

Telly's hand raised, as did his butler's. Stanley turned from the windows, smiling and joining the ranks of confessors. Harcourt, seated upon the piano bench, propped up an elbow and waved.

North was the only hold out. Then carefully, slowly, he raised his hand, but in a more defensive manner. Damn him if he didn't feel as if he was the only man in the room who erred in knowing her secret.

"Now wait a moment, Livvy." He raised his other hand to the fore as well since she began stalking toward him. "Why am I the only man in trouble here?"

Her eyes narrowed. She didn't speak. She kept coming.

He would try a different tone.

"Livvy. Stop this." He took a step sideways toward the door.

She took two quick ones to head him off. The light from the fire lit her face from below giving her decidedly sinister demeanor.

He laughed. She did not. He stopped smiling.

"Blame The Rat, Livvy. He gave you away that first day. And the scarlet ribbon of course."

She stopped. "You have known since that *first day*?" She looked horrified by the news. "But not before you tried to kiss me."

"Correct. I started falling in love with you before I knew. Does that aid in my defense?"

She shook her head and started walking again, until her skirts covered his shoes. His heart jumped with hope that she might kiss him. He even lowered his head, to make it easier for her.

She tipped her head back. Dark curls fell behind her shoulders.

"Lord Northwick?"

"Yes, darling?"

"I am sorry, but I am freeing you from any obligation you might feel for me."

"I do not love you out of obligation, Livvy."

"That is beside the point. You are free to do as you please." She was smiling. He finally felt safe smiling back.

"Then it pleases me to marry you, Livvy." He could dive into the depths of her eyes.

"I worry you do not understand what is going on here, sir."

"What? Fine. Explain it to me. What is going on here?" He wished their audience would be so kind as to slip from the room, but his sneaking into her room recently made such kindness unlikely.

"Ahem," Ashmoore intruded. "May I?"

She smiled and nodded at the man, then stepped back.

North frowned at his amused friend.

"North, old man?"

"Yes?"

"She is setting you aside."

He looked at Livvy, now two steps away. "You would not. You love me."

"I am afraid it is already done, Lord Northwick." She turned toward the doors. "Hopkins can inform me if there is anything special I need to know about the funeral."

Hopkins opened the door for her, then closed it again.

North looked around the room. Stanley and Harcourt were standing before the windows performing pantomime in the light from the sconces. Harcourt was pretending to pick up someone by their shoulders only to turn and set them down again. The shoulders, he noted, were a bit broader and higher than the first time he had done such a thing.

Stanley was playing the part of a fish, being pulled about by his own hooked finger, then removing the finger and grinning at him.

Ashmoore slid onto the couch and leaned forward to put his face in his hands.

Telly frowned at Stanley and Harcourt as if they'd lost their minds. Once they noticed his concern, they stopped their miming, but continued to giggle like girls.

Telly then looked at him and shook his head.

"Almost had her, young Birmingham. Yes, almost had her."

CHAPTER TWENTY-NINE

The Scarlet Plumiere climbed the stairs, feeling quite satisfied with how fate had delivered her enemy into her hands. He had set her aside with the morning paper. She had taken his heart and handed it back to him, tied up with a scarlet ribbon. All in all, she felt completely vindicated. And on a day like today, vindication was a balm for her soul.

The drawing room door flew open and she spun about on the landing, expecting North to come flying up the steps to demand she take him back.

It was North, all right. But he gave the stairs not a glance on his way through the foyer. He didn't so much as pause or look over his shoulder before stepping into the darkness and slamming the front door.

Chester stood at attention, staring forward. Hopkins summoned the boy back to the drawing room.

The Scarlet Plumiere continued on her way, finishing her grand exit in solitude. Unfortunately, she was merely Olivia Reynolds by the time her bedroom door closed behind her. She was too tired to cry, however, and let a numbness settle over her instead. It was done. All the frivolous paths were now closed to her. No more temptation. Just the path she had always intended to travel.

She spread her skirts and seated herself before her mirror but did not look in it. She had no interest in who might be looking back at her. Instead, she examined her mother's jeweled brushes, ensuring the beads were secure before brushing out her hair. The strings were discoloring with age.

A long quarter of an hour later, a movement caught her eye. A shadow crouched at her balcony door, fiddling with the lock.

Feeling too vulnerable by half, she dared not stay lest North persuade her to remove the chair Stanley had wedged against the handles. So, since she was still dressed, she rose and left the room.

Without North there, she felt no need to avoid the drawing room, so she slipped inside to see what grand ideas her would-be heroes had come up with.

Ashmoore was seated on the couch with a man leaning nearby. She knew that head. It belonged to Northwick.

Northwick!

Her heart burst inside her chest.

"But! But! But you are not here!"

He looked up, unsmiling. "I did not get far before I remembered about Wilbur T. Franklin."

"B...but the man on my balcony! I thought it was you!"

"What?" Ashmoore and the rest jumped to their feet.

"There is a man trying to break into my room!" She said it to their backs as they were already flooding into the hallway.

"Stay in this room, with your father and Everhardt," said North as he passed her.

She locked the door behind him. Everhardt moved a heavy chair in front of it. Her father slipped a sword from inside his cane.

"Seat yourself at the piano, Livvy. If someone gets in, you make as much noise as you can."

She obeyed and prayed the King of the Hill was not about to lose his life trying to protect her.

*****

After ten minutes of torture, they heard shouting in the hallway. The handle rattled.

"Lord Telford, it is I, Northwick. You can open the door now."

Everhardt moved the chair and her father unlocked the latch, then opened the door.

A disheveled Earl of Northwick stood in the doorway. She had never been so relieved.

Her father replaced his small sword. "Who was harmed, sir?"

Northwick dropped his eyes. "Peter was struck on the head. We've sent for the doctor and took the liberty of putting Peter in one of your guestrooms."

"He survived it then?"

"Thus far."

"Thank God for that. Did you catch the devil?"

"We did not. We saw no one. Someone damaged the lock on your daughter's balcony door. She should sleep somewhere else tonight." Northwick barely glanced her way, then bowed and disappeared.

She ignored the pain of his indifference and hoped it would only prove to strengthen her resolve. There were preparations to make, for the plan she'd formulated while cowering behind the piano, but she wished to check on Peter first. She found Northwick and Ashmoore hovering at the foot of Peter's bed. The injured man's eyes were closed, oblivious to the cook wrapping cheesecloth beneath his chin.

Ash looked up and gave Livvy a brief smile. "North? I propose we move to the study and let our brave friend sleep until the doctor arrives," he said.

North noticed her, then looked away as he walked past her and out the door. It felt as if he'd taken with him all the warmth from the room considering the cold, painful chills that filled her lungs. She thought she might be able to manage only a few breaths more before she shattered. *Harden your heart, Livvy. Hard, then harder still.*

"How can I help?" she asked Ashmoore.

"Take care of your father, Livvy. He has endured a difficult evening; he will need you tonight. Have a cot taken to his room. You will be safe in there." He winked and left her.

Cook finished her task and sat beside the bed, her hands kneading at her knees as if restless for a bit of busy work. Mrs.

Wheaton patted the woman on the shoulder and also quit the room.

Livvy could not take her gaze from Peter's still, large form. If Lord Gordon were capable of taking down such an opponent, what might be in store for the rest? She visualized the line of people standing between herself and the villain. First, Ursula, the woman he believed was The Plumiere—the only person the man feared. Next, Peter, the first man in his way. Who would be next? Her father, so intent on protecting her? What chance had Papa against a foe that could best Peter? How could she bear to stand by while the men she loved were sent toward Death's door, or through it?

She told herself Northwick was merely one of many men standing in that line. Just another man she would not allow to be murdered in her stead.

It was time to remember who she was, time for Lord Gordon to come face to face with the real Scarlet Plumiere.

As soon as the lion emerged from his lair, the prey would go hunting...and the lion would die.

CHAPTER THIRTY

North took a seat in the dimly lit study and waited for his friends. Ashmoore entered with Stanley and Harcourt. Milton slinked in behind them, then moved to the window and peered around the heavy curtain.

"Close the door, would you Harcourt?" North did not wish to worry about who might be listening in the hall.

Ashmoore sat in the chair behind the desk, but looked to him to begin the conversation, which was fine by him.

"As soon as Gordon shows himself in public, I'm going to call him out," he said.

Stanley nodded, bless him. Harcourt whistled dramatically. It was no surprise when Ash shook his head.

"And why not?"

"Because that only works with honorable men, or men who want to be perceived as honorable. That Gordon has come back before rumors have settled shows he no longer gives a damn about his reputation. He wants vengeance and he wants to get away with it, I'm sure. Unlike Marquardt, he still has a fortune and an entailment. Unless he is found guilty of a crime, he can live as he likes—little more than a corrupt officer of the court."

"So you believe he will not accept a challenge?"

"I am almost certain of it. And if something unfortunate happens to the man, heaven forefend, all of London would know you were recently looking for his blood. That, added to the letter found with Ursula, and the constable would be a famous man. The man to hang Mr. Lott."

"Then what do you suggest?"

"You no longer wish to call him out?"

"No. I see your reasoning. I will think of an alternative."

"Good. Then I see no harm in telling you—"

There was a soft knock at the door. If it was Olivia, he was doomed. It had taken all his strength not to take her in his arms when her father opened the door to the drawing room. He'd had to hold his breath to pass by her in Peter's room. He was too weak to keep his distance at the moment.

And he must!

She was The Scarlet Plumiere, for pity's sake. She had taken down men like Gordon for two years and survived. She refused to give up that role for the simple life of an earl's wife, and one day her luck would run out. With his own bad luck, he'd not be around to save her—or worse yet, he'd be at her side and fail. And after that morning, when the constable said The Scarlet Plumiere had been murdered, he knew just how his heart would react to losing her; it would simply stop. So it was purely for his own survival, as selfish as it was, that he must now harden his heart.

The fact that he was honoring her wishes did not signify.

His luck held, however. It was not Livvy, but her maid that brought in a tray.

"Coffee, gentlemen?"

"Hopkins is as good a mind reader as my man Callister. Give him our thanks."

The maid smiled and nodded, then proceeded to pour.

"So, North, I see no need to keep it from you now. You were not present when Chester shared with us a bit of news he'd forgotten in the excitement."

"Yes?"

"Gordon has recalled his staff. You have a footman who once—"

"He cannot have the lad back. I will not have any of my people near the man, no matter how helpful it might be for us." He took a cup from the maid.

Ash nodded. "I told Chester you would say just that. But there is more. Gordon has been seen...going inside Merrill's Gentlemen's Club...tonight."

"A bit early in the day," Harcourt observed. "Wanted plenty of folks to see him, most likely. And he will have plenty of witnesses for his alibi, even if the patrons of the place are a bit shady."

Stanley smiled at the maid and took his cup. She got caught in his charming snare and nearly landed in her own tray trying to walk out the door. But at last she was gone. They could speak more freely.

"There is one thing that puzzles me." North sat forward and lowered his voice. "If Mr. Wilbur T. Franklin is in Gordon's employ, and he is trying to find out where we all shall be during the funeral, why move now? Why strike at Livvy in the midst of a well-guarded house?"

"I hate to be the one to suggest it," said Stanley, "but perhaps Ursula was forced to give Livvy up."

Ashmoore shook his head. "She was stabbed from behind, surely taken by surprise. My apologies, Stan."

"Perhaps he has hired more assassins than he can manage," said Harcourt. "Perhaps he has offered a bounty and plans to remove another queen from the board only if someone hasn't beaten him to it."

Ash's face dropped for a heartbeat before he recovered. North had never seen that happen, through all their years together, and it frightened the hell out of him.

"How many assassins can one man afford?" Stanley asked his coffee.

"You do not want to know," Ash answered.

"This could go on for a very long time then." Harcourt held up his hands. "Not that I mind, of course."

"No. It will not go on much longer." North took a generous drink of his coffee. "Only until I kill Gordon. Assassins do not work for free, gentlemen."

"And Marquardt?" Ash watched him over the steam drifting from his own cup. "Will you clean the world of The Plumiere's victims, as she makes them? Correct me if I am wrong, but I do not remember such an executioner in the tale of Robin Hood."

"Marquardt will believe The Plumiere has been murdered. He has no reason to come after Olivia Reynolds."

"If he believes the papers," warned Stanley.

"I pray he does. But what do you want me to say? That I am willing to send my soul—if indeed there is anything left of it—to Hell to keep Gordon from getting to her? Yes, I am."

"Even if she won't have you?" Harcourt asked it gently enough.

"Yes. Even then."

Stanley set aside his cup. "We cannot sit here and plan a man's murder."

"No, we cannot," Ashmoore assured him.

From that point on, they tossed about an array of possible solutions, including getting Gordon to confess within hearing of the constable, committing Gordon to an asylum, and sending him to the same fate as Voltaire's *Man in the Iron Mask*. The most reasonable, and unreasonable option was to catch the man in the act of trying to murder Livvy.

"Oh, please let us think of something else," North pleaded.

But they could not.

***

Olivia had no time to quibble. She thought she would have to enlist Lady Malbury's aid to find where Gordon was hiding himself. But her little spy had returned from the study with just the information she sought! Never mind the late hour. She knew where to find the lion, for the moment at least. She had to move quickly. There was no time to plan.

"Stella, I have no alternative. You must go. Say only that John is to bring 'round the carriage and wait. Then come straight back to me."

"But my lady—"

"Stella. Lord Ashmoore is not your employer. Nor is Hopkins. Nor any of the rest. You work for me, or not, depending on your next action."

Her maid stared at her, trying to discern her sincerity. She'd never threatened anyone with dismissal before, and by the stubborn look on Stella's face, she did not truly believe herself in jeopardy. But she turned and left in any case, not happy to do it, but neither did she quiver a lip or weep.

It usually took John and the groom thirty minutes to ready the carriage and team, so she went first to check on her father. Hopkins was busily chatting away about the excitement of the evening while he tucked Papa into bed. His eyes closed when his head touched the pillow, but opened again when the butler touched him on the arm.

"Miss Olivia has come, my lord."

Her father gave her a smile. The man was still himself.

"I have come to say goodnight, Papa." She leaned down and kissed his whiskered cheek.

"Those boys will keep you safe, Livvy. But I am a bit too tired to stand sentry."

"You were marvelous tonight, Papa. And all the protection I needed."

"I will rest at ease only when..." He rubbed the back of his head against the pillow and his eyes closed again.

"Only when?" She would not have pressed for the last of his thought had she not been so curious as to what might bring his harried mind some relief.

His eyes remained closed, but he spoke. "Only when I've killed Gordon for you, Livvy."

Hopkins sniffed and turned away.

Livvy might have shed a tear, but she was not Livvy tonight.

She quietly strode to her mother's dressing room and removed the glorious-but-old crimson cape from its hook. The matching muff was not so large as current fashion, but it would do. The black fur coming out the ends matched the fur lining of the hood, adding just the right touch of drama.

Back in her room, she donned the red velvet gown she'd ordered merely to get Northwick's attention, to drive him mad wondering where she might wear such a thing. The neckline was cut far too low, far too wide for her to wear comfortably in public, but the opportunity to tease the man had been too much to resist, especially with Ashmoore egging her on. For tonight, it was perfect.

She knew all about Merrill's. She laughed at the little thrill of fear that she might be mistaken, even for an instant, for a light skirt. But of course, she was counting on a second or two of confusion in order to get her through the door.

She considered wearing her mother's pearls, but she did not wish to defile them.

Stella stepped back into the room and gasped.

"Close the door, then come sit in this chair." She pointed to the little Queen Anne before the fire. She'd just put a log on. The girl would not get cold. "Please do not dally, Stella."

The maid walked to the chair and sat heavily, then folded her arms, as if to say she would be of no further assistance. But Livvy only needed her to stay quiet for a few moments.

"I'm tying you up, Stella, so the gentlemen cannot be angry at you for not raising an alarm." She draped soft cords around her maid, cords she had taken from her bed drapings. The knots were secure and she poured water over them to make them doubly difficult for the maid to untie.

"Open your mouth, please."

In spite of showing Stella the perfectly clean handkerchief, the maid bit her lips and shook her head. Livvy had only to pinch the girl's nose for a moment to get her mouth open. Then she tied another cord around her head to keep the kerchief in her mouth.

"I am sorry. But you wish to be believed, do you not?"

It was probably for the best she could not understand her maid's response, and avoided the girl's gaze while she placed a shawl over her shoulders and a rug across her lap before hurrying to the door.

"Please do not fret, Stella. I've got a pistol in my skirt and Daddy's hidden sword."

When the maid's eyes flew wide, she realized those were details she should have kept to herself. The more worried her maid, the more she would try to be discovered. And though she hardly had time for it, Livvy took another moment to secure the woman's ankles to the legs of the chair. That way she could not merely stomp about on the floor until someone came to discover the source.

She descended the stairs quickly and hurried to Ian, who stood by the front door, peeking out the side window, probably trying to discern why John had brought the carriage 'round. She only hoped he hadn't had a chance to rouse the others.

"Ian, you must help me. I need to get into the carriage without being seen. Can you dowse the lights for me?"

"I'm sorry, Miss. Can you tell me where you're off to at such a late hour? Lord Ashmoore told me nothing—"

She pretended embarrassment. "Lord Ashmoore does not know. Lord Northwick and I are going to meet...we need to...have a private conversation, he and I. And so he has left out the back. He'll be with me. I won't be unprotected. And I'll have John, of course." She put a little bit of a whine in her tone. "Please understand, Ian. We're desperate to...see each other." Her blush was quite authentic by the time she'd finished.

Ian shook his head before she'd even finished speaking. "Understanding has nothing to do with it, my lady." He started walking away from the door, waving for her to follow. "Let's just talk this through with Lord Ashmoore."

"But don't you see? He's the one keeping us apart."

Ian smiled. "Then you definitely can't leave, my lady. I take my orders from Ashmoore."

She summoned her best look of begrudging surrender.

"Fine, then. But you must tell Lord Northwick why you would not allow me to leave. And if you make him wait all night, he will not be pleased. You'll find him at The Ivy and Stone. A small Inn on—"

"I know it, my lady. I'll just tell John to take the carriage back, then I'll send a man to let Lord Northwick know he can stand down." The man laughed as he slipped out the door.

Livvy hurried through to the back of the house, only slowing before the library door, unable to pray and run at the same time. If the door opened, she was finished.

The kitchen was dark but for the glow of coals in the fireplace. She slipped out the door at the same time she was searching her brain for an excuse to give the next man to stop her. But there was no man at the door. The stars were bright enough to show footprints in the mud that led to the left. He must be making rounds. She struck out through the garden, praying for her luck to hold and made it all the way to the carriage house before the conveyance came into view. Beyond its bulk, she could see the shadow of Ian headed back to his post. What he would do once he got there, she could not worry over. She only needed a little time.

She flagged John down without a sound. He leaned toward her.

"What is it, my lady?"

"Shhh! Ashmoore snuck me out here so I could board without being seen. Lord Northwick is going to meet me, away from the house, so no one will suspect we are together."

"He what?"

"Lord Northwick and I would like a private conversation. Head for Drury Lane and hurry. I'll let you know when to stop."

She opened the carriage and jumped inside. Thank heavens the lamps were not lit. Once she was seated, she held her breath, waiting for the carriage to move, but it did not. Her stomach dropped. Threatening John would do her no good at all. And she doubted the big man would let her tie him up.

Never in her life had her father's house seemed more like a prison than at that moment.

The carriage began to move. She was so surprised, she squeaked. And she did not trust it, so she peeked through the curtains to be sure John was not standing by the drive having been unseated by Lord Northwick. But she saw nothing.

Perhaps it had taken John a moment to accept his disappointment in her.

Livvy would like to think she was incredibly clever to have escaped the house, but she was not. She had not had the time to be clever. After all her deception, it was very likely that Lord Gordon would no longer be at Merrill's. She would almost certainly be locked away for her own good once she was caught by Ashmoore, so she would do what she could with the night she had claimed for herself. And she would be forced to make her decisions as she went.

Her fabricated story had been plucked from a wish, that was all. She had not thought of it until after she had her maid tied up and was heading out her bedroom door. How could she not have realized sooner that leaving the house might be as difficult as getting in?

Directing John to Drury Lane had been a little stroke of luck. Of course she did not have the names of many roads on the tip of her tongue these days, so she hadn't many alternatives, but there were numerous entertainments along the road, even at that hour. And though she was interested in none of them, there would surely be hacks for the hiring. If John was not willing to go along with that plan again, she hoped the road might be so clustered with carriages, her own would be forced to stop a time or two. And if she was very lucky, she could exit the conveyance without John knowing.

Unfortunately, Drury Lane at midnight was not nearly as busy as she'd hoped. The carriage clipped along at an easy speed and she suddenly panicked at the prospect of running out of road before she'd gotten away. There was nothing for it but to stop the carriage herself.

She knocked on the wall.

The carriage slowed and pulled to the side of the road. Suddenly her heart was in her throat, much as it would have been if she really had been off to have a private meeting with Northwick.

John handed her out. It was easy to act excited. She looked off to the right and saw exactly what she needed.

"Northwick waved, then got into that hack. I must hurry." She jumped from John's reach and started backing away. John looked very much as if he was going to follow. "Go, John! You must get the carriage away before it is recognized. He will see me home safely. Keep our secret, John!"

She turned and walked briskly and confidently toward the hack on the other side of the street, praying no one would hire

the thing before she reached it, praying John would not clutch
her billowing cloak from behind. If John noticed her standing
alone in the street, waiting for another hack, he'd hunt her
down. The man looked enraged already—likely at Northwick
for arranging such a thing.

Well, damn the earl for not arranging such a thing.

She reached for the hack door and glanced up. Her hood
fell back.

"'Ere now. What do think...pardon me, miss. I thought
you was someones else—I mean to say—"

"Take me to Merrill's."

"Aw, now, what would a lady—"

"Can you take me to Merrill's or shall I find someone
who can?"

"Yes, Miss."

She opened the door and climbed inside as quickly as her
skirts would allow. She dared not look to see if John had
moved on. If he were behind her, her heart might stop. She
only hoped the hack was out of sight before he could turn the
larger carriage about and follow. With the big man's tendency
to be overprotective of her, she could imagine him bellowing
through Merrill's like a mad bull if he could not catch her
before she arrived.

She turned from that unpleasant thought to another—
what she planned to do with the sword and pistol if Gordon
was still at Merrill's.

CHAPTER THIRTY-ONE

With no solid plan in hand, North suggested they all find their beds. Surely, after the first attack, there would be no further disruptions that night. Of course, they were taking no chances. They had agreed that someone should sleep in Livvy's room that night, but since he didn't like the idea of another man being in there, he had been reduced to volunteering for the duty himself. It would drive him mad, of course, so he decided a bracing bit of cold air might clear his mind before he entered the torture chamber.

Ian sat next to a window by the front door.

"I will be outside for a few moments if you would care to stretch your legs." He stepped outside and shut the door, but it did not remain so. Ian stepped outside as well.

"Back so soon, my lord?"

"I beg your pardon?"

"The Ivy and Stone Inn is half way across London. I only wonder how Everhardt found you so quickly, my lord."

"The Ivy and Stone Inn?" North wondered if he was so weary he'd forgotten something.

Suddenly a coach and team turned off the street and into the drive. It was Telford's big driver, John. Who might have sent him on an errand at this time of night?

The man pulled roughly on the leads and the horses complained, but stopped. He jumped to the ground without the carriage completely secure, and the look on his face made North take a step back.

The big man raised a finger. "You! You ain't supposed to be here!" And without slowing, the man ploughed a fist into his jaw.

When he opened his eyes against the pain in his face and shoulder, North found himself propped on the couch in the drawing room. He flinched when he realized the big man stood on the opposite side of the room, his anger barely restrained, with no one close at hand to stop the man from felling him again.

At least he'd blacked out the old-fashioned way.

"You aren't supposed to be here!" The big man's voice boomed through the room.

"That was just what I was about to say when you rode in, John." Ian's face suddenly appeared before him. "My apologies, my lord. Ashmoore and the rest will be here in a trice."

Ashmoore pushed Ian out of the way. "What has happened?"

The driver pointed at North again. "He is not supposed to be here! He's supposed to be with Miss Reynolds. And if he's not with Miss Reynolds, then who is, I'd like to know!"

North struggled to stand. "Damn her! Where is she?"

"Last I saw her, she was getting into a hack on Drury Lane. A hack that you were supposed to be sitting in. She said she was meeting you...for a private word." He sneered at North as if he'd actually been guilty.

"Obviously, it was not me she was meeting, my friend. Could you cease trying to murder me for a moment at least?"

The big man seemed to consider it, then nodded.

"She told me the same." Ian chimed in. "I told her she could not go without Lord Ashmoore's approval, and she told me to go to The Ivy and Stone to tell you the bad news, my lord. I sent Everhardt."

It finally sank into his aching head that Livvy was out in the city somewhere, in the dead of night, unprotected.

"Who the devil would she be meeting?" Stanley stood against the wall near the door.

His jealous mind raced, but no name came to mind. She'd just left behind all the men she had recently met, and there were no gentlemen in her past—

"Gordon." The name fell from his lips without him thinking it. "Who else could it be? Surely Lady Malbury would not have expected her to leave our protection to meet with some poor chit who did not like the way her new fiancé kissed her glove." He could not keep the sneer from his own voice now. "And let us not forget who we are dealing with here. It is certainly not poor sweet Olivia Reynolds. Oh, no. We are dealing with The Scarlet Plumiere, the woman willing to take on the most powerful men in the British Empire, single-handedly. This phantom has never known danger until I brought it to her door. She has no need of us. It is Gordon needing protection now."

"North. That's enough." Ashmoore sat and put his head in his hands. "If she went looking for Gordon, she had a reason."

"One that would only sound reasonable to a woman." He forced himself to sit calmly, instead of flying out into the night as his body seemed inclined to do.

"Do you know what you are doing, North?" Stanley straightened away from the wall. "You are making her the villain, so she cannot hurt you anymore."

"I beg your pardon!" A slap across the face would not have surprised him more.

Stanley advanced while he spoke. "I doubt you will pardon yourself, if you do not charge out that door and go after her."

North closed his eyes. "She was not in the room when you told Gordon's whereabouts." He tried to remember past the pain in his jaw. "But her maid was!"

"She has gone to Merrill's, my lords!" Hopkins panted in the doorway. "She tied her maid to a chair and took a pistol and her father's cane."

North threw his hands in the air. "Well, Ashmoore, you had best go collect her. Provide her with transportation home at least, after the doorman disarms her."

"I cannot go. Harcourt, you see if you can diffuse the situation. Take Milton with you." Ash turned to the butler. "Did the maid say what color she is wearing?"

"Scarlet, my lord. That new red dress and her mother's red cloak. Scarlet from head to toe."

North's head exploded. "Idiot! The city believes The Scarlet Plumiere is dead and instead of taking advantage and letting her enemies think they have won, she has to rub their noses in it!" Then his brain caught up with his ears. "What do you mean you are not going, Ash?"

"Peter may die tonight. I will not leave him to die alone when there are others who can find Livvy." And with that, Ash quit the room.

That damned red dress. He could keep the other images from nesting in his mind, but that red dress was already there, setting up housekeeping, waiting for the right time to torment him.

A moment later, he climbed in the carriage after Milton.

"You are coming?" Harcourt grinned.

"I go only to make certain she has that damned dress well and truly covered." Or so he told himself.

CHAPTER THIRTY-TWO

Livvy's stomach turned when the hack stopped, but she swallowed hard and refused to cast up her accounts—not that there was anything in her stomach to begin with. The driver asked if she wanted him to wait, then laughed when she shook her head. She tossed the rude man's coins on the ground and turned away. By the time she reached the top of the steps, she'd managed to put her embarrassment to good use.

"I'm sorry, my lady. This here's a gentlemen's club. You want me to whistle for your hack to return?"

"Of course not. You permit mistresses in Merrill's, do you not?"

"Yeah, but you ain't no mistress, my lady. You look like someone's wife. No wives allowed."

"I'm no man's wife. Lord Gordon sent for me. Do you really wish to anger Lord Gordon?"

"Ain't no Lord Gordon 'ere, miss."

"Then go ask the man who looks most like Lord Gordon why he summoned me here if he did not intend to have me admitted?"

She parted her cloak to place her hands on her hips, but it also served to display her low neckline. If Lord Northwick's reaction hadn't been enough to tell her the dress was inappropriate, this doorman's reaction did. She had to squeeze her own hips to keep from letting her hands fly up to hide her cleavage from the disgusting oaf.

"Let's just see what the man has to say." He turned and opened the door. Dear heavens, she was about to be caught in one of her lies. After all she had told that night, she should not

have been surprised. But the consequences of lying here might
be a bit more dire than those at home.

Walking into the foyer of Merrill's was like stepping onto
a smoky island. Through the white fog, she saw bodies, mostly
women, sprawled across settees lining both sides of the
hallway. A dark shadow moved beside one woman and she
realized that there may well be many men here as well, but as
they were dressed mostly in black, they were harder to see.

A newel post appeared and she had the sudden urge to
run up the steps to get out of the fog. As it was, she tried not to
breathe too deeply, lest she be affected by the odd taste in the
air.

The rear of the foyer opened up into a large room filled
with tables for gaming. In turn, the tables were filled with men
who eagerly stretched forward to rake chips toward them, or
tossed their cards about, hardly paying heed to the chips on the
table in favor of the women perched on their laps, or the laps
of their neighbors.

She had read once about a villain who preferred to keep
his back to the wall, to prevent others from sneaking up
behind him and doing him harm. Or perhaps she had read it
about the Earl of Ashmoore. She could not remember. But she
had expected the oaf to lead her to the rear wall where such a
villain might hide. She was therefore surprised when he
stopped in the center of the room where the loudest card game
seemed to be taking place.

And there he was.

He was larger than she remembered. Having Northwick
and his friends about had created a sense that no other men
could measure up to them. But as far as measurements alone,
Lord Gordon looked as intimidating as ever. When she first
met him, she'd been awed. After overhearing his plans for her,
she'd been sickened. But all those feelings had faded a little
with time. And all those feelings came flooding back at the
mere sound of his voice. That voice she had heard in the
garden, at her own engagement party.

She had been told her fiancé was outside chatting with
friends. She'd gone to find him, but failed. On her way back to

the house, she passed a trellised gazebo and recognized his voice. Not wanting to interrupt a man who so intimidated, she'd waited for a break in the conversation.

The first man's words confused her.

"How will you get an heir off her, darling?"

"Oh, I will have my heir and a spare from the little monster. But I think you will have to do the deed, my pet. You have always been able to lie with a woman. I will have to watch, of course. My heir, my bed, you see? And you will stay on, of course. My heirs will need to look alike."

She'd gasped then, giving herself away. When Gordon stepped out of the gazebo, straightening his clothes, he'd frowned until he saw who it was who had overheard his conversation. Then he'd laughed and shooed her toward the house, as if she had not the significance to cause him concern.

"Well, if it is not The Little Monster!"

"She says you summoned her, my lord." The oaf held his hands at the ready to lay hold of her if given leave to do so.

"She did? Of course she did." He jerked his head to indicate the oaf should go away.

The man nodded and turned, but not before taking a second look at her chest. She was thankful she had recovered herself.

There were no women sitting on laps at Gordon's table. Neither were there faces she recognized. Or so she thought until a blond man scooped up his chips and excused himself. His face was a little familiar, but she did not know the name. The fact that he walked with a cane and a terrible limp was no help, though he obviously recognized her.

Gordon laughed at him as he hobbled away, then turned back to her. His nose curled at one corner and erased any remnant of his handsomeness. "To what do I owe the pleasure, Miss Reynolds?"

She would need to be much closer if she was going to do the deed she'd come to do, so she poked at him the only way she knew how.

"You tell me, Gordon. You summoned me, remember? And what do you mean threatening my father like that?"

She could feel, more than see, ears straining in her direction. If anything happened to her or her father, at least Gordon would be suspected.

He laughed. "Surely you do not mean to slander me the moment I am back in town, young lady."

"Slander? I do not understand. Are you trying to lure me into some sort of trap here tonight? I will admit that I was surprised to hear you were back in town, but when I got your message..."

He stood abruptly and she took a breath to cover her panic.

"I worried you wanted to reconsider our engagement. But of course I cannot. After the scandal last time, I was sure you would have no interest—"

"Here, now. What is all this? I sent you no message, Miss Reynolds." Gordon came 'round the table to stand before her. She resisted the urge to step back, reminding herself she was The Scarlet Plumiere—the only thing the man feared.

And there must have been many eyes on them if he was suddenly treating her so formally.

"Oh, you sent me a very clear message, my lord." She took a breath for courage, then stepped close and lowered her voice. "Killing Ursula was just another of your many mistakes. Hurting my people was your last." She'd been careful. No one could have heard.

"I had nothing to do with the whore's death, but I see you two must have been fast friends," he sneered. "After all, you look as if she has been making your clothing selections."

Livvy looked down. As soon as she'd put her hands on her hips again, the cloak had parted, so she immediately dropped them to her sides. Her left wrist reminded her of the cane hidden in the folds. With her knee, she felt for the reassuring weight of the dueling pistol hanging in the right pocket of her dress.

Not yet. The time is not yet right.

"You want me to believe you didn't kill Ursula?"

"I don't care what you believe. I thought I made that perfectly clear at our engagement party."

She refused to allow the shame and horror of that night control her reactions now.

She laughed. And laughed. The longer she laughed, the louder and more maniacal she sounded. When she finally stopped, she'd put some distance between them.

"Surely you do not mean to threaten me here, my lord, in front of all these people. I certainly did not share your secret with anyone. I am insulted that you would think me so cruel. But then I wonder how many others you might have insulted since your return. Am I safe, even standing near you, if there are men waiting around every corner to answer those insults?" He advanced on her, his jaw flexing. She circled the table, clutched at the shoulders of those men still seated. They seemed to cringe from her touch as she imagined Gordon would. "Please, gentlemen. Be careful. Protect yourselves."

"You say they need to protect themselves from me? If that is not slander I do not know what is!"

"No, my lord. They should protect themselves from your enemies. I dare not stay. Having my name linked with yours again will doom me."

And with that, she hurried from the room, putting as many tables as possible between them as she wended her way back to the foyer. Then she paused, looked Gordon in the eye...and blew him a kiss. The man should have been sufficiently enraged by now. And no matter what happened hereafter, he would remember that for tonight, she had played the tune for his dancing.

Once again, she plunged into the smoke-filled corridor. But now it was more crowded. If Gordon followed her, he could find her in this smoke and wring her neck without the people nearest her being able to identify her killer, even if they were so inclined.

She pushed on a shoulder, trying to part the pair in her path. When she tried to slip between them, she was caught by their entwined hands.

"Hey now!"

"Excuse me. Please. Let me through," she urged, trying not to raise her voice. Finally, she shoved the woman into the

man and escaped around her right side. Someone clutched at
her cloak and held, then laughed and let go. Others took up the
game, eager to torment her by slowing her progress.

She was suddenly surrounded by dark shadows. Not a
woman in the lot that she might push aside in order to escape.
They plucked at her cloak, turned her in a circle. She reached
inside the pocket and pulled the sword from the cane.
Allowing herself to be turned, she held out the foot long blade
as she went, feeling it slice cloth and something else.
Something warm splashed on her hand. The sound of air
sucked through teeth. Cursing.

The hands dropped away. Her cloak was nearly freed.
The smoke swirled ahead from the opening of the door. She
moved toward it.

A hand grabbed the back of her neck and held. Her
shoulders shot up to hold the fingers in place. With her left
hand, she fumbled at the clasp at her throat. When she relaxed
her shoulders, the cloak fell away. The fingers lost their grip.
She ran at the oaf, who did not see her coming, then slammed
her body hard against his side. The doorway was clear, then
filled with the face of a disfigured man. She stifled a scream
and moved smoothly around him. With her eyes stinging from
the smoke, she was lucky she could see the steps before her.
She commanded her feet to move, her skirts to stay out of the
way.

And then she was on the sidewalk. The air was clear.
There was room to run if she needed it. Men were staring.
They stopped to watch her pass. She slowed. Her heart beat
too loud for her to discern if someone followed, so she forced
herself to look over her shoulder. No one. A dozen black
figures were headed for Merrill's front door, not in her
direction.

Dear heavens, what now?

The winter air lay upon her exposed skin like heavy ice,
but she welcomed the shock; it served to clear the smoke
lingering in her head. She'd lost the cloak, and with it, the
cane and her mother's reticule. Looking down, she realized
she still held the sword. Blood dripped from the tip and onto

her dress, disappearing in the dark red folds. *No wonder they had stared.*

No cloak. No money. A hack driver would demand payment first, considering the way she was dressed. If she could only borrow a carriage!

She searched the markings on the parked conveyances as she passed. The Count Germaine's decidedly French crest was clear. The next, a coat of arms she recognized as the one that might have become her own—Gordon's!

She glanced up at the driver, but there was no one there. Was he standing with the horses to keep warm? Waiting inside the coach for a summons? *Only one way to find out.*

There was no one left on the sidewalk. The crowd in front of Merrill's had forgotten her. She spun around once more. Her sword caught on her skirt. Depending on what might happen inside that carriage, it would likely be unwise to have her father's blade left behind.

She went back to Count Germaine's horses. His driver was fast asleep, huddled in a mass of blankets. He took no notice when she bent down and slid the sword onto the tree that ran between the animals. It was flat and the perfect width upon which to rest the handle which was carved in the shape of a horse's head, *Telford* was engraved along the mane.

Later, when the weapon fell from the wood, it would hopefully be far away from Gordon's carriage. No one would have a reason to suspect her father.

Sorry, Papa. But she'd already lost the cane.

She walked back to Gordon's carriage. Still no sign of the driver.

She opened the door and tried not to think of the fact that she may not make it out of the carriage alive. But hopefully, neither would Gordon.

CHAPTER THIRTY-THREE

Livvy had stumbled upon a perfect plan to see that Gordon would be found guilty of murder; she was going to freeze to death in the darkness of his carriage, and it was going to take only ten minutes for her to do so! The man had been in Merrill's for the entire evening; so of course there would be no heat. Neither could she find a blanket. *Perhaps the driver is curled up beneath it somewhere.*

Her head was clear, she had the pistol in hand, but she worried she'd be caught off guard at Gordon's arrival if only from the loud chattering of her teeth. She considered pulling her skirts up over her head, hoping her many layers of underthings would keep her lower half warm, but her decision was postponed when a carriage pulled up alongside Gordon's. Her hand raised to the curtain, but she thought better of it. The murmurs of numerous men made her consider for the first time that Gordon might not enter his carriage alone. And if he had company, that company might enter the carriage first, giving the blasted man sufficient warning to get away!

She had one shot. She had to be very sure it entered the correct man. Since she might need to do a bit of bluffing before brandishing her weapon, she held the gun next to her leg, concealing it with her skirt. She'd not be using the thick yards of fabric for warmth after all.

The other carriage had not moved. Surely it was blocking the street.

Gordon's carriage rocked as if the driver might be climbing up to take his position. The time was at hand! She knew it reeked of blasphemy to pray for help killing the man, but she did so anyway.

The door opened slowly, but no one entered. Her heart must have beat a dozen times while she stared at the square of light, waiting.

"Miss Reynolds, please leave the pistol on the seat and climb out."

Northwick? Northwick! Why could it not have been anyone else?

The world got suddenly colder, and it had naught to do with the door remaining open.

"No." She was lucky to have said it without her teeth knocking together.

She heard a familiar growl just before the carriage rocked again.

"I'm coming in. If you shoot me, I shall wring your neck before I die."

He deposited himself across from her and unfortunately, someone beside the door held up a lantern. She had to fight to keep from raising the pistol and shooting out the light—or shooting Northwick so she need not endure the look on his face.

"Where is the gun?" He held out a hand.

She lifted a brow.

"Damn it, Miss Reynolds. You have surely drawn enough of my blood this evening to satisfy even you."

She didn't understand. Drawn his blood? When she had set him aside? Was he hurt so deeply then?

He growled again and turned his arm. Dark drops made a trail across his cuffs.

She met his gaze with confusion, but when she opened her mouth to ask him when she could have done such a thing, her jaw protested. The chattering from her teeth moved into her bones and she lost the ability to control anything.

"Damn it!" Northwick lifted her left hand, then released it and pulled her right arm from beneath her skirt. The pistol was heavy, but she could not release it. She watched, detached, as he pushed the tip toward the floor. "Stand back," he called to the one who held the lantern.

A fierce shiver racked her body just then and the gun went off. There was a spark of fire, a puff of smoke, and that was all.

The look in Northwick's eyes was murderous, but it hadn't been her fault. If he would have left her alone, he would have been in no danger.

He peeled the gun away a bit roughly, then jerked her forward. Shards of pain cut up her fingers, then up her arms when her body slammed into his. She was the ice now, far too thick for his warmth to reach her. One of his arms slid behind her bottom and down to her knees and suddenly she was flying sideways through the carriage door and back into the slightly more frigid air. Her chin was numb and she held it away from him, fearful her face might shatter if it were bumped.

He whisked her around Gordon's carriage to the one stopped in the street. It was her own. She need not glance up to know that John would be there. His disappointment in her was something she could not bear at the moment. She had to get away. She had to get her pistol back and reload it. She had to get back into Gordon's carriage. Surely he would be arriving any moment.

"Get inside!" She looked at Northwick's face, but he was looking at someone else. There was that lantern again.

The lantern went inside.

"Hold her, Harcourt. Get her warm."

She was tossed into the carriage like a sack of wheat and she feared what bones might break when she hit the floor, but she was caught and lifted onto someone's lap. She dared not look up to see if it was Harcourt. She was mortified, held like a baby.

The door closed. A heavy blanket was tucked around her. She breathed in warmer air, but then it went cold again when the door reopened and in flew another small blanket.

"Use this as well," Northwick grumbled. "And do not give her this." He extended her father's intact cane to Milton. The dark horse's head was unmistakable—the handle of the sword she'd placed on Germaine's carriage. He could not have happened upon it. He had to have been watching! And as

Milton spread the smaller blanket over the top of the first, she realized it was her mother's cloak. The fur trim tickled her lips. The cloak had been taken by... Taken by someone whom she'd possibly cut with a sword.

North had followed her into Merrill's.

He likely heard every word she'd said, perhaps been one of those to have laughed at her as she fled. Why, oh why couldn't he have just left her in Gordon's carriage?

She prayed that when the blankets were lifted away, they'd find no trace of her. Surely her overwhelming sense of 'nothingness' would reduce her to dry bits that could be scattered on the wind.

Her face stung, as did her toes, but she did not care. The heat from the man holding her overcame her chills and she stopped shaking at least. Her teeth still rattled, but not incessantly. She held herself away from him until her arms tired. She tried to resist, but the man she believed was Harcourt pulled her close and tucked her head beneath his chin.

"Harcourt?"

"Yes, Olivia."

"Would you mind running that small sword through my heart?"

"Yes, Olivia. And Northwick would also mind, I promise you."

"He was there? Inside Merrill's?"

"He, Milton, and I."

Oh, dear lord!

"You were terribly brave, and terribly clever. You reminded me of your father's dog, though much prettier of course."

"Barking mad?"

He laughed. "No. Just terribly brave considering your size."

"If Northwick hates me so, why did he come? And why could he not just leave me in Gordon's carriage?"

"Because he is willing to sell his soul to see you safe. He does not hate you, Livvy. He hates the risks you take. He fears he will not recover if something happens to you."

"I cannot allow Gordon to eliminate everyone who prevents him from murdering me."

"Anyone, man or woman, would be foolish to assume that burden alone."

The carriage slowed to an abrupt halt. Behind her, Milton cocked a pistol and aimed it at the door. Harcourt pulled her tighter.

Two knocks. "It is Northwick."

"Come," Harcourt said.

The door opened and Northwick motioned Milton outside.

"You too, Harcourt."

"I do not think—"

Northwick gave Harcourt a look that stopped him from finishing.

"Please, Presley," he whispered.

Harcourt looked at her with regret. Then lifted her away from him.

She shook her head. "No!" But her arms were tangled in the blankets and she could not reach for him before he deposited her on the opposite seat.

"Sorry, Livvy." Harcourt kissed her head and was gone.

She tore at the blankets and swung her feet to the floor. As soon as Northwick's bulk was out of the way, she lunged for the door, but he pulled it closed. For the longest time, she stared at his fingers gripping the handle. She would not look at his face; one more fierce look from the man would kill her. She could feel the hardness of his eyes boring into her and turned away from him, into the seat, pulling her legs up, crossing her arms over her chest, willing the great weight of her embarrassment to stop her heart and have done.

Mercifully, he dowsed the light.

Shivers crashed over her, but she would not reach for the blanket. She could survive the cold until they arrived home. Ten minutes. She could last ten minutes more. Within the darkness, he would never see the silent tears escaping down her cheeks.

There was no need to cry, she told herself, over and over again, but the tears continued.

The blankets rustled and she stiffened, but it wasn't blankets that touched her—it was Northwick's hands, feeling her shoulder, wrapping around her waist, sliding beneath her knees. She told herself to resist, but her dread made her boneless.

What can he possibly do to me now?

Once again, she was sitting across a man's lap. His clothes were cold. She could not sense his customary heat. Again, the blanket came 'round her, was tucked here and there against the cold air. Another shiver rolled through her and on into him. Was he shaking as well?

A hand touched her hair and slowly moved to her cheek. She held her breath as her head was tilted back, then nearly sobbed when his mouth descended upon her own. In her weakened state, she relished the contact, reveled in his attention in spite of what he might think of her. She needed this, and she reached for his head, to show him just how dearly she needed it.

Her fingers brushed into his hair. Her palm settled against his cheek—his *wet* cheek. Had the man been shedding tears? Impossible! And yet, there they were.

The thought slipped away, however, lost in the onslaught of warm lips and warmer breath that chased away her shivers. His tongue held her complete attention, demanded it. And there, in the dark, nothing else mattered. There was no yesterday or tomorrow. There was only that moment, and she would have given all the rest to make that moment last.

Their breathing was the only sound. The creaking and clopping of a carriage and horses faded into darkness. He pulled her closer, until she could move no closer. And yet, it would never be close enough.

His lips moved to her jaw, then her neck. His fingers moved across her shoulder, then traveled along her neckline. She moaned as she remembered back to that encounter in the darkened dressing room, how she'd lost her senses there as well.

His hand froze. He pulled back, but only far enough to set his forehead against her own. His breathing slowed along with hers.

"Marry me, Livvy. Set aside your heroics and be my wife. I beg you."

"When this is over—"

He interrupted by kissing her again and while he did so, he pulled the blanket over her, tucked it between them, then held her close before ending the kiss.

"I would do anything you asked of me, Livvy. But I am taking back my promise. I will not marry The Scarlet Plumiere. She lives too dangerously. Let her die, with Ursula." He kissed her forehead, then whispered against it. "Marry me, Olivia Reynolds. Marry me."

There he was, waving to her from that path she wasn't to take. She had already made this decision. She knew she must resist that beckoning hand and turn away. But her reasons were different now. This time, running into his arms might cost him his life. Turning away from him would only cost him his pride, and perhaps a very small piece of his heart.

He held very still, waiting for her answer.

"How can I?" She could only whisper. "How can I tell Lord Gordon and the world that the surest way to hurt me is to hurt The Earl of Northwick? I will not do it. Do not ask it of me."

"Then promise me, just here, just now, between the two of us. Tell me you'll be mine, Livvy. We will tell no one. But you must give me hope. You must tell me you will never do anything so foolish as you did tonight, sneaking away from your own protection. Dear God, if you had not frozen to death, you would have been at Gordon's mercy!"

"I would have shot him. I might have ended up at the mercy of the courts, but the rest of you would have been safe."

"Livvy." His voice changed. "The pistol misfired. If I had not stopped you, it would have misfired when you aimed it at Gordon—if you'd been able to catch him off guard. Then you

would have only succeeded in making him more angry than he
was already."

"Misfired?" She remembered the flare, the smoke. But
there had been no painfully loud report. No wonder he thought
her so foolish; she had failed to load the weapon properly!

The carriage rolled to a stop. She was home, safe for the
moment at least. But none of them were safe for long. After an
atrociously long day and night, she'd failed to make any
difference whatsoever.

Northwick seemed not to notice they'd arrived.

"Yes, misfired. So now will you give me your promise?"

She pushed away from him and got her feet to the floor
before the door opened into the breaking dawn. She lowered
one foot to the step, but turned back to answer.

"I believe you would regret it, my lord. Marrying such a
fool."

She hurried into the house without looking back.

***

North dragged himself to bed with a numb head, a numb
heart, and his soul had slunk back to wherever it usually went
to hide, but this time, without the aid of expensive brandy. He
expected it would curl up and die once and for all, now that he
would no longer be in need of it.

On the morrow, he would murder Gordon, in cold blood
if necessary. On the morrow, he would buy The Scarlet
Plumiere a reprieve—a few more years on this Earth, until she
enraged the next dangerous man. But next time, he would not
be around to protect her.

Peter had lived through the night and given the doctor
hope. Ashmoore had left word not to be disturbed unless it
was a matter of life or death. The matter of a soul hardly
qualified, even if North felt the need to talk about it, which he
did not.

The house quieted. The soldiers took advantage of the
snowy Sunday, to recover from a battle lost, to store up
strength for the battle ahead. Ursula's funeral. And there was
where the war would end, if there was a breath left in him to
·see to it.

Who gave a hang what happened afterward?

CHAPTER THIRTY-FOUR

They gathered in the drawing room early Monday morning. Livvy entered like Bloody Joan of Arc, but instead of chain mail, she was draped in black crepe with a demi-veil already over her eyes. She may as well be bearing the company standard on the end of the lance considering the reaction she got from the room at large.

What were they thinking? That she'd escape them all Saturday night only to save them from the dragon?

Of course they would think just that, damn them. They'd all end up falling on their swords for her before the day was through, if they did not come to their senses.

Good lord, I already planned to do the same!

But there was nothing for it now. He only hoped Saint Joan would be haunted, for a very long time, by the memory of their final embrace.

"Is everyone here then?" She looked around her. "I thought Harcourt would be coming with Stanley and me."

"He'll be along," said Stanley, covering his smile with a hand.

She turned her back as another woman in black entered the room.

"Anna! I did not know you planned to come, but please reconsider. It cannot be safe!"

The figure's dark brim lifted, but it was Harcourt, not Anna who stood before Livvy.

"We've teased about it enough times. 'Bout time it came in handy." His voice raised painfully high. "Allow me to introduce my brother, Harcourt."

Anna walked in dressed in a morning suit, her curls close to her head. If North had not been in on the masquerade, she might have fooled him from across the room.

"I will stand in the rear, so anyone counting Kings will believe they are all accounted for. Besides, there would be no keeping me from this funeral. It will be a crush, I am sure."

***

Anna was correct. Drury Lane was impossible to penetrate. They eventually gave up and walked the final two blocks to the theatre, she and Harcourt on either side of Stanley. Harcourt had protested, but she assured him that the only way he would be believed as a woman was if he held a man's arm. It was bad enough Stanley was the shorter of the two, but Anna was supposedly well known for her height.

Northwick, Ashmoore, and Anna were only steps behind them, having come in Ashmoore's carriage. Northwick had insisted she travel in his unmarked vehicle. John and Everhardt shared the meager driver's seat and their discrepancy in size had caused the box to list to one side the entire journey. On any other day, she would have laughed.

On any other day, her father would not have come to her room, handed her a short sword and sheath to strap to her leg, and demonstrated how to run a blade into a man's heart.

"Throw your weight behind it, Livvy. If it glances off a rib, follow it through."

Harcourt kept glancing at her skirts as they walked.

"Anna!" She shook her head. "Stop doing that."

"I was only wondering if you have any of those dainty treats in your reticule—those little surprises you carried last evening."

She could honestly say, she did not. Northwick had certainly not returned them. When she shook her head, she could have sworn Harcourt looked disappointed.

"Well, Livvy darling, I have some. If you get hungry of course."

Stanley glared up at Harcourt, then rolled his eyes.

As they walked beneath the portico, Stanley dropped behind her and Harcourt pushed ahead. All she could see was his broad back covered in a black shawl much too small for him. Glancing down, she realized an entire foot of black fabric had been added to the bottom of a rather pretty dress. She hoped, in the sea of black around them, no one else would notice.

Men stood on the stairway, directing the crowd through the main doors and away from the boxed seating.

"Ursula would have loved this." Stanley gave her a watery grin. "She missed the stage, and the audience."

They entered an empty row near the back, but Mrs. Malbury hurried up to them.

"Viscount Forsgreen, please. We've reserved seats near the front for you...and your companions of course." She hardly looked Livvy's way, but gave Harcourt a hard stare before she remembered herself.

They followed the Newspaper Queen to the fifth row and seats with 'reserved' markers draped over them, and suddenly a parade of people lined up to give Stanley a nod. Men and women alike.

Livvy leaned forward to cough, then glanced sideways to see how Harcourt was faring. Thankfully, the man was slouched in his seat with his hat brim down. One look at Stanley's moist eyes and she remembered the man was not attending only to protect her.

She squeezed his hand and gave him a wink before settling back in her seat. He gave her skirts a nudge with his knee in answer. But then he stiffened and she realized he'd sensed the weapon beneath her crepe skirts.

"Now, Stanley. Do not get excited," she whispered. "My father gave it to me, just in case. That is all. I am not planning anything."

He relaxed just a bit and took a deep breath.

A coffin was carried onto the stage and the audience rose. Ursula's last grand entrance.

A man with a dramatically curled mustache stepped to the edge of the orchestra pit and cleared his throat for attention before bidding them all to be seated. He introduced a friend of Ursula's who gave a short, flattering account of Ursula's life. For a moment, Livvy feared the woman might list all the gentlemen with whom Dear Ursula had *fallen in love,* but instead, she hinted at the woman's determination to fight for the rights of women through her *writings.*

"Oh, please," she whispered to Stanley. "The woman makes her out to be a regular Mary Shelley."

Stanley smiled. "I believe Mary Shelley would view The Scarlet Plumiere as a welcome friend."

Livvy rolled her eyes, but was quietly thrilled at the prospect.

Next presented was a small man who spoke more through his nose than his mouth. He claimed to be the deceased's cousin, though many tittered when he made the claim. He read Lord Byron's poem, *And Thou Art Dead, As Young And Fair.* She nearly came out of her seat when he recited,

> *"I know not if I could have borne*
> *To see thy beauties fade;*
> *The night that follow'd such a morn*
> *Had worn a deeper shade:*
> *Thy day without a cloud hath pass'd,*
> *And thou wert lovely to the last,*
> *Extinguish'd, not decay'd;"*

Stanley's hand descended and squeezed her forearm. He was practically shaking with laughter, but not at the poem; he was laughing at her.

"How dare he?" she hissed. "He would rather she died young than died ugly?"

"It was one of Urusla's favorites. Or perhaps Lord Byron was one of her favorites. But you needn't get your hackles up. The poem has been read at every young woman's funeral for years."

"Really?" The last funeral she had attended was her mother's, and the poem had certainly not been read then.

"I beg your pardon. I forgot you have been in hiding."

He patted her hand and moved his own away. Lucky thing, that; she would have liked to take a bite out of it. She had hardly been hiding. She'd merely chosen to remove herself from Society, that was all. Surely they did not believe her to be a coward.

Surely.

A musical number followed the nasally poet. Beethoven's Concerto No. 5 was played on the pianoforte, sans orchestra. Just as it was ending, Lady Malbury stood and made her way to the stairs, then up onto the stage. Livvy slid lower in her seat, pulled by a heavy dread in her stomach that seemed to grow with each of Lady Malbury's steps. When she realized what the woman held in her hand, she groaned aloud.

A red feather.

The woman led the applause for the musician. Applause—at a funeral! Then she cleared her throat, twice.

"Ursula will be missed. But every time we see a scarlet feather, let us remember she fought for us. Let us remember to fight for ourselves."

A few men booed, but eventually stopped after a mean glare from the powerful woman who could easily take up the gauntlet and expose their secrets herself.

"Ladies?" Lady Malbury backed a few steps and walked to the coffin. She laid her feather on the top and stepped to the side.

Livvy realized black dresses were lining up to her right, to take the steps to the stage. They all carried red feathers.

"Good God!" Stanley sat forward. After a moment, he turned to her and whispered. "Did you do this, Livvy?"

She could only shake her head.

Stanley looked about them with his handsome mouth agape. Livvy closed both eyes tightly, but she did not last long. She opened one.

The female mourners paraded slowly across the stage and placed their feathers on the coffin as if Ursula had been their dearest friends. Many wept. But they did not know Ursula! Most of them would rather have died than speak to the woman, but they were willing to overlook her profession

because they thought she was The Scarlet Plumiere? It was not
Ursula they mourned at all! It was her!

She shot to her feet. Not even Stanley's insistent tug
could have bent her knees. She wanted to run up onto the stage
and set it all to rights. They had to know they weren't alone.
They still had a champion. Their champion was not lying there
in a coffin! She was alive and kicking, and willing to stick
around and fight for them.

But that was a lie. She was not planning to stay on and
fight for them at all—she was willing to hang, and soon, to put
her own monster in his grave. The Scarlet Plumiere was
nothing but a selfish imposter. What these women needed was
the real thing.

Or did they?

What had Lady Malbury said? *Remember to fight for
ourselves?* Was it a call to arms? Would these women heed
that call? Was it possible there was no further need for a
champion?

She watched the parade, the determination on their faces
after each woman placed her red feather on the pile that now
scattered and swirled around the coffin. There were dozens
and dozens of them now, like so many roses tossed on a
grave—a tribute to what The Plumiere had done for them.

It was over.

She spun around and searched the audience. She had to
find him. Had to tell him, somehow, with just a look, that it
was over. She could let The Scarlet Plumiere go now. But she
could not see him in the dark waves that moved through the
seats, headed for the stage.

There, against the wall, stood a woman with a sack. She
was handing out feathers to the women as they passed. That
was her solution! He would see her tossing some metaphoric
dirt on The Plumiere's grave. He would surely understand
then.

She tried to sidle past Stanley and he grabbed her.

"Let me go, Stanley. I must do this. It is not as if I am
leaving the room."

"Harc—Anna will go with you," he murmured.

North noticed a woman a foot taller than the rest queuing up for the parade and realized it was Harcourt. A search for Stanley's white hair confirmed the man sat alone, so he looked back at Harcourt to find Livvy. It was nearly impossible to tell them all apart in that unrelenting black sea of crepe, bombazine, and lace. If he did not see her soon—

"There," Ashmoore murmured. "She's with Anna."

Finally he noticed the woman to whom Harcourt was clinging.

"What the devil are they doing?"

"I believe they are bidding farewell to The Plumiere along with every other female in the theater."

Ashmoore could not know how his choice of words gave him hope. Could it be? Had Livvy had a change of heart? Was she willing to give up her dangerous game as he'd begged her to do in the carriage?

"Of course it might have looked suspicious," Ashmoore whispered, "had she not shown a bit of appreciation for what The Plumiere did for her."

Ash was correct, as usual. Livvy was only playing a role, damn her little black heart.

Livvy and Harcourt reached the stage and moved to the coffin behind a woman with a long peacock's feather bobbing above her head. Harcourt paused, allowing Livvy to go before him. It was unfathomable that he had fooled anyone at all, standing with his hands behind his back. He may as well have been standing at attention, saluting. Were they all blind?

Livvy was the opposite, of course. She was soft, rounded, elegant. She looked about at the mess of red feathers, then carefully placed her offering on the coffin. She paused for a heartbeat, then turned, looking directly to where he stood with Ash and Anna.

He heard her promise as if she had whispered it in his ear.

"Livvy," he breathed.

She stepped to the side and waited for Harcourt. Lady Malbury strode to Livvy, took her hands, then leaned and said something. Livvy frowned and shook her head. Lady Malbury looked horrified.

Again, Livvy looked in North's direction, but this time, she was frightened. Harcourt took her arm and they fell into the path of the other women, exiting to the left of the stage. Only when North lost sight of them did he realize he was already running down the center aisle. The flow of women re-emerged through the side doors and fanned out into the seats, so he watched for her to do the same.

Not yet. She would not have had time to reach the doors yet.

"Lord Northwick." Gordon stepped into his path as if he had not noticed his hurry.

"Another time, Gordon." He stepped to the side, but so did the other man.

"I was under the impression you would not be attending today."

"Did Mister Franklin misinform you? He is in my employ, you know."

Gordon's eyes lit with rage, but it was quickly hidden. Good. Perhaps Mr. Franklin would receive his just desserts from the hand that fed him.

Over Gordon's shoulder, he saw the feather of a peacock bobbing up the aisle. He looked to his left where Ashmoore stood searching the crowd. His friend looked over and shook his head.

"Pardon me, Gordon." North feinted to the right, then to the left, then easily stepped around the bastard. "Whatever has been done to her, Gordon, will be paid back a hundred fold!"

"I do not know who you mean." Gordon's denial was followed by a guttural laugh that stopped North's heart. Luckily, his feet were still able to move.

Finally he and Ash broke through the side door and into the hallway. The stage door was open, but blocked by a steady stream of female mourners—none of them overly tall. He sidled through at the first chance, then ran up the steps to the stage.

Lady Malbury stood fretting near the heavy red curtains.

Livvy and Harcourt had disappeared.

He ran out again. Ash was already heading down the hall toward the dressing rooms. North searched every shadow as he ran, then noticed the large door leading outside.

"Ash!" He pushed through the door and saw a hack exiting the alley. He charged after it, willing the ground to move faster beneath his feet. He reached the corner but his momentum got the best of him and the snow he stepped upon gave way to mud. He went down on one knee. The hack had already turned again and was gone.

North threw his head back and bellowed his frustration against the lowering clouds. The street before him quieted. Somewhere, Livvy was moving further away from him.

He closed his eyes and almost hoped the darkness would take him, but it did not.

Someone tapped his shoulder and extended a black gloved hand.

"You cannot despair. She still has Harcourt," Ashmoore said.

His friend hauled him to his feet and together they ran back to the theatre door. They found Stanley and Anna leading a shaking Lady Malbury from the stage. Stanley raised a hand to stop them.

"Gordon is gone, but we know where he is headed. Milton followed."

At least he could take a moment to catch his breath and discover what the blazes had happened on that stage. He fought the image of that hack moving further and further away, then he realized the idea of it reaching its destination was even more frightening. To keep his fears in check, he imagined the single horse plodding slowly down the lane.

Once they found a quiet room, Stanley found the distraught woman a chair.

"I got a letter under my..." Lady Malbury bit her bottom lip. "That is to say, I got a letter Saturday evening through Livvy's usual means. Of course I assumed it was from her. The hand was a bit different, but I supposed she had written in a hurry. I had no reason to think anyone else would use...our usual means."

"And what did the letter say, my lady?" Anna was the epitome of patience.

"That she wanted all the ladies of the ton to come to the funeral, to line up and place a red feather on the coffin, as a tribute to The Plumiere—like they had done with the willow branches at the park. She suggested it might help them stop leaning on her and begin standing up for themselves. When she came on stage, I asked her if she was pleased her feather idea had been such a success. She said she had no idea what I meant!"

The woman covered her face dramatically with a handkerchief. Anna opened the woman's black fan and tried to give her a bit of air, but Lady Malbury dropped her dramatics and frowned. She looked at Anna's morning suit, her subdued curls, then rolled her eyes. She took her fan from the girl's fingers and applied it to herself for a moment before she continued.

"I realize someone else must suspect her, to have written that letter. I will never forgive myself if I have been the one to give her away."

"Nonsense." Stanley gifted the woman with one of his most charming smiles. "You have been brilliant, Lady Malbury. Truly. We shall find Miss Reynolds and send word when she is safe and sound. Will that do?"

Lady Malbury only smiled and nodded, then left the room in the traditional Stanley-induced daze.

Stanley grabbed North by the arm. "I'm so sorry I failed you."

North clapped the man on the shoulder, then shook him a little.

"Nonsense. No one can stop her. You know that. And she should have been safe enough, stepping up on the stage for only a moment."

Stanley nodded, though his frown showed no relief.

"It seems Gordon is not our only problem," Ash said. "If he arranged all this, he must have known Livvy was The

Plumiere. So why would he kill Ursula? They hardly moved in the same circles."

North nodded his agreement. "Someone else killed her then. Even after we've dealt with Gordon, we will have some hunting to do."

Stanley sighed. "Poor Ursula."

For a moment, they stood in silence, all staring at the floor.

Ashmoore cleared his throat, then gestured toward the door.

"Well, North? You still want Livvy then, warts and all?"

North grinned, remembering the message she'd been trying to send him when she placed that feather—a veritable nail in The Plumiere's coffin.

"Warts and all," he said.

"Thank God," Ashmoore said with a sigh. "So let us go find this warty, troublesome female."

North stepped into the hallway and paused.

What is that noise?

Someone moaned. It came from the stairwell to the left, from the steps that led beneath the stage. Even before he looked, he knew in his strangled heart, it would be...

"Harcourt!"

CHAPTER THIRTY-FIVE

John brought the carriage 'round to the stage door and they got Harcourt inside. Thank heavens he wasn't harmed nearly as badly as Peter. He pulled off his black bonnet and found a devil of a goose's egg on the back of his skull.

"Three men. One of them waved us over, then told us we would have to go along with them if we wished to see Lord Telford alive. Apparently, they decided to rescind my invitation before we got out the door."

"We will take you to Telford's. Doctor Kingston may already be there, and we can discover if Telford has been taken. Perhaps the good doctor might have an efficient method for extracting confessions." He turned to Stanley. "Where is Gordon? He delayed me on purpose. Even if someone else is involved, he will know where to find Livvy."

Stanley shook his head. "That will be much easier said than done. He has surrounded himself and announced he'll be holding a wake for the remainder of the day."

"At Merrill's? Surely we can slip an unconscious man out through that hall of smoke."

"No." Stanley shook his head and grimaced. "White's."

"Damn!" Everyone would be on their best behavior at White's. Gordon would have to tread carefully. And so would *he*.

***

Lord Telford was entertaining company.

As relieved as North was at finding the man home, hale and healthy, he was frustrated beyond bearing that Stanley's fiancée had come to call. They had no time to pay Irene any heed, and so she hovered over their shoulders as they carried Harcourt up the stairs and got him put to bed across the hallway from Peter. North sent Everhardt to collect the doctor, and told the man to encourage Kingston to bring along anything that might help get a confession from a criminal. Of course he was not to mention that criminal might be a Peer of the Realm.

Finally, when they began stripping off Harcourt's clothes, Stanley took Irene by the shoulders, removed her from the room, then closed the door.

"Listen to me, gentlemen," said Harcourt as his dress was removed carefully over his damaged head. "I am perfectly capable of keeping myself alive until Kingston arrives. Go find Our Livvy."

"I wish everyone would cease calling her that," North mumbled, then cast the trousers aside with disgust.

"Would you rather we called her *Our Plumiere?*"

A gasp sounded from the hallway, then the door flew open. Irene stood with her mouth agape, her face quickly turning an emphatic red.

"What? What?" She shook her head, frowning in confusion. "Olivia is The Scarlet Plumiere? Olivia is The Scarlet Plumiere!" A vein suddenly protruded down the center of her forehead, warning of an impending fit.

Stanley went to her, reached for her, but she recoiled.

"Why did you not tell me?" Her volume forced Harcourt to cover his ears. "How could you have let me believe that Ursula woman was The Plumiere? I could have forgiven her for crawling into your bed, or I could have forgiven her for being The Plumiere, but not both! Not both!" She turned to Ashmoore, her hands up, beseeching. "You understand. She could not ruin his soul, then turn around and ruin his name as well. She went too far!"

North's stomach turned as he realized Gordon was not to be the first making a confession that day. Irene had murdered Ursula!

Ashmoore stepped forward and wrapped his arms around the woman. She curled into him on a sob.

"She went too far," she whispered again and again. Her knees began to give way, but then she recovered herself and pushed away from Ash. She then turned to North and the ferocity in her eyes made him take a step back. "But it wasn't Ursula after all! And it was your fault! You gave her the letter. You practically waved it under my nose!"

She flew at him, fingers clawed, digging into his lapels. He caught her as gently as he could.

"You were just trying to trick me, so your precious Olivia would never be punished for her sins! But she will be punished now, Northwick. Whoever has her will be able to make her pay more dearly than Stanley's whore."

"Enough!" Telford stood at the door, shaking with rage. "Stanley, go collect Lord Goodfellow. Ashmoore, take this woman from my sight. Keep her safely away from me until her father can deal with her. Northwick." The man closed his eyes and swallowed, then looked for North's soul. "Go find my daughter. Do whatever you must, but allow me to send the man to Hell."

CHAPTER THIRTY-SIX

Livvy woke to pain.

Her head hurt so intensely it actually caused a noise—a droning, maddening noise. Through that noise, she sensed a sharper pain near her left temple. She remembered that man bringing his morbid cane down upon her as soon as she'd been forced into the hack. She remembered the horror of watching the enormous stick descend, knowing it would hurt, fearing it might be the last thing she might ever see.

But before that, just a flash of the man's face—the blond man who had limped away from Gordon's table at Merrill's that night. Familiar, but not familiar enough.

Now the pain in her neck and shoulders demanded her attention. Her arms were tied behind her. She'd lain in the same awkward position for far too long. She moaned before she could think better of it.

A boot kicked her in the belly! How could a man do such a thing? How would she ever breathe again? But eventually, she did breathe, though it hurt to do so. In fact, the stabbing pain combined with a screaming soreness told her he'd kicked her before. She thanked God she'd not been awake for it all.

Her stomach turned. She swallowed bile, swallowed again, then she remembered no more.

***

North sat on the side of the large card room opposite Gordon. It was the safest place, really. Any nearer, and he would be forced to listen to Gordon's incessant chattering, be driven beyond endurance, and be forced to strangle the man in front of all and sundry. It was bad enough he had to endure the laughter that reached him from time to time.

But he sat calmly—ever so calmly—thanks to years of studying Ashmoore while the man learned how to control his features. For all anyone could tell, he was whiling away the hours waiting for an annoying relative to quit his house so he might return to it, or any other silly reason gentlemen of the *ton* availed themselves of White's. Gordon could only guess what torment he was truly going through. North hoped to annoy Gordon into leaving the club and eventually leading him to Livvy. There were men watching Gordon's only known residence, men scouring the docks, others watching the main roads out of town. He only wished he were one of them so he could at least feel as though he was doing *something*.

Landtree happened by at one point and played a few rounds of *Vingt-et-un*. Now that he no longer sought to lose his Scottish property, the man was a bit more careful of his wagers and took North for five pounds before he moved on. The fact that North played a few casual hands of cards put Gordon in a foul mood, like a child who was not receiving enough attention.

Of course North noticed this all in a mirror on the wall and rarely turned his head in Gordon's direction.

How he wished he were one of those American cowboys so he might toss a lasso 'round the man's torso and drag him from the building. The guns at his hips would deter others from interfering, and he would deal with the authorities after his woman was safe and the coward was swinging from a high branch.

He tried to remember where, in Hyde Park, he'd seen an appropriate branch.

"Lord Northwick?"

He turned to find Gibson standing over him.

"A missive for you, my lord. The man asked that I deliver it to you directly."

He took the paper from the doorman.

North, return to Telford's straight away. Three more are now watching the bastard. No word on L, but there has been a development. –Ash

***

The drive in front of Telford's resembled Drury Lane.

The doctor's barouche was the lead in a stationery parade, followed by Goodfellow's coach, and a rather ancient wagon. North's unmarked coach brought up the rear. Thankfully, Goodfellow's rig pulled away as he approached the house. Stanley stood at the open door, watching it go.

"I am so sorry, Stan."

His friend offered a sad smile. "Her father vowed she would pose no danger to Livvy. He will see to it."

North had not harbored such a worry until Stanley mentioned it. They had never considered Livvy might be in danger from a woman since there were so many men to worry over.

"Do you know why Ash sent for me? I confess I was on the verge of dragging Gordon from the place just as the message arrived."

"Gordon can wait, I think. Come. The drawing room."

Gordon can wait? Like bloody hell he can!

Livvy was out there, at the mercy of Gordon's henchmen, and she had been for nearly three hours! Whatever this development, if it was not a better clue to finding her, he was going to stomp back to White's and do just as he'd imagined. Only he would see Livvy safe before taking Gordon to Hyde Park. In fact, they may find a perfectly good branch somewhere closer to hand.

Too bad that pear arbor was not a bit taller.

They who waited in the drawing room were a bit of a surprise. He could not fathom how an undernourished urchin and a stout woman in a man's coat might actually trump Gordon in importance, but he was willing to listen—for perhaps two minutes—before he went in search of a length of rope.

"North! Thank God." Ashmoore appeared more agitated than he had all day, which made him feel quite ill with dread. "No word on Livvy yet. I am sorry."

"So you said." He waved the note still clutched in his fingers. "And who is this?"

Introductions were made. The Frenchwoman in the large coat was named Maude, the girl was Sarah. They'd delivered yet another patient, a Mister Thomas, to Telford's slap-dash hospital wing—a patient whom Ash employed to follow Marquardt.

"Marquardt? Now we must worry about Marquardt?" North paced to the window and back again. "If that murderer has shown his infamous face in the city, why have the papers not discovered it?"

"Thomas had a hard time finding the man because he's lost a great deal of his girth. Says he is hardly recognizable," said Ash.

"Well, that should make things easy." He noticed the young girl watching him as she would a mad dog, so he gave her a wink. He also removed the snarl from his tone. "So what do we know of Marquardt?"

"'E has been injured, Monsieur," said the Frenchwoman. "I sewed shut his leg nearly twelve days ago, the same day he struck Monsieur Thomas with his terrible cane. It seems he has used that cane upon the other gentlemen upstairs, *n'est ce pas*?"

He realized why Ash had called him back. "You believe it is Marquardt who has Livvy? Not Gordon?"

His friend nodded. "Maude here practices her medical arts in Paris."

"Gordon was in Paris. They could be working together!"

Ash nodded. "I am sure of it. Thomas said the man had no means until earlier this month."

"After the lottery."

"Precisely." Ashmoore slumped into a chair.

"And so, while Gordon dances about in public, he'll have Marquardt do his dirty work."

"I fear so."

Hopkins entered and bowed to Ashmoore.

"You asked for me, my lord?"

Ashmoore sat forward. "We need the help of the staff, Hopkins. Lord Marquardt is back in London. We must discover where the man might go. Does he have family? His entailed property was seized—"

"Pardon me for interrupting, my lord, but I know where you will find his mother. My cousin serves as butler to Lady Marquardt."

CHAPTER THIRTY-SEVEN

Livvy woke to chills racking her body. The chattering of her teeth was made impossible by the cloth in her mouth, but she was grateful for it. The last time she made a sound, she'd paid dearly for it.

The sack was whipped from her head and the cold air assaulting her face made her nearly wish for the stuffy thing back.

"So, The Scarlet Plumiere awakens."

She turned her head and found the blond man leaning over her from his carriage seat. In the dim light, she realized she was lying on the floor, his boots just inches away from her sore middle. She moved her leg slightly, trying to discern if her papa's blade was still strapped to her leg. There was no reaching it with her hands tied behind her, but it would give her hope.

"Looking for this, Scarlet?" He held up something that flashed in spite of the shadows. Her dagger. "Imagine my surprise at finding your pen was not your only weapon. I admit I rather enjoyed removing it."

She closed her eyes and refused to imagine it.

"I will not be ignored, Scarlet." He threw the sack at her face.

She winced and shook it away, then looked at him again.

"Surely we should be on intimate terms, after I've been beneath your skirts, as it were." His smirk dropped away. "Your damned suitor has ruined my rather brilliant plan. I had hoped to leave your body at Lord Gordon's tonight, so he could have the fame he deserves. It was all his doing, you know. He paid a great deal to have you murdered, the more fool he—I would have gladly done it on my own had he merely given me your name. But I believe he planned, all along, for me to hang for it. His thoughts are so easily read, and yet he believes the rest of us illiterate. He thinks I take him at his word, thinks the world will believe any tale he tells. And yet, it is he who is oblivious.

"I have imagined the look on his face when he discovers your body. He would be confused, of course. Then instead of believing anyone might betray him, he would tell himself that I made some mistake, that I misunderstood his instructions. We are all just idiots in his path.

"But Ashmoore has the place surrounded!" He pushed a curtain aside and looked out the window. "I can't so much as drive past without being stopped, damn him."

He dropped the curtain and dropped his eyes to hers. The hatred in them, combined with a slow grin, had her bracing for another blow, but it did not come.

"Don't worry, Scarlet. I have the perfect location in mind. Tried and true, you might say." He laughed. "You wanted to know what befell those maids of mine. Soon you will know."

This is Marquardt? Dear God, help me!

Darkness engulfed her, but it came with softness and warmth. He'd tossed his carriage blankets on the floor, and thus, onto her. By the time she worked the edge off her face, the carriage door was opening. Marquardt got out. A moment later, the hack rocked as someone climbed to the driver's perch, and then the floor lurched beneath her. Perhaps her captor was also her driver. If so, he would not be back to do more violence as long as they were moving.

Her gag, her aches, the coldness of the floor meant nothing; she had a blanket. She would survive a bit longer. She would find a chance to fight her way free. And since her would-be heroes were watching Gordon and not searching for Marquardt, she would simply have to rescue herself, like any self-respecting Plumiere.

She only hoped it would be a nice long ride.

***

North found Lady Marquardt's residence an hour west of London. It had been the family estate of her parents and so not part of the entailment lost to her son when he fled murder charges.

Ashmoore stayed at Telford's. With so many eyes searching for Livvy, someone needed to stay in the city in case the woman was found elsewhere, or if Gordon made a move. So with Harcourt injured, it was just himself and Stanley who arrived on Lady Marquardt's doorstep, only to drop their jaws on the snowy ground when the door was opened.

Hopkins stood in the doorway.

North's mind reeled with the impossibility of the man arriving ahead of them, but when the butler lifted his nose in the air and acted as if they'd never met, he realized the Hopkins cousins might possibly be twins separated at birth. Same nose. Same bushy eyebrows. Perhaps a bit thinner in the face.

The country Hopkins was none too pleased to hear that Lord Marquardt had returned to England, but even less pleased to tell his mistress what business had brought two lords from London to her door. He took their cards, however, and begrudgingly allowed them to wait in the drawing room instead of the cold front steps.

"I like the other Hopkins better," Stanley whispered as they waited for the footman to get the fire started on the grate.

North decided pacing would better serve to warm him and to keep him from tearing the house apart. If Marquardt had been staying there, the butler could not have been as surprised as he seemed. But the violence of breaking through a few doors would do North's heart some good.

"She will not see you, my lords," the country Hopkins announced, as if he'd warned them she would not. It rang a little familiar, since both Hopkins cousins seemed to also share the same voice. How he wished he was merely waiting for Livvy to come downstairs as when he'd last heard such an announcement.

He dropped himself into a chair and tried the direct approach.

"Then I have some questions for you, Hopkins. Your cousin assured us you were a trustworthy man who would be happy to help us rescue Lady Reynolds." If this tack failed, North would begin dismantling the house, starting with Lady Marquardt's boudoir.

The man's face flushed red, only to blanch white again.

"Miss Olivia? Lord Marquardt has Miss Olivia? Why did you not say so straight away, my lord? What can I do to help?"

Northwick thanked God for loyal servants.

Hopkins eventually told of a small island on the lake and a small hunting lodge in the center that was rumored to be haunted. Lord Marquardt was the only one brave enough to go there. No one had crossed the causey since the man had left the country a year and a half ago.

Northwick and Stanley maneuvered across the snow-covered road to the island to check the small cottage but found nary a human footprint. The building itself was sound, but filthy. Dust blanketed every surface. Nothing had been disturbed. There was no reason to check the remainder of the island. No boats could reach it with the ice encircling it as it did.

An hour later, North and Stanley were headed back to London. Country Hopkins had assured them he and the staff had seen no sign of Lord Marquardt, but they would keep a horse and groom at the ready, to send word should the evil man show his face. They were very aware of Marquardt's suspected crimes and feared the man might have disposed of his victims somewhere on the property, but no bodies had ever been found.

His mother would likely hide in the attic until the man left England again.

Riding quickly for the city, they were no closer to finding Livvy, and darkness was descending like a purple curtain before them. North prayed Marquardt had misplaced that blasted cane of his. Then, ignoring his own lack of soul, North prayed to God, promising all manner of improvements in his life, and in Livvy's, if the woman could just be spared.

As they neared Telford's home, North's prayer turned a bit more general.

Please, let there be news.

When he imagined Livvy might, by some miracle, be waiting inside, he nearly flew up the stairs and into the house without touching a snowy step. But there was no laughter and joy to greet him, only the sound of men arguing—and one of them was Ashmoore. He followed the heated conversation to the kitchen and found his friend toe to toe with the original version of Hopkins. Something was terribly wrong.

"What has happened?" He almost hoped there was no news of Livvy, for only bad news could have caused such an argument.

Ashmoore turned to him and took his shoulders. "Did you not find her?"

North could only shake his head. Ashmoore's grip tightened, but could not compare to the grip of fear on North's heart. One more squeeze there and he wouldn't survive it.

Stanley joined them. "They will be watching for Marquardt. The moment the man shows up, the other Hopkins will send a fast horse. I assume you have no news either?"

Ashmoore glared at Hopkins. "Oh, there is news, but not about Livvy." He released North and sat back on the cook's table. He hooked a leg over the corner and folded his arms. "Why don't I let Hopkins tell you?"

Hopkins color rose, but he did not cower. "Lord Telford went to White's this evening, my lords."

"And?" North knew what was coming.

"And he insulted Lord Gordon. Lord Gordon then called him out. Lord Telford will duel the man in the morning." The man cleared his throat, then waited.

"Like bloody hell, he will." North turned to Ashmoore. Surely his friend was as outraged as he.

Ash nodded. "Just the discussion you interrupted."

"I will serve as his second. I will go in his stead." North's chest expanded from the anticipation. He found it difficult to exhale.

"I already tried that. Telford will not have it. Hopkins here, is his second."

Hopkins' nose rose even higher in the air. The man might topple over backward if he was not careful.

North shook his head and wandered to the hearth where he found enough of a shelf to sit upon. "You said Gordon would never accept a challenge."

Ash snorted. "If two old fools are to be his opponents, what can he possibly fear?"

"I see your point. No offense, Hopkins."

The butler offered him a stiff bow. "None taken, my lord."

Five minutes ticked by with a great deal of neck rubbing and frowning, but no suggestions materialized. North picked up the fire iron and swung it into the fire pit. It rang like a church bell. A white cloud of ash rolled out from the darkness. "How do we get the devil to leave his minions and come out in the open?"

"We can do nothing. He feels he is safe," said Stanley.

"So what would make him feel unsafe?" North began to pace. "No longer safe to sit by and wait."

"If he believes Marquardt has failed? That would make him worry." Ash began pacing in earnest.

"The only way to convince him that Marquardt has failed, is to produce Livvy," North said.

Ash spun on his heel. "Then we produce her."

Stanley shook his head. "I'll not be the next one to don a frock, gentlemen."

North smiled. "We should only need to produce the rumor of her. Let word spread that Livvy miraculously returned to her home. Gordon will be forced to look for himself, wherever he has hidden her. And naturally, he will not be taking witnesses along on the chance she may still be there."

"A word to Lady Malbury should do it, and quickly. Then we need only follow Gordon," Stanley said, his excitement growing.

North groaned. "But even if it only takes half a day, we cannot just sit and wait!"

Ash moved to his side and clapped a hand on his shoulder. "Then when the sun rises, by all means, tear the city apart. Surely there is nothing more we can do tonight. Gordon's house is surrounded. Milton and Everhardt have people searching the city, slice by slice. Get some sleep." Ash turned and frowned at Hopkins. "And you!"

The old man's stubborn face melted away like wax near a hot fire.

"If you care at all for Miss Reynolds," said Ash, "you will march up those stairs, relieve Dr. Kingston of laudanum or something comparable..."

"Yes, my lord?"

"And you will drug Lord Telford's tea."

"Tonight, sir?"

"Tonight."

"He is not himself, tonight, my lord. I fear the excitement of the day has taken its toll. I doubt the man will rise until noon tomorrow, and therefore miss his appointment with Lord Gordon at any rate."

"Tonight, Hopkins. We will take no chances."

After the butler groused from the kitchen, Stanley laughed. "You will have to drug Hopkins too. Or perhaps you could just tie him to that pink chair in Olivia's room."

North swallowed painfully. "And do not forget to wet the knots."

CHAPTER THIRTY-EIGHT

Livvy took back her wish that the carriage ride might be a long one.

She'd rolled and scooted enough to get part of the thick blanket beneath her and thanked heaven she'd been able to do so. Without its slight cushion, she would be little more than a bag of bruised bones by now.

It must have been nearly an hour and one half since Marquardt had left her alone, but the past twenty minutes had been torture. Certainly no road could be as rough on a carriage, let alone a person lying against the violent floor. When the beating ceased, she took a moment to enjoy the stillness before allowing fear to take hold of her once again.

"Nearly there, Scarlet." His voice accompanied a rush of cold air that filled the hack. He tugged the blanket from her and swung it like an actor's cape, allowing it to settle upon his own shoulders. Even with the heavy covering, he shivered violently. She was merely glad to see he'd suffered in some way.

He grabbed her under the arms and pulled her to the door, then he loosened the tie around her head that held her gag in place. She spit the cloth from her mouth and awaited a chance to scream when it would not be so easy to replace the damp thing before she could empty her lungs. He slipped a scratchy rope around her neck and she realized how little real pain she'd suffered thus far. Achy joints were hardly a frightening burden to bear. The prickles of the rope digging into her skin could not be ignored, however, and they served to rouse her foggy mind to the horror of the night. Had the maids he murdered been trussed up in the same manner?

Leaving the rope to dangle, he hoisted her to her feet, then removed the ties from the back of her hands. Moving slowly, lest he feel the need to subdue her again with his cane, she lifted her shoulders and stretched her sore limbs.

They were in a forest. The trees allowed little snow to fall between their branches. How he'd driven a hack so deep into them, she could not guess.

"If you scream, I will pull the rope. But there really is no need. No one will hear your cries out here."

"You mean to hang me then?" Her throat was dry, her voice little more than a whisper.

Marquardt laughed. "Hanging? Only if you insist. But I rather thought you would prefer to live until tomorrow. What say you, Scarlet? Do you wish to live to see tomorrow?"

She nodded emphatically, not wishing to be misunderstood in the dark.

"Good girl. You will need your hands to keep your balance, I think. And to swim, of course, if you should happen to fall into the lake. The winter has been mild. If the ice has not frozen a path to my little island, I give you my word as a gentleman to reconsider your suggestion of a hanging."

He laughed again, adjusted the blanket on his back, then took up the end of the rope. He clicked his tongue as if encouraging a horse, then pointed down the hill. She walked ahead, feeling carefully for the ground as she placed each foot. There were few stars peeking through the storm clouds, but if she watched the falling snowflakes, they seemed to light her way a bit. The dark stripes before her were certainly trees, but she held out her hands to defend herself from what she might not see.

Her foot slipped and she went down on one knee. The rope jerked and tightened around her neck instantly. She jumped back to her feet to pull it loose again, to pull those tiny spikes out of her skin.

"Not my fault, Scarlet. I merely tried to help you remain on your feet." He clicked his tongue again and she started moving again.

The slope ended at the shores of a lake. The snow fell into the water and disappeared as if they had never been. She wondered if her fate would be the same. He'd spoken of an island, but all she could see was darkness at the edge of the ice forming along the shore.

"Go ahead then." He shoved at her back.

"You're mad," she whispered. "I will not walk into a lake."

Suddenly the whites of his eyes and the slash of his teeth were before her. The light wood of his cane loomed just above his shoulder.

"I am not mad, Scarlet. Angry, yes. Not mad." He moved to her side. "If you will but look, you will see the path of ice. Tread carefully. If the ice breaks beneath you, I promise to pull hard on the rope. If it breaks beneath me, I will do the same. Either way, your survival depends upon us both reaching the island. Do you understand?"

She nodded, though she had yet to see the path he spoke of. She edged forward and prayed the man had better vision than she. But once on this island, would he leave her there, to freeze to death?

A white line appeared on the surface of the water. A snow-covered tree or a path?

She stepped to her left, lining up with the image. Two steps forward and she understood how the ice had formed a bridge stretching out into the darkness. The center of it was wider than the span of her arms and she allowed a swallow of hope into her belly. The whiteness tapered away slowly. The entire expanse might be seven or eight feet wide!

She felt with her toe and found the path quite firm, so she took another step. Marquardt clicked his tongue again and flipped the rope. In defiance, she walked ahead quickly. Even when all slack was gone in her tether, she pressed forward. Marquardt only laughed, so she slowed. She'd not risk her life further just to amuse him.

They'd been walking so long she suspected there was no island at all, that he was urging out to the end of some iced-over pier and planned to push her into the sea. She'd even begun to brace herself for the imminent fall when she saw the shadows looming ahead, higher than the water. He had not lied about the island!

Her next step sounded far different from the ones before. She felt the ice give a little but kept her pace. Perhaps Marquardt's greater weight would break through. She lifted her hands to her neck, sneaking her fingers beneath the rope as Marquardt stepped upon the weakened spot.

She heard the ice crack that time and whipped around to see how the man was faring at the same time he yanked on the rope. Her feet flew out from beneath her and she landed hard on her right shoulder. The impact crackled beneath her and it was her turn to laugh like a madman. She was going to die, but she would take the monster with her.

She inched back toward him, where he stood frozen on the weak spot. Leaning on his cane, out to one side, had likely saved him.

"Stay where you are, damn you. If anything happens to me, your father will die by Gordon's hand."

She stopped laughing, moving, breathing. The man had to be bluffing. As the other man had pushed her into the hack, at the theatre, he'd admitted he'd lied about her father. But she knew not what to believe. She simply needed to escape this man and find out for herself.

"You are bluffing," she hissed.

"Am I?" He took a small step and the ice crackled again. "Move!"

She pulled her feet beneath her and leaned back, scooting until she felt the path was firmer again. Then she stood, hating the way he clung to the rope, staying just behind her, waiting for her to fall into the water so he might choke her while she fought to stay alive.

She stepped onto hard ground before she realized the water to either side had disappeared. She could have kissed the icy mud in spite of how it froze her feet. A moment later she was thanking God for the shelter she saw at the top of the hill.

Once inside, Marquardt tugged again on her tether.

"Let me remove your rope. Then I will help you remove your wet shoes."

She stood still and waited. As the cane crashed against her head, she should not have been surprised.

***

When North had not a prayer left to pray, when he found himself repeating himself for the hundredth time, he settled his head back against the couch and rested his swollen eyes while he waited for morning. As soon as it was light, he was going to tear the city apart.

He had not intended to sleep. His dreams were muddled, desperate, unfocused. There were ghosts of Marquardt's two murdered maids. The groom that never seemed to arrive at Telford's house, despite his fast horse. There was a boat, trapped in the ice. And far too many Hopkins cousins.

He woke with terror in his belly. Dawn was breaking on the other side of the floral curtains. And somewhere, Livvy waited for him to come for her.

And thanks to his dream, he was afraid he knew just where to go.

His horse seemed to share that sense, for he barely gave the beast any prompting at all and still ended up on that road back to Lady Marquardt's. A month before, he would have never trusted himself to go in search of the bastard on his own, but today he felt as capable as any of his friends. Perhaps their confession had affected him after all. But at least he was doing something. If he had to sit around all day waiting for Gordon to take the bait, he would end the day searching for a bed at an asylum.

Lady Marquardt's staff might think him foolish for checking the property yet again, to be truly certain Livvy was not there, but even the thought of turning his horse made him sick to his stomach. What if Marquardt had arrived and taken his mother's household in hand, what if he stopped any messenger from leaving the estate?

What if he was already there, on that damned island, and no one knew it? What if he, himself, had been so close yesterday and walked away?

He suddenly understood why his friends had kept their secret from him, how ashamed they'd felt for coming so close to finding him in France, and yet giving up. There would not have been nearly enough liquor in the whole of the country to help him forget, if he'd done the same. He only hoped that Livvy was found in time, just as he'd been.

His mount seemed to sense his urgency and increased its efforts without so much as the brush of his heels. He ignored the light morning drizzle and kept his horse to the turf beside the road instead of the thick mud in the center. Traveling the same stretch for the third time in less than a day, made the trip seem shorter and he thanked God for it. He came upon the entrance to the drive long before he'd expected it.

Instead of going to the manor, he turned to the left, toward the causey that led to the island, leaning to the side to study the ground. There were many more footprints in the day-old snow. But they only led up to the causey and no further. Hopkins was having the place watched then. Excellent.

He looked over his shoulder at the residence. A woman in a dark dress stood at one of the upper windows—either a maid or Lady Marquardt, it was impossible to tell which. But he'd been spotted. He lifted his fingers to the brim of his hat and bowed. A heartbeat later, the woman was gone.

Would Cousin Hopkins appear with footmen, with orders to toss him off the property?

He looked back at the island. The roofline of the small lodge was visible between the trees that crowded the center of the island as if they sought shelter from the ice encroaching upon the banks in frozen waves. If Hell were snow and ice, instead of fire and brimstone, it would appear the Devil had his sights on pulling the island to his bosom.

No smoke rose from the chimney.

North imagined there was fine fishing out so far. Even in winter, the fishing might prove brisk from the edge of the ice that collared the island like some spikey frill from Queen

Bess's time. The wind blowing down from the hills, as it was that morning, was likely what kept the ice from freezing all the way to the mainland. But on the lee side...

On the lee side, there would be no stirring wind! On the lee side of the island, the ice might span the entire distance, creating a natural causey across which a man might reach the shelter with no one from the residence any the wiser.

Surely there was someone in the house that knew—the gilly at least. But by the time he found the man who hunted for the estate, he could make it 'round the lake to see for himself!

A glance proved there was no sure footing along the bank, but then he wouldn't wish to have his intentions known by anyone hiding on the island. There had to be a road to the other side. Surely there was a road.

He was so agitated by his new realization, he was caught off guard by the approach of the groom.

"My lord? Lady Marquardt would like me to assist you in any way I can."

He looked back at the window. The woman had returned. He brought his fingers to the brim of his hat once more.

*****

Livvy woke sitting upright on the floor. Each of her arms was tied to the opposite ends of a bedframe. She was merely grateful to have awakened at all. Another day of living, then. An entire day, if she were lucky.

She remained as quiet as possible. Marquardt snored from the bed behind her. Her shoes and socks had been removed, but if he'd made a fire in the night, it had died out long ago. The large room was cold as stone. With the sunshine lighting the windows, it was difficult to believe the nightmare of the previous day, but she knew, as soon as the wicked man rose, anything was possible.

She wasted no time fretting, but turned instead to prayer. She needed a miracle. She needed strength to fight. She needed to work the stiffness from her arms without making a sound. If she was fortunate, a plan would come to her before the monster stirred.

That thick cane with which her head had become too familiar leaned next to the fire. Pity the thing hadn't caught fire and burned to ashes. But there it stood, taunting her. Never out of her sight, but completely out of reach.

The fire iron lay even further away. Even if she stretched out, she'd never reach it with her toes. What she could do with it then, she did not know.

The structure was round, with the fireplace in the center. The bed on one side, the hints of a kitchen on the other. No doubt she could find all sorts of weapons there, but she would need to be free to find out.

She turned her hand, to peek at the knot on top of it. The rope squeaked lightly and she froze.

Marquardt yawned dramatically and her stomach turned. She pulled her legs to one side and would have liked to curl into a ball to protect herself, if only from the memory of being kicked in the stomach.

"Good morning, Scarlet."

She jumped at the nearness of his voice. His head hovered above her.

"I haven't slept so good for a long while. Much easier to sleep in one's own bed, don't you agree?"

She said nothing and breathed carefully, trying not to inhale the dust stirred into the air with his movement.

"Come now, be civil. We have endured so much together, you and I. We very nearly died together last night. That should bond us in some way, surely."

He toyed with a lock of her hair. She did not pull away, lest she anger him.

"I will find us something to break our fast, shall I, Scarlet?" Then his voice changed to falsetto. "Why Lord Marquardt, how gallant of you."

He stood and walked away, laughing. She waited until he'd gone 'round to the other side of the fireplace before she tried to wrench her hands free. With all the banging around the man was doing in the kitchen, she felt safe in using all her efforts. When the noises stopped, she settled back to her original position, though she was a little out of breath. She willed herself to breathe deeply, slowly, quietly.

"I fear I have not been 'round much lately to stock the place, due to no fault of my own, of course. So if all I have to feed you are nuts, you can only blame yourself." He bent in front of her and held out a handful of almonds, as if she might eat from his hand. "Here, now. Do not be ungrateful. If your stomach would not have growled so, *I* might have slept a bit longer, and *you* might have lived a bit longer. Again, no fault of mine. Now eat."

She opened her mouth and waited. He narrowed his eyes and looked into hers for a moment. She tried to appear obedient. Satisfied, for whatever reason, he picked some nuts from his palm and tossed them into her mouth. They were rancid, but she ate them. He ate some as well and gave no indication he tasted anything wrong. She wondered if he was used to such spoiled fare, or if his mind was too occupied with horrible ideas that he had no attention to spare for such details.

When the nuts were gone, he cleared his throat and spit toward the fire, but the white stuff fell short. He didn't seem to notice that either.

"So, would you care to know why the servants believe this place is haunted?"

She watched him carefully, remembering how much he disliked being ignored.

He laughed and a lock of hair fell across his face. He might have been a charming boy at one time. "It is not haunted, by the way. It was only the screaming they must have heard on the wind sometimes..."

His attention caught on the bed behind her and remained there. His words trailed away. His breathing changed. His nostrils flared. He acted as if he'd just run a great distance.

If he wanted her on the bed, he would have to release her. The time to fight was at hand. As soon as he untied one arm—no, two; she'd need both.

Finally, he looked at her, but not at her face. He bent down and scooped her up. She thought he might have forgotten the fact that she was tied to foot of the bed. But he hadn't forgotten. She feared he meant to rip her arms from her body, but he merely tossed her legs up over her head. She landed on the mattress, on her belly. The bruises from his boot stole away her breath, as did the realization that he'd gotten her onto the bed without having to untie an arm!

For the first time since she'd been abducted, she considered the possibility that The Scarlet Plumiere might not be able to rescue herself after all. Marquardt acted queerly, to be sure, but his actions were practiced. He'd done this before. He'd tied a woman to the foot of his bed and had stolen away her hope with a clever trick. Perhaps his two maids had not been his only victims. And perhaps he was already familiar with all the ways in which a woman might try to escape him, and he knew just how to prevent it!

He leaned over her and a chill racked her body. Then she could not seem to stop shaking. The strange sound he made, sucking in air between his teeth, told her he was pleased with her reaction to him, so she took a deep breath, then another, willing her body to relax, willing her mind to think rationally.

Perhaps her only hope was to be rescued. And if that were so, someone would need to know she was there.

She raised her head and screamed...quite pitifully. She'd never been able to sing Soprano and her scream was loud but low—more like the bellow of a cow in need of milking.

Marquardt gasped in surprised, then laughed so hard he backed away from the bed and against the wall for support. She tried again.

He laughed again, shaking his head. "Sorry Scarlet. No wind today, I'm afraid. And those screams of yours won't carry far."

If it kept him crippled with laughter, she thought, she might be able to scream for a good long while. However, when she took a deep breath to do just that, she heard a squeal—the high-pitched squeal of a woman. She looked at Marquardt, to see if he had heard the same, fearing she'd imagined it.

He lunged toward the fireplace and grabbed his wicked cane, then raised it above her head. She winced and tried to duck her head beneath an arm, but it was no use.

"Please," she cried. "Forgive me!" She truly believed she would not survive the blow.

But it did not come.

She twisted her head to look at him, then bit her lips and shook her head slowly, giving him some promise that she would not scream if he would spare her.

His arms held steady while he glared into her eyes. His jaw flexed, then flexed again. More voices added to that of the woman, as if a band of merry makers was headed for the island. He glanced at the door, then raised the cane a little higher; it would end now.

Still, she did not scream, kept her eyes on his.

With one hand, he reached into his trouser pocket and pulled out a white handkerchief. Still holding the cane above her, he forced the cloth into her mouth. She did not resist. Finally, he lowered the end of the weapon to the ground. He then propped the thing against the footboard, only inches from her hand, then moved to the side of the bed.

Was he tempting her? All she could do was knock it to the ground, so she held still.

Something heavy was pulled from beneath the bed. The sound of it, dragging against the dirt on the floor, seemed louder than her scream had been, but he didn't seem to notice.

The dragging stopped, followed by noises she could not identify. Her heart jumped when Marquardt's weight pushed on the mattress beside her, but the only thing that touched her was a rope placed across her mouth, forced between her teeth like a bridle, then tied behind her head. She winced only when her hair was caught in the knot. Then his weight was gone. Her hair pulled painfully when she turned to watch him. He picked up his cane and peeked out the door. After a final glance at her, then at whatever he'd dragged from the under the bed, he slipped outside.

Livvy began to shake. She thought it might be relief. Then she realized she was crying, sobbing soundlessly into the cloth. She didn't want to die.

Please, God, I do not want to die.

The door opened so soon she nearly inhaled the handkerchief in surprise. If he caught her crying, he'd take no pity. Besides, if her nose clogged with tears, she'd not be able to breathe.

She wiped her eyes on the dusty blanket beneath her chin and faced him.

Only it was not Marquardt, but Northwick closing the door. He turned and froze.

She started shaking again.

He placed a finger against his lips while, with his eyes, he drank in every horrible detail—her gag, her tied hands, her bare legs—but he did not go to her. Instead, he headed around to the far side of the fireplace...and disappeared.

Had she imagined him? How many times had she been struck on the head? Had those nuts poisoned her? Northwick had to be an hallucination. There was nothing that could have brought him to this hellish place.

"Nothing to fret about, Scarlet," Marquardt said cheerfully as he entered a heartbeat later. "Just some servants collecting ice from the causey. I fear that means you'll have to wear your gag for a bit longer. But I am certain we can find a pleasurable diversion while we wait for them to finish."

He walked toward the cold fire, his every step echoing in her chest as if he trod upon her body and not the floor. He leaned the cane against the wall nearer the bed this time, as if to promise her she would not be able to stay his hand again should she scream.

Livvy looked past him and imagined Northwick appearing around the corner of the chimney, coming to her rescue, but he did not. Obviously, she was hysterical.

Marquardt crouched before the coals, held out his hands as if there was some warmth left for him there, then he rubbed them together as if over a hearty flame, as if he imagined a bright fire burning there. Was he taunting her, reminding her of the cold? Of her position on the bed, powerless to curl into herself to save her own warmth?

Or was he mad—imagining a flame where there was none? She still tasted the bitterness of the nuts that still clung to her teeth and tongue—a bitterness he'd seemed not to notice.

She found him staring at her then, his jaw dancing, his eyes enraged, as if she'd questioned his sanity aloud. She quickly blanked her face, as she'd seen Ashmoore do, but it was too late. Marquardt jumped to his feet and headed around the bed, to her right. She waited for his weight upon the mattress, but it did not come. Instead, he was rummaging through the thing he'd slid from under the bed.

Chains sang a brief song as they piled onto each other, hinting at a more permanent bondage. She pushed the thought aside. Just as she had with Gordon at Merrill's, she refused to allow the man to control her with terror.

Chains? Fine. But there would be no more cowering. If once again he lifted that cane above her head, she would not plead with him. There would be no more fear for him to savor.

She turned her head, to test herself, to see if the ominous staff would bolster her courage or tempt her to have done with it all. But it could to neither. It was gone!

Her gag stifled any gasp that would have escaped her lips. Her first thought was that Marquardt might punish her for the thing going missing. But how could it be missing unless Northwick was truly there? She could see enough of the floor to know it had not fallen. Even if it could have done so without making a noise, the gnarled knot at the top would have prevented it from rolling more than a half turn.

She was so flooded with hope she barely noticed when the mattress moved beneath her. Hands grasped her around the waist and flipped her over, onto her back. Her arms twisted above her head and pain arched through her shoulders and remained, like a well-aimed blade. She fought with her legs to turn back onto her stomach, to relieve the pain, but he grasped her left knee, his fingers digging into her exposed flesh. The

bruising grip distracted her attention from her shoulders and
she stopped kicking.

A heavy, bitter-cold manacle clamped around her ankle
but she refused to react. Marquardt stilled, staring at the door
as if listening. Again, there came a merry shout, but no
different than before. No closer than before. His head turned
toward her, then shook back and forth.

"Scarlet, Scarlet. You must save your strength. We have
yet to begin." He brushed the dust from his fingers. "I have
suffered a good eighteen months. I have lost my previous girth
thanks to my Plumiere-induced poverty. So much so that no
one recognized me when I returned." He poked her in the
chest, then slid his finger down the center of her belly. "Your
fault."

Had he a sharper fingernail, it might have cut the fabric
and her skin with the pressure of it.

"So you see, you have brought about your own demise.
Had you kept your little pen out of my business, I would be fat
and happy. You would be... Well, you would hardly be here.
And now, the only question is, how long can you hold on?"

He leaned forward, bringing his face within inches of her
own, one hand pressed into the mattress along the right side of
her body. The slight contact repulsed her, but she refused to let
it show.

"I think, perhaps, you will *not* die today." His voice was
low, his breath foul. "'Tis a fact, I would consider your little
debt to me paid in full, and I would go so far as to let you
go...if you managed to last, say, *eighteen months.*"

She did not react.

He frowned. His nostrils flared, but his voice remained
pleasant as he sat back. "No. Too long. You could never last.
Truth to tell, I could not last so long without tiring of you.
Eighteen days, though? I think we might both last that long.
And to give you hope, I shall make a little mark upon my
beloved cane. One mark for every day you survive. In fact,
you have survived an entire day already." He stretched a foot
to the floor and started to rise, then he froze. His eyes searched
the short wall where his cane had been. His frown intensified.

He looked to the door, then back at the fireplace, as if retracing his steps. Then he looked at her, as if expecting a confession.

Again, she did not react.

As he walked away, she peeked around her arms, not daring to lose track of his whereabouts. His fingers traced the spot where he'd rested the cane, then he moved to the door and slipped outside again. Perhaps he finally questioned his own sanity.

Someone patted her hand and she jumped. It was Northwick.

"Livvy darling, I am cutting the ties, but leave your arms where they are. Do you understand?"

She nodded. He was there. She'd felt his touch, and but she dared not celebrate, even silently. The devil was still among them. But she was not alone. And if she could have chosen one man on Earth to have come through that door, it would have been Northwick. It was the perfect moment in the middle of a perfect nightmare.

The tension disappeared from first one rope, then the other. A fleeting squeeze of her hand and he was gone. It was difficult to hold her arms in place, but she did so. The ache in her shoulders moved to the inside as her muscles struggled to maintain the pose. She dreaded what might happen next, while at the same time thrilling at the proof that Northwick was indeed there with her.

A quick peek showed her would-be rescuer poised behind the door, the wicked cane raised above his head.

The door opened. She watched between arm and footboard as Marquardt slid inside. He frowned at her, then looked to his right. His arms flew up in defense as his own weapon descended upon him. She heard it crack across his arm before it glanced away.

The cane came at him sideways, but he bent and blocked it with his shoulder. The wood fell to the floor with a rumble. The zing of a blade leaving its sheath made her pray it was Northwick's. Everything was upside down to her. She watched the two forms crash into each other, then stumble away, beyond her vision. Then she remembered her hands were free.

Her body cried out at a dozen sharp pains as she sat up. She pulled the cloth from her mouth, around the rope, then reached back for the knot. The rope tasted of rot. Her arms were too sore to hold up, but she had no choice.

Finally the knot came free and she flung the disgusting thing away.

"Go!" Northwick's voice boomed into the rafters.

She would love to have obliged him, but the manacle remained around her ankle. She tried to ignore the struggle going on behind her so she might concentrate on freeing her leg, but she could not help but look to see if Northwick was all right.

Marquardt had his weapon again and stood grinning, using his cane to block Northwick's dagger.

"Where is Lord Ashmoore?" He took a swing at Northwick's head, but it was easily avoided. They separated. "Why would he send another man to collect his woman?"

"She was never his," Northwick said, then took a quick step forward.

Marquardt swung out. Northwick's blade followed behind the swing and sliced a short trail up the other man's arm. Marquardt backed against the wall, hissing in a breath. He looked at the gash, then laughed.

"Then whose is she?"

"Mine." Northwick raised his blade and slashed down toward the other's neck, but the blade hit wood and stuck. He freed the dagger and stepped back before Marquardt could take advantage.

"Wrong again, Northwick. She's mine." Marquardt pulled back his club and swung with all his might, grunting as he changed direction to come up under Northwick's chin.

Too late to avoid the blow, the latter blocked the attack with his arm. The cane crunched the underside of his forearm. The dagger flew from his hand. He only grunted, though his arm had to be broken! His left hand clutched onto the cane, just below the knot, and forced it upward. Marquardt changed the direction of his efforts yet again and the knot struck an oil lamp hanging in the center of the room. The glass shattered. The oil splashed from the fireplace to the footboard.

Livvy turned her attention to the shackle. She had to get free and help Northwick!

A large trunk lay open upon the floor; the thing Marquardt had dragged from under the bed. There were other manacles there of various sizes, the smallest of which were stained brown. In fact, everything in the trunk suffered from the same stain. She looked for a key, but found nothing but tools; a chisel, a sledge, and a saw.

Then she realized the rot she'd tasted on the rope might well be blood!

"Why do you not go?" Northwick shouted.

"I am chained!" She rolled and pushed off the bed. Her left foot barely touched the floor, but she was able to reach the truck. She forced her hand amongst the gory collection and grasped the handle of the saw.

"Funny thing," said Marquardt. "She has a manacle about her ankle. I just tossed the keys into the lake a moment ago. But I'll be fair. If you can convince her to let you remove her leg, you can take her home with you." He laughed so hard he lost his balance and in a trice, Northwick had him up against the wall with the cane across the madman's neck, holding the thing in place with just his left hand, his arm leaning heavily against it.

Livvy could not risk watching any longer. She turned to the headboard. The end of the chain wrapped numerous times around the thick wood before the links were caught in a lock. She pulled on it, but the metal was secured. She placed the saw against the top of the rail that held her captive and worked quickly. Each time the teeth caught, pain jolted through her shoulders, but she kept on, fearing what might be happening behind her.

A few more pulls, then another, and the saw jerked free. She'd done it! But the new cut was far too thin for the chain to fit through, so she turned back to the trunk and grabbed the sledge. It was so heavy she had to drag it from the box and while she did so, she looked toward the men still wrestling for control of the cane.

Marquardt dropped a hand from the weapon and struck out at Northwick's damaged arm. The latter cried out but did not let go. Marquardt was tiring. He grunted and gasped for air. Northwick pressed on.

Suddenly, Marquardt slid sideways along the wall, then out from behind the cane and dove for the floor. By the time Northwick was able to swing the mighty weapon with only one arm, Marquardt was rising again and scrambling toward her with the dagger in his hand.

"Bid farewell to The Scarlet Plumiere, Northwick!" Marquardt kicked the handle out of her hand and threw his body against her, pushing her onto the bed. With the dagger suddenly at her throat, she dared not move.

Northwick was right behind him but paused and held out the cane. "Here," he said. "Take it."

Marquardt looked from the cane to her and back again. He pushed the point of the blade into her flesh with his left hand and held out his right for his precious stick. Northwick obliged by placing the end of it in his hand, but did not release it.

"Toss the blade and I will let go."

Marquardt grinned and lifted the blade from her skin. Northwick slid the wood further into the other man's grasp. Then Marquardt slung the dagger away from him, to the other side of the bed while he wrenched the cane out of Northwick's grasp.

North backed away with his good hand raised.

Marquardt glanced at the headboard, then pushed away from her and advanced toward the man she loved. She lunged for the sledge, and tried to lift it to strike Marquardt, but was not fast or strong enough. She could not lift it high enough to even throw.

In horror, she watched the monster first strike Northwick's injured arm, then lifted the club above his head. She screamed in warning.

Northwick ducked away, but not far enough. The wood caught him and spun his head as he crashed to the floor, his arms caught beneath him.

Hope died in Livvy's chest at the same moment a flash of yellow light flared in the fireplace. It managed to lure Marquardt's attention from the body at his feet. He frowned at the bright, living flame and she remembered him explaining they could not risk a fire during the day. Would that the smoke from such a small blaze had already brought attention to the island, and help for Northwick!

The flame jumped to another spot of oil. Then another. It appeared as if the fire itself had decided to walk out of the ashes. Small tendrils of smoke rose into the room instead of the chimney. The bold flame sprang forward and flared, then turned in Livvy's direction, following the splatters.

Marquardt turned toward the door. The voices outside had changed. A hue and cry!

Thank God!

The fire moved beyond her vision, toward the foot of the bed. The light from it grew, proving how pathetic were the morning rays that had seemed adequate before now. Perhaps the dust had caught fire. Perhaps the floor. But at least it was moving away from Northwick. If they hurried, their rescuers could get him outside before the smoke became deadly, but they would need to hurry. Their voices were still so far away!

She'd nearly forgotten Marquardt. He watched her, his face vacillating between regret and satisfaction. She dared not move until he moved.

Finally, he shrugged his shoulders. "I will leave you both to it, then," he said. "I think I'll herd the servants back to my mother's house and pay a call." He bowed, then walked out the door, whistling.

She screamed as loud as she could, then bent back to the trunk to find a tool she might be able to manage. As soon as she was free, she would worry about dragging Northwick out the door—a neat trick if she could barely lift the hammer.

Marquardt's whistling began to fade.

She could not imagine what to do with the chisel, so she turned back to the headboard. Kicking the wood frame apart would be impossible with bare feet, but she could brace them against the wall and pull on the chain!

She jumped back on the bed and did just that, screaming as she pulled with all her might. The wood gave a little. She checked the size of the gap she'd created. Not much progress, but progress just the same. She pulled and screamed again.

"Livvy, sweeting. Stop shouting."

She sat up and turned. Northwick's magnificent dark form stirred against the floor!

He lived! God was in his Heaven! Northwick lived!

Slowly, he arose, one arm hanging against his body. His other lifted and he gingerly felt his head. "I have had worse hangovers, I believe."

Her view of him was suddenly interrupted by flames jumping between them and licking over the edge of the bed to the very place Livvy's hair would have been had Northwick not spoken.

Their eyes met in panic, then he hurried to the side of the bed. She scooted to the edge and stood while he pulled the blankets off and tossed them onto the fire. The flames only grew.

"We need to leave," he said.

"I would prefer to take my foot with me."

Northwick pulled up his cravat and covered his mouth. "I hoped he was lying about the key." He bent to the trunk and began digging.

She coughed and covered her face with her sleeve. The smoke curled into the rafters like a gathering army. He slammed the trunk closed, then grabbed the chain. Just as she had, he tested the lock, then looked closely at the headboard. Over her shoulder, she watched orange light crawling up the wall on the far side of the bed. It captivated her, but she forced herself to look away.

"You should go." She had to yell to make her voice work.

He frowned at her, then noticed the hammer. With his good arm, he swung the thing as if it weighed no more than a pencil, but when it struck the wood, she felt it in her bones. After half a dozen such strikes, the rung she'd sawed through cracked and twisted away. Northwick slid the loops of chain off the top and handed them to her, then led her quickly, but carefully to the door.

She glanced back at the accursed bed and was glad it would soon go up in flames.

Northwick leaned down to kiss her but coughed instead. His smile promised he would try again later. She grabbed for the latch, to get him out of the smoke, but the door did not open. He moved her to the side and kicked it, but it held firm. He jumped over the flames nibbling hungrily on the dusty floor and returned with the sledge. She stood to the side and watched in awe as he attacked the door. How Marquardt had ever fought this man and escaped was a conundrum.

The heavy hammer broke through the wood and sunlight poured in the hole.

Northwick looked out, then back at Livvy. "He used the damned cane again! I'll try to move it from the door."

His arm fit through the opening, all the way to his shoulder, and while he was concentrating, she could not stop herself. She lifted her face from her sleeve, stepped close, and kissed him squarely on the mouth.

He smiled, then growled at her. "Livvy. We are about to burn alive. What can you be thinking?"

"I am thinking you have rescued me so often I had best begin thanking you for it, else it will take a lifetime to do it justly."

"A lifetime? I rather like the sound of that."

He extricated his arm and pushed the door open. Fresh air flooded past her skirts and the smoke chased them outside.

She was happy to hobble across the snow considering where she might be at the moment, had Northwick not rallied. Every bruise announced she was still alive. Every step, placed next to his dark boots, reminded her that God had spared the man she loved. That beloved hero led her toward the shore and a little path he promised would lead to the causey. He also promised to carry her over his shoulder before her toes froze.

Their path was blocked, however, by Marquardt, but the man took no notice of them as he was backing from the land-bridge, facing a mob of servants armed with pitchforks, among other things. And at the head of the mob, advanced Hopkins, sword in hand!

At least she thought it was Hopkins.

Marquardt chose that moment to turn away from his pursuers, but stopped moving altogether when he saw the pair of them cutting off his escape. He glanced at the cloud of smoke billowing into the heavens, then back at the cane now in Northwick's hand.

Expecting an attack of some sort, Livvy braced herself. Northwick stepped in front of her, but Marquardt gave them a wide berth as he ran around them and back toward the cottage. After a stunned pause, Northwick followed.

"Stay here," he shouted, but of course she could not.

The broken door was ablaze, as was the rest of the dwelling. The heat made it impossible to approach; the men could not possibly have gone inside. By the time she and the mob of servants reached the other side of the small island, Northwick was standing on the shore, at the edge of the ice across which she and Marquardt had made their frightening journey in the dark. Looking upon it now, it was yet another miracle she had survived. The traces of their original crossing wove across the expanse of ice not four feet wide. Half a step in either direction would have led her to a watery grave.

A third of the way across the lake, staying carefully upon the footsteps from the night before, went Marquardt.

"He is getting away," cried a woman.

Northwick glanced at the crowd, then at Livvy. "No. He is not." He looked at the sunny sky and so did she.

"Warm day," she whispered.

Northwick nodded at her, then turned his attention back to the lake.

Marquardt was nearly halfway across, but he'd stopped. His feet stood wide apart. His arms flung out. Then slowly, ever so slowly, he stepped back. A few steps more and he turned.

"Ho," Northwick called. His voice traveled clear and strong across the water.

Marquardt looked up, grinning.

Northwick tossed the cane straight up, then caught it round the middle. The heavy knot dipped low over his back just before he threw it, like a javelin, toward Marquardt. Livvy thought it would run the man straight through, but it missed him; the tip of the thing seated itself deep in the ice between his feet, the sound of it ricocheting to shore and back again.

He laughed. "If I were a fatter man, Scarlet, I would have been dead by now! Your fault again, I'm afraid!" He wrenched his cane free, then turned toward shore. Holding his weapon out for balance, he hopped along the path he'd tried to take before, but this time, he did not pause.

But even as they watched, the ice began to shift beneath the villain's feet.

Northwick pulled her to his side. "Do not watch, Livvy."

She lowered her head, but watched just the same.

Marquardt lunged for a more sturdy piece of ice, but it shattered at his touch and he sank completely. His cane flailed wildly for purchase but only served to destroy what it touched. Marquardt resurfaced, gasping, laughing, only to disappear again.

A rather large man stepped up to Northwick, nodded, then lifted Livvy into his arms. A woman covered her feet with her shawl and she was born away from her nightmare, her eyes closed against the brightness of an unusually sunny February sky.

CHAPTER THIRTY-NINE

Northwick simmered in frustration and dread all the way back to London.

Due to his injury, he was unable to wrap both his arms around His Livvy while the coach carried them home, thus his frustration. What he dreaded was informing her of her father's encounter with Lord Gordon. It was a fact he'd left Telford's home without checking the old gentleman's bed. Drugging the butler had been a resounding success if the sounds from his quarters had been any indication. He knew not if Hopkins had been successful at drugging his lord.

And so, rather than confess his oversight of not checking on her father, North decided to wait until they were but a block from her home before telling Livvy anything. And so he did.

She could hardly keep her seat, of course, proving he'd been right to put it off.

"Lord Northwick! I asked you nearly three hours ago how my father fared! You lied to me!" She glanced at the woman assigned by Lady Marquardt to be their chaperone, then blushed.

"I did not *lie* to you Livvy, my love. I told you only that your father would be much happier once you are home and hale. You would have fretted yourself ill—more ill than you are already—and I have saved you from that. Another lifetime of gratitude added to your bill will do." He shook his head when she opened her mouth to speak. "And you will call me North, Livvy. I will hear it from your lips before I allow you out of this carriage. I swear it."

She smiled at him then. In truth, he knew not whether to brace himself for a kiss or a slap.

"Ramsay, my love." She looked to be sincere. "A half-truth is a lie where I am concerned. I will teach the same to our children. It would be best if you did not attempt to teach them otherwise."

Ramsay? The woman was out of her mind if she supposed he would answer to his Christian name, but he would explain that later. When a kiss from her lips might ease the ache in his arm, it was hardly time to give her proper instruction on how to best please him.

He was unaware they'd stopped. Her borrowed blue skirts were disappearing out into the sunshine before he realized he'd closed his eyes in anticipation of that kiss. He decided to add that to her bill as well.

Livvy stood inside her father's foyer as if uncertain of being welcomed in her own home. Or perhaps she was merely afraid to hear word of her father. She jumped when North placed his arm around her. If he had to touch her a thousand times to erase the memory of Marquardt's hands, he would do so and gladly. If she recoiled from him, he would stand at arm's length for the rest of their lives if need be, but no further.

To his utter relief, she pulled him tighter to her. He could have shouted for joy. Instead, he shouted for Ashmoore.

His friend ran out of the drawing room in stockinged feet, sliding for a bit on the marble floor before changing direction and launching himself at Livvy. No doubt the woman was as shocked by his friend's appearance as he, for she allowed the man to take what embrace he would.

Northwick cleared his throat and when that failed to end that embrace, he flicked his friend's ear. "What the devil is wrong with you?"

Ash finally stepped back. His eyes were rimmed in red. He wore no cravat. More than one button was missing from his black shirt, and his curly dark hair looked as if it had never known a brush. All this since last night?

"What is it, Ash? What's happened?"

Ashmoore looked at Livvy with all the pity in the world swimming in his eyes. He opened his mouth to speak, but closed it again.

"Good God!" Stanley's voice rang out from above. North turned to find his other friend collapsing on the stairs. "That runner of yours told us Livvy was safe, but I refused to believe it until I saw her for myself. He also reported that Lord Marquardt died from a sudden gain in weight, so of course I knew he'd gotten his facts wrong." He waved his fingers. "Welcome home, Livvy. Such as it is."

"Thank you, Stanley." Livvy gave him a weak smile. "I take it my father is not at home?"

"Not yet!" Harcourt beamed from the head of the stairs. "I would put nothing past the old man. He is Livvy's father, after all."

"That is true, Presley. Thank you." Livvy's smile remained sad and North wished he could run back and kill Marquardt all over again.

Harcourt frowned at North in confusion. "Did she just call me Presley?"

"I fear she did," Livvy said. "Now, where should we look for my father?"

North dropped his chin to his chest. If their children took after their mother, his life would be a constant goose chase—a glorious goose chase, but exhausting just the same.

"I would turn the house upside down. He absolutely must be here somewhere." Lord Telford stood grinning while a footman took his heavy coat from his shoulders.

"Papa!" Livvy walked delicately toward her father. Her body jerked a bit with each step, but she waved North away when he attempted to support her.

The older man frowned and pulled her carefully into his arms. "Daughter. What have they done to you?"

"I'll be happy to tell you the whole of it just as soon as you tell me where you've been."

Telford looked none too repentant.

"I was busy slaying your dragon, Princess." His eyes glistened over a mischievous smile. "I insulted Lord Gordon.

L.L. Muir

He failed to imagine what a marksman an old soldier might be. I quite surprised him. Just before he died, of course."

"Papa!"

"I've been with the constable for most of the day. But I'm afraid it hasn't been a very good day, Livvy dear." He winked at his daughter then. "Hard to put a doddering Peer in prison for dueling. Especially when he doesn't even remember his own name, let alone the duel."

Harcourt was the first to laugh. Stanley next. North was sure his outburst was due to relief alone, that the last known danger to His Livvy had been removed. Lord Telford led her into the drawing room and the gathering sobered as they each found a seat—all but Ashmoore who struck a familiar pose, glaring into the fire. North sat far too close to Livvy to be proper, but the only acceptable alternative would be for her to sit upon his lap. He was being far too generous to Lord Telford as it was; if Livvy did not need some time to recover from her ordeal, they would have traveled first to Gretna Green before returning to London. It was too bad of him to have asked for her hand while she was so grateful to be rescued, but a man clever enough to keep up with The Scarlet Plumiere had to take advantage where he could.

Hopkins stood at attention near the door looking as if blinking caused him pain. Hung over, no doubt. Poor man. North could not help but laugh, but stopped when Ashmoore glared at him. Was he hung over as well? Then a thought struck.

"Ash? Did you happen to get the drugged tea meant for Telford?"

Telford laughed. "He did not. My tea went in the chamber pot. Hopkins is a terrible actor, if you must know."

Ashmoore rolled his eyes, then came to stand before North.

"I have been of some service to you these last weeks, have I not?"

North nodded. "You have, and I'm grateful of course. But why do I have the impression you are about to offer me a proposition I will not like? You cannot have Livvy, Ash. She has agreed to marry me. You will have to find another."

"I would like payment for services rendered." Ash crossed his arms and waited.

"Payment? Of course, my friend. Name your price. Any price but Livvy."

Everyone laughed but North. His gut remained clenched while he waited for the guillotine blade to fall.

"The Scottish Property." Ash lifted his chin as if expecting a challenge.

"I beg your pardon?"

"I am certain you heard me correctly." Ashmoore blushed—before God and man, Ashmoore blushed.

"Do you know something about this property that I do not? Have they perhaps found gold in the fleece?"

"I know nothing about the place, other than it is far away from you lunatics. I need a rest. I cannot remember the last time I truly slept. If the estate is merely infested with The Plague, it will be a welcome change."

"How soon would you go, Earnest?" Livvy looked at her fingers, which were entwined with North's.

Ashmoore frowned at her, but ignored her sudden use of his given name.

"I will not miss the happy event, if that is what you ask."

Livvy raised her head and gave him a generous smile. "And how long will you be gone from us?"

Ash looked at his stockinged toes and put his hands behind him. "A year perhaps."

"A whole year? But what if... That is to say..." She looked at North for help.

"Worry not, Livvy. We will send him word when... Er..." Dear lord, how did one word such things?

"No!" Ash rolled his eyes and spun away from them. His hands came 'round to dig themselves into his hair. "Do not send word when you find you are with child, Livvy. I will not return until it suits my purpose."

Stanley laughed. And he kept on laughing until North was sure the man had lost his senses. Finally, the future duke spoke.

"Ashmoore has been infected, but not with the plague."

Ash growled in warning. Stanley pointed an accusing finger at him. North worried that finger might not be strong enough to hold the darker man back.

"All this romance has turned his head. He only wants to go to Scotland—"

"Stanley," Ashmoore warned.

"He wants to find that Scottish lass who stole his heart in France."

Ashmoore pounced, laying His Grace low, then sitting on him and pounding on his shoulder. They were boys in the dormitory again. Lord Telford laughed until he had to wipe tears from his eyes.

When North could breathe again, he took pity.

"Yes, Ash. You can have The Scottish Property. Since it was your lot that was drawn, it rightfully belongs to you. And do not forget the thousand pounds from me, and a horse from Strothsbury."

"I will take it all, thank you." Ashmoore grumbled. "I assure you, I do *not* go in search of that Scotswoman who led us to you. She is still in France for all I know. I seek only rest and a bit of diversion."

North suppressed a smile. "You said she wore a mask?"

"Yes."

"Sounds like another Scarlet Plumiere to me, Ashmoore. Heaven help you if you find her."

THE END

If you enjoyed Blood for Ink, please consider leaving a review.

Thanks for reading!

Excerpt from
BONES FOR BREAD

The Scarlet Plumiere Series, Book 2

Scotland, 1816

"I regret to report, Lord Ashmoore, that the stock was taken last eve." Allen Balfour stood with hat in hand, though to Ash he did not appear the least bit regretful. Balfour had been making himself at home in the manor when Ash had arrived a week ago to take control of the Scottish property. Being demoted to the position of shepherd had perhaps soured the man's disposition. But no matter.

"I am sorry to hear that, Balfour. Pray allow the Frenchwoman to see to your wounds."

The man laughed, as did his two sons, one perhaps twenty years, the other half as old.

"I received no wounds, me lord. They tied me up, but dared not harm *me*." Balfour's chest lifted, as did his nose.

"Then allow the woman to treat the damage done by the ropes." Ash gestured toward the kitchens where the Frenchwoman proved she was just as talented a cook as she was a healer.

Balfour frowned and waved his wrists in front of him. "No damage."

Ash folded his arms and narrowed his eyes. The older son took a step back, but his father stood his ground. The young one merely watched.

"So. You did not try to free yourself? To raise a cry?" Ash took a threatening step forward, which usually sent men running. The fact that Balfour remained unaffected, after losing a hundred head, meant the Scot would need to be cowed another way. Ash would have to make an example of him in order for the rest of his stay in Scotland to be relatively peaceful.

Balfour rolled his eyes. "I dared not struggle, me lord."

"I thought you said *they* would not dare harm *you*," said Ash.

The older son glanced nervously behind him, at the open doorway. The boy laughed. His father clouted him on the ear, though gently. And just like that, Balfour exposed his weakness.

"It be The Highlander's men that took 'em," he said. "None can be expected to fight against The Highlander. You will learn that soon enough."

Actually, I will not be the one learning today.

Ash looked at the boy. "What is your name?"

"This is me own lad, Fin." Balfour took half a step to the side, clearly ready to protect his son.

Ash looked at the nervous one. "And you?"

Balfour answered again. "My oldest, Martin. Fought against Napoleon. Came home a hero."

Martin blanched. Ash would bet the young man had either told his father tales, or the father lied on his behalf. As expected, the question served to get the man's attention off the one called Fin.

"Come here, Fin."

The boy stepped forward eagerly, oblivious to his father's grasping fingers.

Ash took the lad's shoulder and led him to his side so they both faced Balfour. "Fin," he said, "you are my hostage until my animals are returned. Do you understand?"

The boy's eyes widened, then he looked at his father, whose face was turning purple. He looked back at Ash and nodded.

"I will ask for your word of honor that you do not try to escape."

The boy's eyes went wider still. He frowned at his father for a moment, then down at his overlarge boots. When he finally lifted his chin, he nodded once, then avoided looking at his father altogether.

Balfour screamed in frustration and headed for his son, but a heartbeat later, Ash had a short blade to the man's neck.

"You cannae have me lad! Take the other one, if ye mun!" Balfour was in anguish. The lad meant a great deal to him; he would learn quicker than expected.

"You cannot have my stock, sir. Return them and the boy will be yours again. Return them not and the boy remains with me, to raise as I see fit."

"You bloody bastard!"

Fin came forward and wrapped his arms around his father as if he were afraid the man would press himself into the dagger. "Dinna worry, da. Just go ask The Highlander to give them back. And dinna forget the pony!"

Ash growled. "They have my horses?"

"Only the pony," said Fin. "They left you the other one so you could leave Scotland faster than if you walked."

Balfour squeezed a handful of his son's hair, then stepped back. The look he gave Ash promised vengeance. "Spill but a drop of his blood, I will kill you for it." With that, he headed for the door, but at the entrance, he paused without turning. "Feed him. He's wee yet." Then he was gone.

Oh, but Ash nearly felt sorry for this Highlander fellow.

***

The Highlander hurried from her tent to interview the runner. The man was seated on a log trying to catch his wind, but jumped to his feet when she approached.

"What is all this about that daft Englishman taking my wee brother for ransom?!"

Acknowledgements

With this book in particular, I would like to thank my husband.

BLOOD FOR INK was not an easy book to write. In fact, it has taken me the longest of all my projects. And through it all, my personal Thor stood by me, pushed me, and gave me more support than I even asked for.

Thanks to him, I now have an office away from home where I can go and play with my imaginary friends. Without it, you would still be waiting for this first book in The Scarlet Plumiere series.

So enjoy. Know that a lot of blood, sweat, and tears went into the making, along with a great deal of sacrifice from my private superhero. I will now go reacquaint myself with my family and pretend to be a non-writer...for a little while, until one of my future characters escapes the dungeon in which I try to contain them all.

Sometimes, in their struggle to get my attention, it gets a little ugly—good thing my husband is not afraid to fight them all. Currently, he is King of the Hill.

About the Author

L.L. Muir lives in the shadows of the Rocky Mountains. Like most authors, she is constantly searching for, or borrowing pens. Currently, she writes paranormal fiction for both adult and young adult readers, and historical romances, both Scottish and Regency.

She loves to hear from readers! You can reach her through her website—

www.llmuir.weebly.com .

Made in the USA
San Bernardino, CA
15 April 2017